Permanent Fatal Error

HADLEY COLT

BETIMES BOOKS

First published in the English language worldwide in 2014
by Betimes Books

www.betimesbooks.com

ISBN: 978-0-9926552-6-6

Cover design by JT Lindroos

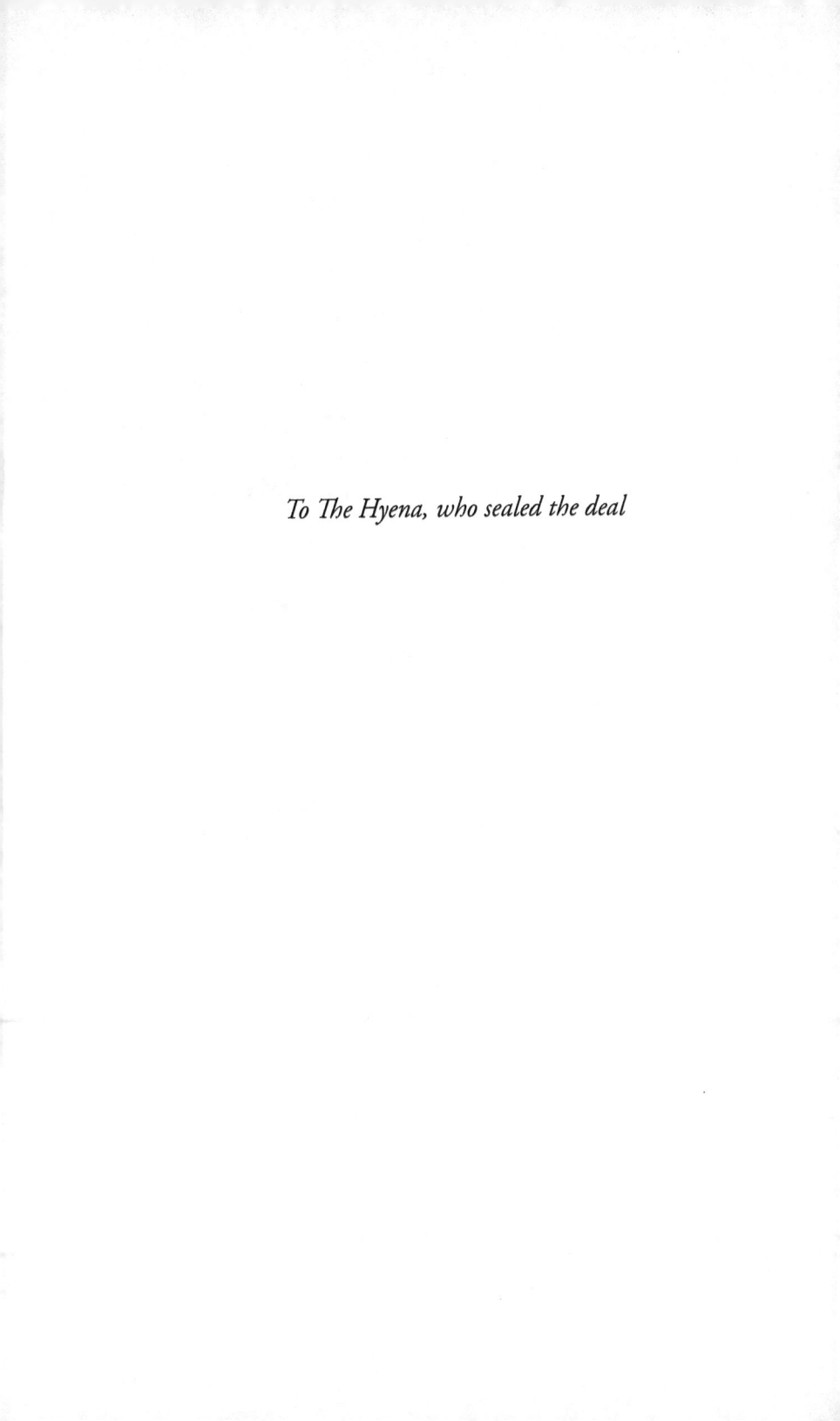

To The Hyena, who sealed the deal

*"On the trail of another man,
the biographer must put up with
finding himself at every turn;
any biography uneasily shelters
an autobiography within it."*
— Paul Murray Kendall

ASHLEY & CHASE

*"I'll tell you all my secrets,
but I lie about my past."*
— Tom Waits

1

It started with an email:

From: writerswife@yahoo.com
Subject: Query Regarding Suggested Life of Author
        Everett Hyde
To: Chase Alger
Reply-To: Amanda Hyde

Chase was accustomed to acquiring editors writing to suggest topics for biographies. The recent PEN/Jacqueline Bograd Weld Award for Chase's biography of Antoine de Saint-Exupéry had resulted in a flurry of suggested subjects for his next book.

But after five consecutive biographies of men of letters, a part of Chase craved something in a different vein.

Still... He stared at the subject line.

Everett Hyde. Son of a bitch!

Chase sipped his first coffee of the morning, still mulling over that name, "Everett Hyde." No denying that interested him. So did the sender's name, Amanda Hyde. Perhaps the legendary author's widow?

He clicked open the email and read on.

Dear Mr. Alger

For the longest time, I have resisted repeated inquiries seeking my participation in various projects and biographical studies of my late husband, Everett Hyde.

After all the years, I have finally resolved to participate in the preparation of an authorized, scholarly biography of my darling Everett. To that end, I'm willing to provide complete access to official documents, typed manuscripts, typed personal journals and other privately held, never-before-seen materials.

I've been quite impressed with your biographies of Richard Haliburton, B. Travern, of Everett Ruess, Ambrose Bierce and so many others.

I am, therefore, reaching out to you as so many have (admittedly quite unsuccessfully!) reached out to me.

I do hope you'll consider my request that you be the one to write my husband's sanctioned biography.

You are my first and only choice for this project.

I very much look forward to hearing your thoughts.

Cheers,
Amanda Hyde

Damn. Chase wasn't sure he could stand to immerse himself in the dusty debris of another novelist's life for eighteen or twenty-four months. Not even one with as sensational and sexy a back-story as Everett Hyde's.

The past several weeks had found Chase flirting with the notion of composing a biography of Sydney Reilly, the legendary 20th-century British Spy alleged to have inspired Ian Fleming's James Bond.

Reilly, it had emerged a few years ago, had in fact been a Russian Jew by birth, and Reilly's audacious self-reinvention and eventual disappearance along the Bolshevik-patrolled Finnish frontier, and the man's still unknown fate, gripped Chase's imagination. Reilly's story resonated for Chase in sundry, idiosyncratic ways.

Some part of Chase also fancied the notion of potentially spending several months conducting research in Russia.

Chase might have ignored the email query regarding Everett Hyde, simply deleted it without a response, but for that *Reply-to* line: "Amanda Hyde," the reclusive late-author's equally reclusive wife. Late author? No, that wasn't quite right, not really. Everett Hyde's fate was as open to conjecture and sinister conspiracy theories as that of Reilly's, in many ways.

Shivering, Chase pulled his robe closer, thinking it was time to finally turn on the heat. Or, better, he should hustle back to bed with Ashley. That'd warm him up, he thought.

He read Amanda Hyde's message over twice more, decided to respond. Chase kept his note back neutral. He didn't commit to anything, but expressed an interest in talking further with Mrs. Hyde. He asked for a phone number and a time when he might call to discuss her proposal.

He read his reply over three times and hit *Send.* Responding in this way didn't lock him into anything. He thought it bought him some time to decide to go ahead with her offer or to find some tactful excuse to pass. A sanctioned Hyde biography was potentially somebody's goldmine; maybe it should be his after all.

Chase then turned his attention to other emails, just getting the gist of what had come in overnight. He was inclined to get back in bed with Ashley, to nudge her awake if she hadn't heard him rise.

The digitized woman's voice from his computer's speakers suddenly chirped: "Mail truck!" The voice startled Chase, nearly made him spill his coffee.

Smiling crookedly at his reaction to the email alert, Chase scrolled back to the top of his inbox and saw a "Failure Notification Notice." He clicked on the notice to see which of his emails had bounced back to him.

It was the reply to Amanda Hyde, marked "Unable to Deliver: Permanent Fatal Error."

Less than a minute had passed since Chase had sent the reply to Amanda Hyde's biography query. He shook his head, went back to his Sent box and reopened his note to Amanda Hyde. Chase hit *Send* again.

Thirty seconds later, he received another delivery error notification: "Permanent Fatal Error."

Frowning, Chase copied the text of his message back to Amanda Hyde and pasted it into a new-message template. He checked Amanda's email address from her original note and this time keyed it in by hand, twice checking what he'd typed against Amanda Hyde's original message.

Chase hit *Send* again, waited a few seconds, then tapped the Send/Receive button of his email client. That perky voice again called out, "Mail truck!" Another failure notice marked "Permanent Fatal Error" appeared. *Damn it to hell.*

Perplexed, Chase ran his fingers back through his sandy brown hair and stood, shaking his head and pulling his robe closer around him. *What the hell? Well...* maybe—*maybe*—it was an omen of some kind.

And anyway, he really didn't want to write about another writer; he was quite sure about that now.

So Chase decided he'd take it as a fortunate thing his email replies to Amanda Hyde's offer had repeatedly fouled-out for whatever reason.

Consider it some kind of half-ass good luck, he told himself.

2

Ashley rolled onto her back, heart still racing. She smiled at Chase, said, "I think we're finally getting the hang of this." She clasped his hand, raised it to her mouth and kissed its back.

He laughed, pulled the covers back up around them and said, "Pretty sure I can still count the number of times we've been together."

Chase had rushed back to bed and Ashley after checking his email. If he'd been working on a book, he'd probably have stayed at his desk until lunchtime or thereabouts. But as it was a chilly November morning, he'd instead brushed his teeth to wash away the smell and taste of his morning's coffee and then slid back into bed, spooning up against Ashley's long, bare body and cupping her left breast in his hand. Within a few minutes, Chase's soft squeezes and his erection had sleepy Ashley pushing her hips back against him.

Brushing tangled hair back from her forehead, Ashley said, "Time to turn up the thermostat, don't you think? It's icy in here now."

"I'm almost comfortable," he said. "Finally."

"I'm freezing." She reached to the nightstand and turned on her iPod for some background music.

Muttering, Chase slid out of bed, his knees cracking and feet cold on the hardwood floor. He crossed the loft and edged behind the sectional couch to flip the lever to heat. He turned the thermostat up to seventy. There was the immediate whir of the blower; the scent of dust charring in the long-languishing ducts soon permeated the loft.

Chase hesitated, glancing at his computer screen before returning to bed with Ashley.

He had five new email messages. They included a note from his agent, two pieces of spam that had gotten by his filters. *Esquire* was proposing an article.

And there was another email from Amanda Hyde.

The query line on this note was the same as the first, but there was a different email address this time. The first query, the one Chase couldn't reply to, had been sent from a Yahoo address. This new email was written from a Hotmail account.

Chase opened the new email and read it over. The text was nearly verbatim to the first note. Chase opened his Sent file again, found his reply to Amanda Hyde and copied it. He returned to her Hotmail note, hit *Reply*, and pasted his answer into the message area and tapped *Send*.

Ashley called to him, "Coming back? And do I smell coffee? If I do, I want some." He could hear the smile in her voice: "Just sayin'."

"A minute," he answered. Chase waited about fifteen seconds, then hit the Send/Receive button on his email and cursed softly as another error message returned to him. He opened it and read through the boilerplate text. The words "Permanent Fatal Error" again leapt out.

Cursing again, he put his computer to sleep.

Chase fetched a couple of mugs and filled them with coffee from the steaming pot. He poured a little cream and sugar into Ashley's mug.

She struggled up as she saw him returning, propping pillows up behind her back and running her fingers through her long, auburn hair. She turned down the sound on her iPod. "You lose your way to the thermostat?" She wrinkled her nose as he handed her the mug. "This isn't early-onset Alzheimer's, is it?"

"You won't think it's funny when you're spoon-feeding me," Chase said, sliding in next to her as she lifted the sheet and comforter for him. "I'm not that old, you know."

At twenty-three, the late forties probably did seem rather old to Ashley, Chase figured. Or he feared it might. She sometimes seemed so young. And her devotion to him scared him a little. Ashley struck him as almost too clingy, or so he sometimes thought—usually when she wasn't around. "I got this strange email," he said. "Someone suggesting a book about her dead, well, her probably dead, husband."

Ashley sipped her coffee, said, "I thought you'd decided to write about the spy. I like that idea." She sipped some more coffee and frowned. "Who's the husband? And what do you mean, probably dead?"

"Another writer, as it happens," he said. "Another novelist."

Chase stroked Ashley's cheek. He remembered she had graduated Wellesley with a degree in English literature. In the course of the past six months, she'd been enjoying increasing publication of her short stories in various literary journals. Her day-job was a copywriting gig for a P.R. company. Gambling she might know more about Hyde than he did, Chase said, "You've heard of Everett Hyde?"

"Had a professor who was mad about him," Ashley said. "I mean really nuts about the guy. Professor Greenwood even wrote a critical analysis of Hyde's works. All three of Hyde's novels were assigned texts for my class. Hyde is, *was,* a little like Salinger or Pynchon. The mystery man, *ooo, ahh!*" Ashley shrugged and the sheet fell down around her waist. She tugged it back up to cover her breasts. "Personally? I always suspected it was a cynical marketing ploy on Hyde's part. The wife's as much a hermit as Hyde was, as I recall. She actually wrote you? That's pretty amazing on its own."

"She wrote twice, from two different email accounts," Chase said. "Haven't decided to do anything about her offer, but I didn't want to just shut the door cold, you know? Hell, it could be a big book, done right. And with her cooperation? Well, it could be bigger still. But each of my responses came back with these delivery failure notifications."

"On both email accounts?" Ashley shivered and pulled the comforter up over her breasts. She sipped more coffee, watching him over her cup's rim.

"Both, yeah," Chase said. "Strange, isn't it? I even wrote a fresh note back and typed in her email address myself. Still no go. Same result."

Ashley nodded. She sat her coffee mug on the side table and slid out of bed, forearms crossed over her breasts and hands rubbing below her shoulders as she padded naked on tiptoe to his floor-to-ceiling bookshelf. Like so many young women her age, Ashley was bare there. That excited Chase. She also had a tattoo of a butterfly at her bikini line, just above her right thigh, some Latin motto across the small of her back. Her tattoos? Chase tolerated those.

He looked again at her iPod set up there on the nightstand. Ashley had lately been leaving more of her stuff around his place, almost like she was gradually moving in with him. Not good. Then Chase looked at her again. Still… And that fine young body of hers?

Over her shoulder Ashley said, "You have any of his novels here? Hyde's, I mean?"

"Maybe, though it's been years, decades, since I looked at them, if I do."

"If you'd only alphabetize your books."

Chase had been in Ashley's apartment just a couple of times. It was a small and depressing place, he thought, but probably the best she could afford in the city with some help from her not-rich parents. Oh, she'd made some attempts with the joint, made it as homey as it probably could be. Kept it neat. And even her rattiest paperbacks were organized by subject, genre and shelved by author's last name.

The thing that has most struck Chase about Ashley's place was the number of family photos littering her apartment, almost a comical number of them. An only child, nearly all of the photos were pictures of Ashley with her parents. She'd pressed him a couple times in recent weeks to pay a visit home with her. So far, he'd successfully deflected each of her attempts. He'd taken her requests as a sign she thought they were moving to the next level. Again, not good. And, anyway, what could he possibly have to talk about with those people?

"Here we go," she said, standing on one long leg, up high on her toes now, a long back and shapely ass. Her toned arm stretched to reach the book on a high shelf. She grabbed her right side briefly, mumbled, "God, must have pulled something at the gym."

Still clutching her side with one hand, Ashley scurried back to bed and curled up against Chase, her feet already grown cold as she snuggled up with him. She kept her hand pressed to her side, over her butterfly.

Wincing at her cold toes poking against his calf, he said, "What's with the book?" It was Hyde's first novel, *Steal Me a Dream*.

Ashley smiled. "Hyde's publisher. I figure it's like a lot of the big authors, you know? A long and exclusive publishing relationship. Since the wife wrote you, and since she's probably Hyde's literary executrix, chances are Hyde's present editor will be able to give you a phone number to reach the wife. I mean, if you decide you do want to pursue it."

It was a good idea. He should have thought of it. Chase checked the book's spine, scooped up his cell and dialed 411. He agreed to pay extra to have the operator dial the number for him and was passed through several desks before being connected to someone named Kathleen DeCarlo. Chase told Kathleen about the two email solicitations he'd received from Amanda Hyde.

Kathleen listened and then said, "I know your work, otherwise I'd accuse you of a sick joke or a scam, Mr. Alger."

"Call me Chase. And what do you mean?"

"When did you receive these emails, Mr. Alger?"

"This morning."

Chase looked at Ashley—the volume was up all the way on his phone and Chase could tell she could hear both sides of the conversation. Ashley's tongue teased her top lip. Her warm, hazel eyes watched him.

A pause, then Kathleen said, "That's impossible, Mr. Alger. Chase, rather."

"Why is it impossible?"

"Because Amanda Hyde passed away two months ago. From cancer."

"I didn't know. Hadn't heard. I'm very sorry to hear that."

"Given it was Amanda Hyde, you wouldn't really have expected to hear about it, would you, Chase?" Just a little acid there.

"No, I suppose not. But these notes were from Amanda Hyde," Chase insisted. "Or at least they purported to be. Did you ever receive any emails from Amanda?"

"Several, but as she's been deceased for nearly eight weeks, what dif—"

He pressed ahead: "Can you open your inbox and search for one of her old notes to you? I just want to see if the address I received my emails from matches yours."

There was some hesitation, then the sound of keys tapping. Kathleen began reading the email address. Chase waited until she reached "at" and finished for her, "Yahoo.com, right?"

"That's right," Kathleen said. "You're not saying—?"

"I am. That's the exact email address my note was sent from," Chase said, feeling gooseflesh on his arms and back. He saw Ashley shiver again. Hearing something strange in his voice, he said, "Did Amanda ever write you from a Hotmail account, Ms. DeCarlo?"

"Kathleen. And never. But that doesn't mean Amanda might not have had one." A pause. "I don't understand any of this. It's very strange."

"Can you tell me who is representing the Hyde estate now, Kathleen? I seem to remember there being at least one child."

"A daughter," the woman said. "I'll need to make a call before we proceed further. If we even are to proceed further."

"I'll give you my cell number," Chase said, "and—"

"I have caller-ID," Kathleen said. "I'll be in touch. Or, I won't. Good morning, Mr. Alger. I mean, *Chase.*"

Chase closed his phone.

Ashley said it for him. "Creepy."

3

While Ashley showered, Chase trawled Google, combing websites for tidbits about Everett Hyde's disappearance or death at age twenty-three.

Opinions seemed about evenly split. One faction remained devout in the belief Hyde was still alive, living anonymously somewhere and perhaps writing for posterity, or even publishing under some other name.

The other half believed as Chase himself inclined. They figured the eccentric young author took himself out, leaving behind three too-hard-to-top novels and an unambiguous, typed suicide note to his wife Amanda.

The fact that something definitively identifiable as Hyde's body was never found fed the mill for the conspiracy theorists and the "Hyde is Hiding!" diehards. (One fan site actually offered that phrase on a Café Press T-shirt.)

Chase heard the floorboards squeak and felt velvety lips brush the back of his neck; this playful nip at his ear followed. He wrapped his arms behind himself and pressed Ashley's thighs to the back of his chair as she massaged his shoulders. She leaned down for a better look at his iMac screen.

She sighed. "God. You're hooked, aren't you?"

"Aren't you at least a little curious, too?"

"The email stuff is certainly very strange," she said, stroking his cheek. "I mean, the fact you can't respond, and of course the fact that the woman who sent them died long before she could possibly have sent them. Maybe someone's playing a nasty joke on you."

"Pretty elaborate hoax," he said. "And how'd they get Amanda Hyde's real email?"

"You're right. And now I'm freshly spooked." Ashley backed away from Chase and pulled a chair up alongside his. She was wearing faded jeans and a soft turtleneck sweater. Big wool socks. Dressed as she was, she looked huggable, like the fetching and outdoorsy girl-next-door from some Orvis catalogue. "Finding anything interesting?"

Chase shook his head. "Mostly finding frustration. Hyde's death was so loud, and so colorful, there's just a lot of crazy stuff out there as a result. Not knowing a hell of a lot about this guy, it's kind of tough to sort fact from myth. Hyde's suicide inspired at least two True Crime books, a PBS documentary, and an HBO docudrama that's being planned for next year. All of them mounted without the cooperation of Hyde's widow, or any of Hyde's fiercely loyal and notoriously tight-lipped friends." He squeezed and then shook her knee. "That professor of yours, he's probably still around, right?"

"Sure," Ashley said. "Should be able to reach him at his office. School is back in session by now. And he'd probably be excited to hear there's some possibility of a book about Hyde drawing on this cache of stuff that's been held back by the wife all this time."

As she talked, Chase clicked on a Wikipedia entry for Everett Hyde. He slumped back in his chair and shook his head. "There's not even a picture of the dude."

Ashley slapped his knee, then stood and wandered to the refrigerator. "No surprise there," she said. "You want some orange juice?"

"Thanks, no. Why no surprise?"

"Told you, Hyde was a lot like J.D. Salinger, like Thomas Pynchon. He totally abhorred publicity. Unlike those two, Hyde kind of went into the fiction-writing business intent upon emulating Salinger and Pynchon's recluse model, right out of the gate. He never permitted dust jacket photos, never gave interviews or even autographed a book. I don't think there's a single confirmed photo of the guy anywhere. If I remember right, neither his publisher, nor his editor, ever actually met Hyde."

Chase's cell phone began vibrating, wiggling across his desktop. He scooped it up and checked the caller-ID. It was Jeremy Hill, his go-to computer geek.

Jeremy said, "Problem? Crash your hard-drive again without backing up a book?"

"God, nothing that horrific this time, Jer," Chase said. "I've got an email problem. As in, I can't respond to a couple of important ones."

"Give me some more detail," Jeremy said. "This all of your emails, or?"

"Just to a specific person, but the problem is happening with two different email addresses for this person. I respond to an email from either address, and I get shot back this delivery error notification, permanent fatal error. What's going on? How do I fix it?"

Jeremy smacked his lips. He was probably already at the beer, Chase figured. Jeremy didn't have a waist anymore so much as an equator. "Could be a spoofed email," Jeremy said. "You know, someone you know gets hit with some spam email with a Trojan horse code that borrows their email address and then spams a bunch of other people with Viagra knock-offs and shit like that. Could also be a thing where some random email address generator happened on an email address for someone you know."

Chase said, "For two different email addresses for the same sender? And here's the other thing, I actually wanted the information in these emails. They were tailored to me and what I do. One's from an Hotmail address, the other a Yahoo account."

Jeremy took a few breaths. He carried so much extra weight he sounded like an asthmatic over the phone. "Okay then, some possibilities for you to consider. This person has some crazy-over-the-top spam filter and forgot to give you a password or some kind of link to get you through it."

"You said possibilities, plural." Chase watched Ashley as she pushed aside some books and parked a hip on the corner of his desk, sipping her orange juice and watching him, cocking her head to better hear Jeremy's side of the conversation.

"Still thinking of the second one," he said.

"I held back the best bit," Chase said. "I made some follow up calls and found out the person who sent me these emails died several weeks ago. Yet the emails came over this morning."

Jeremy paused. "It's possible to set an email for transmission at a stipulated date and time. But why do that? Someone else could be using the email addresses. Maybe posing as this dead person. Possible?"

"Possible," Chase said. "But again, why not do it in some way so I can answer the mails?"

"Maybe you answered your own question, pal."

Chase said, "What do you mean, Jer?"

"You said the author of the emails died. Maybe whoever's handling the estate pulled the plug just after the messages went out. You know, some lawyer closing out a clients' old accounts. Shutting down the infrastructure. Could explain how both email accounts shut down about the same time. And if whoever cancelled the accounts didn't know about the emails that were sent to you this morning?"

"It would answer a lot," Ashley said softly to Chase.

Chase cupped a hand over the phone so Jeremy wouldn't hear. "Sort of answers some questions," Chase moved his hand from the receiver and said, "Jer, thanks for this. I owe you a carton of something higher-end than your usual Budweiser. What about Molson?" Chase wasn't a beer drinker himself, preferring red wine as his alcohol of choice.

"How about Heineken?"

"Done." Chase tapped his screen to end the call. He shrugged at Ashley. "Like I said, Ash, answers some questions, but not the really big ones. Who is pretending to be Amanda Hyde? What exactly are they trying to rope me into? And to what end?"

4

While Ashley roamed the stacks, Chase sat holed-up in the periodical section of the library, sifting through magazine articles from the period of Everett Hyde's vanishing.

The announcement of Hyde's apparent suicide rocked the literary world and left dedicated readers shaking their heads.

It seemed all along the author, who fans somehow collectively and inchoately had come to believe lived somewhere in the arid west (all those piercingly described desert settings? How could it be otherwise?), had in fact always been holed up in northern Kentucky.

Hyde made off with the family's only car, a rusted-out Monte Carlo with bankrupt brakes and a warped plank of wood where the rear bumper should be. He'd driven down to Miami in a sprint fueled by caffeine and diet-pills. Vast quantities of Mountain Dew, too. The abandoned car was littered with cups and green aluminum soft drink cans and wadded-up fast food bags.

The cult author had torn down through the Keys on the overseas highway until he hit a dead-end at Key West. There, Hyde mailed a suicide note to Amanda. Mrs. Hyde was then pregnant with their first child.

Hyde's stated plan was to steal a friend's boat from its slip and sail out into the Gulf of Mexico where he vowed to drown himself.

Distraught, Amanda had called Kentucky police who in turn called the Key West cops.

The friend's boat had indeed proven stolen.

Several days' breathless news coverage shifted focus when the boat was found adrift near Sanibel Island. No sign of Hyde was found. None of the author's personal possessions had been discovered on the derelict craft.

In July of that year, a decomposing torso had washed up on a Sanibel beach in a storm's wake. One arm remained attached to the rotting trunk. On the biceps of the arm that was severed just below the elbow was a partially legible tattoo that might have read, "Amanda, Always."

Mrs. Hyde confirmed—according to police reports that were public record and so accessible to the tabloid press—that her giddily drunk husband had gotten the tattoo on the board-walk at Wildwood, New Jersey. It was, she contended, a dubious celebratory gesture on the night they'd become engaged.

Doubters argued Amanda Hyde had lied about the nearly illegible tattoo to rush a settlement of her husband's substantial estate that remained frozen in escrow and probate purgatory, awaiting compelling proof of his death.

The lack of photos of the author, the lack of a complete and undisputable corpse, the absence of any samples of Hyde's DNA to check against that of the ravaged, decomposing torso and truncated arm—all of these fueled conspiracy theorists' wild conjectures.

A sudden shaking in the pocket of his leather jacket momentarily startled Chase. His cell phone was vibrating again.

It was Selma Lindscott, his über literary agent calling. The trades and lit-bloggers called Selma "The Hyena." Selma so relished the nickname Chase had come to wonder if she'd maybe started the whole thing herself.

He answered his phone and said softly in a library voice, "What's shaking, Selma? Did you get me a good French deal on the de Saint-Exupéry?"

"We're very close. And remember, *good deal* in the real and the literary worlds are decidedly not synonymous. That said, the award came at just the right time. But that's not why I'm calling. I'm calling because I'm a little angry with you, Chase. No, that's understating it. I'm royally pissed off at you, honey."

"Christ, what did I do?"

"It's what you didn't do," Selma said. "How do you fail to give your agent first heads-up on this Everett Hyde project? We should have strategized this before you ran off half-cocked."

"What Hyde project?" Chase tried to figure out how in hell Selma could have gotten wind of anything involving Hyde and himself. "I'm still leaning toward the Reilly book," he said, voice sounding rather shrill to his own ears.

He winced at Selma's long, pained sigh. "I wish you would un-lean that way, Chase. Frankly, that one scents of hard sell and meager foreign rights potential. Also, I think we've hit the 19th and early 20th centuries hard enough with the past few books, don't you agree?"

Chase shifted in his chair, rubbing the back of his neck. It really didn't sound like a question coming from Selma's mouth. She'd recently been dropping hints sales of the Saint-Exupéry biography were very soft despite the award and that the publicity attendant to the prize hadn't translated into a U.S. sales bounce of any magnitude.

Selma said, "Everett Hyde, if not contemporary, is at least *fairly* current. I also sense this is as close as I'm ever likely to come to getting you to take on a potentially *huge* project in terms of sales potential and some excellent prospects for a film option. This is *commercial.*"

That was probably all so, he thought—the sales potential, the possibility for a movie deal. Christ's sake, it had been one of the first things out his mouth to Ashley when he told her of the initial emails. But again, how did Selma have wind of the Hyde prospect? He put the question to her, ruing the exasperation in his voice.

Selma sounded exasperated, too. "Hyde's editor, this Kathleen DeCarlo, called me. She told me you two talked this morning. I needed to be out in front of this, Chase. For God's sake, this project should have gone to *auction*. I think we could have gotten high six figures, easily."

That made Chase's stomach hurt. He said, "How can there be an auction, Selma? I haven't said yes to anything." He explained briefly about the email queries he couldn't return, about Amanda Hyde's several-weeks-passed death.

"A tad eerie all of that, yes," the Hyena said, cutting Chase off. "But you're no crime fiction writer so we'll just have to save the intrigue and the ghost story stuff for the eventual screenwriter."

Chased managed to squeeze in, "Selma—"

"Important thing," she said, cutting him off again, "is the daughter, Shelby Hyde, has green-lighted your book proposal." Chase bit his lip, tasting blood. Proposal? Damn it—

"Unfortunately," Selma said, "Kathleen DeCarlo, the clever bitch, no sooner got the okay from the daughter than she leaked an item about our project to *GalleyCat*. Kat tried to make it sound in the blog announcement like it was a done-deal. I'm thinking Kat did that to stop me from shopping it and keep our book in-house with her."

Chase said, "Will you stop with these terms like *our project* and *my book proposal?* I got an email asking me to consider writing the damned book. I couldn't respond to anyone to say yes or no to the proposition. I haven't even got the stomach to write another book about another writer. I—"

"Well, I suppose, the fix is in and always was," Selma forged ahead. "I mean in the sense Kathleen's got the Hyde publication rights locked up until sometime into the next century, and she's between me and the mysterious and reclusive daughter. This relative stuff is a new wrinkle in my handling of your materials, Chase. It's not like your other biographical subjects, apart from Saint-Exupéry's nephew, have had immediate heirs or copyright issues for us to sweat. We're just going to have to play ball since the daughter is clearly entitled to pieces of all the action that would otherwise be wholly ours."

The Hyena's one-sided conversation reached something like a pregnant pause, enough at least for Chase to insert, "This thing is screwball, Sel."

Chase was suddenly aware of Ashley at his side. He wondered how long she'd been there. He also wondered how much she had likely overheard. Ashley extended an index finger, then began stroking it with her other index finger in a scolding motion. Clearly, Ashley had heard enough to deduce Selma's mood.

He said, "Selma, like I said, I'm really not sure I'm up to writing about another author just yet."

"Do it for me, Chase," his agent said. "Don't screw this up, because there won't be another opportunity like this for the two of us. Do it for me, Chase, darling. Think of my retirement needs. Do this, and I swear I'll positively break my back for your spy book."

Selma didn't wait for Chase's answer. She said, "Great! Now, here's what you do. Stay away from your email and don't answer your phone except to me. Just please, for God's sake, do what I say for twenty-four hours. Let me do my thing without throwing any more hurdles in my way, yes? Maybe I can still salvage mid six-figures out of this."

"Selma..." Ashley was smiling and shaming Chase with her fingers again.

He sighed.

"Promise me," the Hyena said.

"Swear," Chase said, frowning and putting down his cell phone.

Ashley cuffed him under the chin. "Guess I won't be needing that copy of *Russian for Dummies*."

"*Nyet*. Not this year, anyway." He found himself trying to remember if he'd ever invited Ashley along to Russia.

"Blast." Ashley arched an eyebrow. "Hey, did the Hyena say anything about my novel? Any nibbles?"

Ashley's manuscript was good, the only reason Chase had dared push it at Selma. The Hyena had agreed it had merit, and she wasn't the type to indulge in mock compliments or kind lies. "I could barely get a word in edgewise," he said. "Besides, you have your own client relationship with her. It would be impolitic, and therefore not Selma-like, to let me get between you and her representation."

"Suppose so."

Chase's cell phone vibrated again.

He checked to see who it was. That *feeling*. No number or name, just, "PRIVATE." Odd. He showed the screen to Ashley.

"Could be Selma, testing you," she said.

"Or it could be someone else," Chase said.

Ashley narrowed her eyes. "Or it could be this editor, Kathleen, trying to do an end-run around your agent. Don't answer it. Listen to the Hyena. Listen to me."

5

The voice was strong, even biting, as it read aloud the letter over the phone:

My dear Professor Greenwood,

All that any man has, all any writer has, is his past.

Our past—our life behind us—is all any of us can truly be said to own. And for a writer maybe most of all, his past is the single most important thing he possesses, drawing upon it as he must for material to write about.

So I'm asking you to lay off me, professor. My past and my life, such as it has been lived to now, is potential source material for my fiction, and by prying into my past you threaten that material, that wellspring upon which I might draw for future fiction, and so, by extension, you threaten my actual livelihood. That, I just can't permit.

I have a family to support, Greenwood. (Do academics and literary critics reproduce? Do they even know how? Or do they simply observe others and dispense advice to those who can while they themselves cannot?)

I support my family with my writing, professor. Each day I have to face the blank page knowing I have to fill it with words I can sell to feed my family and keep us in a home. I have no tenure, no stipends or grants or even a base salary.

Facing the blank page is challenge enough without academics and journalists hounding me, searching for me, dogging my steps and haranguing me through my publisher with fool questions and prying inquiries.

Taking time to write you now is costing me time I could better spend writing the books you claim so enthrall you. Like you probably only claim to, I truly care about my novels, and it is my choice to stay out of the way of each of my books and let them speak for themselves.

You should respect that if you're truly the admirer of my work you claim to be. Lord knows you have Mailer and Vonnegut and so many other preening pretenders if you secretly prefer the poseur and celebrity-boy schools of writing.

So a last time: lay off me, professor, and be grateful I'm asking you in writing to do that. (No doubt you'll one day sell this letter to some collector, perhaps for much money, *if* I live long enough to write two or three more books as good as the first three.)

Know this, professor. If I met you in some bar or on the street, I'd use my hands to deliver this message, but my hands would be closed and you would be left bleeding hard.

— Everett Hyde

Ashley's former professor drew a deep breath and said, "Tough stuff, isn't it? I received it, via his publisher, about three months after the publication of his third novel, *Rain Dogs*. About a year before the death, as I recall it. I was asking his publisher to pass along to Hyde some questions for a biographical section I originally envisioned opening my book on Hyde and his first three novels. This is what I received instead."

Chase had placed the professor on speaker-phone after Ashley had called Adam Greenwood, engaging him in a bit of small talk and reminiscing about classes with him before explaining about Chase and his new project and then passing the phone to Chase.

Rubbing his jaw, Chase said, "*Rain Dogs*. That's an interesting title. What's it mean?"

Ashley narrowed her eyes, then raised her hands in a, "Why are you asking *that?*" gesture.

Professor Adam Greenwood hesitated, then said, "You haven't read any of Hyde's novels, Mr. Alger?"

"The first, I think, but it's been a long, long time," Chase said. He squirmed in his chair, trying to avoid Ashley's eyes. "Rest assured, I'm knuckling down to re-reading them soon. I was freshly struck by that title when you said it just now."

"Tom Waits, the singer-songwriter, used it for an album title not long after Hyde's last book appeared," the professor said. "Maybe it was done in homage to Hyde. Anyway, it's from an obscure turn of phrase. In New York City, or any large urban area, the dogs may wander the streets at will, but sometimes the rain comes, hard and unexpected, and the dogs lose their trail for the path back home, the scent washed away. So they wander around lost and stray, or *rain dogs*."

"Evocative," Chase said. "Was there any reaction from Hyde when your book eventually appeared?"

"Oh, Hyde was at least two years gone when my book was finally published," Greenwood said. "Unhappily, it didn't have much reach past academia. Never tapped into Hyde's mass popular audience, I'm sorry to say." He hesitated, then added, "Once you're in the family's good graces, and have access to Hyde's papers, perhaps if you could put in a good word about me—?"

"I'll certainly try," Chase said, rolling his eyes at Ashley and making a hand gesture to simulate masturbation. The crass display angered Ashley. "I will do that," Chase lied. "Do you know much about the daughter?"

"Nearly nothing," Greenwood said. "Hyde, his wife, the child—they're all essentially enigmas. Even as long as I've been studying him, Hyde remains ultimately unknowable to me. I'm sorry I couldn't be more helpful to you, Mr. Alger."

"Chase. Thanks so much for sharing that letter, professor. It truly gives me some flavor for the private Hyde. The call was worth it just for that."

"Well, I wish you all good luck, Chase. Certainly better luck than the last of Hyde's prospective biographers enjoyed."

Chase chuckled. "Well, Hyde's safely gone now," he said. "I don't foresee any angry letters from him threatening to beat me to a pulp or shoot me down in the streets. He certainly won't be terrorizing me like he menaced you, Professor Greenwood."

"Oh, I wasn't thinking of myself," Greenwood said. "I was just proposing a short, biographical sketch all those years ago. No, I was referring to Hyde's biographer, Carl Thompson."

"Carl Thompson?" Chase arched an eyebrow at Ashley. She sipped some wine and shrugged. Chase said, "Who is Carl Thompson?"

"Who was he, don't you mean," Greenwood said. Some hesitation, then, "You really do come fresh to Everett Hyde and his story, don't you?"

That almost got Chase's back up. Ashley's teasing nod in commiseration with her former professor didn't ease tensions. She caught Chase's irritation and mouthed, "So sorry."

Oblivious, the professor said, "Well, perhaps it's best you do have an open mind regarding Hyde, Chase. Lord knows, there are enough crazy and dark things out there about him to try and sort through. Perhaps you're uniquely poised to cut through the fog and hyperbole about Hyde in a way that an aficionado like me never could."

"Maybe," Chase said coolly. "I put it to you again, professor. Who is, or was, Carl Thompson? What's the story there?"

Greenwood sighed deeply. "Poor Carl. We corresponded quite a bit. Carl was working on a book-length biography of Hyde. For a spate there, Carl had a good bit more success ferreting out facts on Hyde than I ever had. Carl came to the project an admirer of Hyde's. Near the end, Carl confessed to me he'd come to loathe Hyde. He claimed that he considered Everett a monster, actually evil. Twisted and perverse."

Chase said, "I thought there was no published biography of Hyde."

"Oh, that's still the case," Greenwood said. "Carl never finished his book. It was a terrible ordeal for him. Apart from the hard work of digging up material on Hyde, Carl was harassed with threats of litigation from Amanda Hyde, a harrowing figure in her own right. One of Hyde's friends there in Kentucky nearly beat Carl to death when Carl drove up looking for those who knew Hyde. He was seeking anyone who might describe what Hyde looked like, how Hyde seemed to those who encountered him around that rural Kentucky town where he'd lived—or hid—for so many years. In fact, that bruiser broke Carl's jaw. Carl had just gotten his jaw unwired two days before he died. I remember he was looking forward to eating meat again. He was always painfully thin, but after weeks with that wired jaw, Carl was like a walking skeleton. Or so I was told."

"And he died?" Chase winced. "Unexpectedly? From the injury?"

Ashley sat frozen now, her wineglass halfway to her mouth.

Greenwood said, "I think it's fair to describe Carl's death as unexpected. At least, to everyone but Carl, maybe. They found his body dangling by a rope around the neck. They found him hanging from the window of his office, about six floors above the streets of Miami."

"My God." Chase pinched the bridge of his nose between thumb and forefinger. He avoided Ashley's eyes. "Suicide, then?"

"Eventually it was ruled to be so," Greenwood said. "But I've often wondered if the Miami police got that right."

Ashley piped in now. "Why? Why do you wonder that, professor?"

"Well, when they found Carl's body hanging there, hanged by a piece of clothesline tied off around the leg of his desk, they also found a loaded gun in one pocket of his windbreaker, and a computer disk labeled 'Hyde draft' in the other pocket."

That raised the tiny hairs on the back of Chase's neck. Spooked, but still thinking practically, Chase said, "What became of Carl Thompson's manuscript?"

Maybe it would save him some time if Chase could lay hands on it.

Greenwood said, "The disk was blank, the police told me. I frankly thought I might pick up where Carl left off, and so made some inquiries with the Miami police. But the directory on the rewritable CD indicated all materials on it had been erased not long before the coroner estimated Carl went out his window."

"And Carl's computer?"

"Shot full of holes with his own gun. Effectively destroyed."

Chase nodded slowly, said softly, "How many years ago did this happen?"

"Actually, just months ago," the professor said. "I seem to remember it being around Christmas time. It rather ruined the holidays for me."

6

"It's true what Professor Greenwood said, isn't it? You really don't know much about Everett Hyde? You haven't really read his novels?" Ashley handed Chase a fresh glass of Cabernet Sauvignon. They had been low, and Chase had walked a couple of blocks to get a new bottle.

He sipped the new wine, said, "I really think I read at least the first one, although I couldn't tell you anything about it, not even with a gun to my head."

Ashley thought about it some more. It was one of the few things that gave her any qualms about Chase. Despite all the books in his place, all the expected classics and a smattering of recent, well-reviewed bestsellers, she rarely saw Chase read anything that didn't tie back to his biographical subject of the moment. She said, "You don't seem to read many novels at all."

Chase hesitated, choosing his next words, then said, "I've never been a fiction reader by nature, Ash. I was always a history buff, for just as long as I can remember. It's always been history for me. Or other biographers' books. The fiction I've read has mostly been by those authors whom I've been writing about. Never read a word by Ambrose Bierce until I decided to write about him. Then I read it all. Same with Everett Ruess. Same with Richard Haliburton, a name I only knew from biographies about other authors until I chose to write about Haliburton myself. And B. Traven? Never heard of him. Oh, I'd seen *Treasure of the Sierra Madre* on TV. Really enjoyed Huston's film. But I hadn't made the connection at the time that it was based on his novel. And the latest, Saint-Exupéry? Never felt compelled to break the spine of *The Little Prince* until I decided to write about its author."

"Missing Men of Letters, every one," Ashley said, licking her lower lip after sipping her Cabernet. "At least Hyde fits your pattern. But you're just not a pop culture kind of guy, are you, Chase? Every time I push back much farther than a few years, you seem at sea. I mean, unless it ties back to someone you've written about." She winced a little and rubbed her right side. This nagging ache.

Chase laughed and said, "So said the sexpot who was born hardly any years ago."

She looked around his place again. Nothing really personal there. Her apartment was filled with family pictures, sentimental objects and keepsakes. Chase's place was anything but.

His cell phone began ringing. It was closer by Ashley and she scooped it up, checked the ID.

"Hey," Chase said, "That's for me."

"You're not allowed to talk on the phone until tomorrow," Ashley said. "Remember what the Hyena told you? But you're in luck. Speaking of the Devil, it's Her."

Ashley lobbed his cell phone to Chase, and he caught it, tapping to answer. "Selma!"

"Chase! Down to cases. Have you been obeying my order to lay low?"

"Completely. Ashley's right here, you can ask her."

"Don't you dare give that little witch the phone," Selma said. "She'll ask me about her manuscript and I don't have any answers back yet, not up or down. I ask about this other, because suddenly this bitch, Kathleen DeCarlo, is playing hard to get."

"What do you mean?"

"Kat's suddenly not returning my calls. For about two hours there, I'd have thought we were high school lovers in the early days of our courtship. You know, panting phone conversations. 'You hang up first'; 'No, *you* hang up first.' Like *that.* That kind of nonsense, you know?"

He didn't but said, "Okay…"

"Now the bitch is positively missing," Selma said. "You haven't talked to Kat since you and I last spoke, you swear, Chase?"

"I'm making myself scarce, just as you ordered, Sel."

"Great. Keep it up then." Selma hung up without saying goodbye.

Chase said to Ashley, "You heard about your book?"

Ashley nodded. "At least nothing isn't a no."

"With turns of phrase like that, you should maybe write poetry." That prompted Ashley to stick out her tongue.

His phone rang again. Selma. Again. She said, "Okay, this is strange. Kathleen, the silly bitch, is fucking *dead.*"

Chase coughed up his wine, staining his sweatshirt. Ashley was wide-eyed. Wiping his mouth, he managed, "Dead? What? How?"

Selma said, "I shit you not. I called her number again. No answer. So I then called a generic number. Some sobbing, wage-slave secretary told me they'd just gotten word Kat died. Seems she fell off the terrace outside her apartment. Happened not far from you, actually. They found a goblet and a mostly empty bottle of wine. They figure she was tipsy and fell off her balcony. Clumsy cow was probably celebrating our deal before we even had a deal, goddamn it! Fuck us harder, yes?"

Chase was still trying to assimilate the information. "This woman, Hyde's editor, she fell off a building?"

"Only thirty-five floors. If it weren't for the theatre marquee below, she'd probably have taken a few pedestrians with her. Don't worry, Chase. This doesn't change anything. I've got the name for someone new to deal with. In a way, this is actually good news, darling. No way this new guy in the mix at that house could know different, so I'm going to swear to him that I and Kathleen were dickering over the number of zeros in your advance. I'm going to say I was holding out because we've had you at five-figures—they don't have to know it was mid five-figures—for some number of books now, and I need to graduate you to the next level. I'm going for as close to a million as I can and we'll walk it back *slowly* from there. I think I'll get something large for us this time."

Chase believed Selma, cold as it was on her part. He almost laughed when he looked up and saw Ashley had her hands pressed to the sides of her head, index fingers extended in Devil's horns. "Go for it, Sel," he said, smiling and shaking his head at Ashley.

"I am," Selma shot back. "This means you now lay low for *forty-eight* hours, Chase. You only answer this phone for me."

"Will do." He tapped to end the call and dropped it on an end table. He let out a long breath. "This has been the craziest damn day, Ash."

"Bloody, too," Ashley said. "I've got to say, Hyde's widow? His would-be biographer? Now his editor? For a guy decades dead, the casualty rate around Hyde is remarkably high, don't you think?"

7

While Chase made dinner, Ashley sat at his computer, surfing and printing out scraps about Hyde for him. She'd read Hyde's books, of course. She knew a bit of Hyde's biography. But the more Ashley explored the myths that surrounded the man and his disappearance and factored those against the string of recent deaths tied to Hyde, the more unsettled she became about Chase pursuing the project.

The dishwasher churning in the distance, Ashley was curled up beside Chase on the couch, sipping her wine and rereading Hyde's debut, *Steal Me a Dream*.

Chase sat leafing through Ashley's notes, really just browsing for high-points or sexy hooks at this early stage in his research.

In many ways, Hyde's path to publication seemed improbably blessed, given all the obstacles before him.

Hyde had purportedly been born and raised in Chicago. He'd dropped out of high school halfway through his freshman year, frustrating latter-day researchers who'd hoped to find at least a graduation yearbook photo that might allow them to consult with photo experts who aided law enforcement, techie gurus in "aging" the photos of missing youths to create digitally-matured composites that might aid investigators looking for long-missing children.

As Ashley had earlier asserted, there were simply no photos of Hyde out there in the world. Not a single one. Even retroactive searches of DMV databases had failed to turn up so much as a blurry mug shot from an operator's license. It seemed entirely probable that Hyde had never been a licensed driver.

Then there was the matter of his astonishing literary arc. Hyde's un-agented first novel was miraculously plucked from a slush pile of over-the-transom manuscripts by one of the major New York publishing house's newer editors, some now-famous and retired literary lion named George Barry.

The intrepid, tyro editor immediately sent a letter to Hyde's stipulated NYC post office box promising to advance him eighty thousand dollars for the novel. It was an impressive sum at the time for an unknown debut novelist, large enough to draw industry coverage, which, of course, was the fledgling and career-building editor's calculated intent. But the resulting publicity was onerous to the reclusive author.

Several weeks passed before the hot-shot young editor received a definitive reply, a note from an apparently obscure New York literary agent explaining he was now representing Hyde and that while the author cheerfully accepted Barry's "generous advance," he would only do so upon the condition that he not be required to provide any biographical information or personal photos. Oh, and he would not tour in support of the book, grant so much as a single phone interview, or sign even one presentation copy.

Take it or leave it.

Chase smiled at that. Seemed to him that Hyde had found for himself some kind of spiritual twin for his own personal shark of a literary agent.

After some lip-biting, the editor, in thrall to the power of the mysterious young author's fever-dream narrative, capitulated, and Hyde was off to the races.

Hyde's next two novels drew still bigger advances, sold quickly to Hollywood, and passed through innumerable reprintings. Yet Hyde remained a hidden man.

There were various rumblings in the trades about what might constitute Hyde's fourth novel, but no substantive details had ever emerged. Not even a working title.

Tired, his eyes burning, Chase pulled off his reading glasses and tossed Ashley's notes on the coffee table. He put his glasses atop them. He drained what was left of his drink and said, "Think I'm turning in."

"Me too, then," Ashley said, standing and stretching, yawning. "What time is it?"

Chase checked his watch. "Nearly midnight."

"God." Ashley stretched again, then groaned and hugged her stomach.

His phone vibrated again. He frowned. "I should ignore the thing."

"At this hour?" Ashley shook her head. "What if it's the Hyena? What form would her wrath take if she knew you blew her off?"

Ashley had called it right—it was Selma. Chase answered his phone, said, "Sel? It's nearly tomorrow. What couldn't wait until then?"

"I just wanted to tell you two things. I think tomorrow we're going to agree on a million dollars. I'm already writing the *Publishers Lunch* announcement in my head!"

Chase could hardly believe it. Still, he managed, "What's the second thing?"

"Oh! That stuff about Kathleen falling?"

"Yeah?"

"Well, our new best friend, Gordon Walsh, your soon-to-be new editor, I mean, he just confided he wrangled from police the fact there was a suicide note found on her laptop. Doesn't make sense to me. I was the last one to talk to her, it seems, and she seemed elated, even bubbly. Guess you never really know what's in a person." A pause, then, "Did I mention she landed face first?"

Chase was truly appalled. "No." He closed his eyes. "Jesus."

"Well, this thing with Kat falling or jumping, it's probably apart from all this with our project. Still, be careful. And *puh*-lease think hard if there isn't some way to use this about Kat in our book."

8

The reddish sun was just casting light around the curtains. Chase had elected to spend the morning in bed. He was avoiding his computer this one time. After yesterday, he actually dreaded what his email inbox might contain.

Ashley propped her chin on his chest. Chase stroked her back. She said, "So, what are you going to do with this insanely lavish advance when the contracts are signed? Buy some crazy sports car? Maybe take me to Europe for a month or two?"

"I'll believe it when the contracts are signed," he said. "That's assuming I really go ahead with this thing. Between Hyde's last biographer going off his head and hanging himself and Hyde's editor taking that bloody plunge yesterday, I'm beginning to think this project is cursed in some way. I mean, even the man's wife is freshly dead. Sort of crawls your nape, doesn't it? I know it does mine."

"The wife died of cancer," Ashley said. "Nothing particularly sinister there, just terrible luck. And this thing with Kathleen is simply sad. Tragic for those who knew her. Maybe she did it as a result of a lover's spat. Maybe she just got some bad medical news that hasn't come to light yet."

Chase's fingers combed through her auburn hair. "Maybe. Seems you've read Hyde's novels in some detail, Ash. Much more than just the casual reader would. You actually studied under a man who's kind of the Hyde expert. What's your sense of the author from his work? What are some of his themes? Any recurring subjects?"

Ashley's fingers traced his lips. "It's maybe dangerous to try and draw conclusions about a writer from what he writes." An uncertain smile that reached some part of him. A sultry smile. "But of course you know that…"

"Granted. Now, what comes up in the books, over and over? Did you leave his novels intrigued about the writer behind them? Did you leave them with a sense of liking the author, or did you get the same sense this dead, would-be biographer of Hyde's ended up with? I mean, that Hyde was evil or twisted in some way?"

"I'm about a quarter through re-reading the first one again, so I'm going mostly on memory," she said.

He stroked the small of her back. "That's fine. Whatever you call to mind will likely be what resonated the most your first time through."

Ashley propped her head on her hand. "There's a lot of dark family history in each of the novels. Stuff about how one generation kind of pollutes or dooms the next. I remember there being some stuff with incest in the second novel, *Spare Parts*, and again in the third, *Rain Dogs*. Lots of psychosexual stuff that left me thinking Hyde was maybe kind of messed up in that area. But not so much of it as to make me think he was actually evil."

"What are the guys like in the books? Does Hyde have the same basic protagonist with a different name from book to book, or is there some variability?"

"Some variation, but like I said, they're all kind of screwed up sexually. The guys are married in the second and third books, and fairly unhappily so. The dude in *Rain Dogs* ends up sleeping with his own daughter after his wife's death. The three have been living in near seclusion—sound familiar?—and when the wife goes, the father and daughter kind of just drift one another's way. The male character is about forty, and the daughter maybe twenty." Ashley shrugged. "You can't really make much of that, though. Hyde was dead before his own first child was born, so it can't be biographical in that sense."

Ashley hesitated, then said, "But there is a kind of air of debauchery that runs through the three novels. A decadence that goes beyond just the sordid sexual stuff. I suppose there's something Baudelarian about all of Hyde's writing, even the six or seven short stories he left along with the published novels. But evil? That might be overstating it. That might be overstating it quite a lot."

Chase said, "When you're done with *Steal Me a Dream*, would you drop that first novel on my desk? Suppose I should read them in order, first time through."

"I'm beginning to believe it is going to be your first time reading him," she said. "And that's kind of odd. Hyde's almost the perfect biographical subject for you, based on your past books. Yet you seem to have missed all this stuff about him. Even missed experiencing his work."

"He was born in the wrong century, I guess." Chase scratched his chest. "You heard the Hyena yesterday. I've been focused primarily a hundred years, give or take, on the wrong biographical sales market sector. I mean in terms of selling books in big numbers." He wished he hadn't said it with such bitterness.

Ashley said, "Still, missing Hyde's stuff, particularly at your age, is a little like someone now not having heard of *The Da Vinci Code*, or J.K. Rowling."

"J.K. who?"

"Very funny." Her fingers trailed through his chest hair. He rested a hand on her thigh.

She reached over to the nightstand and checked her phone. "Seems I had a call." She tapped the screen, said, "It was from Selma. Maybe she got an offer on my novel. Is it bad luck to hope for that?"

"May not be what you think." Chase made a face like, *Don't kill me*, then said, "I turned my phone off after her last call around midnight. Partly to sleep and partly just to avoid any more crazy news that might keep me up. It's possible she might be trying to reach me through you."

"She called about twenty minutes ago but I had my ringer off." Ashley held her phone up to her ear, stroking her hair behind her other ear with her left hand. She said, "Selma? Hey there. Doing good." There was some small talk then Ashley said smiling, "Really? That's *great!* No, it's a first novel, so I think that's very fair. More than I expected, frankly. No, I agree we shouldn't say yes, just like that. Sure, I can wait." Ashley nodded her head a few times and said, "Well again, that's better than wonderful news. I'm thrilled!" A pause, then, "He's right here." She passed her cell phone to Chase. He had to smile: Ashley was glowing.

He said, "Selma?"

"Hey. You may have gathered if you were in earshot, there's been an offer on Ashley's novel. We're not going to say yes, just yet. I think I can leverage a better offer from a slightly more prestigious publisher now with another offer on the table. Now, the *important* news. We got our advance. I've already posted to *Publishers Lunch*, so I'm expecting the film folks to start circling. Remember, anything like a side offer tied to this, you come straight to me with it, right?"

"Of course." He could hardly fathom the money involved with this crazy gig.

Selma said, "We're going to be dealing with a guy named Shawn Dalton. He's the Hyde daughter's representative. Him, you can talk to. He'll probably be in touch today or tomorrow. I gave him both your phone numbers, as well as Ashley's, just in case. He'll arrange your travel—whatever is going to be required in terms of security and getting you to the Hyde estate, whatever. You'll probably be purposely run around a bit. Seems the daughter is about as nutty as her old man was about privacy and so forth. They'll kind of spin you around or run you in circles by air or car or something, according to Shawn. Just so you won't know exactly where you are so you can't compromise her privacy when it's all done."

Chase said, "Kind of weird, isn't it?"

"A million dollars' worth of weird," the Hyena said. "Don't lose sight of that, right?"

"Right. Well, Selma, all I can say is thank you so much. I'm stunned by the money."

"It's more than just the money, Chase. It's the raised profile and the other things this might bring our way. Just don't screw it up. Smile and think about the money. And all you have to do now is write a fucking masterpiece."

He laughed, said, "No pressure."

Selma's smile went out of her voice. "No, Chase. No alternative. After your last book, frankly, you were nearly radioactive."

Stung, stunned, Chase passed Ashley her phone, then remembered and kissed her. "Congratulations on the offer for your novel, darling," he said. "Sounds like it can be improved. The advance, I mean. And if that can be done, Selma is the one to make it happen for you. The woman's relentless."

"Congratulations to you," Ashley said. "I'm over the moon, but I'm getting chump change compared to your deal. I heard some of the rest. It is a little frightening, isn't it? Being bundled off in some car or plane to parts unknown somewhere? I don't envy you the trip."

"I can't deny it." Chase decided he'd better turn on his cell phone again. It played a little music as it powered up, then immediately began ringing. Chase frowned. "It's my old agent," he said, "the guy who handled my stuff before Selma, Bryan Dane."

He tapped the screen with his thumb, said, "Bryan? It's been a long time."

"Hey, Chasers! Just calling to congratulate you on scoring the mother of all book deals. I saw it on *Publishers Lunch*. Must admit, I'm jealous. I hoped we were going to get that deal with Hyde's daughter. I'm representing Christopher Bruce now, you see."

Bruce was another biographer, one who tended to run more toward True Crime-style bios. Tawdry tales of bluebloods who had their wives murdered after finding some hot young thing at a party in the Hamptons and getting this itch. Sleazy stuff like that.

Chase said, "What?"

"Yeah, I was negotiating with the Amanda Hyde's fellow, Shawn, for the past several months. All very hush-hush, of course. We took the project to them. Nobody ever said no, not outright, so I held out some hope. When Amanda died, it all just sort of seemed to fizzle, if it was ever really going anywhere. We had hoped to strike a deal with the daughter after a respectful period of mourning. But all was silence after Amanda's death except for a curt no from the daughter. Guess that's because you'd gotten to her first. How, I have no idea. I didn't know you were even in the hunt, but after your other books, it makes sense you'd inevitably get around to Hyde. Anyway, congratulations again, Chase. Always knew you'd score big, in time. Just sorry we couldn't get there together." He laughed and added, "I'm really sorry, now."

Chase ran his fingers back through his hair. "Thanks for the well-wishes, Bryan. I appreciate it." His ex-agent was a nice guy in an old-school way. He'd always liked Bryan. He tapped his screen to end the call. Ashley was watching him, clearly she had heard both ends of the conversation.

Chase said to her, "Now I'm even more curious about this family and their interest in me being the one."

9

George Barry, Everett Hyde's original editor, sipped his martini and said, "The veal is hardly ever less than excellent."

"Thanks, I'll think about that," Chase said. "I appreciate you doing this on such short notice. I'm told I could be hustled onto a plane at nearly any minute and flown off into the hinterlands, to some secret place somewhere, to meet Hyde's daughter. It's all kind of nerve-racking, in its way."

The retired editor smiled. "It's no problem and my days are hardly crowded lately. It helps that we both live here in the publishing capital of the world. Of course, I tried to lure Everett here a couple of times. Just so I might get a glimpse of this writer whose work I was so intensely involved in presenting to the world. But Everett just wrote tersely back how much he hated big cities and therefore would probably hate New York most of all."

Chase sipped his red wine, said, "Is that how all of your exchanges were handled? In writing, I mean? Did you ever speak on the phone?"

The old man nodded. "Just once. That so-called exchange was something resulting from a medical emergency between novels two and three. Everett desperately needed an advance. I was quite startled when the call was passed through and the man on the other end said he was Everett Hyde. I mean, I have to believe it was Everett, though he could perhaps have put somebody else up to calling in his stead. But given the nature of the call, his shyness and embarrassment to ask for an advance against an unwritten third novel, I believe it was Everett."

"What did his voice sound like? Deep? Masculine? Thinner than maybe you expected? Surprising in some other way?"

"It sounded matter-of-fact, I'd say." George lifted the speared olives from his vodka martini and shook them dry over the glass and plucked one from the end of the plastic sword skewer and popped it in his mouth. "It was a fairly unremarkable voice. Hyde had an accent about like you do. By that, I mean he had no accent to speak of. You're from the Midwest, aren't you?"

"Uh, sure."

"I'm guessing Everett was a Midwesterner too. Not Chicago, as has been claimed. Maybe originally from Indiana or Michigan. Maybe Ohio. Someplace with no remarkable accent or dialects. Everett was pretty laconic during that phone call. Just used the words needed to put across what he wanted. What he craved. Nothing showy. Everett didn't chin himself on his vocabulary the way some writers can in conversation. He wasn't going for effect."

Chase toyed with his cocktail napkin, said, "I've been reading a bit about Hyde's last days. I mean, trying to get a sense of what can be trusted amidst all the crazy stuff out there on the Web now. Looking for anything that might have foreshadowed an intended suicide." Chase hesitated, then said, "Did you see it coming?"

The old man sighed. "Well, of course Everett's books are littered with suicides and characters contemplating all forms of sexual self-abasement. That, and then, self-destruction."

"Of course." Chase sipped more of his wine as distraction. He still hadn't read all of Hyde's novels, and he saw now it was probably not just stupid, but possibly an affront to sit here with no first-hand grounding in Hyde's body of work, but still presuming to question the man who had edited and first published all of Hyde's printed works. Chase thought of Ashley. He regretted now not having asked her along to lunch.

Chase echoed what Ashley had earlier said to him. "Of course, one never wants to confuse an author's persona and personality. There's the writer and then there's the man."

"No, of course not, though I'd likely forgive you that in Everett's case," Hyde's former editor said. "I mean, there's nothing really out there about Everett to measure against. And since Everett's detractors—not that there were many, mind you, but those who cropped up were vocal and they truly angered Everett—they claimed he essentially wrote the same book three times."

"That's not your own opinion, I take it?" Chase figured that was safe enough.

George shook his head. "Not at all. Lord, no. Most worthy artists have certain touchstones and themes, certain recurring scenes or conflicts that surface time and again in their works, but in different contexts. Sometimes those repetitions are intended to mirror or to re-contextualize their cousins. Honestly, you could say John Ford kept repeating himself, but I love his Western films, even if they are full of echoes and familiar scenes and even if they give me terrific rushes of déjà vu at times."

"I was thinking of some of Hyde's more uncomfortable, but dwelt-upon themes. All that incest, for instance." Chase raised his goblet again, looking over the top of the wine glass for some reaction.

The old man cleared his throat, mustering up the edge needed to say the next. He sighed and did that. "Yes, well… I've wondered if Everett wasn't perhaps, well, let's say, familiar, for lack of a better term, with his mother. The maternal figures in Hyde's books are of a piece, of course, too. Earthy and very sexually aggressive, even toward their sons. All those scenes of these women flaunting their bodies in front of their young boys, usually when alone in the house with the lads, when they could as easily close a bathroom door or throw on a robe after showering and bathing." The old man waved a hand, uncomfortable to talk about it, despite his role in publishing the materials. A couple of older women at an adjacent table had ceased their own conversation, clearly hanging on Chase and George's rawer exchange.

"Anyway, all of it is supposition," George said, apparently oblivious to their elderly eavesdroppers. "Soon, you'll know more than I know or ever hoped to learn. I can't wait to read your book. And when you get back, you must let me treat you to lunch here. Then you must tell me, off-the-record, of course, about the papers you were privileged to see, Chase. The possibly complete, unprinted works and stories." He smiled and said, "I don't suppose you'd let me pay you to tag along as an alleged research assistant?"

According to Selma, Ashley was already cleared with Shelby Hyde's representative to fulfill that role for Chase. The fact was Chase couldn't abide the prospect of being stranded in some unknown, remote place with nobody for company but the reclusive daughter of the reclusive author. He was also a little uneasy about going off to a mysterious place alone. He'd lately begun to find Ashley's near constant presence around him cloying, yet now he desperately wanted her along for this trip, if only for carnal distraction.

In his mind, Chase had begun to visualize this hellish and decidedly Gothic few weeks for himself, marooned in this crumbling, remote family house with a couple of bent and elderly servants and Hyde's shrewish daughter. She would surely be some pale and bulging-eyed neurotic Chase envisioned as an unsettling cross between Flannery O'Connor and Emily Dickinson. Ashley would be a sexy diversion if all his worst fears were realized.

Chase said, "I'm afraid I've got someone else coming along for that research role. Sorry."

The old man waved a hand. "I was joking anyway. I'm too known to that family, and they'd never let me get near Everett's unpublished works. That's a goldmine for someone, in the end, and I expect the daughter will not want to share any of the money to be made if it's eventually published. Not even with Everett's kindly old editor."

Chase smiled, said, "Tell me, George, how much editing did Hyde's works require? Were you doing the Max Perkins-Thomas Wolfe thing and cutting down vast swaths of prose and organizing it, almost co-creating? Or was it more just tweaks and typos and so forth?"

"Much more the latter," George said. "Actually, Everett's manuscripts arrived fully-formed and remarkably clean. There was little if anything I could think of to bring to the table, and I frankly think Everett would have balked if I'd tried to tinker with his stuff in any substantive way."

"And the fourth novel? Any hints or sense of what form that might have taken?"

"None at all," George said. "I really wasn't privileged to see that side of Everett. By that I mean the planning and plotting and his steps taken toward a novel. A few months would pass, with no way for me to reach Everett directly, no word from him. Then a manuscript would simply appear. It went that way for the second and third novels. One sorry day it stopped." A snap of fingers. "And then he was dead."

The old man chewed on another olive, said, "Of course, conventional wisdom is his inability to write a worthy fourth book is what drove Everett to suicide."

Chase said, "Is that a theory you subscribe to?"

The old man thought about that and shrugged. "Having no alternative? I suppose I must."

10

Chase folded his long black overcoat and draped it over a chair. He checked his watch, then ordered a bottle of wine. He had some time before Ashley arrived.

She had picked the restaurant for their celebratory dinner to mark the signing of their book contracts. Selma had indeed succeeded in getting a larger advance from a second house for Ashley's debut novel. It was a respectable sum, what agents called, "A nice deal," in their loony lexicon—a turn-of-phrase for telegraphing the general range of money paid to an author for a book without getting *too* concrete about it.

Chase also hoped to settle with Ashley on some fee he could arrange to pay her for research assistance. She'd demurred when Chase first suggested it. She said it was enough he cover her expenses, "Whatever those might be there at Thornfield Manor or Xanadu or whatever they call this secret place we're going to be spirited off to visit." She'd not used any vacation at work for the year, and so took her full allowable three weeks off to accompany him.

But he'd insisted upon some kind of salary for her. Chase saw Ashley as invaluable to his book's factual integrity with her far deeper knowledge of Hyde's novels, particularly since he wasn't sure there'd be time to complete a first reading of all three of the books before being hustled off to Shelby Hyde's mysterious sanctum.

In theory, he should just be able to plunge in and plow through the three novels. But he had this aversion to doing that he couldn't yet figure out. Maybe some of it was the seedy, sordid subject matter everyone said typified Hyde's novels—stuff well outside the content of the works of the other authors whom Chase had chosen to write books about. Maybe it was the magnitude of the book deal that had him cowed. There was so much on the line with this one. He'd chosen his other biographical subjects based on passion, but this one had chosen him, so to speak. He couldn't shake a sense he was doing this one for the money. Still, it was *a lot* of money. He imagined it a sum to change his life forever.

Chase thought more about this secret location where the daughter was awaiting him. He smiled to himself. In his mind, he had begun to envision this crazy, Hitleresque, "Wolf's Lair" chalet hidden somewhere in a remote range of mountains. Some place like the bunker he figured Dick Cheney had been hustled off to in the first days post-9/11.

Chase had stopped at a bookstore after his lunch with George Barry to pick up another copy of *Steal Me a Dream*.

Chase took another sip of his wine, Château Margaux—splurging now that he had this magnificent book deal. He opened Hyde's novel, sighed, and set to it. He shook his head at Hyde's opening line:

> *I know exactly this much about family—*
> *it can destroy you. Blood is poison.*

Chase read on for a time, getting a little under four chapters into the novel.

Hyde's narrator was Dash (short for Dashiell) Hunt, a twenty-something, lanky moper and dreamer who had this way with words. Dash was trapped in his dusty hometown and hostage to family who couldn't fathom—let alone appreciate—his artistic inclinations.

Home was some wide-spot-in-the-road where a couple of state routes haphazardly crisscrossed in the desert. It was a place called "Why" in Pima County, Arizona.

Why was hard up against an Indian reservation and about thirty miles shy of the Mexican border.

Dash Hunt took refuge in library novels and fiction books collected by a relative, a school teacher, all the while trying hard to steer clear of his father, Jed Hunt. Jed was a harrowing and fearsome son of a bitch. He made his living as a Ranger at Organ Pipe Cactus National Monument, tooling around the Sonora Desert in his state-provided pickup and finding his way home three or four nights a week just to touch base, have rough sex with his dishy and neglected wife Iris, and maybe to cuff his sensitive son for being a "goddamn no-account bookworm."

Iris Hunt. Good God. Just a few pages in, Chase could already see how she typified the mothers in Hyde's books as described to Chase by Ashley and Hyde's editor. In a desert hellhole with a population of less than a hundred—mostly drunken Indians, old folks or co-workers of Jed's—there were scarce options left to Iris when it came to exercising her prodigious carnal urges. She was a barely repressed nymphomaniac. Iris found sex with sadistic Jed to be little better than a spur, something to make her crave more intense and satisfying couplings in which she dominated. But likely prospects for a better sex partner were scarce in Why.

Inevitably, Iris's carnal focus began to turn to her son.

"Hey, finally digging in, huh?" Ashley smiled and bent over to kiss Chase on the mouth. She tasted her lip with her tongue. "That's pretty good stuff you're drinking."

Chase closed the novel and poured Ashley some of the wine. "I think I need a shower," he said, nodding at the paperback. He picked it up and placed it on the empty chair beside him. "This is sordid as hell. I'm hardly into the book, and already I can see the mother and son are going to end up between the sheets."

"Not in that novel," Ashley said, "but I don't want to give you any spoilers." She sat down, rather carefully, Chase thought. "Hyde toes up to that tawdry line but doesn't quite cross it," Ashley said. "For the actual incest, you have to read *Spare Parts* and *Rain Dogs*. Especially *Rain Dogs*. God. Yet, pretty effectively erotic in its dark, wrong-headed way."

Hm. Ashley wasn't that adventurous in bed, it seemed to Chase—another sticking point for him when it came to the matter of her growing attachment. Maybe he'd skip ahead to the good parts of those second and third Hyde novels. Perhaps see what "darkly erotic" things turned Ashley on in those books and that he might impel her to try.

"It's well-written, and the characters are all vivid and effectively drawn, but I'm not really liking any of them," Chase said. He sipped more wine. "Despicable and unsavory as this book is, at least so far, I'm a little surprised Hyde's so popular."

"Well, like you said, you're hardly that far into the novel." Ashley sipped her wine, smiled, and said, "This is very good. And you've been at it a while, haven't you? I hear it in your voice. As to Hyde's debut, you have to hang in there for a couple more chapters to really get a taste for the book and Hyde's appeal as an author. Remember, it was written at a time when readers still had attention spans. Novels could go for the slow-build, relative to now. And at base, Hyde's just a natural storyteller, a guy who knows how to spin a sexy, slow-burn yarn."

Hyde's books have that thing so many novels now lack. You know, a plot."

He smiled. "You two would have gotten along great then." Ashley's novel also had a strong narrative arc. She'd confessed to Chase her fear that her old college-writing chums would loathe her novel because, as she sheepishly put it, "something actually happens in my book."

Ashley said, "By the way, some drunken nut evidently has gotten your landline's number. I was sitting there trying to write and, for about half-an-hour, the phone would ring every five minutes, and this guy would just rant and rave about your book in progress on Hyde, and how he should just shoot you." She smiled and shrugged. "Think it's that other biographer your old agent told you about? Maybe he's pissed you got his big money?"

"Or maybe it's just some other nut who subscribes to *Publishers Lunch*," Chase said. So Ashley had been back in his place, writing. Chase wondered if there wasn't some subtle way to get his apartment key back from her. After this trip, he was going to have to set down some rules, he decided on the spot.

She squeezed his hand. "Thank you so much for the dinner," she said. "For celebrating with me. My folks are excited, but they don't know what this means to me in some ways. I'm lucky to have a writer boyfriend to share this first sale with me."

"My pleasure," he said, looking at the wine bottle, weighing what was left.

She shook her head. "Those phone messages, they were rough. Kind of scared me to hear them coming over like that. In real time, I mean."

He tried not to let that rattle him. He waved a hand and said, "I'll listen to 'em later. Tonight, we celebrate."

11

Chase's hand hovered above the answering machine power switch. Angry, he was thinking about turning it off. Maybe even unplugging the thing for a few days. He wished he had waited until morning to listen to the recorded threats. Confronting them now was a stupid mistake. He should have taken slightly drunk Ashley straight to bed. He should have deferred checking the damned message machine.

But it was too late for that. The messages were just as Ashley described them—a drunken, non-descript voice ranted slurred threats and profanities. The caller threatened Chase with the sight of his own blood and cursed him for agreeing to write a book that could "only hurt Everett Hyde's reputation and obscure his three perfect novels. Lay off him, Alger! I'm warning you nicely! Ignore these warnings at your own peril, you parasitical son of a bitch! Just lay off."

Chase thought he'd delete the messages, then he hesitated. Maybe it was better to retain them, he decided, just in case it might be more than some drunk's harmless rant.

He scooped up his cordless phone and punched in STAR-69, thinking he'd see about maybe getting the drunken man's phone number. Fruitless: the caller's number was privacy-protected.

Suddenly, there was this other voice on the answering machine tape. Chase hung up the phone and bumped the volume up a couple of settings.

A voice said, "Chase? Shawn Dalton. I represent Shelby Hyde. Sorry I missed you. Afraid I seem to have taken your cell phone number down incorrectly when your agent gave it to me. I wasn't comfortable using the number for this Ashley person, even though your agent insisted it'd be okay to use it. Some piece of work, that one! I'd leave you my number, but I think it probably best I call as I'll be in and out until early morning. I'll try you again tomorrow around nine. I'm here in the city. I see from Google Maps you have a Starbucks just around the corner from your place. Maybe we could meet over coffee. By then I'll definitely need the caffeine. Hope to talk to you soon."

"Hardly any accent there," Ashley said, slipping off her jacket.

"Nah, sounds Midwestern to me," Chase said.

"But there is a slight accent, just on some words," she said. "Like maybe he's lived in the South for a while. Otherwise, he sounds about like you, yeah, plain. Colorless."

"Well, I guess tomorrow we'll know the plan," Chase said. "I'm thinking it might not be the worst thing in the world to start packing in the morning."

"Maybe," Ashley said. She wrapped her arms around his neck, aimed for his mouth, but kissed his chin. It had taken a second bottle of wine for Ashley to catch up to Chase, and now he was enjoying her slight drunkenness. He would enjoy it even more once he got her undressed and into bed. Maybe he could get her to let him do some of the things with her that up to now she had resisted when he tried.

Ashley tugged off his jacket and tossed it on the sofa behind him. She began fiddling with his shirt buttons. "Problem with packing for this trip now is we don't know where we're going and so what weather to prepare for," she said. "And we also don't know for how long."

"All true things," he said. "So I suppose we should find something else to do with ourselves, shouldn't we?"

About eleven, coming down off a fairly intense Château Margaux buzz, Ashley decided she wanted another glass of wine to savor while, "waiting for you to recover, so we can go again."

Chase certainly hoped he could recover for that. He gave her another look. Despite her buzz, she'd rebuffed some of his more exotic overtures. Still the small-town girl that way. Frowning, Chase poured two glasses of red wine, then put on Bryan Ferry's *Bête Noire*. He hesitated by his computer, then sat down the wine goblets and bumped the mouse waking it up.

There was a single email sitting in his inbox. The subject line read EVERETT HYDE. Chase checked the sender line: UNKNOWN. Swallowing hard, expecting something just like what confronted him when he opened the email, though not expecting the exact content of the message there, Chase read the terse threat and felt his elevated pulse in his ears that throbbed and began to burn.

> Bastard!
>
> You drop this thing and lay off Everett Hyde while you've still got your teeth and looks to impress that hot young beauty you're sleeping with.
>
> Trying to write a biography of Everett Hyde can be a very unlucky thing.

If you doubt that, ask around after a dead son
of a bitch named Carl Thompson.
Lay off, Alger. That's all, simply lay off.

Chase slowly let out his breath.

That phrase, "lay off"—Chase's threatening caller had
used it, too.

And now that he thought more about it, Chase remembered the same phrase coming up at least a couple of times in
the angry letter Everett Hyde had sent Ashley's professor so
many years ago.

"Lay off."

That simple phrase gave Chase terrific chills.

Cursing softly to himself, Chase pulled out his chair, sat
down naked, and tapped the reply button. His response was
visceral:

FUCK YOU!

Then, thinking of Hyde's three novels and their recurring
Oedipal motifs, Chase impulsively added:

&
FUCK YOUR MOTHER!

Chase hit *Send*. He wasn't sure what would happen since
the email's author had somehow sent the note under an anonymous account.

Thirty seconds later, his computer called out, "Mail
truck!" This time it didn't surprise Chase to see the familiar
jargon when he opened the delivery notification alert:

"Permanent fatal error."

Seething, he put his computer back to sleep and retrieved the wine goblets. Ashley reached out to take her glass, smiling. Her smile dimmed as she looked at his face. She said, "God, what's wrong?"

"Nothing," he said, not wanting to spoil anymore of the night. It was Ashley's night to celebrate a book contract too, after all, and her first—there was nothing more exciting for an author.

He slid into bed with Ashley and sipped some wine.

She leaned over and kissed his shoulder. Playfully bit it. "You're sure?"

"Nothing to worry about," he said. "Nothing at all."

12

By seven a.m., Chase had showered and brewed fresh coffee. He sat in front of his computer, pounding out a first draft of his envisioned opening for his biography of Everett Hyde.

Working from stuff on the Web, stuff he'd confirm, augment or punch up when he had access to primary sources and people, Chase opened with Everett Hyde tearing down the highway to Key West in his beater car, jacked up on diet pills and gallons of coffee and cola, intent upon taking himself out. The cult author was all cold sweats and shaking hands as his would-be biographer described it.

At eight, Ashley wandered out, buttoning up one of Chase's flannel shirts found in his closet. Showing a lot of leg, she groggily twisted up the sleeves as she made her way to the kitchen. She poured herself some coffee and ran her fingers through her tangled auburn hair.

He said, "Sorry, left the sugar—"

"No, taking it black this morning," she said, her eyes narrowed to slits and brow furrowed. "I've got a pretty serious hangover. Going to sit in bed with my laptop and finish a short story. Something I'm submitting to *Glimmer Train*. Then I'll hit the shower. This mysterious Shawn dude call yet?" She stretched and rubbed her side.

"Not yet, but it's too early. You okay?"

"Just hung-over, like I said. What are you working on?"

"Some rough-draft stuff on Hyde."

"Shouldn't you read his novels before you start writing your book?"

Chase shrugged. "I read some more of the first novel early this morning before sitting down to type. I must have read the book sometime back, because what I read this morning seemed somehow familiar. I always had this sense where it was going. Vague but accurate."

Chase didn't confide to Ashley the dark and vivid nightmares he'd had after finally falling asleep, still sprawled half atop her. Strange sex dreams driven by Hyde's book. Stuff about incest with a dishy mom. Even worse stuff about his fearsome father beating Chase with little or no provocation. The mother and father were both faceless in Chase's dreams, as they always were.

"I'm going to cross my fingers this Shelby chick lives somewhere really warm," Ashley said. "I'm losing my tan lines. And I'm already getting tired of the cold weather."

"But the cold's hardly started," Chase said. He was glad to be pulled away from his recollections of his night's twisted dreamscape.

"I know, and that's a very strong sign," she said. "A sign, I mean, that I need to live in the Florida Keys. Not one of the name Keys where the property rates and the cost of living are insane. I'd be fine with some obscure island. Some garden that's overgrown with palm and fruit trees. A bungalow sandwiched between some Hummer-driving drug-runners and an alligator farm, maybe. You know, local color."

"Sounds idyllic," he said to Ashley's back as she padded away, sipping her black coffee and squeezing the back of her neck as she rolled her head side-to-side. A few minutes later, he heard water running in the bathroom.

His cell phone rang. Chase checked the screen, then said, "Selma, you're up early."

"Giving you a vital heads-up," his agent said. "I'm changing my home phone number. This book of yours is becoming a kind of hemorrhoid. My machine was full of these *crazy* phone calls. Some foul-mouthed drunk threatened me. I'm not exactly in the phone book, you know, not my private number, so I don't know how in hell he got it. Probably it's just some other agent who's pissed we got the deal he thinks he should have had, or something. Maybe he looked me up in a trade journal of some kind. Anyway, I'm not fooling around waiting for the asshole to lose patience and give up." Selma read Chase her new home number.

He said, "I've had several similar calls. An email, too. I—"

"Just some jealous losers," Selma said, not waiting for Chase to finish. "I've even had some lurker, according to my doorman. Tried to get through the front door here last night. God knows what he wanted or thought he'd try if he'd gotten inside."

Chase said, "Did your doorman get a description?"

"Nothing useful. Just some white guy, late forties or early fifties." Selma paused. "Chase, don't get paranoid on me just because Kat fell off that roof the other night. Just because of those strange emails you got that started all this. It's background noise at best. If these threats are sour grapes, they'll pass in a couple of days."

Chase shook his head at that. "Did I mention there was another guy who started a biography on Hyde? They found him with a blank computer disc in his pocket, hanging from a rope around his neck outside his office window last Christmas."

"Really?" Chase thought he maybe finally had Selma's attention. He was half right. She said, "That's an *excellent* and sexy thing for our book, Chase."

"Honestly, Selma, if we're both getting threats, we should probably take them at least a little seriously, don't you think?"

"I'm changing my home number," Selma said. "That's a major pain in the ass. So how's that for serious? My doorman's being extra vigilant. Besides, in an hour I leave for Washington, D.C., for a couple of days. The National Book Festival. My last chance to hang with the First Lady, maybe. I'm after her for a memoir idea I have. Gotta go now, love, but you can reach me by cell. Oh! Did Shawn ever get hold of you?"

"He's supposed to call me in a few minutes."

"Great! Good luck!"

Chase sighed and turned back to his opening pages on Hyde's Key West suicide run.

Ashley was probably right that he should get Hyde's novels under his belt before tackling any real composition of the biography. Chase was about to put his computer to sleep and get back to *Steal Me a Dream* when the voice once again chirped "Mail truck!"

The email was from George Barry. It was a short note that read:

"Very curious this. Sending along just in case you didn't see it."

It was followed by a link to some article from *The New York Times* website.

Chase clicked on the link, sipped some coffee while he waited for the *Times'* page to load.

A headline and a subhead appeared first on screen that caused Chase to swallow wrong, scalding his throat:

Screenwriter Roger Daniels
found hanged in Village apartment

Scribe's work-in-progress was HBO biopic on cult novelist Everett Hyde

13

The latest story in the *Times* about Kathleen DeCarlo's death was decidedly sketchy. There was nothing much beyond what Chase had learned from Selma.

The woman went off her apartment balcony and fell screaming to her death. A marquee several stories below Kathleen's recessed terrace spared pedestrians being crushed by the falling editor, just as Selma had said. It happened not far from Chase's place, roughly between his neighborhood wine shop and the closest Starbucks.

Kathleen *had* been drinking.

There was no sign of forced entry into her apartment, and no mention of the suicide note found on her computer.

The article didn't go ahead and state it, but the way the story was framed conveyed a sense the reporter at least assumed the woman had been drunk and accidentally tumbled to her death. It was a sloppy piece of news writing.

Still, better that prospect of an accidental fall than the possibility Kathleen had been pushed. Right?

His landline rang. Chase braced for some drunken madman's threatening rant, said, "Yeah?"

"Hey, at last we connect! It's Shawn Dalton. Am I catching you at a bad time?"

"Not at all. Still want to meet for coffee, Shawn?"

"I've been up twenty-one hours. That is to say, *yes*. Desperately."

"How soon can you meet me at that Starbucks?"

"I'm already nearly there. Or here. I'll have mine in front of me before you arrive. Depending on how fast you are, it may not be my first. Or even my second."

It started drizzling, so Chase jogged the last half-block and ducked into Starbucks, slicking his damp hair back.

One man was seated alone at a table near the faux, gas-fed fire. He raised his cup and said, "Told the barista to give you whatever you want, buddy. Indulge yourself, no worries. You can't possibly exceed what I gave her and her tip. Honestly, can you believe what we pay for coffee these days?"

Somehow Shawn looked a bit familiar to Chase, though he couldn't quite think why that should be, beyond a superficial resemblance to himself. The other man was tallish, slender. Sandy brown hair graying at the temples. Hazel eyes that recalled Ashley's.

Chase ordered China Green Tips tea—*grande* size—then walked over to where Shawn was seated, switching his scalding cup from hand to hand as he made his way from the cash register. He quickly sat his tea down on the table and stuck out a stinging hand. "Sorry, skin may still be hot. And how'd you know it was me?"

Shawn stood and smiled, taking Chase's hand and pumping vigorously. "Your dust-jacket photos." Regardless, he intently studied Chase's face.

"Oh, sure, right."

Shawn had a firm, but not crazy-strong grip.

They both sat down. Shawn gave Chase another long, hard look. "You seem familiar to me, I mean beyond the photos on the flaps of your books."

"Probably just have that kind of face." Chase gave Shawn another appraising gaze. There seemed to be nothing quite so familiar there now.

"Well, I've got to say, given some of the candidates in the running, I'm relieved my young client chose you to write this book about Everett," Shawn said. "I've read all of your biographies to date. You'll give Everett his due in a book the also-rans would never have attempted to write. And if they had *tried* to write it, they'd have screwed it up, with handles. I really believe that. If this biography must be done—and I'm frankly not convinced it does—it needs to be done right."

"Well, thanks." That seemed like damning with faint praise, the more Chase thought about it.

Shawn smiled. "No. Thank you. I've been grinding my teeth over some of these fools Amanda was courting. Thank God Shelby seems to have some taste in biographers that the late Mrs. Hyde, God rest her sometimes misguided soul, lacked." Shawn shook his head, warming his hands on his coffee cup. "You see, among the many responsibilities Everett left me is, well, protecting his literary legacy, so to speak. It's a part of my job to nurture the Hyde literary estate. To see he stays in print, well-promoted and so forth. And I'm to slap down some of the sillier and exploitative side projects people try to mount from time to time, to tie the mercenary bastards up in endless and potentially devastating litigation."

Chase carefully sipped his piping green tea, then said, "Did you ever meet Amanda Hyde? In the flesh, I mean? Have you met Shelby?"

Shawn scowled. "Never laid eyes on them since becoming Everett's legal counsel. Everett found me not long after his third novel was published. After his death, Amanda and I communicated in writing, and, later via email. I only started corresponding with Shelby after her mother's death. Now, the daughter? She seems sharp. And harrowingly ambitious. Really, I'm still taking her measure. I have this feeling she's also taking mine."

Chase thought about it, then said, "It's the strangest thing how I got involved in this gig." He explained about his unreturnable emails, about his call to Kathleen DeCarlo and her revelation regarding Amanda's death from cancer.

Shawn listened intently, nodding. "God, I wish I could explain it. I wish I could."

That inspired Chase to share computer geek Jeremy Hill's theory regarding executors and closed-out email accounts.

"I'll have to make some calls to some of my people on that front," Shawn said, looking serious. "That's not the kind of thing I tend to handle personally. There is some possibility there. I mean in terms of your computer friend calling it right. God knows, failing that explanation, it gets more than a little unsettling, doesn't it?"

Chase smiled thinly and shrugged. "That's soft-soaping it, Shawn. Especially after Mr. Hyde's current editor taking the plunge. And just a few feet from here, at that."

Shawn shrugged it away. "She was tipsy, the papers said. All giddy, perhaps, from the notoriety coming her way over this book deal she sealed with you. Maybe she was just three-sheets-to-the-wind. Frankly, she struck me as pretty flighty. Maybe bi-polar. Kathleen was proposing all kinds of dubious stuff involving Everett once she got word Amanda had died. She wanted to reissue Ev's novels in annotated form with introductions from all these flavor-of-the-moment young novelists. She had this crazy idea about reformatting Everett's third novel with an alternate ending he'd cut before the book went to galley. Everett would never have stood for that in his lifetime. I doubt Amanda would have, either. I was getting ready to move on Kathleen for that one. The daughter was definitely against it."

Chase frowned and said, "And now there's this thing with the guy writing the script for the HBO flick about Hyde hanging himself. I only recently heard about Carl Thompson's death. And his screenwriter found dangling, too? That's got to give you pause, doesn't it?"

"Pause? Sure, I suppose. But not enough to pull out, right?" Shawn arched an eyebrow. "No. Of course not. Me either. That is to say, I've had similar thoughts, but Everett's oeuvre? Let's face it, it's dark stuff. *Very* dark. In that last book he goes all but pitch black, or so the damned critics say. The ones who are most drawn to his writing—drawn to it sufficiently to want to write books about it, to dramatize his life, even though there's nothing in the public domain to hang your hat on—they're likely to be dark and destructive types, too, wouldn't you think?"

Based on his scant reading of Hyde's canon, Chase was hard-pressed to deny it. He sipped more of his tea, said, "Given the number of years you've been serving the family, it's just amazing to me that you've been in contact with the Hydes this long, yet the women remain essentially strangers to you."

"Call it a testimony to a penchant for a certain degree of privacy." Shawn hesitated, then said, "The Hydes, all three of them, set great stock by their solitude. Or so it would seem."

Chase was checking out some comely young black woman at the counter. He saw Shawn catch him looking, smiled crookedly and said, "And they wonder why dogs snap their chains, huh?"

"Suppose." Shawn checked his watch. "Listen, I've got one more appointment before I can hit the sack. We leave tomorrow afternoon, and I still need to squeeze in some sleep. And yet you probably have a thousand questions."

"Probably. At least." Chase smiled. "My—" he almost said girlfriend, caught himself, and said, "assistant wants to know how to pack. She's hoping for some place tropical."

Shawn laughed. "Don't we all? I really don't know myself. I mean, I don't know exactly where we're bound. I've just been told to pack like I'm planning to be in New York in, oh, December. Or maybe upstate New York. That is to say, expect something brisk."

On his way out, Chase decided to veer right to pass by Kathleen DeCarlo's building. He didn't know what he expected to find there, and really found little other than some barricades set up to discourage people from walking under the now-twisted canopy of the theater's marquee.

14

Ashley had narrowed her choices to three winter coats she thought might be suited to "someplace with trees and a sky, a place you can see the stars when night falls." At least that was how Chase described Shawn's second-hand characterization of the place.

She was uneasy about the trip. All the deaths cluttered around Hyde unsettled her. Chase was obviously obsessing over them, too, yet pressing ahead. He was more mercenary than she might otherwise have guessed. It had to be so: given Chase's own stated concerns about these hangings and deaths-by-falling, it was the only explanation for Chase forging ahead with the project.

The timing could certainly be better, too. Here she was, on the brink of her own literary debut, and instead of bunkering in to work on addressing any notes her editor might have regarding her first novel, she was tagging along to keep Chase company while he worked on *his* book. Yet Chase seemed eager to have her with him, and given some of the mixed signals she had sensed him sending in recent weeks, she decided she'd better go along. He was smart, charming and attractive. And even though he was writing nonfiction, she cherished having another author to talk things through with. Ashley was confident in them as a couple. Chase, she sensed, was still deciding.

She stacked the three coats on a display table by a tri-paneled mirror to try them on again. Shrugging off the first coat and reaching for another, Ashley saw a man reflected in one of the mirrors. The man was rather tall, six-feet, maybe six-one. The man kept his back to Ashley as he sorted through blouses.

From something in his demeanor, the way he held himself, Ashley guessed the man was in his mid- to late-forties. He had a hoody on under a long black overcoat and the hood was up. A clerk leaned in toward the man as Ashley watched them in the mirror. As she shrugged on the second coat, Ashley heard the clerk ask if she could help the man find something. Ashley heard only a word of the man's answer: "Browsing."

Even at that, there was something familiar about the voice.

Ashley slipped on the third coat, a suede number, turning a bit to inspect it from different angles, but as much watching the man who still kept his back to Ashley. Looking at herself once more in the mirror, she settled on the third winter coat. Another clerk who had been helping Ashley earlier was suddenly at her side. The clerk said, "That's the one, for sure. It looks great on you. Leave the other two and we'll put 'em back."

Nodding, Ashley checked her watch and saw it was ten to nine and evidently near enough to closing time as another clerk had partly pulled down the metal, garage-style door that dropped into place to protect the shop's glass façade overnight.

As the clerk rang up her new coat, Ashley stole a look back over her shoulder: the man was gone.

Probably nothing menacing, she thought, but with the emails, phone threats and so many violent deaths that tied back to the Hyde family, Ashley had to allow that some of Chase's mounting fears had infected her own thinking.

The clothing shop was connected by a breezeway to an adjacent shoe store. Ashley grabbed a black baseball cap from a display by the register and asked the clerk to ring it up, too, as well as to remove the price tags along with the security buttons from her new coat and hat.

Ashley slipped her old coat into the store bag and donned the new one. She tucked her hair up under her ball cap and tugged the brim low. She pulled up the collars of her coat around her cheeks, then left through the front door of the shoe shop, head down and walking briskly.

Her father was always after her to carry mace. He even offered to buy her some self-defense key ring he'd seen in a mercenary magazine. The thing looked like a metal dagger and could be driven into the eye or soft tissue of an attacker.

Her parents were still back in their small town in Pennsylvania. Thomas McKnight viewed Philly as something just short of Hell. New York exceeded his vocabulary to adequately disparage. He was always at his daughter to leave the city. He'd say something in variation of, "You can write *anywhere*, *can't* you? Isn't that what writers do? Write about other places and people from imagination? These science fiction writers don't have to go to the moon to write about it. Why God invented computers. Everywhere has been photographed by now, hasn't it?"

Her parents had grudgingly come around to Ashley's ambition to make her living as a writer. They'd yet to reconcile themselves to the notion of her forever doing that in New York City. When she first told them of her dream of living in New York City as a fiction writer, her father had laughed scornfully. When he saw the look his reaction put on his daughter's face, he'd gathered her up in his arms. He'd wiped at her tears with his big and callused thumbs, vowing to find a way to get her to the city.

With this strange stuff swirling around her, this stranger maybe stalking her in the clothing store, she wished she'd gotten that mace from Daddy—that she had let her father buy her that wicked key ring.

In the angled glass of shop-fronts, Ashley checked for glimpses of anyone who might be following her, but the reflected images were too indistinct to settle her mind one way or another.

About twenty yards up the street, a cab was pulling up to the curb. A couple was climbing out. Ashley ran and squeezed into the back of the cab ahead of some cross-looking dude in an Italian suit with a cell phone pressed to his ear.

It was less than three blocks to her apartment. Ashley had the driver circle the block twice, just trying to see if she could spot a possible tail.

Satisfied nobody had followed her home, she paid the driver but took the precaution of asking he wait to see her pass through the security door of her building before driving off.

She wasn't confident the cabbie spoke enough English to even get the drift of her request, so she ran to her front door and quickly slid through. Turning, Ashley saw the taxi driver leaning down to wave at her before driving away. Ashley waved back, then pressed her hand to her belly, frowning at some pain that had come again there, wondering if she might not be getting an ulcer.

Ashley threw home the deadbolt on her front door. Then she called Chase.

She said, "Hey."

"Hey," he said back. "You home? Or are you coming back here?"

"Locked in here, safe and sound," she said. "Only thing was—"

This beep—a call waiting. She said, "I've got take another call, it's Mom. Have to take it."

"Of course. Quickly then, are you coming back tonight?"

"It's late, and I have to pack, so I think I'll sleep here tonight," she said. "Call you in the morning."

"Right." Ashley frowned. Chase hadn't put up much of a struggle about her staying home.

Ashley talked to her mother for about forty minutes, talking about her book deal. She already dreaded the prospect of her mother or her father perhaps actually reading her novel, especially the sex scenes, which were raw if honest. Hopefully, Dad would take them for figments of her imagination.

But then there was the stuff about her hometown and some thinly disguised family members that her mother might recognize and blanche at reading.

She did tell her mother about her impending trip with Chase and a little about the mysterious legend of Everett Hyde. She didn't confide to her mother about the threats, or about Hyde's murdered agent and two hanged would-be biographers.

As their conversation wound down, Ashley stripped to her bra and panties, intending a shower. She felt her right side again, pressing her fingers to the butterfly tattoo—the relic of a tipsy whim she now regretted. God, if Daddy knew about those tattoos?

Still probing, she found there was no pain in her belly now, but it was warmer there, she thought. She got a small bottle of Perrier from the refrigerator and pressed its cold plastic to her side.

She leaned over her battered old white-pine desk and powered up her laptop. Saying her good-byes to her mother, Ashley piggybacked a neighbor's bleed-over wireless signal and clicked to check her email. Rubbing her lower right side with one hand, now cold to the touch from the frigid water bottle, she clicked at her mouse with the other.

While she waited for her email to boot up, she opened up her iTunes library and clicked on Lucinda Williams' *Passionate Kisses*. She was intent upon drowning out the sound from her neighbors. The couple to the east were banging their headboard against the wall, the girl groaning over and over, "Oh yeah! Oh, baby, just like that!"

To the west, the Culversons were arguing again. Mrs. Culverson always had bruises she tried to hide with long sleeves, caked face powder, and too-big-for-her-battered-features sunglasses.

Ashley's email account finally opened. It was mostly mundane stuff at first. Amazon.com free-shipping offers, some items kicked her way by a Google news and a blog alert she'd created for the name "Chase Alger"—probably stuff about the recent book award and the new Hyde book deal.

And a single email with no subject line, sent by "UNKNOWN." This one had come through the email attached to the official website she'd established recently to promote her own works.

Ashley went straight to that email, took a breath, then opened it.

The message was pithy and to-the-point:

> *"Don't you think it odd a man who writes books about the lives of others has no past of his own?"*

What the hell?

Deliberating, Ashley read the message a couple more times. She let out a deep breath, finally decided in her mind: she tapped the reply button.

Ashley typed, "Elaborate." She hit send.

A minute passed, then she got a message back:

Undeliverable.

She opened the notification error, grinding her teeth at the message:

Permanent Fatal Error.

More craziness.

And yet? The creepy email message stirred qualms Ashley had sometimes entertained about Chase, but never until now so *deeply*.

Chase's strikingly bland personal space—his apartment devoid of photos or family heirlooms or *anything* that connoted a personal history—suddenly took on a sinister patina.

The biographer who lived to ferret out the secrets and family lives of others *never* spoke of his parents.

Ashley realized again she didn't known anything about his origins. He'd claimed to have no siblings. She'd once been talking about lost, beloved pets and asked if he had dogs or cats. Instead of answering simply, Chase seemed to grope for memory of some pet of his own before saying, "Nah... I mean, not that I recall."

She stared at the message on her screen a long time before sighing and hitting delete. She looked around at all her own childhood pictures and family portraits, trying to imagine Chase as a child, as a teen... as a young man.

She came up short every time.

SHELBY

"The finished man among his enemies?
How in the name of Heaven can he escape
That defiling and disfigured shape
The mirror of malicious eyes
Casts upon his eyes until at last
He thinks that shape must be his shape?
And what's the good of an escape
If honour find him in the wintry blast?"
— W.B. Yeats

15

Ashley and Chase were riding their second airplane of the day. They'd been hustled off a small prop-job and urged into a jet by Shawn Dalton, far from sight of any terminal or signage that might give them a clue as to where they had touched down.

Chase's only observation, whispered to Ashley, "A jet means someplace far away, potentially. Craft like this might be able to go some real distance on a tank."

Now Shawn sat with them in the rear compartment of the smallish Gulfstream jet, his very presence discouraging that flavor of out-loud speculation regarding destinations.

Dalton was about Chase's age, Ashley guessed. He had similar height and hair color to Chase. Shawn wore black pants, a dark shirt and sweater under a long black overcoat. He was attractive enough, she thought. In some ways, Chase and Shawn might even be confused for siblings, though Shawn was maybe more classically handsome than her writer boyfriend.

Shawn had been waiting at Chase's loft when Ashley arrived with her luggage. Shawn had also shared an airport shuttle with Ashley and Chase, leaving her no opportunity to raise the issue with her lover of the strange email regarding his allegedly shadowy past.

And Ashley had to admit that now there were other, fresher concerns nagging at her—these truly dogging her thoughts. She pressed her hand to her side again. She had a burning ache about halfway between her navel and right side and wondered if the dark and strange events of the past couple of days might not indeed be stoking ulcers.

She had tried to beg off the trip at the last minute, thinking out loud she really should see a doctor, but Chase had shamed her along.

Maybe it *was* just an ulcer—something reasonably treatable. Lord knew she was stressed. No disputing it, things were strange about this trip. Strange, and more than a bit troubling.

Ashley kept catching herself cataloguing her concerns.

First, there was the matter of the cell phones, or rather, their lack of phones now.

Ashley and Chase had been instructed—no, ordered—by Shawn to leave their cell phones at Chase's loft. Their phones were turned off and left to gather dust there on Chase's writing desk.

Shawn had been nonchalant in his explanation for that. He said, "Miss Hyde really is very protective of her privacy, you see, and our security consultant for this transaction—we'll meet him there; quite an impressive guy—alerted Miss Hyde to the concept of cell phone pinging. You probably know all this, though I have to confess the technical aspects of much of this still flat out confounds me. So far as I understand it, your cell phone constantly emits a signal that bounces off any cell phone tower in its range, leaving a kind of recorded and therefore traceable footprint, so to speak. It seems if you're in range of several towers simultaneously, and more or less stationary, as we'll be at Miss Hyde's compound (that word had made Ashley shiver, a little), your location could potentially be triangulated to within a few inches."

As Ashley had started to raise a finger following Shawn's fairly unnecessary explanation of cell phone tracking, Shawn had quickly held up a hand, shushing her, and said, "Please, Miss—?"

"McKnight, but Ashley's fine."

"If it's any consolation, Ashley," Shawn said smiling, "I've been directed to leave behind my own cell phone. It's not that we're not trusted. It's more the fear that some agent, some editor—or maybe some conniving publicist at Everett's old imprint—might try to use this technology to track down Shelby Hyde. Maybe try to make a fast buck selling the location of her private estate to *Entertainment Tonight, People,* or *The National Enquirer.* The last thing Miss Hyde wants is her privacy shattered by a bunch of skulking paparazzi or mouthbreathing *stalker*azzi from *TMZ,* or the like."

Chase had said, "I understand that. Really, I do. But I also do require daily contact with my agent. We're in some delicate rights negotiations now, foreign rights negotiations. Also, Ashley needs to be in constant reach by her mother, who is ill." That last had been a lie, but under the circumstances, Ashley would allow it. Chase then had added, "And Ashley just sold her first novel and there are still details to be worked out. Papers to be signed and maybe mailed against deadlines."

Shawn had paid a good deal more attention to Ashley after hearing about her novel. Smiling, he asked, "You're a novelist, Ashley? What kind of novel? Not some genre effort, or...?"

Ashley had shaken her head. "No, it's a literary novel. But I'll probably be slaughtered for it. Against current vogue, my novel has a plot. Sometimes, I think I was born twenty or thirty years too late. I think I'm maybe a Modernist throwback."

Shawn had smiled and squeezed her arm, drawing a frown from Chase. Still holding her arm, oblivious to Chase's scowl, Shawn had said, "No worries on losing contact with your agent, Ashley. We'll all be issued pre-paid, disposable cell phones at the other end. Those are untraceable, I'm told. The reason terrorists favor the things."

At last letting go of her arm, Shawn had said, "I'll look for your novel, Ashley. Be very nice to read something new and literary that actually tells a story for a change. So much written now just doesn't... well, cohere. Doesn't really go anywhere." He winked. "And don't worry, if we need to, we will find a way to get any documents back and forth between you and your publisher, I promise. Lord knows, I know how to move contracts."

Now they were hitting turbulence. The jet's bucking had Chase and Shawn hunching a bit in their seats in apparent fear of otherwise banging their heads against the crowding fuselage as the plane plunged and rose sharply.

Ashley thought the turbulent air rocking their jet might be the result of updrafts from the mountains below them. Through breaks in the cloud-cover, she saw occasional flickers of their plane's shadow across the canopy of trees growing thick on the mountain tops. They were flying low enough now that Ashley suspected they must be on a landing approach; the painful popping in her ears certainly indicated descent.

Because of the verdant mountains, Ashley also figured they must still be somewhere east of Missouri. The mountains were too wooded to be the Rockies or even the Sawtooth ranges, in her estimation.

And although they had been flying for some time between the prop aircraft and this one, Ashley strongly sensed they were flying in great, lazy circles. The late afternoon sun had shone through both sides of the jet's compartment, so Ashley had deduced they'd arced west before eventually doubling back eastward.

Ashley looked away from the window. Chase's head was down and he was pouring over a Hyde novel, the second one, cramming to better cope with Hyde's daughter. Chase had one leg crossed over the other. His white knuckles on one of his seat's arms the only indication other than his stooped position he was even aware of the roughness of their flight now.

Shawn suddenly reached over and shook Chase's foot. Shawn said, "Everett's second novel, how many times have you read it?"

Ashley held her breath, hoping this time Chase would have the good sense to lie.

Chase closed the paperback, marking his page with an extended index finger. "God, I've lost count. Since this started, I've been going back through them. It's amazing how you find new angles, new elements each time. Of course that's true of all the best books, so many layers and nuances."

That almost elicited a wince from Ashley, who anticipated Shawn's next question. Shawn indeed posed it. "For instance?"

Chase brassed it out. "I'll save my take for the biography. Like the man said, the book you talk about is the book you never write."

That somehow seemed to satisfy Shawn. He smiled and said, "In that, you almost sound like Everett."

Ashley said, "You met Everett face to face?"

Shawn shook his head. "Lord, no. But we talked on the phone a few times. I tried to draw him out on writing. I'm something of a frustrated fiction writer myself." He made a face. "But given my background and training, if I do ever put something together, it'd probably read like John Grisham. That's if I'm lucky." Shawn smiled at Ashley then.

"When you put these writing questions to Everett, he'd clam up on you?" Evidently deciding his reading was done for a time, Chase folded the corner of the page his finger rested upon to bookmark his place. He slipped the paperback into the pocket of his own black overcoat. "His editor made Everett sound pretty tight-lipped about his writing process."

"Every time I put such a question, it was met with silence," Shawn said. "Everett never talked about works-in-progress, which I do kind of understand. And I've read enough interviews with other authors, and handled some business for several other writers, to know it's a common enough attitude. Take you, for instance, Chase. But Everett wouldn't even talk in broad generalities. Wouldn't even talk about writing routines, nothing like that."

There was some crackling, some static, then a voice came over the radio. "So sorry for the rough ride, folks. Mr. Dalton, you wanted to be alerted when we began our final approach. That would be now."

That confirmed Ashley's suspicion, almost as much as the popping and piercing pain in her ears that had plagued her for the past five or ten minutes. She had extremely narrow ear canals, and air travel was frequently an unpleasant, sometimes even an agonizing experience.

Shawn said, "This is a little strange, I know, but I have to ask you to put these on now."

He reached into a plastic bag and pulled out two pairs of black sunglasses. They looked a bit like vintage aviator's glasses, perhaps even antique welding goggles. The shades had black plastic panels that wrapped around the sides of the glasses, effectively precluding peripheral vision. There was also an extension at the top of the glasses that firmed up against the forehead, just above the eyebrows, making it impossible to peer over the tops of the glasses.

Chase tried his glasses on, then pulled them off, frowning and looking at the black lenses. "I can't see anything other than my feet."

"That's pretty much the point," Shawn said, smiling a bit sheepishly. "Miss Hyde really is adamant about protecting her privacy. The glasses are her security advisor's inspiration. It was these, or blindfolds, which frankly would have been a little over-the-top and could cause problems with authorities if civilians were understandably alarmed at seeing blindfolded people being led around the airport grounds. Again, if it's any consolation—" Shawn pulled out a third pair of glasses—"I have to be wearing these when the cabin door is opened. The two pilots and the security chief will be there to offer us each an arm. They'll see us into the back of the van that will take us on the next leg of our journey. And before you ask, yes, I'm told there are no windows and a curtain will be closed between us and the windshield."

Ashley and Chase exchanged uneasy looks and then slipped on their black sunglasses. As she sat there, effectively blind, Ashley moved her jaws and swallowed repeatedly, trying to get her ears to stop hurting. She mumbled, "This is all a little scary."

She felt a hand bump her thigh and then rest there, squeezing slightly in a gesture of comfort. She reached for the hand and rubbed her thumb across its back, feeling small hairs.

This sudden chill: she tried to remember if the backs of Chase's hands were that hairy. Uncertain now, she moved her thumb away. She felt the hand lift from her thigh.

A moment passed, then a hand closed over the back of her hand, squeezing it reassuringly. The hand was warmer now and the pressure seemed familiar. She squeezed back once, then tipped her head back against the seat, gritting her teeth at the pain deep in her head as her ears throbbed, at the duller ache in her abdomen that seemed to come and go in shorter intervals.

16

The pilot, or maybe co-pilot—Ashley hadn't heard either one say enough over the radio to be certain—said, "Ma'am, I'm going to take your arm now and lead you out of here."

Ashley extended her left arm. "Can we make it this one?" She found pressing her right palm to her abdomen slightly eased the occasional pain in her side.

Someone took her left arm and said from below Ashley, "Sure. Duck low now, Ma'am. First step of seven down is coming right up."

So far, it didn't seem much colder outside than it had when they left New York City. The tarmac stank strongly of fuel and the jet's roar covered any telltale sounds that might have given a clue as to where they had landed.

The voice again. "Okay, Ma'am, we're getting into the van now. Just a step up, but please keep your head low again. Don't want you to brain yourself."

The stranger turned her around inside the van and said, "You can take off your glasses now and grab a seat."

The van had bench-style seating along each side of the rear compartment. As she sat down, Chase was taking off his glasses and sliding onto the seat next to her. Shawn was just stepping into the van, slipping off his glasses as one of the pilots flipped on an overhead dome light in the back of the van. "So you won't be in darkness for the rest of the ride," he said. "I'm told it won't be a terribly far drive." He closed the van's back doors on them.

Shawn had taken up a seat across from Ashley and Chase. He smiled and shook his head. "That wasn't so terrible, was it?"

Chase kept up small talk with Shawn. Ashley held to the edge of the seat with both hands to steady herself against the van's motion. The pain in her belly, whatever it was, had eased a good bit. She started thinking maybe she had actually somehow torn a muscle at the gym and the discomfort from that was at last subsiding.

It felt as though the van had been climbing for a time, twisting on embanked, inclined roads. Or it *had* felt that way. Contrary to what the pilot said, the trip was turning into a very long one. Ashley guessed they were in heavy traffic now, crawling along at hardly more than idling speed. Every few feet, a volley of horns sounded. Occasional obscenities shouted out by other drivers bled through the van's walls.

Shawn said, "If the road was flat, I'd guess we're on the Vegas strip."

Through the closed curtain, a voice, low, gravelly, said, "Just a couple more blocks, then we'll be asking you to put back on those funny glasses, folks."

This time, a very strong hand took Ashley's arm. "Here, sweetie, duck that noggin'. I've got you." It was the gruff, low voice that had instructed them to put back on their glasses. The man's hand moved down and took Ashley's hand and then urged her to bend her arm. Another hand closed over the back of her forearm. "Nice and easy now," he said. "I'll guide you and don't worry, beauty, I'll remember to walk for two. No steps to worry about. There's just a kind of ramp, but I'll tell you when we get there."

Ashley could feel a gustier wind across her face. It was a good bit chillier than it had been on the airport concourse. It was dark now, too, so far as Ashley could make out around the bottoms of her sunglasses—at least she could see her feet and so maybe wouldn't end up tripping. She also felt snow on her skin, tasted it on her lips.

They moved inside a building, and she could hear what sounded like passing families, adults and children chattering. She heard something about a "slalom." She realized she had cocked her head to hear better, and the man with the gruff voice suddenly made small talk, deliberately she thought, trying to inhibit Ashley's efforts to eavesdrop on passers-by, to get some other clues as to where they were now.

The voice said, "Must be a little unsettling, all these precautions. Don't worry though, honey. Once we get up top, all this cloak-and-dagger shit stops. It's a swell pad up there. Very swanky. And now here come those ramps. They zigzag, but just you trust me. I won't let you fall."

Ashley put out her left hand and felt a cold metal handrail. She let her fingers trace across its stinging surface as they walked on, veered left, then went on another twenty or so yards before a sharp turn to the right.

They passed through several switchbacks like this, as if they were in a cue for some amusement park ride.

Another voice she didn't recognize said, "Here she comes."

Some other voice—maybe a father because Ashley heard excited children, too—said, "God, we just made it in time!"

Ashley's guide called back, "Uh, no, sorry, you *didn't,* pal. Last public ride up and back ended five minutes ago, pal. This is a private charter, one way. Sorry, folks."

She could feel a slight breeze against her cheeks again. There was a sound of some heavy machinery coming to a sighing rest, then Ashley could hear the wind again and felt a much stronger gust of air that fingered her hair. Her guide said, "Going outside again, but not for long."

There was a pneumatic sound, like an automatic door opening. Through the narrow space at the bottom of her glasses, Ashley could see she was stepping off a concrete pad onto something covered with nonskid rubber. There was the subtlest sense of motion under her feet, as though whatever they were stepping into was buffeted by the blustery wind.

The rocking increased in pitch as the wind grew harder. She heard the sigh of an automatic door closing again. She could hear a fan blowing and felt warmer air coming her way. Her guide took her hand and placed it on a rail. "Hold tight now. In fact, sit down, why don't you? Bench is right behind you." He held her arm as Ashley felt with her other hand, patting an upholstered bench and then sitting down.

"If your eyes were open," the gruff voice said, "you'd be fine, but with them closed, well, the first couple of pylons, particularly, can really rock this mother. With those shades, boat's motion might knock you off your feet."

There was a sound of whirring machinery from somewhere outside whatever they were *inside,* then this jerking and rocking motion, forward and back. There was a sense of some swinging, then a steady, forward momentum that sent Ashley leaning backward a bit. There was a slight bounce now and then, too. A few seconds passed, then the gruff voice said, "Hold tight now love, this is the first and rockiest of the pylons."

There was a tremendous lurch and then sway that sent Ashley bumping back against what felt like very cold and tempered glass. There was also a slight stomach-fluttering sensation, a little like the drop you experience on a roller coaster. Then they began their forward motion again.

"One more pylon, and then we'll let you all take off your glasses for a few minutes. We'll be out of sight of landmarks for most of the time it takes to get up top."

There was silence for a few more moments, then, "One more now. Hold on tight."

This lurching jerk wasn't as severe as the first had been in Ashley's estimation. When it was over, the gruff voice said, "Okay, folks, you can take off the glasses. At least until we get near the top."

Ashley pulled off her shades, blinking a few times to adjust to the low light. They were in some kind of a large tram. She looked out the window behind her. She saw the lights of mountain homes glowing far below, headlights on twisting roads and snowcaps on the mountains glowing in the light of the nearly full moon. She could see the play of an opposing cable and the dim lights of another tram coming down from the mountaintop as they climbed to meet it.

She exchanged glances with Shawn and Chase. The gruff-voiced man said, "Not so frightening once you know what you're inside, is it?" He was tall, at least six-four, maybe even six-five, Ashley thought. Guy was way too into his own physique, she could tell that from his severely tailored clothes. He was wasp-waisted and broad-shouldered under a leather bomber jacket.

The man's head was shaved and he had the gray-blue shadow of a beard and moustache, just stubble really. His eyes were pale blue and he had a scar that started high up on the left side of his forehead and trailed jaggedly down, disrupting his rather bushy black eyebrows, and resuming at his cheekbone. The scar terminated just below his lower lip. It looked like whatever caused the wound had severed some nerve. The man's mouth drooped a bit on the left side. The resulting expression looked like a perpetual sneer on him, where it might have resembled the effects of a stroke on a less malevolent-looking face, Ashley thought.

The man smiled his crooked, drooping smile and said, "Christ, my manners. Well, I haven't any! That said, I'm Joe Arick. But call me Brick, everyone does."

Shawn said, "Brick. Really?"

Chase slipped the arm of his glasses down his sweater neck. "Swell, Brick. Good skiing in these parts?"

Brick winked and smiled at Chase; not a pleasant smile. "Very clever, buddy—fishing for some clue as to where we are. Well, stop that stuff, and I mean fucking now. Ms. Hyde asked I make it clear up front that as much as she values your services, all of your services, she'll take a dim view of anyone's attempts to undermine security. She'll take a dim view. Me? I'll take a much more boisterous view."

Shawn, scowling, said, "Boisterous. That a threat?"

"Just setting terms, counselor," Brick said. Still smiling, he looked over his shoulder. "Another pylon coming up. We've still got some distance to go."

That wasn't pleasing news to Ashley—her ears were already popping.

She looked through the back window of the tram—the thing seemed big enough to hold nearly a hundred—but it was all gloom and snow flurries that direction, same as up front. So Ashley turned her attention to the side window, where she could look down and occasionally see rooftops covered with snow, scattered landscaping lights. She could see some interior light through a few skylights. Through one of these, she saw a couple sprawled nude on a bed, making love.

Chase walked unsteadily over and sat down next to her. "You still feeling okay?"

"Better now," Ashley said evenly, watching the couple until they disappeared from view. It was true that the pain in her side, whatever the hell it was, had subsided again, at least for a time.

He took her hand and she squeezed it back. Remembering then, she looked at the back of his hand and got this shiver—it was smooth—nearly hairless.

She glanced over at Shawn, but his hands were in his pockets.

17

"Like a mini-blizzard, isn't it?" Brick was holding tight to a chrome center post as the tram rocked side-to-side. That lateral motion, combined with the heavy and stomach-dropping back-and-forth sway as the tram's arm passed over the intermittent pylons, was harrowing. Chase said, "How much longer?"

"To the top, of course, but that's the next-to-last one," the security chief said. He looked over his shoulder again, there was a hazy light visible up there now. "Yep, time to put on those crazy shades again, kids."

Ashley looked at Chase, shrugged, and slipped back on the black glasses. "For all this weirdness I'm enduring, you better write a great biography," she said softly. She added, "And you better take me some place with palm trees and sunlight after this."

Brick again had Ashley by the arm. She watched her feet through the tiny slit at the bottom of her glasses. She saw they were again stepping onto concrete. "No maze this time," her guide said, "but another ramp."

She could again hear voices, what sounded like families. Someone muttered, "They must be blind people being trained how to get around."

Someone else, a teenager maybe, said, "Then shouldn't they have canes or dogs?"

From what sounded like somewhere below them, Ashley heard excited chatter, a few young squeals of delight. She also heard a scraping sound that seemed familiar, but which she couldn't quite place. And now, as those scraping sounds grew louder—and so presumably closer—there was a slight sense of colder air, a *rising* chill. The scraping sounds were more intense, and now there was an expanse of white visible through the bottoms of her glasses. As she focused on that white patch, she saw someone's head far below; saw the back of a calf and a foot. Then Ashley knew: they were walking by an ice skating rink perhaps ten or twelve feet below.

Ashley's escort must have realized she might see what they were passing by because he suddenly urged her away from the skating rink's perimeter. All she could see now were her own feet and gray concrete. There was the chatter of some more excited children. Brick said, "Going outside now. Be careful, people. There's going to be quite a few steps and ramps getting to the next van, and it's icy here. Already about two inches of snow on the ground, they say."

Ashley held onto a metal rail while Brick steadied her by her other arm, telling her as they were about to take each step. They walked slowly across slick pavement to another van.

This van they entered through a sliding side door. Ashley went in first and scooted all the way across the seat, settling in behind the driver to make room for Chase and Shawn. Once they were in the van and the door was closed, Brick, sitting up front in the passenger seat, said, "Glasses can come off—there's not much lighting or scenery, and with all the snow, you're not going to see much anyhow."

Ashley slipped off the glasses and passed them to Brick who dropped them in the console compartment between the driver and passenger seats. He threw Chase and Shawn's glasses in behind hers. Blinking as her eyes adjusted to the light, she saw that Shawn was sitting next to her. Chase was seated behind the passenger's seat, staring at the back of Brick's shaven head.

Shawn checked his wristwatch. "Almost ten—assuming we're still on Eastern Standard Time."

Brick twisted around his seat to see them better. Ashley found herself searching the van's dashboard for a clock. There was a piece of duct tape slapped over the portion of the dash above the radio/CD player, just about where she would expect there to be a digital clock display. Brick said, "Give me all your watches, on that note. We'll give 'em back in the morning. When you wake up, and your watches are returned, then you can trust whatever time they say is the time it is where you are."

"Been some time since I last ate," Shawn said, sour-faced as he slipped off his watch and passed it to the security chief. "A time since any of us have had anything." Shawn nodded at Ashley pressing her hand to her belly, confusing her belly pain for hunger pangs. "See," he said. "Starving."

"There's a cook on duty at the compound," Brick said. "She'll make you all whatever you want. Ms. Hyde's away this evening, but she'll be back here in the morning to meet you all after breakfast."

"You're sure she'll even be able to get here?" Chase said, "I mean with all this snow? Looks like it's going to come down all night."

"They're used to snow here," Brick said. "And I'm told this isn't so much snow at all for these parts."

They rode in silence for perhaps twenty minutes, Ashley guessed. Brick said abruptly, "And here we are."

They were on twisting, climbing, snow-covered road. The light, dry snow moved in serpentine eddies across the pavement, stirred by the wind.

The van driver pressed the button on a console clipped to the passenger's side sun visor and a black, wrought iron gate swung inward. They pulled through and the man pressed a second button on the console to close the gate behind them. Through the snow, and in the low light, Ashley couldn't make out much of the house. It seemed to be a mix of stone and timber, one-story and not particularly imposing. The house was surrounded by tall old trees and old-growth furs and pines that topped out at perhaps thirty or forty feet, looking like trees that might find their way to the White House lawn or Rockefeller Plaza some future Christmas.

As they moved around the van, motion detectors kicked on several exterior floodlights. Now Ashley thought the house looked a bit like a ski-lodge—a sense that was undermined by the surrounding fence with razor-baling wire running along its top, by the security cameras that slowly panned left and right and back again from pole-mounts or from the corners of the steeply-sloped, cedar-shingle roof.

"Smallish-looking," Shawn said. "The house, I mean."

Brick shook his head. "Nah. It's spacious enough. Joint's built into the mountainside. Spreads out and goes down from the front here. It's actually several stories tall." He slipped out and then opened the sliding door of the van to let them out.

"We'll have your luggage and laptops to you shortly," Brick said nonchalantly. "Bags are coming in a second van, coming up the slow way, via roads. You were all too valuable to risk on the ice, so for you, it was the tram."

Ashley couldn't resist looking back over her shoulder at all the empty space behind their seat. There was more than enough room to transport her own, Chase and Shawn's luggage. Maybe Brick read her mind. He said, "Since 9/11, bags aren't allowed on the tram. When we get inside, we'll see to taking any orders for food, drinks. We'll show you to your rooms while we wait for your luggage to catch up." He shrugged, "Or, if you're like me and you sleep in the raw, well, you can crash, pronto."

Ashley arched an eyebrow and leaned forward a bit to exchange a look with Chase. Shawn said, "Gonna be a strange few days, sure enough. And this guy's a major-league asshole."

Chase said, "A pretty polite way to put it."

18

A shley said, "This Brick guy, he's really a piece of work, isn't he?"

"Well, he's way too into his stupid nickname, that's for sure," Chase said. "What a clown."

Ashley kicked off her shoes and stretched out on Chase's bed. She rubbed her right side as she sipped a diet Coke. Looking around, she saw there were no clocks, not even an alarmclock radio. No television, either. Ashley shook her head at that: probably it was because one local newscast would tip them to where they'd been taken.

As a result of their pretense she was along as Chase's research assistant, they'd been given separate, anonymous-looking rooms. They were little better than hotel rooms: the same basic color scheme, the same maroon upholstery on the chairs, and even the same paisley duvet spread across the identical king-size beds.

Each of the rooms had a couple of landscape paintings of forested glens that Ashley was fairly certain were mass-produced. Each room was also equipped with an intercom console next to the bed. Ashley's room was across the hall from Chase's. Shawn had been placed in the room to the left of Ashley's.

The interior portion of the house that Ashley had so far seen reminded her even more of a ski lodge, lots of dark exposed timber, stone and hardwood floors covered with throw rugs. There were no personal photos in the public spaces they had seen so far. Evidently, Everett Hyde's aversion to photos encompassed family portraits, as well. Ashley hadn't even spotted a photo of any women, young or old, who might be Shelby or Amanda Hyde.

The sofas and chairs were all covered in distressed leather. The tables and armoires were made of artificially distressed and dark hardwoods.

It seemed hours had passed, and Ashley, Chase and Shawn were still awaiting their luggage and laptops.

Brick had explained some reckless retiree had rolled a motor home on the single icy road leading up to the Hyde compound. He said it might be three hours before the wreck was moved far enough off the pavement for the van with their luggage to make it around the accident scene.

"Looks like we may sleep commando after all," Ashley had said dryly when that news was delivered to them at the bar. She immediately regretted the remark when Brick smiled and winked at her. She regretted it more as he gave her a lingering and leering, head-to-toe look.

They were alone in Chase's room now. He sat down next to Ashley. Chase cupped a hand over her hand as she massaged her side. "Hurts again, huh?"

"Yes," she said. "Sometimes it's nagging, sometimes pretty sharp. And sometimes there's no pain at all."

"Here," he said. He unbuckled her belt and then unsnapped her jeans and pulled down the zipper about half way.

Ashley said, "Uh, not sure that just now I'm feeling up to—"

"It's not like that," he said. Chase slipped his hand down her jeans and under the waistband of her panties. He pressed his palm over the butterfly tattooed there and said, "It is warmer there. And not just because of your hand having been pressed there so long, I think." He slipped his fingers from under Ashley's panties and pressed them to her slightly damp forehead. "You've got a fever. Doesn't feel like it's too high, but definitely there."

"God, like I need to be sick."

"I'm really afraid it could be appendicitis," he said. "Ever had problems like that?"

"Never. God, I hope you're wrong. What if it bursts? God only knows where the closest hospital is."

Chase pushed the intercom button and asked for the cook. He asked that some Motrin be brought along with the soup and sandwiches they were already expecting. He let go of the intercom button and said, "We'll see if that helps. We'll watch this. If the pain seems to worsen, let me know and I'll get you to a doctor if I have to carry you down the damn mountain myself."

He smiled crookedly and added, "Whatever damned mountain we're on. You're right, I owe you, darling, for coming along on this crazy gig." He did, truly. But why'd she have to go and get sick on him like this?

Ashley hesitated, then said, "We haven't gotten to talk much since I left your place yesterday. Listen, something strange happened last night. I went out shopping for some stuff for the trip, my new coat, for one thing. While I was in the store, trying on coats, there was this man I'm sure was watching me. Couldn't really see much of his face, but he was about your height. He was wearing a black overcoat and he—"

Chase bit his lip and then shrugged. "It may be nothing. Probably, it was nothing. I mean, all this strange stuff going on? The threats? They probably just got your mind going. Not like this guy tried to talk to you, right? Not like he followed you, so far as you can tell."

She nodded and then smiled uncertainly. "Maybe. We do have every reason to be paranoid." She thought then about mentioning the hairy hand that had touched her thigh so familiarly during the second plane ride, but as Shawn had been cleared of suspicion once, she thought it might be a mistake to cast fresh doubt on him.

And if it had been Shawn copping a feel, well, it couldn't help Chase's work to be at odds with the Hyde family attorney this early on. No real harm had been done, and if it was Shawn who'd grabbed her leg, well, Ashley promised herself to be more vigilant. She wouldn't put herself in any position for a sequel.

Ashley sipped more cola and thought about raising the issue of the strange email she received alleging some mysterious past for Chase, but the moment still didn't seem right.

There was a soft knock on the door, then a voice, "Food's ready."

Chase stood up and headed to the door, calling ahead, "Just a sec."

"The Motrin helped?"

"Tons," Ashley said. "Vino probably isn't hurting either." They had ordered a bottle of Chilean wine. Their dinner dishes had been taken away, but they were still sitting opposite one another at a small table in the corner of his room. Chase had the gas fireplace in the corner of his room turned up. The fire provided more atmosphere than heat. He'd set up his iPod and its speaker-base. An old tune, 10cc's *I'm Not in Love*, was playing.

Chase reached across the table and pressed his palm to Ashley's forehead, feeling for her temperature through her careless auburn bangs. He pressed the back of his hand to her right cheek. "Fever's gone, at least for now."

"Maybe it really is just a pulled muscle," she said.

"The pains from those don't usually come and go like this. And they don't cause fevers." He arched an eyebrow. "Dinner was okay?"

"Hit the spot, though just about anything would have done that," she said. "But the soup was really good. Great comfort food and good with this weather."

They'd been served some kind of frothy, thick and spicy version of tomato soup.

Chase was drawing his hand away from her face when Ashley clutched at it and squeezed. She held his hand, rubbing its back with her thumb. "You know, I don't think I care what anyone thinks. I think I might just stay here with you the night through. Let the servants talk, you know? If word gets out about us, it'll also keep the lady of the house at bay. I mean, just in case she's not the frumpy hermit you've envisioned. May also keep Brick from putting any moves on me. That's reason in itself."

Chase frowned. "Why? You think he might do that? Has he already tried something?"

Ashley smiled a little and shrugged. "Could happen. Brick strikes me as the type."

"Okay." Chase stroked her cheek. "I really want you to stay with me here anyway. I would have insisted if you hadn't offered." That last was a lie, but a kind one, he told himself.

19

It was hard hearing their conversation over the music on the iPod.

Shelby Hyde cursed, thinking she'd have to order Brick to install another sound pickup somewhere closer to the bedroom door, far from the nightstand and the iPod now sitting atop it.

And that damned sorry excuse for "music" that Chase had turned on? It was stuff that would have been popular decades ago, maybe. Back when there still was such a thing as "popular" music being played on AM radio.

The Hollies, Ambrosia and the Three Degrees. And *worse*.

Good God! Now it was *The Air That I Breathe*.

All of these vintage tunes he favored—that was kind of further proof to Shelby, in its way.

But how could they intend to fuck to such music? Shelby leaned in closer to the monitor. She wished she could hear more clearly what Ashley and Chase were saying to one another between kisses.

They'd dimmed most of the lights in Chase's bedroom and that made it harder to see, too. Shelby flipped a couple of switches to change camera angles, to get a broader view of Chase's bedroom. She toggled levers to focus the cameras on the bed.

Chase was undressing his "assistant," now.

Ashley had a pretty body. She kept herself fit. And she had a good ass, or most men would say so, anyway.

The fact that Chase and Ashley were a couple was no revelation to Shelby. She'd learned that from her investigators weeks ago.

Ashley and Chase were naked now. They were both slightly drunk and laughing. Their hands roamed over one another's bodies. Ashley stretched out on the bed first, giggling. She was punchy from the pain medicine and the wine.

Shelby kidded herself that she might luck out and the little bitch would overdose.

Sitting in her chair, Shelby shrugged off her silk robe, one hand on the console board, the other straying.

Ashley was shaved or waxed down there. Shelby assumed Chase must like that. Hell, most men liked that, didn't they? Judging from their porn proclivities, it certainly seemed so. Shelby drew her nails through her own groomed pubic hair. Well, she could take care of what was left easily enough.

Her breath coming a bit harder, Shelby studied Chase's body. She focused on him until Ashley rolled out from under Chase and swung a long leg over his torso to straddle him.

Ashley was astride him, but her back was to Chase now, going "reverse cowgirl" on him. It was one of *those* porn positions: one that probably would never have occurred to most couples until DVD's and pay-per-view dragged the hardcore stuff into every bedroom. Hot to look at, no denying that. But in Shelby's experience, that position was hell on your quads and backside and didn't do anything near enough for your clitoris. At base, it was a sop to the dudes. Still, Shelby watched them and kept touching herself.

After a while, Ashley shifted onto all fours. She had something tattooed in Latin just above her tailbone. Whatever it was, it seemed to draw Chase's attention as he took Ashley hard, doggie-style.

Tattoos? So far, Shelby had avoided any body art, though she had fleetingly opted for a tongue piercing for a long-gone lover with a mutual oral fixation.

But if *Chase* jazzed on tats? God only knew, there was no shortage of tattoo parlors in the tourist hellhole down the mountain.

Chase reached around with his right hand now to touch Ashley between the legs. Shelby figured he must be getting close, the way he was working at Ashley with his trembling hand. Shelby was close to peaking herself, trying to convince herself her fingers were actually his fingers, Chase's hand on her there.

He said something to Ashley. She responded in a firm voice, so Shelby could actually hear this time. *"No,* Chase. You've got a woman, why would you want *that?"*

They both climaxed shortly after that. When it was over, Ashley rolled off Chase, rubbing at her side. Served the bimbo right, Shelby thought, her own heart still racing. Stupid porno positions—what good were they but to warp a man's expectations and pull a woman's muscles?

Shelby watched a minute or two more as the couple lay there, spent and panting. She flipped a couple of switches to activate the night vision software on her spy cameras. Chase and Ashley's nude bodies glowed eerily green and white, their eyes like those of demons.

20

S till stretched out naked atop the sheets, Ashley reached over and turned off the iPod on Paul Davis' *I Go Crazy*.

"Enough of that stuff, okay? Your taste in tunes is not exactly what I'll call aphrodisiacal. Maybe some Lana Del Rey?"

"Still feeling okay?"

"Yeah, I think I am," she said, rubbing her belly. "But of course I'm also buzzed."

"That's good to know."

She arched an eyebrow. "Yeah, well, I'm spent for this night, so don't be getting worked up again." The muscles in the backs of her thighs were still quivering from the strain.

Chase smiled and extended an arm. Ashley raised her head, then settled into the crook of his arm. He said, "Been meaning to ask for a while now. That tattoo above your backside. I've got no Latin. What does it mean?"

Ashley blushed. "*A bene placito.* I won't tell you what it means. I was fairly drunk. I mean, like, Spring Break-style blitzed. I'm very seriously thinking about having both removed, the one in front and particularly the one in back. Also, now that everyone has one, or practically everyone, what's the point?"

"I hear you."

She'd almost toed up to it so many times. Ashley decided to finally take the plunge. "Listen, I got this very strange email last night before I went to bed."

She felt the muscles in Chase's arm tense. He said, "What kind of strange email?"

"It's actually more than strange," she said softly.

Smiling, Shelby leaned in closer to the monitor. She turned up the volume on the microphone hidden in the headboard. "I couldn't return the email," Ashley said. "When I tried to respond, I got this notification back, permanent fatal error. Sound familiar?"

Chase frowned. "Sounds all too familiar. What did this message say? Did they threaten you?"

"Not really." Ashley hesitated, then went for it. "It said, 'Don't you think it odd a man who writes books about the lives of others has no past of his own?'"

Ashley half-smiled and shrugged. She realized she was rubbing her side again. That dull throb had returned. "You hardly ever talk about your past," she said, soldiering on. "When you do talk about old times, it never seems to reach back very far. Not much beyond the time I was born. When I was just a child. You've never talked about your parents, Chase. I'm not sure if they're even alive. There are no personal photos around your place."

Ashley tried to keep it light, nonchalant.

She didn't mention she had Googled Chase after the unreturnable email message had come through.

Of course, when they'd met, after their first impromptu date, Ashley had run a quick Google search on Chase's name.

But during that initial and cursory search she hadn't noticed how thin the biographies on Chase's publisher's and his own official Web site ran. And that first time she hadn't gotten out her credit card to run a criminal background check. She hadn't run a dead-end public records check on Chase's name like the ones she'd run last night.

Fruitless searches, all.

After a few false starts, pregnant pauses, and conversational cul-de-sacs, Chase said, "This might not be the best time to talk about this, Ash. Maybe in the morning, when you're feeling better." He might have added, "When we're both sober."

Searching his eyes, Ashley shook her head. "No, I think now might be the perfect time. *In vino veritas*, right?"

He tried to make a joke. "Okay, that Latin I know."

"Don't try and laugh this off, Chase." The sudden and shrill edge in her own voice surprised Ashley. "What's your mother's name, Chase?"

Chase almost flinched at the hard, accusatory edge in her voice.

For a moment, she sensed he was trying to conjure up some name. All the while, he kept looking her in the eye. That somehow endeared Chase to Ashley, despite all the tension she felt now.

He said finally, "I don't know."

"Your father?"

Softly, "I don't know."

Ashley sighed. Frowning deeply she said, "Any siblings?"

"Not that I know of."

"What *do* you know?"

"I'm Chase Alger."

"Middle initial?"

"L."

"What's that stand for?"

After a time, Chase shrugged. Ashley said, "How long have you been 'Chase'?"

"Twenty-five years."

"How old are you, Chase?" She couldn't help it, letting a little more gravel go into her pronunciation of his now obviously adopted first name.

"Best guess is mid- to late-forties."

Ashley suddenly realized she was cold. She raised herself up on her elbows, wincing at the pain that caused in her side, then lifted her legs and pulled the sheets and comforter from under them. Shivering, she pulled them tight around herself.

Chase tugged the covers up to his waist. Ashley remained seated now, beyond easy reach of Chase's hands. "Were you ever going to share any of this with me, Chase? When were you going to tell me that you really do have no past? That you don't truly know who you are?" She shook her head. "And isn't that some crazy kind of irony given the men you write books about?"

Now Chase couldn't face her. Head down, he said, "I guess irony is one word for it."

She reached over and tipped his chin up with her thumb and forefinger. "Talk to me, Chase. Tell me what you do know about yourself. You owe me that much, right?"

21

*M*ea *culpa*: another of the rare Latin phrases Chase could claim.

Miami, that's where they found him. They said he was cowering in an alley, bloody and missing teeth. He had heard someone, maybe a paramedic say, "Severe head trauma. Think this poor son of a bitch may well end up a vegetable."

He had no wallet and no identification, when they found him.

His clothes were unremarkable: Levi's jeans, well-worn Rockport shoes and a bloody Polo shirt sporting two bullet holes—one through the left arm, just above the elbow, the other higher up in the left shoulder. He still carried those scars and passed them off to various lovers as the remnants of a mugging.

Ashley had accepted that story the first time she'd studied the scars on his arm after making love in something less than low light. She had bought his story just as the others before her had believed when he told them that fiction. Well, maybe not a fiction: for all he knew or could remember, it might even be the truth.

The Miami-Dade cops later told him that they took his fingerprints as he drifted in and out of consciousness those first days in the hospital. The prints were fed into various data bases but produced no results, except, maybe, the half-assed peace of mind of knowing he was no criminal. Well, at least not the kind of criminal who had ever gotten caught.

The doctors were split on the cause of his memory loss. Some pointed to his head injuries. The neurologists insisted his amnesia had some psychological root. The shrinks had sided with the doctors who had blamed his head injury. Either way, his memory never came back. Not a flicker. Not the nagging, foggiest hint of a single memory.

The picture of his bruised and swollen face printed in the newspapers never brought anyone forward claiming to know his real identity.

Because of that, he figured he must not be from around Florida, at least. He had no way of knowing what other newspapers outside the Sunshine state might have written about him, or if they had even printed that picture.

After three weeks with no prospects of improvement in the state of his memory—his wounds healing and his face back to what must have been normal and now sporting pristine dental implants—he had simply walked away from the hospital.

He started drifting north; took some odds jobs here and there.

Along the way he met various women who made local newspaper work in Georgia attractive for a time. He took on some more freelance journalism assignments in South Carolina.

It soon enough became apparent that he had an inherent flare for writing. He thought maybe he'd been a writer of some sort before that blow to his head robbed him of himself.

Whatever the case, he decided to exploit those writing skills.

He moved into magazine work. He scored some good gigs profiling novelists, athletes and politicians for *GQ, Esquire, Rolling Stone* and *Playboy*.

He spent a lot of time in libraries in those early days. One of his habits was wandering the stacks, and opening up random books. Fiction or nonfiction, it really didn't matter. He'd flip to the rear interior dust-jacket flaps, working on the premise he might open a book one day and find his own face looking back from some author photo.

One afternoon, browsing the stacks, he ran across a slim biography of Ambrose Bierce. He decided he could have written a better book—could in fact write the definitive Bierce biography. He was certain of that.

So he wrote a book proposal and fired it off to a dozen different New York publishing houses. His pitch drew interest from an editor at one of the NYC majors.

Realizing he needed a professional to secure the offered publishing deal, he selected Bryan Dane to represent him. He pulled Dane's name cold from a second-hand copy of *The Writer's Market*.

By the time his book proposal was picked up, he'd more or less settled on a name for himself. He had also finally stayed in one place long enough to establish a mailing address and to wade through the drudge-work resulting from being an adult needing some kind of acceptable proof of identity, a Social Security Number and other identification documents in order to forge his new life.

His new name... *Chase*: a kind of joke on himself, figuring he was doomed to be the man who'd always be seeking his true identity. His first name, he thought, should reflect that strange quest. *Alger*: after "Horatio," of course—the fictional poster child of self-made men. He needed a middle initial for one of the documents and simply selected "L," figuring to come up with some name to go with it later. But he'd never gotten around to that. Leave it to Ashley to ask.

Shaking his head now, Chase slipped from the bed. He padded naked into the bathroom and turned up the tap. He bent over the sink and splashed lukewarm water on his face.

Ashley followed him into the bathroom, wrapping herself in the bed's down-filled comforter. She was emphatic. "Don't you *dare* walk away from me, mister. You owe me some answers. You really do, you know."

"Yes, I do." He looked at himself in the mirror. His face dripped water. "But I can't have this conversation just now, Ash. I just don't think I can."

In a room above theirs, Shelby cursed and slammed a fist down on her desk. She rued the lack of sound pickups in the bathroom, the lack of cameras. And Shelby cursed the running water that thwarted the expensive microphones in the bedroom.

Ashley persisted and eventually broke Chase down.

He told her all that he remembered.

When he finished—all too soon, Chase could tell from the expression on Ashley's face—she bit her lip and then said, "So you were found in the same state where Everett Hyde disappeared? Found at almost the identical time he went missing? My God, you might be Everett Hyde." Ashley was pale. "Do you grasp how my skin is crawling right now?"

Chase hung his head, unable to face up to the stricken expression on Ashley's face.

"*No.* No." Staring at his feet, he said, "When this opportunity came up to write Hyde's biography, as I came to know more about Hyde and the timeline for his disappearance, I went back and I checked on some things. There was a period of about a day when I thought maybe I might be Hyde. But it doesn't gel. Not when you look at the dates when I was found, at my time in the hospital. It misses by days, yes, but it misses.

I couldn't have mailed that suicide note from Key West, Ash. I was in the hospital and mostly in a kind of coma or fugue state when that note was written. Also when that boat was stolen. I am not Everett Hyde. That's for certain. I know I'm not. I promise you."

"But even if that is so, you don't know who you are," Ashley said. Her heart was racing. Everything about their relationship and the future she envisioned for them was now uncertain… no, *worse*. She couldn't imagine how they could go forward from this unbelievable revelation.

She left the bathroom. She tossed the comforter on the bed and scooped up her underwear; began dressing.

"I'm going back to my room tonight and don't try to change my mind," she said. "I have to think. I just have to think, and I need to do that for a while away from you."

He stood naked, framed in the doorway of the bathroom, little more than a silhouette.

He watched Ashley dress, then said an unanswered "Goodnight" as she slipped into the darkened hallway.

22

Ashley almost bumped into Shawn as she turned in the common corridor after shutting Chase's door.

Shawn put a hand to Ashley's shoulder to alert her before she slammed into him. He said, "Easy there, honey. You're up late, too, huh?"

She was momentarily startled, then ran her fingers back through her hair, gathering it behind her head. She pulled a hair tie from her pocket and twisted it around to make a ponytail. "We're allowed to roam the house, huh, Shawn?"

"Very probably not," he said. He smiled and shrugged. "But who cares if that's so? Our luggage is finally here, I'm told. Say they'll bring it down to us in a few minutes. I was really just trying to lay hands on one of those disposable cell phones they promised us."

Ashley pressed her hand to her right side; that damned ache was there again. "Any luck with that?"

"No. I'm told we'll get those in the morning. Maybe. That grates, I'll tell you. I've got some sensitive calls to make. Phone calls I should have made hours ago. Confidential calls. And given this whack-job of a security chief's zeal for his job, I'm not exactly trusting this joint's landlines to be at all private."

"Probably wise to be wary that way," Ashley said. She put a hand on her room's doorknob. "Well, goodnight, Shawn."

"Night. Sweet dreams. And do stay warm."

Ashley locked her door and then stripped off her clothes. She twisted the shower knobs and put her hand under the spray. She pulled it back and briskly shook it out to lessen the sting from the scalding water. Someone needed to turn the thermostat on the hot water heater down a few clicks, she thought. She fiddled with the shower's hot water knob and put her hand under the spray again. It was just bearable.

As she lathered up her hair and body, she thought about Chase's expression as she confronted him.

On balance, he'd seemed annoyed to be pressed.

Couldn't he, even for a second, put himself in her position? Couldn't he imagine what it was like to learn the man you'd become so attached to, the man who'd helped to kick-start your own literary career and whose life you wanted to share, was nothing more than a façade?

How could he possibly expect anything less than the reaction he'd received?

Ashley was reeling, in a kind of mounting panic. The combination of these strange, worsening pains in her side, this bloody fortress with no clocks, phones, radios or televisions, and now these revelations regarding Chase, or whoever he was, were too much.

God, but it was all such a mess. Two days ago Ashley had been so happy, everything seemed approaching perfect. She had Chase, had her dream city, and she had her heady first book deal.

Ashley finished washing off the soap and turned off the water. She stepped out and looked at herself, naked in the mirror. Her chin trembled and she began to cry.

Ashley finished patting herself dry with a plush towel. She wrapped the towel around her head like a terrycloth turban and walked naked back into her bedroom. She stopped in her soggy tracks, frowning.

Her luggage was now piled on her bed.

That angered her. Ashley had locked the door to her bedroom before getting in the shower. Of course, the polite thing to do when she didn't answer a knock would have been to leave her luggage outside her bedroom door. The presumption to enter her bedroom was made more unsettling by the fact that Ashley hadn't closed the door to the bathroom while she showered.

Cursing, she tugged the towel from around her head and wrapped it around her torso, mostly succeeding in covering only her breasts. The towel was about an inch short of reaching her thighs. She checked the knob of her bedroom door. The lock was engaged again.

Ashley wiped at her eyes with her knuckles and dropped her damp towel. Angrily, she spun her suitcase around and unclasped its latches. The sweat pants and T-shirt she was rooting around for were on the right-hand side of her suitcase. When she'd packed, she'd placed them at the bottom of a pile of clothes she'd wedged into the left side of her luggage. She supposed the piles might have been swapped during an airport inspection, but somehow she doubted that was where the switch had occurred, particularly since they were on private charters. She wanted to scream.

The waistband of her sweats caused her some discomfort in the lower right side of her belly. Ashley pulled the sweats down a bit so they rode lower on her hips and loosened their drawstring. She slipped on the T-shirt and dragged a comb through her hair with one hand while unloading her laptop with the other. She placed the computer on a writing desk to the right of her bed. There was a Post-It affixed to her laptop case that gave instructions for acquiring the compound's Wi-Fi signal.

Ashley booted up her machine. The computer's clock indicated it was midnight, Eastern Standard Time. Of course there was no way of knowing if the clock had been reset by Brick or his crew.

Then Ashley got this inspiration. In a fit of optimism, she had recently contracted with that Web designer who specialized in author sites to design Ashley's own official Web presence. Her site was fairly meager stuff at the moment: links to some of Ashley's online stories and literary magazines that had picked up her material. There was a biography, a blog and links to some admired writers. Soon, at least, she'd be able to post a page focused on her debut novel.

But apart from the site itself, there was a Web traffic summary report she checked in on once or twice a week, even though visitors to her site were still sparse. One of the summary report options provided server locations for her Web site's visitors. To date, there had been only three consistent, recognizable visitors to her site that showed up on that report. One was herself; the second was Ashley's mother back in Pennsylvania. The third was her Web site's design maven, who was based in Colorado.

Ashley called her Web site up, closed the browser window, then opened it up again and went straight back to her site. She then checked her traffic summary report, calling up the page that recorded "visitor paths."

In the past twenty-four hours, her site had been visited twice—both times in the past five minutes. According to her site statistics, Ashley's own laptop had accessed her official site from somewhere in the state of Tennessee.

Ashley closed her traffic summary site and opened up Google. She typed:

tennessee tram ice skating

The resulting search came up with numerous hits for something called "Ober Gatlinburg Ski Resort & Amusement Park." It seemed to be the only tram in Tennessee.

Ashley smiled and said, "Gotcha!"

23

"The spyware did its job," Brick said. "Mirrored her computer screen on mine. She's a clever little bitch, I'll give her that. She used a Web traffic report site to get her own general location here in Tennessee. From there, she used the state name and the word 'tram' to figure out she's in the Smoky Mountains. Hell, Gatlinburg has the only tram in the entire region. Like I said, clever, you have to admit."

"Very clever of her, sure," Shelby said, biting on the chewed-up end of a Bic pen cap. "Has she had a chance to share her discovery?"

"No. Shortly after performing that search, she logged off. Looked on camera like she was in a good bit of pain. She phoned down for more Motrin a while ago. Last time I checked the monitor, she was still in bed. Sometimes she's wrapped in a ball with the covers pulled up tight under her chin. Sometimes she's spread out naked there on top of her sheets, bathed in sweat. Based on things overheard, I'm convinced she's got acute appendicitis."

Shelby sat back in her chair, one eyebrow arched. "And if it should burst?"

"She might die without immediate treatment. Peritonitis."

"Doesn't hurt they've argued with one another," Shelby said. "So let's try to keep her alone then, right?" Shelby smiled at Brick, closed a hand over his. "You on board with that?"

The security chief nodded and smiled. Shelby had found Brick through a quarter-page display ad in *Soldier of Fortune Magazine*. He was a nasty enough piece of work. A mercenary in every sense of the word.

Brick didn't disappoint her now. "So long as your money keeps spending, sugar, sure. Whatever you want, darling. Anything." A wicked grin. "Hell, not like it'll be our first together, right? Not even second or third."

24

Chase was about to tap on Ashley's door. Brick called down the hallway, "Whoa there, sport! Don't."

Scowling, Chase said, "Something wrong?"

Brick closed the distance and slapped Chase's right arm. "No, nothing to worry about. Your assistant called down a few hours ago to say she was up late writing and wanted to be allowed to sleep in. Said she'd take breakfast in her room alone, later."

Christ, Chase thought, she's really pissed at me. Well, like it was really his fault. The way she had gone at him? The way she'd pressed it all? He said, "Ashley's been ill. I should check on her, anyway."

Brick shook his head; this strange smile. He said, "Damn. This is… awkward."

"What do you mean?" Chase frowned. "What's awkward?"

"Uh, Ashley, Ms. McKnight, specifically asked you not be permitted to bother her. Sorry, brother. I don't know what's up between you two, but she was pretty pissed. Like I said, this is awkward." Brick smiled again, friendlier this time. "Anything you want to talk about? Need an ear? Maybe some advice?"

Chase drew a deep breath. He could feel his pulse in his ears. He was furious with himself for the rage he knew must be written all over his face. He was madder still at Ashley for giving that message to Brick to deliver. He managed a hoarse, "No. But thanks anyway."

"Hell, I'm sure she'll get over it, buddy," Brick said. He slapped Chase's back hard enough to sting a little and began guiding Chase down the hall with his palm still pressed to the biographer's burning back. "You must be starving, huh? How's a Bloody Mary to wash down your eggs sound?"

Chase cast a glance back at Ashley's door. How was he going to patch things up if she was avoiding him? If she wouldn't answer the door?

And what was she thinking, confiding about their argument to this idiot steroid junkie?

Brick said, "Huh? How about it—Bloody Mary hit the spot?"

"Let's make it a screwdriver," Chase said sourly. "At least then I can kid myself I'm getting the vitamin C."

Brick winked and gave him another stinging back slap. "That's the spirit, my man. Now, hang close and I'll give you the nickel tour of this dump on the way to the bar."

When they finally reached the dining room Brick said, "Back in a minute. Bar's right there, so help yourself. Go for the heavy pour. I would, I was you."

Chase saw Brick put the arm on some muscle-bound young stooge in a black T-shirt. Chase figured the young security flunky for another steroid abuser: no amount of pumping iron could build muscle mass like that.

Brick leaned in close to his underling's ear and said, "I wouldn't want to monitor 'em either, but those are the orders. Sound pickups in the bathroom. A camera, too. And for God's sake, try and install it so we can hear over the sink water."

The young guard nodded and said, "And the woman's bathroom, too?"

Biting his lip, Brick thought of the last image he'd seen of Ashley, naked and sweating, curled up in a ball and clutching her side, in obvious agony, sometimes softly calling for help, her voice a hoarse rasp. "Might not be necessary after all," Brick said. "I'll get back to you on that. How's she looking, by the way?"

"Fucking hot," the younger man said, smirking. "I mean, you've seen that righteous body and face of hers. But she's hot literally, too. I think she should be in a hospital. She's rambling now. She might be talking in her sleep, but it's more like she's delirious. Really out of her head." The young guard hesitated, then asked, "Should I send for a doctor?"

"She hasn't asked for one, has she?"

"Well, no, but—"

Brick leaned into his flunky's face. He snarled, "If she asks, then you ask me again. Got it?"

The security chief didn't like the look on the young man's face. Nevertheless, his underling nodded and said, "Yeah. I hear you, boss man."

25

A shley felt better after her second scalding shower. Now that she knew they were in Tennessee, she trusted her computer's time setting... Particularly after checking in on some online sites that helped travelers and business people to convert their present time of day across various domestic and international time zones.

It was noon where she was now—she trusted that was fact.

She switched off the hair-dryer. As the whining fan in the thing wound down, she heard someone banging on her door. Ashley pulled the top of her robe closer and tightened its belt, grimacing a little at the discomfort that caused her, though it was nowhere near the pain she'd experienced during the night. There was an hour or two when she had really thought she was in grave condition.

She leaned close to the door and said, "Who is it?"

"Shawn. I'm just checking on you, Ashley. Missed you at breakfast, and Chase said you weren't feeling good last night. I just thought someone should look in on you." A pause. "Sue me—I was concerned."

Well, he was more concerned than Chase, evidently. She said, "Just a moment," then unlocked and opened her door. Shawn smiled. "Thank God. You look... so fine."

There were a couple of ways she could take that. Probably just as Shawn intended.

"Just out of the shower," she said. "Feeling much better now. At least for the moment. Thanks for checking on me, though. That's very nice of you." Ashley hesitated, then motioned him inside her room. "So, have the rest of you met the mysterious Ms. Hyde?" Her voice was still a bit hoarse.

Shawn looked around her room, said, "Yours is bigger than mine." He peered out the window above her writing desk. "And you have a much better view, too. Mine's blocked by this big fat tree trunk. Infuriating." He walked closer to the window for a better view down the mountainside.

His back still to her, Shawn said, "You were asking about Shelby Hyde. No, she's not around yet. We were told she was held up wherever she is. Breakfast was just me and Chase and that fool who calls himself Brick. And Brick talked for all three of us. Consider yourself lucky to have missed that repartee. I had no idea you could fit the word 'cocksucker' in so often, in so many sentences. It's a kind of art unto itself."

Ashley smiled despite herself and sat down on the foot of her bed. Shawn spun around the chair from her writing desk and straddled it, resting his arms across the top of the chair's back. Ashley said, "Did you ever get your disposable phone?"

Shawn smiled and shook his head. "Yes and no. I was given one. It was completely useless. Seems there's only one viable cell tower around these parts. The guy who bought the phones for us bought them from the wrong provider. Or so the story goes. Not sure I really believe it. Regardless, Brick has sent the guy back down the mountain on the ice to buy phones compatible with the tower up here. Wherever here is."

Wanting to share her discovery, to gloat a little, Ashley blurted out, "Oh, I know exactly where we are. Well, to within two or three miles, anyway."

Shawn narrowed his eyes. He smiled and said, "Really?"

"Oh, yeah."

He was still smiling, but seemed a bit incredulous. "Honestly?"

"Honest."

"How in God's name did you figure it out, kiddo?"

She finished explaining and Shawn said, "That's a kind of genius, Ashley. Too bad we can't let on to Brick that we know. I'd relish sticking it in his eye."

"It would be satisfying," Ashley said. "That dude's a major idiot."

"No arguing that." Shawn stood up and stretched. "I'm just here distracting you, probably from your writing." He inclined his head at her laptop. "But you must be starving."

Ashley nodded. "I could eat a little. I think I'll just have something sent up. She wasn't sure she could face Chase yet. She certainly didn't want to risk doing that in public. The notion he'd kept his own ambiguous past from her still hurt.

Shawn seemed to think about it before offering. He said, "Listen, this whole affair is screwball, even unsettling. And maybe even a little bit sinister. By that, I mean this isolation. Keeping us in the dark as to where we are, though you found your way around that quickly enough. Then this stuff with the phones. I need contact—unmonitored contact—with clients, with partners." He paused, then said, "I hope you don't think I'm crazy or paranoid for saying this, but I think my luggage was searched."

"Mine certainly was," Ashley said. "Piles of clothes were reversed."

"Well, there you go." Shawn turned and looked at her laptop, again. "Damn. I should have mentioned it sooner." He was chewing his lip, rubbing the back of his neck. He looked agitated.

"Mentioned what?"

"Your computer," Shawn said. "It really is ingenious what you did. But I'm thinking now it was maybe also a little dangerous. After seeing my luggage was gone through, I ran a virus check on my computer. Someone loaded it up with spyware last night. All kinds of monitoring and screen mirroring programs. If they did that to mine..."

Ashley looked at her computer. "Oh, God!"

"Yeah. You're not online right now, are you, Ashley?"

"No. Not this second."

"Good. Don't go back on until I can look your computer over. Some of these programs are made to upload their discoveries when you log on to a server. Maybe your surfing history last night hasn't been uploaded yet."

"Damn!" Ashley realized her underarms were damp now; not fever—fear.

"Yeah," Shawn said again. "Particularly in view of Brick's warning about trying to figure out where we are."

Shawn bit his lip. "Look, I've got some wine I ordered last night and never got around to opening. I could use a lunch companion. Well, drinking companion. How about while you eat, we have some of that wine, and I'll clean up your computer if it was messed with? I'll tear off anything they might have put on, purge your history and cache of anything incriminating. Just in case Brick is more than bluster."

Ashley hesitated, thinking about his offer. She wasn't particularly tech-savvy. She wasn't sure she could do herself what Shawn was offering to do for her.

He said, "And you're here to learn more about Everett Hyde, right? I'll tell you what I know while I purge your computer of spyware. Because, well, I'm leaving here real soon, I've decided. You and your beau are going to lose access to any of the stuff I can give you on Hyde when I go. At this point, I just want to stick around long enough to meet Shelby in the flesh. I want to do that as much out of curiosity than anything else. Then I want to get back to New York. I don't like being treated like some Gitmo detainee. On that note, let's set up some proper password protection on your computer, too."

Ashley said, "Great. I'd really appreciate you fixing up my laptop. I'll dress while you fetch that wine." She smiled, said, "I sure hope it's red wine."

He smiled. "Is there really any other kind?"

26

Chase again had his hand poised to knock at Ashley's door. He paused when he heard laughter. A male voice that sounded like Shawn's said, "More?"

Ashley, cheerful sounding, said, "More would be really nice." A long pause, then, "This is really nice."

He was lying on his bed, staring at the ceiling when the intercom next to his bed buzzed.

A husky female voice said, "Chase? It's Shelby Hyde. Just got home and I'm so eager to meet you. Won't you please join me for a drink?"

Chase wasn't expecting the attractive young woman who greeted him. She was tallish, maybe a shade under five-ten. She had a slender, athletic build, reminiscent of Ashley's physique. Her straight, sandy brown hair just reached her shoulders. Shelby wore a little black dress that reminded Chase of a dress that Ashley had worn to the launch party for his most recent book. Shelby's legs were long and shapely. He thought some of their calf and thigh definition might come from roller-blading in the good weather. But then he thought about how hard it would be to roller-blade in the mountains—the roads were far too steep for any of that.

Maybe Shelby kept in shape with ice-skating instead, perhaps at that very rink Ashley had told Chase they had passed while being led off the tram in those blackout glasses.

Shelby smiled and put out a hand. She had a firm grip. "First, thanks so much for putting up with my, well, let's call 'em privacy demands, Chase." There was a slight southern accent there, he thought. She had wicked, playful eyes… this animal allure.

"Privacy seems to be a family tradition," Chase said.

She slowly released his hand, almost as if reluctant to let it go. He savored her touch. "Exactly." Shelby searched his face. "I'm thrilled you'll be the one writing my father's biography. I know it'll be sublime."

"Nice of you to say," Chase said. "We'll see. Your father certainly left a hell of a story to tell. I'm looking forward to viewing his manuscripts. Any holographs or fragments. Perhaps journals or diaries, if he left any of those behind."

Shelby smiled and took his arm, leading him toward the bar. "Of course. And you will. Very soon. But first I want to learn some more about you, Chase. And about your methods. Your habits. Work habits, I mean. Have a drink with me?"

"Sounds great."

"What'll it be?"

"Red wine for me," he said.

"Of course," she said. "And I'll have the same."

He said, "My assistant. She's been ill. I wonder if you—"

"She must be feeling better," Shelby said, handing Chase a bottle of wine and a corkscrew. "Ms. McKnight ordered a late breakfast for herself and Mr. Dalton. A bottle of wine, too. She's probably gathering notes about my attorney's memories of my father, don't you think?" This sultry smile. "Probably pumping him."

Shelby smiled at his frown and lifted her wineglass. "I meant pumping him for information, you know?"

27

"**B**obby Bristow," Shawn said. "Bobby was Everett's closest friend. Maybe his only real friend in the world. They were like brothers. Bobby was even with Everett when he made that last dash down to the Keys."

Ashley said, "I've never heard of this Bobby Bristow. Never run across a single mention of the name."

Shawn freshened their glasses from their second bottle of wine. "Of course, it would never have gotten out about Bobby from Everett. And Everett's friends, even the most casual ones, if such a term even applies in this case, only remained Everett's friends so long as they kept their mouths tightly shut."

She sat back in her chair and crossed her legs, sipped and savored more wine. Running her fingers through her hair, Ashley said, "That begs the question how you know about this Bobby Bristow, doesn't it?"

"You sound like a cross-examining lawyer, and I know those types." Shawn smiled and shrugged. "As I told you and Chase on the ride here, a few times, here and there, I got calls from Everett. Usually late at night, and usually when he was on a bender. Hyde was a red wine fiend, I'm told. Amanda said he used to drink gallons of the stuff. Well, one night, about a week after the third novel was released, Everett called me up. He woke me up, in fact. He was clearly in his cups and started talking about his life. I let him go on because what he shared fascinated me and because I sensed I was maybe the first to hear much of it. And I didn't know each time I hung up if it would be the last time I'd be graced by a phone call from Everett. So we talked for perhaps an hour. No, that's not the way to put it. I listened while Everett talked. A lot of it was about this lifelong friend of his, Bobby."

Ashley rested her chin on her palm, all attention. "So who was Bobby Bristow?"

"Seems they grew up together," Shawn said. "Only-kids-in-the-neighborhood kind of stuff, you know? Seems when they were fairly young, Bobby's mother and father left little Bobby with the Hyde family while they went to handle a family emergency. Something was wrong with Bobby's mother's mother.

"It was winter," Shawn said, his eyes going far away now, his gaze drifting to the window over Ashley's computer. It was snowing again outside, and the wind whipped the snow into squalls. "They left in bad weather and drove into the heart of a wicked storm. Their car missed a turn and fell into a ravine. The car landed on its roof. Bobby's parents were crushed inside. Probably killed upon impact. Or at least one hopes."

Ashley said, "That poor, poor kid."

Shawn nodded. "Yeah. The only other family Bobby had was that ailing grandmother that prompted his parents' star-crossed trip. She passed away the same night that Bobby's parents were killed. So the Hydes adopted Bobby. Everett said his parents took Bobby as their own. According to Everett, his mother, particularly, always wanted a second child, but there were severe complications with Everett's birth. His mother couldn't have more children of her own."

Shawn paused, sipped some wine. "Everett said the funny thing was that Bobby looked like he really could be his birth brother. They had the same coloring and body types. Same hair and eye color and were about the same height. Most around where they lived believed the two boys were truly blood."

"It's just so strange to be learning about Bobby now," Ashley said. "I actually studied with Professor Adam Greenwood. He wrote a book about Everett Hyde's works. I don't think he ever knew about Bobby."

"Greenwood, yeah, I've read that book of his," Shawn said. "It's okay. Maybe the best of those kinds of books about Hyde that I've come across." It was true. Shawn had read it all, the good and the bad. Greenwood's book had some real insight; he did grasp much of what their author was aiming for with those three published novels.

"I was in touch with Professor Greenwood recently," Ashley said. "If we talk again, I'll tell him of your high opinion of his book."

Shawn shrugged. "And you'll tell him about Bobby Bristow, no doubt."

"That's a revelation for Chase to report in his biography," Ashley said.

"Anyway, do you think an academic would really care what a lawyer thinks of his work?"

"Given whose lawyer you are, and what you know about Hyde that others don't—well, yeah, I think he would."

Shawn shrugged. "Either way, it's okay. If this book of Chase's goes forward, Bobby's existence isn't going to be secret much longer."

"Chase will do a great job with this book, trust me."

"He may be worthy enough, but I sense your knowledge and appreciation of Everett's works goes much deeper than your partner's. And, as a writer, as a fiction writer, you have the potential for insight into Everett and the pressures of his creative life that a mere biographer might lack."

Ashley said, "Chase is a writer, too."

"He's a nonfiction scribe," Shawn said, curling his lip just a bit. "Calling a glorified journalist a writer is like calling a house painter an artist. I revere talented fictions writers, really savor their work. Nonfiction writers? Journalists?" Shawn waved a dismissive hand.

She picked up her wine glass, held it about halfway to her lips, said, "I don't agree with that assessment. Not at all."

"You're loyal. I admire that trait, generally. But you should be careful. The book markets are much stronger presently for nonfiction than fiction books. I'd hate to see you pulled in. Would be a terrible thing for you to get knocked off course from writing the stories and novels you're gifted enough to write."

Ashley said, "Pardon me, but you have no way of knowing how good or bad my fiction writing is."

"Actually, I spent a couple of hours surfing last night after I cleared off my computer. I found a number of your stories online, *Mississippi Review*. Those sorts of online literary sites. You've got the chops, that much is certain." He smiled and said, "At least, this lawyer thinks so. I think you're a major talent. And to have your ability and voice at such a young age?" He smiled. "Now that I think about it, you're actually about the age Everett was when he published his debut novel. Promise me you'll never veer into writing the kind of stuff Chase does? That'd be a tragic waste of talent."

Ashley smiled at Shawn over the rim of her glass. She said, "No worries about me derailing. I'm just here to help gather materials. The writing of the book is all on Chase's back."

"Glad to hear it." Shawn bit his lip and said, "You writing fulltime?"

"Can't afford that," she said. "Not even close. Still have a day job."

"Maybe that will change soon. It should. Any work you do that isn't toward the page is a waste of time and talent, Ashley. You're a comer. I'm only sorry you're coming into the market at this crazy time."

"What do you mean?"

"I mean all the strange demands placed on writers, these days," Shawn said. "I used to question Everett's aversion to publicity. His refusing to have any public profile at all. Lately, I wonder if Everett wasn't right. Perhaps even a visionary. All the crazy things required of authors now, blathering on those stupid blogs. Virtual launch parties and tours and interviews and book trailers on YouTube. SuperPoking one another on Facebook. Stalking customers on Twitter. And you know as well as me that a fair number of mediocre writers get contracts based on their looks or their so-called platform." Shawn smiled and said, "I won't hold it against you, but did your agent have a glossy of you to shop around with your first novel?"

"Absolutely not," Ashley said sharply.

"Well, I don't want to break your heart, honey, but if your agent had had a picture of you, with your looks, well, I bet he or she could have doubled whatever advance you're getting. You're pretty and you have a voice like a late-night FM deejay. You're solid gold in today's fiction market before ever printing a word."

Ashley just shook her head.

"You know I'm right," Shawn pressed.

"Maybe. But that's not how I got my book contract." She saw his glass was nearly empty. This time Ashley handled the refills. She said, "You said you're a frustrated fiction writer. Any complete manuscripts of your own? Any short stories?"

"A few of the latter." He stared into his glass. "Had some stories published in literary magazines here and there. You know, the kind that pay you in copies. The kind that seem more amenable and appreciative of your works if you're one of their rare subscribers."

"What about a novel?"

"A few in a footlocker. Embalmed with rejection letters. The letters all read about the same. 'I very much enjoyed your novel, but I didn't *love* it, etc., etc.'"

"Have an agent?"

"Thinking about trying again soon." He smiled again. "Anyway, I'm thrilled for you, Ashley. Can't wait to read your novel, particularly after reading your stories. You're a stylist, no question, but the prose isn't distracting, doesn't wave a finger at itself like some I can think of. The story comes through hard and clear. Perfect balance. If you write like this at, what? Twenty-three? Twenty-four? Can't imagine what kind of writer you'll be at thirty, at forty. The ear you have for dialogue and voices is amazing. And your characterization is so economical, yet piercing. And like you said, you've got story, character arc."

Ashley hardly knew what to say. She tried to deflect the talk from her own work: "So, veering back to Everett Hyde and all these secrets of his you've been keeping…"

Shawn smiled and tapped her glass with the rim of his goblet. "You're modest. Don't like talking about your work? I get it. Right. You've got questions. Fire away."

"Whatever happened to Bobby Bristow?"

"Oh, he died. Or it's likely he did. As I said, he was along for Everett's last ride down to the Florida Keys. The working assumption back in the day was Bobby had some kind of suicide pact with Everett. That Bobby died with Everett down there somewhere in the Florida Panhandle or thereabouts."

Shawn paused and shook his head. "Well, at least so far as Bobby's fate goes, it's about the same enigma as Everett left us. That is to say, no body was ever found. No real resolution to the mystery of Bobby's fate. Expect there never will be."

28

Chase felt a bit buzzed. Between them, they'd put away a bottle-and-a-half of red wine. He said, "It's strange how all this started for me. I got these emails from your mother's account. I mean, after she had... well, passed."

Shelby licked her lips and tapped the bar with her nails. "Yes, Kathleen told me just shortly before her accident."

"If it was an accident," Chase said. "I've heard rumors there was a suicide note."

"I hope that's not true," Shelby said, her brow furrowed. Her right hand was resting very close to Chase's hand, close enough he noticed. She pressed her other hand to the small of her back. She had grimaced in pain the few times he had noticed the base of her spine touching the padded back of the barstool. He wondered if back problems ran in the Hyde family.

Shelby poured him a little more wine despite his raised hand, then said, "Listen, please, don't get all worried about the emails, Chase. I ran across those notes of my mother's to you while I was going through her computer. I was looking for anything I might need to know. Business or bills to handle, and so forth. Her notes to you were in a draft file of her email client. She had written them some time back. And she had written similar notes to some other biographer named Christopher Bruce. And to perhaps five or six other potential biographers. I had no idea she was contemplating a sanctioned biography of my father. I knew your work. I didn't know anything about the others. It seems mother also had some background checks run on you and five or six of what she perceived to be the top contenders for the job."

"She must not have liked what her investigators turned up about me since we never really connected," Chase said. "Not that there's much of anything to turn up."

Shelby smiled. He noticed now she had dimples. "So it seemed from the file I found in my mother's papers. On paper, you seem to be a straight arrow, Chase. A guy who's left very few footprints." Now he couldn't read her expression. "But in person?"

She brushed her sandy hair back out of her eyes. Shelby's hair was very close in hue to Chase's own. "Anyway, when I saw you were among the ones she was considering, I just went ahead and sent the email to you from her account. I called up her second email account and pasted the message in there and sent it again, just to cover bases. Turns out all of mother's email accounts were configured to be one-way, so to speak. She'd send out messages and then in the body of her message direct recipients to answer her through Kat. It was another way of keeping things private, of keeping the world at bay. I only found this out about mother and her email screenings from Kathleen the day she... you know."

She squeezed his hand. "I'm sorry my ignorance about that technical stuff with Mom's email took on a sinister patina. Who knew there'd be all this other dark stuff going on at the same time?"

"In a way, all of that kind of hooked me on the project, odd as it sounds," Chase said. "This strange fouling out of all my attempts to return the message just drove me on in the end." Then he thought of the email Ashley had gotten. When Ashley had tried to reply to it, she too, had received a "permanent fatal error" notice.

Chase said, "Why didn't *you* sign those emails to me? They were still carrying your mother's name."

"Yeah, another silly thing. Call it attention deficit disorder or something. I didn't touch the body of the email, didn't change a word of my mother's, but I did mean to change the name." A funny smile. Shelby said, "So sue me."

"I'm just relieved to hear there's some kind of rational explanation behind those emails," Chase said. "They were a real worry in tandem with all those death-by-hangings of other would-be biographers of your father's."

"Yes, that is all very disturbing. Sometimes I think my father's works appeal most strongly to borderline personalities. And the ones who seem to delve deepest into Daddy's writings seem to be the ones who are the most borderline of all. Thank God you're breaking that sorry mold."

He said, "So when do we start work on this book, Shelby?"

She smiled. "How about right now? I'm going to take you down into the study where my father's manuscripts are stored. There are typed drafts of about a dozen unpublished short stories. Four complete typed novel manuscripts and a novella. And the typed manuscript of an unfinished novel. Frustratingly, I think that might be the very best manuscript of all. But it's unfinished. Anyway, you can have a peek now, whet your appetite."

That got Chase's attention. "All that stuff? And none of it ever published?"

"I didn't know until a few weeks ago any of it even existed," she said. "My mother kept it from me. I'm not sure if her death hadn't caught even mother by surprise. She thought her cancer was in remission. But it so wasn't. When I should have probably been mourning, instead, I was holed up, savoring this cache of my father's writings. That's how potent it is. Amazing stuff, all of it."

"What are your plans for all these works?"

"Publication, of course," Shelby said. She took his hand and led him down a flight of stairs. Chase let himself be led. She said over her shoulder, "Well, publication after you publish your biography to stoke even more interest than already exists in Daddy's works." She smiled. "After all, there's a generation that hasn't truly made Daddy's acquaintance, yet. We need to fix that."

29

Brick and his flunky were drinking spiked coffee and watching the monitor. The younger one said, "So what do you think, boss? We save this footage of the chick and the lawyer gabbing for the boss lady?"

Brick poured a little more whiskey from a flask into his coffee, drank and made a sour face. Acid reflux. Well, booze and coffee was no antidote for that. Once again, he thought about how much he missed the carefree recklessness of his long-gone youth, a golden time when a man didn't spend all his time stewing about spots on his skin, esophageal cancer and how many times he had to wake up in the night to take a stingy leak.

"Fuck it," Brick said. "We ain't got that much tape to spare, and I don't relish trying to drive down that icy trail in this unending goddamn snowstorm. So, no, we recycle this video."

"What about from earlier? The stuff where's she sick in bed?"

"The nude stuff? Save that until last for re-use. Haven't really gotten much time with that footage yet. Want to see for myself this hot body of hers you've been going on and on about all morning."

Ashley was stretched out on the bed. She'd propped some pillows up behind her and was massaging her side. The pain was a dull throb again now, not the stabbing sensation she'd endured earlier.

Shawn was sitting at her writing desk. He claimed to have found a frightening array of spyware programs loaded onto her laptop overnight.

Then Shawn had stumbled across the manuscript of her debut novel and had pressed her until Ashley had given in and agreed to let him read a couple of chapters.

He had read all the way through to chapter seven now. Occasionally, he'd look back over his shoulder to say something like, "This is magnificent stuff," or, "God, you're a marvel, Ash." Here and there, he'd read a line aloud and say, "Wonderful... wonderful."

He turned around in chair all the way this time. "My God, but you're a monster talent, Ashley. Accomplished as your short fiction is, this is something else again. Mature. Perfectly formed. You frighten me a little, you're that good. You need to be doing this fulltime. You're going to be huge." He narrowed his eyes as he watched for her reaction. "And I've been too liberal with your time. Not feeling well again, are you, Ash? Maybe you'll feel better when you wake up."

Ashley said, "I think I do need to sleep."

"Yeah, clearly. Listen, I'm gripped by your novel. Mind if I shoot myself a copy of this to my computer? I promise to trash it after I finish. I just need to read it all through, right now. I'm that hooked, Ash."

Ash... again. That reminded her of Chase.

Ashley shrugged, said, "What could it hurt?" She managed a smile. "You're really enjoying it?"

"Savoring it. Admiring it. It's the first thing I've read in a very long time that makes me want to sit down with its author and a good bottle of wine and talk about the book. Deep talk. What the Spanish call *charla profunda*. Delve into the process and the inspirations and tactics you adopted to tackle some of the harder stuff. Writer talk. There are stretches in here, well, I just can't figure out how you brought them off so magically."

Shawn hesitated, then said, "Don't take this wrong, but you're a throwback to the good old days of fiction writing for me. If you'd been born twenty-five years earlier, I think they'd maybe be studying you in school now. You've got two short stories that are destined for some Norton anthology not too long down the road. I'd wager real money on that. This novel is going to get you starred reviews across the board. I'd make book on that, too."

Ashley smiled and shook her head. "And now I think you're drunk, Shawn." Drunk or trying to seduce her. But she searched his face and decided he was sincere.

He said, "No, I'm not drunk. Too practiced, takes too much now to get there these days. But even if that was so, it's been a pleasure murdering the late-morning-into-afternoon with you, Ash," he said. "I'm not wrong about your writing. You have the potential to be one of the ones that matter."

Shawn scooped up the vial of Motrin on the nightstand by her bed and said, "Better take a couple of these now, and drink a glass of water or two. Head that pain off before it can get a good grip on you." He shook some pills into her palm then filled her empty wine glass with water from the bathroom tap.

Taking the glass, she said, "Thanks. For the pills and especially the company. And for the nice words about my writing." She smiled and said, "And of course for the wine, too."

"All my pleasure, entirely." He meant it. He was fascinated by her and staggered by the depth of Ashley's prose and power of her storytelling abilities at such an early stage of her writing career. He said, "I want you to know, I meant every word I've said about your writing. I hope you believe that, because it's the truth."

He waited until he saw her take the pills, then reached over and shook her big toe through her sock and let himself out, setting the door lock from the inside.

Shawn was startled as someone grabbed his arm, squeezed hard. Brick said, "How is she?"

"So nice of you to worry," Shawn said. "She's good. Well… seems okay at least."

"That's real fine to hear," Brick said. "That's real good." Shawn wasn't sure he believed Brick. The security chief slapped Shawn on the back and said, "C'mon, counselor. Ms. Hyde wants to have you and Chase sign some papers. Make this biography thing all official and the like."

"We'll need a witness," Shawn said. "A competent witness."

"And that'll be me," Brick said, thrusting a thumb at his chest.

"You? Really?"

This back-slap that stung. Brick grinned and said, "Who else?"

30

"She's looking bad again," Brick said. "She's calling out for help, but appears she can't reach the intercom to contact us. Doubles up with pain every time she tries to move. It's actually surprisingly hard to look at."

Shelby checked her watch. She flopped back in her chair, then squealed and said, "Damned tattoo."

Brick raised his eyebrows. *"You* got a tramp stamp? Back there?"

She regretted saying it. "Forget that," Shelby said. "Okay. Let's get Dalton and Chase in the van and take them down the mountain for dinner somewhere where we can control the scene. Someplace with a private party room would be best. We'll say Ashley is hanging behind. You'll make it clear to Chase that Ashley's still pissed at him. While we are at dinner, I want you to go in and check on her. Then insist on taking her to the hospital."

"And...?" Brick couldn't believe she really wanted him to get the girl medical help. So he wanted to make Shelby say it, the haughty, bent bitch. She'd given him a tumble, exactly once. She'd left nail marks in his ass cheeks; she'd made him come on her belly. But then no repeats, the cock-tease.

"And then you take care of her," she said. "I don't want to know the details."

He nodded, said, "This is really going to cost you, you know."

"We already set terms for that eventuality, remember? I know exactly what it's going to cost me."

He smiled. "In *cash*, sure you do. What I mean is—"

"Just do your job," Shelby said. "I know what I want. That's all that matters."

"I think it's my appendix," Ashley groaned. She was curled up in a ball on the bed, her back to Brick. She'd sweated through her blouse. It stuck darkly to her shoulder blades and spine.

Brick was hunched over her computer, typing in the letter Shelby had written for him to send to Chase, ostensibly from Ashley.

He hit *Send*, said, "Yeah, I think so too, honey. I'm going to get you in my car, and we're going to get you down the mountain, *muy pronto*."

"I need my computer to come with me. My luggage." Ashley flexed her right hip again, it seemed to offer slight relief.

"I'm already gathering it all up," Brick said. "No worries."

Hell, he had to bring along her stuff, all of it. He couldn't risk anything of Ashley's being left behind to find. It had to look like the vixen had bolted, run off in a snit.

With the weather, he couldn't bury the body — the ground was just too hard for that. So he would have to drag it off into some remote woods and let the animals, elements and time have their way with the corpse. Her luggage and laptop he'd drop in various dumpsters around Gatlinburg and Pigeon Forge.

Zipping her laptop into its bag now, Brick said, "Okay, I'm running your stuff down to my car. I'll be back in about two minutes for you, love. Then I'll carry you. I promise, I'm going to take real good care of you."

She said, "Does Chase know? He should come with me." Hell of a time to try and face up to him after his revelation, but sick as she was?

"He's away for now. Some research trip with the boss."

"What about Shawn?"

"With Shelby and Chase. Sorry, sweetie. I'll get them to the hospital to visit, soon as I can. Now I'm going to load the car. Back in a jiffy."

It seemed a lot longer than two minutes to Ashley, even in her feverish state.

Ashley held up a hand as he reached for her. "I can walk." She did find herself leaning on Brick as they made their way through the house and out into the snow flurries. Brick held her hand as she eased into the passenger seat of his car. He helped her with seatbelt and shoulder harness, pushing the lap strap down low to avoid putting pressure on her belly. That was just salve for his conscience, he knew.

He slid in next to Ashley and gunned the engine a few times. Brick's car seemed extra loud to Ashley. Some kind of muscle car, probably. She'd hadn't really gotten a look at the model through the blinding snow flurries, just saw it was glossy black and a two-door. It was also very low-slung.

Brick said, "Here we go," then got the car in gear. Even moving, its exhaust thrummed loudly. The interior of the car shook each time he stepped on the gas. Glass packs? Ashley had a boyfriend in high school who'd had those stupid things on his vintage junker. Riding in his car could all but loosen the fillings in your teeth. In the country, you could hear it coming from two miles away. Ashley's father hated that car, hated that boy.

Despite the cold, Ashley was sweating. She dragged the back of a shaking hand across her forehead to keep her perspiration from running into her eyes. She said thickly, "We're going higher. Hospital's downhill, right?"

Brick shot her a look, licked his lips, and said, "Just these crazy mountain roads, sweetie. Some are one-way. *Real* one-way. Like this one. Gotta go up to go down, baby."

Ashley said thickly, "Oh. Okay. Just please hurry."

Her pain seemed to be coming in cycles again, and she was in one of the intervals where the stabbing in her side was subsiding. She was able to focus a bit more. Ashley looked around the interior of the car. Her bags and computer were piled on the back seat.

And there was something wedged under Brick's thigh.

She looked at that object tucked under the burly man's leg for a time and realized what she was seeing—the butt of a gun.

Brick was stealing glances at her. He obviously saw what she had seen. He shook his head, almost solemn. "So sorry, honey. Yeah, it's like that. Hoped to just do it and spare you the scare. That's the God's honest truth. Now? I swear I'll make it fast, darling. Fight me, and I'll make it *slow*. And maybe try to enjoy myself with you before I finish off, too. Understood?"

Ashley couldn't believe it. He really meant to kill her? She said, "What? Are you serious?"

"You know what this is," he said. "You know what's going to happen. I see it in your face. Before we left, I sent your boyfriend a *Dear John* email from your computer. Given your last fight with him, he's going to fall for it, just fine. Your bags are dumpster-bound."

Ashley played a bit sicker than she felt. She groaned and pressed her hand to her side again. "What are you saying?"

Brick gave her this sad smile now. It was nowhere near comforting with that severed nerve pulling it down on one side. "Lover-boy's bedroom back there, and yours, is wired and bugged and riddled with cameras, baby. I've got film of you being boned by that bookworm I could put up on an amateur porn site and retire on, I think."

That admission made Ashley freshly nauseous. She said, "Why?"

"Search me. Ms. Hyde seems to have some obsession with your boyfriend. Between things she's said, things of her father's I've read, and my own imagination, I think Shelby Hyde thinks Chase is her old man. And I reckon she has the hots for Daddy. With all that incest in his books, she probably thinks the twisted yen is mutual. Or will be. She had me do some deep background checking on your boyfriend. I know all about his invented identity. About Chase's amnesia or whatever he chooses to call it."

Brick pulled the gun from under his thigh. He was steering with his right hand, splitting attention between Ashley and the road, pointing the gun at her torso with his left hand.

"There are a lot of people who know I'm here," Ashley said, fighting to control her rising sense of panic. Her chin was trembling, her breath starting to come in ragged heaves. As her blood pressure mounted, she could feel the pain starting to gather in her belly again. "I emailed my agent," she lied. "Told her we're in the Smoky Mountains." She tasted her tears salty in her mouth. Ashley realized she was crying.

"And your agent will think you left these mountains in a huff, just like Chase will believe," Brick said. "Come spring, whatever is left of you will be buried." He shrugged. "In the end, you'll be another missing writer, sweetheart. Maybe a subject for another biography for your boyfriend. Now don't get stupid on me 'cause I've done a lot of work on this car and I don't want the inside all fucked up with blood where I might have to trash it for fear of Luminal inspection by some redneck Tennessee cop who's seen too many episodes of *CSI*, got me? This is going to happen. You don't do anything stupid, and I'll make it painless, I swear I will. You're a good kid. Shouldn't have to suffer none. Believe me, I don't like this anymore than you."

Ashley nodded, wide-eyed. "Please, mister! Please don't do this to me! Please?" The snow was coming down harder now. She could see some lights up ahead of them, some kind of large structure. There was an old and buckling stone wall running along Brick's side of the road, something once intended to stop skidding cars from going down the mountain side. Now it looked ready to tumble over.

Ashley weighed her options. She saw only two: die at Brick's hands, or die trying to save herself.

Squealing at the pain the exertion caused her, she flung herself toward Brick and grabbed the steering wheel with both hands, twisting it toward the old wall. Brick cursed and tried to right the car, dropping the gun to use both hands.

Ashley let go of the steering wheel and ducked low as a dislodged stone shattered the windshield and landed on the seat between them. The nose of the car dipped, headlights shining on snow-covered pines and bare oaks.

Then they were airborne. Ashley felt her stomach drop as they began to fall. Snow and sleet whipped through the hole in the windshield and stung her eyes.

Ashley ducked down low again as the car dove down the side of the mountain.

31

"All this material, and none of it has ever been published?" Shawn sat back in his chair, shaking his head. He seemed all but flattened by the revelation. "This could be worth a fortune," he said to Shelby, some bitterness in his voice. "That's what you're thinking, isn't it?"

She nodded, glaring at Chase. He squirmed and bit his lip. Clearly Shelby hadn't meant to share the existence of her father's material with the family attorney. At least not yet.

"Admittedly, it's not on quite the same plane as Daddy's three published works," Shelby said. "Although the unfinished one, what's there of it, is up to par, I think." She stared at her plate. "That said, the other novels are better than anything any of his contemporaries have published since Daddy's death. That's not just a proud daughter's observation, either. I'm being very frank about this. And coldly objective, I think. By anyone's standards, it's extremely potent material."

"I've read a bit of each now," Chase said. "Shelby's right. It's some powerful stuff."

Shawn wadded up his napkin and threw it across his plate. "I'm truly floored." He tugged on his ear lobe, said to Shelby, "Your mother, Amanda, swore, she swore that she had obeyed some order your father had given her to burn all of his letters and manuscripts. She was to destroy any scrap of writing he left behind unless he left specific instructions behind for its publication."

Shawn hesitated, then said, "Did Everett do that? Did he indicate he wanted any of this stuff out there?"

"Of course not," Shelby said, a bit wary-sounding to Chase. She crossed her arms and glared across the table at her attorney. "Do you honestly think my mother should have obeyed Daddy's wishes to burn his writings? That would have been a crime against literature! Think about what would have been lost."

Shawn dug his knuckles into his eyes. His eyes still closed, he pinched the bridge of his nose between thumb and forefinger and said, "I'm of two minds, here. As your attorney, I'm seeing big dollar signs for your estate as I sit here working my mouth. And, frankly, I see a big commission for your humble attorney. But as your father's appointed guardian of his reputation, the one he left legally in charge of protecting his estate and literary legacy, I'm just trying to get some assurance this stuff will enhance and not harm Everett's critical reputation. I want that for the sake of my own conscience, too. Look at some of the Hemingway stuff that's been published, and the effect some of the posthumous stuff had on his literary stature. The first rule in maintaining a literary estate is to do no harm. Your father was very keen on that point and made it clear I was to make that my priority."

"It's good," Shelby said, her voice a rasp that unsettled Chase, just a bit. "The material is good."

Shawn held his ground. "How good? How good is it?"

"Like you said," Shelby said, "'Big fucking dollar signs' worth of good."

32

The headlights of Brick's car had been taken out by sturdy branches not long after the stone from the crushed wall crashed through the windshield.

Ashley had the sense they still hadn't fallen too far from the road.

There was a stinging slap against her face, and she realized the passenger-side airbag had deployed.

They were stopped now, just the sound of whatever was left of the engine winding down and wheels turning on twisted axles. That and the nostril- and eye-stinging stench of gasoline.

Ashley lifted her head and tried to press the airbag away from her bruised breasts but found it had little give.

She looked over and saw Brick was slumped forward, his bloodied face buried in the tattered folds of his own airbag. A tree branch had come through the windshield. It had snaked its way through the steering wheel, puncturing the airbag and driving itself through Brick's torso, just below his left collarbone. Ashley twisted her neck around for a better view and saw the jagged end of the tree branch protruded several inches through Brick's seat. Blood dripped *pat pat pat*, on the man's twitching, muscled thigh.

Still smelling gasoline, afraid of being burned alive, Ashley wedged an arm around the airbag and groped for the car keys.

She turned off the ignition, hoping she'd done so in time to prevent the spilled fuel from catching fire.

Gasping, Ashley pulled the keys loose and gathered them between her fingers. She began poking and shredding at her own airbag with the keys. There was a pop and the airbag at last deflated. Ashley pushed against the punctured bag to speed its emptying. She wrestled to free herself from the seatbelt and shoulder harness. Several times, she tried to open the door, then realized the impact had probably twisted the car's frame, jamming the doors permanently shut.

Ashley looked at the stone on the seat between them and hoisted it. The effort caused her pain, but adrenaline kept her focused. She threw it back through the windshield in the other direction, widening the hole. She kicked loose the last shards of glass and fished around in the backseat until she found her purse. She slipped it over her shoulder and wrestled her laptop and suitcase from the back seat.

Brick was groaning lowly: unconscious, yet clearly in a great deal of pain. Ashley shoved her suitcase and laptop out onto the accordion hood of the car and crawled out and slid down onto the sharply sloping, snow-covered ground. The snow drifts nearly reached her knees.

Brick's muscle car, a Mustang, she saw, had squarely hit a big old pin oak.

The moon was full, otherwise she'd be nearly blind in the winter woods. She could see up the slope a good ways, could actually make out the silhouette of what was left of the wall she'd steered them into.

Ashley struggled with her bags, waded back up the hill, and leaned against the back of the Mustang, panting and clutching her side. She was afraid the impact and the seatbelt had conspired to rupture her appendix. The pain was different now, duller and not so localized.

She rested her laptop case and suitcase on the trunk of the Mustang and waited until the burning there subsided a bit. While she did that, Ashley strategized.

Presumably, Brick was carrying a cell phone. Ashley decided to risk it.

She slogged back down through knee-deep snow to the front of the ruined Mustang and recovered the stone that had crashed through the windshield when they'd torn through the retaining wall. The rock was wedged between the folds of what was left of the hood.

Hefting the rock between her cold hands, she struggled back up the hillside, around the back of the car, and back to the driver's side window.

She drove the rock against the window's glass three times before the fractured glass finally collapsed into Brick's lap. The noise seemed to be bringing Brick back around.

Ashley bit her lip and thrust her hands into his nearest coat pocket and found nothing.

She patted at his interior pocket, just under the bloody branch. All she got for that effort was a bloodied hand. She wiped her hand down on Brick's pant leg, then reached across his torso to feel for his right-hand coat pocket. His hand closed around her wrist.

Brick turned slowly her way and snarled, "You bitch!"

His left arm was moving—she saw he had the gun clutched in that hand. She raked at his eyes with her free hand and felt something wet on her nails. Brick screamed and let go of her wrist. She fell back onto her ass in the deep snow. The first of two gunshots whipped over her head.

Ashley scrambled up the hill to the back of the ruined Ford. Staying low, she groped over her head and pulled down her purse, laptop and suitcase. She started climbing up the hill. She soon realized she couldn't do it with all her bags, not with the pain in her belly as it was now. She slipped her purse's strap over her head, and then followed that with her laptop case's strap, getting it under her left arm, the bags' straps crisscrossing her chest like bandoliers. She decided to leave her suitcase behind when she heard more shots behind her.

Hauling herself up the hill, her bare hands burning from the snow, she wondered at the shots Brick was taking. With that tree branch pinning him to his seat, he couldn't possibly get a good shot over his shoulder.

She heard a scream behind her, turned, and saw Brick fall face first through his broken window into the snow. It clicked for her then: the tough bastard had shot through the tree branch to free himself.

The mercenary struggled up onto his knees, trying to draw a bead on her. Ashley threw herself behind the trunk of a tree and felt it take the shock of another couple of slugs.

She screamed for help, slogging up the hill in a straight line, trying to keep the fat tree trunk between herself and Brick's shots.

Ashley could see the ruins of the wall. Groaning with pain, she rolled over the remains of the wall and onto the shoulder of the slick, dark mountain road. Any hopes of flagging down a passing car seemed remote. The road was snow-covered, and there were no tracks in either direction except those left by the Mustang.

Through the stinging flurries, Ashley could see the lights she'd seen just before the wreck. They were maybe two hundred yards further up the steeply inclining road. She could hear the crunch of snow behind her; snapping branches. Despite his wounds, Brick seemed intent upon catching up to her.

Her hand pressed to her side, Ashley set off in a staggering shamble up the icy road toward the hazy lights flickering through the flurries.

33

"I can't believe she just left me like this," Chase said, sitting on the foot of his bed. "Just took off, cold, like that." Chase snapped his fingers and shook his head. In a way, in the fleeting moments he let himself think it, it was almost a *relief* as he found himself increasingly drawn to Shelby.

On the other hand, it stung to be dropped so abruptly like this. Vanity, sure, but there it was...

Shawn shook his head. Not the picture of commiseration, Chase thought. "Yeah, well, like you said, rightly or wrongly, she was angry at you. Seems you screwed up big time." Shawn sat in front of Chase's laptop, reading over Ashley's good-bye letter again. While Chase was distracted, Shawn had taken the liberty of opening some of Ashley's earlier emails to Chase.

Shawn was interested in Ashley, there was that. She was pretty, yes. Smart, too. But her writing beguiled him as much as her pretty face and body. More, really. Yes, he was increasingly infatuated with her. He was, therefore, nosey.

But Shawn also was left a little thrown by Ashley's email kiss-off to Chase.

Shawn had read enough of Ashley's prose now that he had a real sense of her writing style, a strong enough sense of

Ashley's voice, even in the casual format of an email. Enough to draw some conclusions.

Ashley's earlier, loving emails to Chase "sounded" like Ashley in most ways, they read as her writing. The voice was not inconsistent with the young woman's prose.

This new email, on the other hand? Shawn had concluded it didn't sound at all like Ashley.

Pressed, Shawn might have confessed to doubting the email's authenticity. But he wasn't going to volunteer his skepticism to Chase. He said, "Want to tell me what was going on between you two?"

"No," Chase said. "No, I really don't."

"Fair enough. Guess I'm out of here, then." Shawn rose and stretched. He pressed his palms to his back and winced as his spine cracked. "I've drunk my fill, or I'd offer to tie one on with you. But I've got some hefty paperwork ahead, so I'll scram."

Chase nodded distractedly. He mumbled, "Can't even call her now because her cell phone's back at my place."

"Yeah, well, that's a real problem." Shawn shook his head and let himself out. He cast a sour look back at Chase, and shaking his head again, pulled the door nearly shut behind him.

Shawn wasn't gone five minutes when Shelby knocked lightly at Chase's just-cracked bedroom door.

She said, "Hi, Chase. I... Well, I was just informed your assistant left in a bit of a huff. Well, I mean, I kind of came to believe, or was led to believe, that she might be more than your assistant." Shelby ended on an ascending note, making her observation sound more like a question, inviting elaboration from Chase.

Instead, Chase looked back over his shoulder, biting his lip. He shrugged. "We should probably get back to work downstairs in the document room," he said. "We should continue going through those manuscripts. I need a better handle on what, and about how much, I can use in my book. Be better, sooner rather than later, to establish all that."

Shelby looked at Chase for a time, lightly rubbing at the small of her back, then said, "Okay. Sure. But how about I stand you a drink first? Glass of red wine?" She smiled a sad smile. "Or maybe you crave something stronger?"

Chase stood and shrugged, his hands in his pants pockets. "No, wine would be very nice." She took his arm and he let her do that.

"Great then," Shelby said, leading him down the hallway. "After a glass or two, we'll set back to work."

"Right."

She was still clinging to his arm. Chase said, "Your security gopher, this Brick guy, shouldn't he be back by now? I mean, it couldn't take long to make a run down on the tram and to put Ash in some cab." He raised an eyebrow. "Could it?"

"Mr. Arick had some other tasks to see to for me," Shelby said.

She gripped his arm a bit harder, seemed to hesitate, then said, "You putting that question to me just now, that wasn't an idle one, was it? You suspect something else, is that it? You suspect that maybe, well, maybe there was something developing between your assistant and my security chief?"

Shelby looked up at him with inquiring eyes.

Chase pulled his arm away. "Honestly? That was the last thing I was thinking. Ashley loathed that steroid jockey, of that much I'm certain. Her standards were way too high to give that fool a second look." This crooked smile. "I mean, Christ, could any woman really want to spend even idle time with that son of a bitch?"

34

A shley was bent over, hands gripping her knees, trying to catch her breath.

The lights she'd been running toward came from a small-ish building with a few cars parked out front. Most of the hazy illumination from the building originated from the side of the structure that faced away from the road.

Ashley let herself in and closed the door against the wind. She'd heard shouts some distance behind her. Brick was still chasing her on foot, though she doubted he could risk barging in after her. Not bleeding from the shoulder and waving around a gun as he was.

But if he still had a cell phone somewhere on him? If he did, he could call in others after her. He might even have done that some minutes ago. If so, they could be getting close.

Frantic, Ashley looked around the interior of the small building. It was crammed with various souvenir items, stuffed plush black bears, tacky jewelry, and gaudy postcards.

A sign advertised the cost of chairlift rides down the side of Crockett Mountain into the heart of downtown Gatlinburg.

"We'll be shutting down soon, honey," an old woman huddled behind the cash register said. She was holding her wrinkled and shaking hands up close to a space-heater. "If you want a ride down, cold as it is, the last ride down will be yours."

"Perfect," Ashley said thickly. She winced, then dug out her change purse and handed over some bills. She saw some souvenir mittens and gloves for sale by the register, woolen ski caps with black bears embroidered on them. Ashley bought a pair of fleece-lined gloves and pulled the tacky, bear-emblazoned ski cap down tight over her ears. She figured she looked like some overgrown kid in the things.

The woman directed her out onto a windswept platform, and a gangly kid with zits positioned Ashley on a painted square. She was swaying in the Arctic wind, feeling as though she was close to fainting.

The teenage ride operator eased her back into a chair and then folded the bar down over her head. Ashley heard the metal locks click into place, then began the frigid and bouncing, bobbing descent down the side of the mountain, her eyes immediately tearing from the stinging cold snow whipping up into her face.

She needed medical attention, she thought. There was something about the pain in her belly that had definitely changed, and she was afraid her appendix was spilling poison inside her, putting her at risk of septic shock and death.

Yet it occurred to Ashley then that if Brick did survive his wounds long enough to get word back to Shelby and her other stooges, they'd likely call around to area hospitals looking for her in order to finish what Brick had failed to do. They had no choice now.

Ashley opened her purse and found a nail file. She slit the interior lining of her purse along its bottom edge, then began sliding into the slit all of her personal identification: her operator's license, library cards and charge cards. Her old student I.D. she'd sentimentally never gotten around to tossing.

She was passing over a fast-running stream. Cars crawled in the gridlocked traffic beneath her feet. She was amazed she'd managed to remain conscious on her freezing ride down the mountain. Ashley closed her purse and checked to see that its strap and her laptop's strap were still securely fastened across her torso. Thanks to Shawn's password protections, she wouldn't have to worry about anyone booting up her laptop to look for clues to her identity. Bless him for thinking of it, for insisting.

Now she was maybe twelve-feet off the ground, her chair in a steep, final descent. She tugged back on her mittens.

A man stepped forward and grabbed her chair. He lifted the bar and took her by the arm to help her off. Ashley promptly fell to her knees. She was almost hit in the back of the head by her ski chair as it bumped along to make the turn and begin its ascent back up the mountainside. Ashley would have landed on her face if the man wasn't still gripping her elbow. This ride operator, some codger, said, "Oh, God, sorry, hon'. You okay?"

"I'm very sick," Ashley said, trying to stand up. "I need an emergency squad, right now! T-tell them it's my appendix! Tell them I think it's burst! T-tell them I'm—"

Ashley felt herself falling forward again. The elderly ride operator caught her up in both arms now. Whimpering, she heard the old man yelling to someone else, screaming for them to call 9-1-1.

35

They were holed up again in the manuscript room.

They each sat with pages of manuscript of Everett Hyde's unfinished novel, reading passages here and there that struck some chord or whose prose construction or rhythms they particularly admired.

Shelby finished reading aloud a longish passage about an older man and a young woman on the verge of intimacy and said, "Amazing, isn't it?"

"It is," Chase said. It was in its way... Amazing, and uncomfortably arousing.

"So unfair," Shelby said. "It's just wrong that this is the one left unfinished. The other manuscripts are good, sure, but this one? I think it might have been his very best of all. Might have been the finest of my father's novels. If he'd only gotten it done."

"Possibly," Chase said. "Maybe that's all so. But it's written at such a pitch, and it moves at such a furious pace at what must have been only about the halfway point, given the length of your father's other works..."

Chase shrugged and poured himself a little more wine and said, "I just wonder if your father simply didn't know how to maintain that pace and deliver on the rest of the book after this wild front end. Maybe the ending eluded him. You know, a lot of critics and other authors have ventured similar opinions of Fitzgerald's *The Last Tycoon*. They think that Scott's brilliant fragment constitutes a clearly unfinishable work. They argue that for such a majestic opening there could be no effective climax. Maybe your father sensed the same thing about his novel."

"God, but that's a depressing thought," Shelby said. "I'd hate to think it could be true. That kind of thinking makes a part of me wish those conspiracy theorists were right with their wild ideas about Daddy faking his death."

Shelby stood and stretched, then carried some more manuscript fragments over to where Chase sat on a smallish leather loveseat. She sat down next to Chase, very close, hip touching hip.

He said, "What do you mean about the conspiracy theorists?"

She smiled and briefly rested her head on his shoulder. "If father was still alive, maybe now, with some years past, he could finish this novel. God, it's just so wrong that it's left like this, simply trailing off into nothingness."

"If these conspiracy buffs had it right," Chase said, very aware of Shelby's hip pressed against his now, of her hair tickling his neck, "don't you think your father would have at least reached out to you? That he would have tried to contact your mother?"

"Sure," she said. "Or maybe. I never met him, of course. So sometimes I indulge in some fantasizing." Shelby smiled and bumped foreheads with Chase. "Confession time. I even bought one of those silly T-shirts a few years ago. Do you know the ones? 'Hyde's Hiding!'?"

Shelby again rested her head on Chase's shoulder. She held up some manuscript pages and said, "God, listen to this passage here, it's a bedroom scene, and it's way sexy, even more than the last one."

36

Ashley lay there a time, listening to the quiet, making sure she was alone.

After perhaps two minutes of that silence, she opened one eye. It was dark and very still.

The hospital room, for there was no doubt it was anything but, was the usual affair—small, impersonal. A TV was mounted high on the wall. There was a hand-held control unit for the TV that included a red button to summon a nurse. The remote control's power cord was wrapped once around the metal rail of Ashley's bed, up near her head.

Ashley could tell she was naked under the ill-fitting hospital gown. She could feel the sheets of the bed against her damp, bare back through the gap in her gown.

She slowly turned her head and saw the vitals monitors by her bedside. Ashley squinted at the glowing digital numerals there. Nothing extraordinary about her pulse or her blood pressure. Her heart rate was steady.

Slowly, Ashley raised her right arm. There was an IV needle thrust into the back of her hand and secured with tape, explaining the cold stinging in that hand.

There was a duller ache in her belly. She could feel a catheter between her legs and smell the faint scent of urine from the bag hanging at the foot of her bed.

She raised her left arm and saw a plastic identification band bound 'round her wrist. Ashley held her left arm up to her face and twisted the plastic band around with her right hand, moving gingerly to avoid increasing the sting from the IV.

The ID bracelet read in part, "Jane Doe. DOB:?"

So. They hadn't yet identified her. Thank God. At least that much was in her favor. If the hospital didn't know who she was, nobody could inadvertently tip Shelby Hyde or her minions to Ashley's whereabouts.

Ashley looked around again. It was indeed a single room, no ailing company. She turned on the television and turned down the volume. Ashley flipped around the channels until she hit the Weather Channel. Assuming she was still in Tennessee—and really, where else could she be?—it was just after nine p.m. It was snowing outside, probably. According to the date at the corner of the screen, it was the evening after the night she escaped from Brick.

She bit her lip, then raised the sheet and tugged up the nightgown until she could see her side. Her butterfly tattoo was obscured under layers of surgical tape and bandages. Ashley's knowledge of anatomy was limited, but the bandages were just about where she'd figure them to be following an appendectomy.

Ashley could hear the squeak of rubber-soled shoes on tile. She flipped off the television and pulled down her gown, then pulled up the sheets. The nurse caught sight of her adjusting her covers before Ashley could close her eyes.

"We saw your vitals fluctuate and figured you were finally awake," the nurse said, smiling. "How are we feeling?"

Ashley checked the woman's nameplate pinned above her rather ample left breast: it read "Jynnifer." Ashley ran her fingers back through her hair. She said, hoarse-sounding, "Where am I?"

"St. Anthony's, in Sevierville."

Nodding slowly, Ashley bit her lip. "Sevierville...?"

"Yes," the nurse said, studying Ashley's face. "You know, in Tennessee. Not far from Pigeon Forge? Gatlinburg?" As if it might solve everything, the nurse wrinkled her nose, said, "You know, Dollywood?"

Ashley played thick: "Tennessee...?"

The nurse scooped up the chart at the end of Ashley's bed and examined it. After a time, she said, "We need to get your name. You were unconscious when you were brought in."

Now Ashley figured she really had to go for it. She said, "Sure... uh..."

The nurse was still studying her face.

Ashley said, "What was wrong with me? My side hurts."

"We had to remove your appendix."

"I do remember my belly hurting."

"Yes, it was severe appendicitis."

"Did it rupture?"

"All but. You were very lucky. But you're going to be just fine. Now, your name?"

"I... I don't know." Irresistibly, Ashley thought of Chase, coming to in some hospital a quarter-century or so before, apparently truly unable to remember who he was. Unable to answer the same questions now being put to Ashley by some well-meaning medical professional.

"You were unconscious for at least an hour before the ambulance could move you through traffic from downtown Gatlinburg last night," the nurse said. "Place is always crazy at night. Gridlock city. So it took time to get you from Gatlinburg, that's where you were found, to the hospital here. Your vitals were still strong when the paramedics reached you last night. That's when you were brought in."

Sounding rather stupid to her own ears, Ashley said dumbly, "My appendix?"

"Yes," the nurse said. "You passed out in the arms of a chair-lift operator. Those chairs you ride up and down the mountainside, you know? The ride operator swore he caught you before you could hit the ground. And, consistent with his story, you show no signs of a head injury, although there is severe bruising to your torso and waist. Those bruises wouldn't be inconsistent with the bruises we might see in a car crash, from the seatbelts."

"I was in a car crash?"

The nurse was near exasperation, Ashley could tell. She said, "That's what we were really hoping you could tell us. A car went off the road last night. It was found a few hours after you were brought in. It was found not far from the chair lift ride you rode down the mountain. We found you with a purse and a computer. There was no identification in the purse, and your computer seems to be password protected. Now, your name?"

"I... I don't know." Ashley leaned into her subterfuge a bit harder: "I'm scared. My God, I don't know who I *am*." To her surprise, the tears came easily. She managed, "I'm so afraid!"

"Easy now," said the nurse, softer suddenly, starting to buy in, Ashley could tell. "Your memory might come back once you get your bearings, sweetie. Probably once more of the medication wears off."

"I want to get up."

"You can do that, I think," the nurse said. "You're allowed to move around a bit, to walk. In fact, we encourage that about now. But first I have to take out the catheter you have inside you."

The nurse did that and helped Ashley to her feet. Ashley was surprised to find she could move around without too much pain. She was just a bit dizzy from the medication that had been pumped into her system.

After a trip to the restroom, Ashley asked, "When can I leave?"

The nurse chewed her lip, said carefully, "Well, if it were a simple matter of the appendectomy, you'd probably be released tomorrow, but…"

Ashley said softly, "And my memory?"

"Yeah… About that— I'm gonna get a doctor for you right now," Jynnifer the nurse said. "I suspect he'll want to have you see a specialist or two. He'll probably order a CAT-scan. We have to notify the police, too. They'll certainly have some questions."

Certainly. Of course they would. But those were questions Ashley was pretty sure she couldn't answer yet. And Ashley didn't have much appetite for having a lot of unnecessary and invasive scans run on her brain; for suffering a bunch of neurologists or the like doing things to her. "Will he be here soon?"

"We're in that shift-change period," the nurse said. "Should be able to have him here in an hour or so. In the meantime, I think we should get you around a bit. You should be able to take care of some things yourself now. While you wait for the doctors."

"I think I am ready to try," Ashley said, driven to get moving. Eager to be freed up to find her clothes, her computer and bolt. But first she needed to know how limber she was. She needed to know how much stamina she had and what effect the medicines might have on her coordination and concentration. She also needed to make some decisions, and *soon*.

Chase, whoever he really was, was still in that insane compound with Shelby Hyde.

Shelby. The crazy woman who had clearly ordered Ashley's murder.

Regardless of his identity, Ashley couldn't just abandon Chase there, could she? She couldn't leave him to the whims and designs of that crazed orphan.

And Shawn? He might be in trouble, too. If they found out Shawn also knew what Ashley had learned about their location, God knew what they'd do to him.

Ashley chewed her lip, wondering at Shelby, wondering what she was like. With her appendix pain, Ashley had never gotten a glimpse of the bitch.

The nurse finished making some notes. She took Ashley's left hand to help her to her feet. She squinted at Ashley's ring fingers and said, "No tan-line or trace of a ring impression there. Not of an engagement ring, or a wedding band."

"No," Ashley said dully, looking at her hand. "Guess that's so. More bad luck, eh?" She lowered her legs over the right side of the bed and got up on shaky legs again. The nurse worked at the back of Ashley's nightgown, tying it tighter, then helped her on with a robe. She got Ashley's left arm through one sleeve and draped the rest over Ashley's right shoulder; the IV in her right hand precluded slipping the other arm through the terrycloth robe's sleeve.

"Any pain?"

"Not really," Ashley said. "I mean, I feel a bit of a pain in my side, but it's more of an ache."

"And some sting from the stitches," the nurse said. "All to be expected."

They walked slowly along the antiseptic-smelling hallway, the nurse holding firmly to Ashley's left arm. Ashley had her right hand wrapped around the aluminum IV stand for support. One of the stand's wheels squeaked as it rolled along, and it had a tendency to drift rightward. Jennifer asked, "Anything coming back to you?"

"Nothing at all." They turned a corner and Ashley could see the nurses' station ahead. They were on the second lap around the ward. Ashley checked the clock as they passed the nurses' station again. Half-an-hour left until the nurse had estimated Ashley might expect the first specialist's visit; a sawbones intent, quite likely, upon putting Ashley through that battery of tests and scans she sorely wanted to avoid.

"I'm feeling very tired," Ashley said.

"We'll go back in a second," her nurse said. "We're headed the right way, anyway — it's a circle."

They were passing the elevator banks. One of the cars' bells rang and the doors slid open. Another nurse pushed a man in a wheelchair from the elevator. Ashley gave the man a double-take: he was bald, looked in obvious pain.

Then it clicked. Of course. It made perfect and terrible sense. They were both going to be classified as trauma cases and so rushed to the nearest available medical center. There already seemed to be a suspicion that Ashley had been in that crashed car that had been found. Presumably, they would have found him much closer to the crash scene.

Jynnifer said to her fellow nurse, "Hey, Laurel, there you are!" With some effort, Jynnifer turned a resistant Ashley around to face the man in the wheelchair. She said to Ashley encouragingly, "This is Mr. Arick. He was hurt in that car crash I was telling you about. The one we thought you might have been in, as well. Does he look familiar to you, honey?"

Brick smiled uncertainly at Ashley, searching her face.

Ashley's heart was racing now. She could feel her pulse in her ears and in the stitches in her belly. She said, "No, I don't know who he is. *Should* I?"

"And still no sense of who *you* are, either?" Jynnifer searched Ashley's face. Brick was doing that too, licking his lips and trying to get the drift of what was going on with Ashley.

Thinking it might buy her time, Ashley said, "No, I still don't remember anything. I still don't know who I am."

That wasn't subtle, but it at least firmly put the notion of amnesia across to Brick. One of his eyes was bandaged. His arm was in a sling and his shoulder swathed in bandages. An IV tree was attached to the back of Brick's wheelchair. Banged up as he looked, Ashley still saw him as a grave threat.

"Well, the doctors will see you soon enough," Jynnifer said. "We'll get to the bottom of this, don't worry." She nodded at Brick and said, "And you, Mr. Arick? Do you know this young lady?"

Brick smiled crookedly and shook his head. "Lord, how I wish I did." He glanced up at his own nurse, Laurel, and said, "She's a looker, just like you said. But, no, I don't know her. Damn it."

Heart thumping, Ashley managed, "So nice to have met you, Mr. Arick. Hope you feel better soon."

Brick winked. "You too, sweetie. I sure hope we meet again. Feel like we will."

Ashley nodded uncertainly and said to her nurse, "I really am very tired."

"Let's get you back to your room, then. It's not far."

As she walked along, clutching her squeaking IV tree's aluminum pole, Ashley couldn't resist the urge to look back at

Brick. The soldier-of-fortune was still sitting there in his chair, his nurse walking away from him to the station desk.

Brick smiled meanly at Ashley and raised his good hand. He pointed his index finger at Ashley like a gun, then pretended to pull the trigger.

37

C hase had burned hours finishing his reading of Hyde's other two published novels.

Ashley had been right about the intensification of the incest stuff, particularly in the last of Hyde's three published works. Feeling a bit sleazy after all that—and made uneasy by his own tumescent response to too much of it—Chase had wandered off in search of some coffee and run into Shelby at the bar.

After a couple of cups of coffee, they'd taken a bottle of wine and drifted down to sample more of Everett Hyde's unpublished works. After a few drinks, Shelby had gotten out her father's suicide note.

At Shelby's urging, Chase had begun reading the typed note aloud:

> Amanda,
>
> It's been a long time since I finished anything I started writing. That, of course, is a part of the problem. Hell, maybe it was even the start of this other.
>
> For better or worse, I guess this will be the last of my completed works—my last full piece of prose.
>
> Even in that, it's probably another mistake.

After all, how many famous writers who kill themselves actually leave a suicide note?

Yukio Mishima is the only one I can think of, and he's regarded as little better than a loon now.

Maybe I should have followed Papa's or Pancake's examples, and gone out in vexing silence.

But there are things straining to be said; scores to be settled and last business to close out.

For what you've done, there can be no forgiveness, Amanda, not from the sorry, obsessive likes of me.

But honestly? I doubt redemption is even within your grasp.

For me, at least, what you have done is truly that terrible.

You have not simply betrayed me. You've burned down everything we shared and built together—set torch to our pretty, private world and scattered the ashes wide. There is no way back for either of us now to the life I thought we cherished sharing. (More the fool am I, eh?)

There are words, darling, words said in anger sometimes, to be sure, but words that can never be taken back or forgiven. There are bells that can't be un-rung. There are calamitous actions whose awesome consequences—no matter how unforeseen in some crazed heat or scalding passion—can't be forgiven or forgotten.

You knew, Amanda, *only* you knew, what happened all those years ago.

That knowing, and what you did in full possession of that terrible knowledge, raises your betrayal to the realm of grand tragedy to my admittedly no-longer-clear mind.

You alone among all the souls in this sorry, bloody world know what he cost me.

You know what he did to my family.

The sheer fact of your treachery in face of that knowledge is all but insupportable.

But that it comes in the midst of this long terrible fallow period? This unending nightmare stretch of failed and unfinished works that pushes me past all boundaries of coping?

Do you really loathe me that much? If so, why? What on earth did I do to justify this treachery from you?

I was down, so terribly down. You knew that. And now you've made my waking horror somehow worse, made it blackly sublime past all comprehension or endurance.

In a very real sense, you've killed me—not just destroyed us—but truly murdered me. You've slain my spirit. I see no future. I'm past all hope of prospect for improvement now. The words won't come and my world has become ashes.

Yet I've seen to your material needs for the years ahead. I've done that mostly for your baby, of course. What happens to you, absent the child, well, at this moment, I truly think I couldn't care less.

I wish I thought I could get around it all. I wish I could convince myself that with time I could forgive you and we could have back our old happy life together.

But I know myself too well. I know the way my mind gnaws at a grievance like a dog worries a bone. I'll never be able to forget, and I'm not wired to forgive. Not this time, anyway. This is all on you.

My attorney, Shawn Dalton, will see to the administration of my published works, and you'll be the beneficiary of his efforts.

All that's taken care of.

The rest of the material I left behind is to be burned, immediately. I say again, burn it, *now*.

Mark this well: failure to exercise my wishes on certain points—destroying the manuscripts, for instance—will void the contracts I've asked Shawn to exercise in your (and eventually your baby's) favor. I would have seen to the destruction of my unpublished works myself, but instead I have to see to Bobby first.

I'm going to see to him before he can hurt anyone else with his selfish hedonism and low animal drives. I'm going to drive that sociopath off the face of the earth before I follow him on down to hell.

They say drowning is the easiest death, so I've reserved that option for myself. I'll steal a boat and sail out past any possibility of swimming back to shore. There I'll dive down as deep as I can and take a big, sweet breath.

And Bobby? Since I'm struggling for words these days, I'll crib from another: nothing in Bobby's regrettable life will become him so much as his leaving of it.

And I promise you, Amanda, a gentle drowning or a quick shot in the head is not in the cards for Bobby. The violence I'm stopping myself from inflicting upon you will instead visit *him*.

I'm intent upon making him see what it is to suffer at least once. I mean even to savor his delicious misery. You'll probably say I'm not that cruel or sadistic. That would be further confirmation of how little you truly know me.

I aim to prolong Bobby's agony, so maybe I'll have time to acquire a taste for his (and your) flavor of cruelty.

So farewell, darling. Good luck, Amanda, you sorry wreck.

I hope your baby eases some of the other loss coming your way.

(Best destroy this note, <u>now</u>, as my stated intentions of suicide will void insurance and other benefits due you if this falls into the wrong hands. See, even in my present state of hate, I'm thinking first of you.)

—EH

The typed note was preserved in a Mylar envelope.

Shelby gestured at the archival envelope in Chase's hand. She said, "Have to ask yourself, what mother did to provoke this letter, don't you?"

Chase said, "Hell, yes. And who the hell *is* this 'Bobby'?"

"Bobby Bristow."

Chase said, "And who is that?"

Shelby made a face and shrugged. "Just some asshole who destroyed everything."

"And what did your mother do to elicit all that anger from your dad?"

Shelby took the suicide note from his hand. A bitter smile. "I have no idea."

38

Ashley closed the door to her hospital room and booted up her laptop. The clothes she had been wearing when they brought her in were in a plastic bag by the bed. With some struggle and pain, she pulled on panties and socks. She typed in her password and stepped into jeans. She grabbed a Wi-Fi signal.

Ashley kept moving between painfully skidding on clothes and prepping her computer. She finished putting on her shoes, wincing at the strain doing that put on her abdominal wound.

She searched a closet by her bed, found some antiseptic wipes and adhesive bandages and set to work removing her own IV. The nurse hadn't reconnected Ashley to a vitals monitor, remarking the specialist would immediately spirit Ashley off to some other ward for her first battery of tests.

With the IV out, Ashley was able to slip on a sweatshirt and sweater, and then shrug on her coat. Doing that, she noticed the tightness setting into her back and shoulders from the crash. She also saw her suitcase sitting on a shelf above the closet clothes rack. Someone must really be convinced she was in that car with Brick. Well, she wouldn't question her luck to have her other belongings back.

Judging by her room clock, she had perhaps ten minutes left before the neurologist would arrive.

She shot off a jiffy email to Chase:

i'm ok; u r in danger
find an excuse and get out of that compound contact
me asap via hyena

She shut down her computer and stowed it back in her laptop case.

Gingerly, she pulled on her coat and zipped it up. She swung her purse strap and laptop strap across her shoulders. An alarm buzzed next to her bed, making Ashley flinch. She stabbed the button on the console at the top of the bed. "Yes?"

"Just making sure you're still awake," Jynnifer said. "Dr. Ford will be there in a few minutes."

"Great," Ashley said. She lifted her luggage with her left hand, looked around and made sure she had everything. Ashley crept to the door and peeked through the crack: nobody was walking the long hallway.

She slid out and made her way down the corridor toward the nurses' desk—the only way to reach the elevators and stairwell. She had tucked her hair up under her souvenir ski cap and turned up the collar of her coat. She kept her head down and shoulders hunched and passed close by the desk so the nurses seated on the other side couldn't see her suitcase.

Ashley held her breath as she passed the nurse's desk. Nobody paid her any attention. Sighing, Ashley stabbed the down button for an elevator.

A nurse pushing a supply cart sidled up alongside and smiled at Ashley. She said, "Visiting hours ended an hour ago."

Ashley smiled back, sheepishly. "It's been such a harrowing thing with my sister. Sue me, ya know?" She hefted her suitcase. "Anyway, she's finally being discharged, thank God. Going to bring around the van to pick her up."

"That's great that she's all better," the nurse said.

The bell rang and the doors slid open on an empty car. Ashley held the door for the nurse as she struggled to push the cart's wheels over the seam between the hospital's tiled floor and the elevator floor. Ashley sensed motion behind her, then turned her head quickly as Nurse Jynny passed behind her.

Ashley slid in after the other nurse, punched the close-door button, then pushed for the second floor at the nurse's request. Ashley selected the lobby button for herself.

She watched the flashing floor lights above the door. The important thing, Ashley thought, was to be outside the hospital when she was discovered missing. Ideally, she'd already be in some cab and a few blocks from the hospital. Then she remembered she was no longer in New York. She wondered how common cabs would be in this mountain tourist-trap town.

The car slowed at the fourth floor and the doors parted.

A male voice: "Son of a bitch! Must be fate, huh?" With his working arm, Brick punched the nurse in the face, sending her sprawling unconscious backwards into Ashley.

Brick slid into the elevator car and stabbed the close-door button, said, "Time to finish it, Hot Stuff. I promised you that, didn't I?"

39

Shelby had excused herself briefly. She returned with a bottle of sparkling water and a plate of fruit and cheeses. She settled in next to Chase again, closer to him than the size of the loveseat mandated, and playfully popped a grape in mouth. "By the way, who is the Hyena?"

Chase made a face. "Why in God's name do you ask that?"

"I had an email from the new editor handling my father's estate. There was some mention of the Hyena that confused me. Juxtaposition led me to believe it might be someone attached to you."

He poured some more wine in both their glasses and said, "It's my agent's nickname in certain publishing circles."

"Nice." Shelby smiled and shook her head. "She must hate that."

"Actually, Selma seems to love it," Chase said. "I'm half convinced she created the nickname herself."

"Sounds like quite a woman. Excuse me for one more minute." Shelby rose and moved briskly across the room. She shot a glance back over her shoulder and smiled to catch Chase checking out her backside. He smiled uncertainly and turned his gaze to his drink. Shelby winked and let herself out.

Chase watched her go, thought about the look she'd given him when she caught him watching her rump. She was sharp and worldly. Chase undressed her in his mind while awaiting her return.

Brick's chief stooge was waiting outside the door. Shelby said, "It's his agent's stupid nickname. So get word out to ours to resume all monitoring of all the taps we were able to get on *that* bitch's phones."

Her flunky nodded. "There's more," he said. "Ashley's email was sent from a Wi-Fi signal at St. Anthony's, you know, the hospital in Sevierville."

"And you were able to delete that message so Chase won't see it?"

The security man smiled. "Got at it through Alger's own Web Mail page. Deleted it and emptied the trash. He'll never know it existed."

"Get over to the hospital now," Shelby said. "Watch her there until you hear from me, or from someone I send."

Brick had confided to Shelby his lieutenant's worrisome weakness for Ashley. Brick had ventured a guess he'd be unreliable if it became necessary to do anything bloody to Ashley. Shelby said to Brick's flunky, "Whatever happens, don't let her leave, unless you follow. Understood?"

The guard nodded.

"Take Franklin with you, all the same." Franklin was feral, according to Brick. Shelby figured Franklin would keep his wishy-washy friend in bloody and murderous line.

40

The nurse crumpled to the floor. With his right elbow, Brick bumped the button to stop the car between the fourth and third floors. There was a lurch, and Ashley and Brick were nearly driven to their knees by the cage's sudden stop.

Ashley's stomach throbbed as she reached for the handrail and hauled herself back up. Brick was having a bit more trouble getting upright with his one functioning arm.

Putting her back to the wall, Ashley kicked the medical supply cart with her left leg. The cart tipped across Brick's legs, knocking him back to the ground. Drawers slid open, spilling bandages, tongue depressors and plastic-wrapped hypodermic needles.

Brick bellowed and kicked the cart back at Ashley. The metal case slammed into Ashley's shins. Screaming, she sprawled across the case, her face nearly landing in Brick's lap.

He knotted the fingers of his right hand in her hair. She slammed a fist into the bandages below his left shoulder. Brick howled, nearly blacking out.

Ashley bit deeply into his thigh, twisting her head side to side; felt flesh tear loose. Brick screamed and wrenched her off himself, slamming her into the wall of the elevator.

Seeing flashing lights and splashes of color, Ashley groped around on the floor with her hand. Her fingers closed around plastic-covered hypos and tongue depressors. She gathered up what she could of those and then swung nearly blind, aiming for Brick's face. There was another animal scream, a howl of pure pain.

Ashley grabbed hold of one of the open metal drawers of the medicine cart and wrenched it loose.

Grasping the tray with both hands, she swung the metal drawer against Brick's temple. She slammed the drawer down again, this time across the top of Brick's head.

The man's terrified screams probably had echoed up and down the elevator shaft. If so, there wasn't much time at all left her now, but she couldn't risk Brick coming after her again.

Ashley grabbed up one of the sealed hypodermic needles. She tore off its sanitary wrapper, uncovered the needle, and then drew the plunger back, sucking in air. She stabbed the needle into a pulsing vein in Brick's neck and depressed the plunger with her thumb. With some luck the resulting embolism would do serious harm to the bastard, maybe even kill him. If so, she promised herself in the moment she'd learn to cope with causing his death.

Ashley reached across his torso and pushed the button to resume the elevator's descent to what proved to be the fourth floor. The doors opened. Nobody was still waiting to get in, thank God.

Ashley ran out of the elevator and down the last three flights of steps to the lobby.

It was snowing outside, a kind of mini-blizzard. A single blue cab sat out front.

Ashley was about to step out into the heavy falling snow when she saw Brick's muscle-bound stooges headed her way.

41

I t felt like telling tales out of school. Objectively, Chase could step outside himself and see that. But that didn't stop him from sharing.

"It was at a reading for my book that came out this past April," Chase said. He smiled and held his goblet out for an offered refill.

Shelby topped off his glass. A little wine dribbled down the side of the glass and trailed down the stem to the base. Chase wiped at the glass with a thumb, aiming to avoid staining his pants and succeeding in doing just that with his tipsy fumbling.

Shelby daubed at the stain on his crotch with a couple of fingers, slowing the motion of her rubbing and smiling delightedly at him as she detected his growing erection.

"She wasn't there to see me," Chase said. Distracted as he was, senses dulled by wine, he hadn't yet detected the change in Shelby's attentions, and not his own reaction to those attentions, either. "She really hadn't come to meet me," Chase said.

That was true, so far as he remembered. Ashley had later told him she'd come to the bookstore looking for a collection of Raymond Carver's short fiction—some damned thing called *Furious Seasons*, if memory served and, in this case, it seemed that it did.

According to Ashley, Chase's wit, his speaking voice and his self-deprecating anecdotes had drawn her in, leading her to slide into one of the too-many empty chairs arrayed before his podium.

Ashley had been one of a half-dozen of the dozen-or-so in attendance to buy a copy of his new release for Chase to sign.

She'd also contrived to be *last* in line. So conversation dragged on a while. When the bookstore's clerks began slamming shut the folding metal chairs, Ashley suggested this bar she knew, "A cozy place, close by."

Chase suddenly felt quite mad at himself, sharing all this with Shelby. Then he realized Shelby probably wasn't listening, or more properly put, wasn't paying him *that* kind of attention.

His belt buckle was undone and his pants open. She was holding his underwear to one side and she began working at him. Chase didn't balk; he tangled his hand in Shelby's hair and closed his eyes.

42

B rick's men hadn't yet spotted her; Ashley was fairly certain of that. She was still wearing her ski cap. Remembering a scene from an old Sean Connery James Bond film she'd recently watched with Chase, one of his favorites, Ashley dropped her bags and pivoted so her back faced the two security stooges.

She was faced up against a shadowed pillar. She wrapped her own hands around her back, stroking at her spine as if she was in a passionate embrace with a lesbian lover. When she heard the pneumatic doors slide open and then shut again, she risked turning around. Ashley saw the guards' backs as they approached the information desk to ask for a room number. It might take some time, she thought—after all, she wasn't Ashley McKnight to the hospital staff, just Jane Doe. But soon enough Shelby's men and the hospital staff would know she'd gone missing.

The cab driver was still sitting out front in his idling blue cab. She picked up her bags and ran. Ashley slid into the back of the taxi, said, "Downtown Gatlinburg, by the Ripley's Museum. Do it fast and I'll pay you more."

Ashley remembered the kitschy museum from some pop-up ad on the Ober Gatlinburg Web page during her earlier browsing. She'd check into a hotel for the night, rest some more. In the morning, she'd see about contacting Selma. She would fill in the Hyena regarding all these nightmarish events. Get a bus ticket or rental car back to New York City.

Ashley would put some safe distance between herself and Shelby Hyde's mountain compound until she could figure out what to do next. Until she could figure out how to best help Chase and Shawn. Those were her initial plans.

But when Ashley reached the hotel, she was wired, edgy and verging on manic.

She paced and then impulsively snagged the room's phone directory and found a rental car agency. She arranged to have the car dropped off in the hotel's lot.

While she waited, Ashley stripped off her clothes and surveyed her body in the full-length mirror attached to the closet door. There were bruises across her waist and torso from the seatbelt and shoulder harness of Brick's wrecked Mustang.

From the position of the bandage low down on her belly, Ashley figured her butterfly tattoo was probably a total loss. Maybe that was an excuse to finally eradicate the thing, whatever was left of it, along with that long-regretted tattoo spread across the small of her back.

Ashley touched the bandage on her belly. She desperately wanted to shower, but was afraid to risk wetting her bandages. She was probably already pushing her luck in the sense of having no antibiotics on hand to stem possible infection from her surgery.

So she put back on her clothes and booted up her computer. Once online, she looked up the address for the mountaintop end of the Gatlinburg ski lifts, then keyed in a Google map search to that place from her hotel.

The medication had nearly worn off, and there was a constant pain in her side now, not like the pain from her appendix, but what she took for a kind of post-operative, stitches-induced keening.

Ashley hit the vending machine next to the elevator for an overpriced Diet Coke, then went downstairs and picked up the keys for her rental car from the front desk. She hung a left out of the hotel's lot and descended down into the tourist-clogged strip of downtown Gatlinburg, sipping her cola.

She palmed the wheel, nosing into the crawling traffic, waiting for jaywalking elderly couples and stroller-pushing younger ones to clear the way.

After a block or so, Ashley glanced left and saw the chair lifts she'd ridden down the side of Crockett Mountain in a daze the night before. Somewhere up there, near the top of the lifts, was Shelby Hyde's compound. That thought, and her determination to intrepidly head back up there anyway, made Ashley's underarms and palms damp.

Ashley crawled through successive traffic lights, taking advantage of the time sitting still to master the temperature and radio controls of her rental Chevy.

Eventually, she reached a mountain-cut intersection and doubled back, drifting off onto the Gatlinburg by-pass that took her higher up into the Smoky Mountains.

Roadside signs warned that any cars proceeding further best be equipped with tire chains, but the roads looked to have recently been shoveled and salted. Steel tube gates closed during the worst road conditions hadn't yet been set in place, so Ashley decided to take her chances.

She tried to discount the many caution signs—the ones that warned of ice hazards, deer crossings, slippery shoulders and bobsled-like descents along serpentine turns.

Instead, Ashley focused on the odometer, doing the math in her head and trying to guess backward from the chairlifts where Shelby Hyde's compound might be located.

43

U nable to ignore the pounding at the door, and detecting Chase's distraction at the insistent hammering, Shelby hauled herself off Chase and combed her fingers through her tangled hair. She smiled and ran the back of her hand across swollen lips and nodded at his wavering erection. "Get your pants back up, huh? We'll get back to this soon enough. That's a promise." Another sultry smile.

As Shelby approached the door, she said loudly, "This better be really important!"

Chase watched her as she talked through the cracked door to someone, then slid out the door and closed it behind her.

She returned a few minutes later. Chase smiled and extended a hand. Shelby took his hand and shook it and said, "Get up, lover. Get packed. We need to move, now."

Thickly, he said, "What? Move? What do you mean?"

"We have to change locations. Just got tipped some news crew is on its way up here to try and interview me. Seems my cover is blown here, suddenly. And that has me fucking livid beyond description."

"What?"

"I'm not kidding, Chase. My privacy is important to me. You know that. Now move your ass and get packing! We leave in a half an hour. I've got my crew gathering father's papers.

We'll go to my other place, south of here. We'll resume our work—" she smiled wickedly, "—and other things, there."

Chase said, "This is crazy! How'd they find you?"

Shelby shot him a look. "You're asking me that for real? Because I blame your crazy ex-girlfriend, Ashley McKnight. According to Mr. Arick, she was trying to determine our location from the second she set foot in here."

Angry now, Chase said, "And on that note, where is Brick?"

Shelby said, "Pack, Chase. Do it now, or we're as good as finished."

44

Through mounting snow flurries, Ashley saw a familiar fence topped with razor-baling wire. The place looked more like a prison than a private home.

She slowed and turned into the driveway footer, pulling up about a foot from the fence. The motion detectors lining the front of the house kicked on then, illuminating the driveway and front of Shelby Hyde's compound.

No question about it, she'd found the right house. Gathering up a notebook and pen, Ashley took down the small, almost subliminal numbers on the mailbox outside the gated entrance. Now that she had a formal address, Ashley intended to pull up a county auditor's Web site and run a property ownership check on the parcel to see if she could find whatever front, pseudonymous shell company, or DBA Hyde's evil daughter had constructed to hide her ownership of the property.

The house looked dark, abandoned. All the lights were off inside, and there were several sets of overlapping tire tracks in the driveway—fresh tracks filling with snow.

Ashley weighed her options. She was tempted to slide out of the car and press the intercom button on the post by the fence, see if anyone answered. Brick was presumably still in hospital. His flunkies were maybe still there, too. But Ashley was unarmed and alone and it was a crazy notion, she knew.

And she was all but certain that Shelby had pulled up stakes. Probably Shelby had been driven to do that when Brick went missing. If that hadn't been cause enough, then Brick's friends would have prompted the exodus, calling, as they would have to, to report Brick had been routed in a hospital elevator and that a "Jane Doe" who could only have been Ashley had bolted about the time that Brick was dying in the elevator. She remembered Brick twitching there on the floor and shivered.

Ashley tried to shake that image, and then shifted into reverse and carefully backed out onto the mountain road. Then she began ascending higher up the road, following the same path Brick had taken in his ill-fated attempt to take Ashley for a bloody last ride.

After a few miles, Ashley passed the ruined stone wall through which Brick's Mustang had barreled. Presumably, the man's muscle car was still down there somewhere on the mountainside, wedded to a sturdy old oak. Ashley passed the chair-lift concession's mountaintop HQ, all dark now.

The grade changed, and she was headed back down to the other end of Gatlinburg's main drag. Ashley was determined to return to her hotel. When she got there, she'd call the Hyena and see if she could provide any assistance, offer any useful advice.

Ashley squinted at the headlights in her rearview mirror.

That was when she realized after so much time alone on the treacherous mountain road there was actually someone behind her.

45

They'd gone down the mountain in two vans: Chase and Shawn in one, driven by Brick's weak-willed flunky who had a crush on Ashley; Shelby in the second van with Franklin, the most vicious of Brick's cohorts.

"The boss is seriously fucked," Franklin said to Shelby. "That bitch jabbed a needle in his jugular and shot him full of air. Could have killed him, just like that. Symbolism, they call it."

"Embolism," Shelby corrected him.

Franklin snapped his fingers with his right hand, steering recklessly on the snow-covered roads with his left. "Anyways, either way, could have killed him like that. Would have been kinder if she had killed him, I think. Instead, the boss had a profound stroke, whatever that means in the end. Pretty much, his left side is all fucked-up right now. They're not sure he'll regain any use of his arm or leg on that side. His face is all slack. Oh yeah, and he may lose his right eye."

"Christ," Shelby said. "What a mess. If she goes to the police, I swear—"

"They don't know who the hell she even is," Franklin said bitterly. "They have her down as a Jane Doe at the hospital. She bolted before the cops could come and talk to her. I did some poking around. Seems the medics think she's got amnesia or the like. Given what she did to the Boss, I'm thinking that's so much bullshit, probably, but if it isn't, no saying what comes next."

She rolled her eyes. Shelby said, "Okay. So the police haven't landed on us yet. That means Ashley is likely still off-footing. Still trying to figure out what to do. She'll hesitate calling the cops, I think. She's probably still trying to think through any ramifications that might have for Chase."

Shelby said, "Once we get to the airport, I want you to call our people in New York. Have 'em watch her office and watch her apartment. See if she has family there. And watch that literary agent of theirs. I'm banking on Ashley heading back to the city if she figures out we've moved from here. She'll regroup there in the city, I think. It's critical for all of us she be put down. Understood? Your sorry ass is on the line as much as mine now."

"Oh, I get that," Franklin said. "I want that bitch dead now as much as you do. I want to put that slut down not just for my own safety, but for what she did to the boss."

"That's the spirit," Shelby said. "You hold onto that conviction. Use your hate."

Chase and Shawn were in the back of the van. There was a partition between them and their driver.

"Trying to put aside whatever went down between you two, I'm not buying this thing about Ashley running," Shawn said. "She was pretty ill, you know. Probably needed medical attention."

"I know that," Chase snapped back. "It didn't help her condition, you filling her up with wine."

Shawn let that one pass. He really didn't want to know how Chase knew he had shared drinks with Ashley. Instead he countered with, "Ashley figured out where we were, did you know that, pal? She figured it out without breaking a sweat."

"So where are we?"

"Gatlinburg, Tennessee," Shawn said softly. "You know, the Smoky Mountains? We're driving down to Gatlinburg now. I checked some maps. It'll be a bit of a drive getting to the airport to be taken to this crazy little bitch's next hide-out."

"Ashley figured this out?"

"Yeah, she did. Bad thing is, Ash did it before I could warn her our computers had been tampered with. Loaded up with monitoring and spying software." Shawn paused, then said, "I think they knew Ashley learned where we've been the past few days."

Chase raised his eyebrows. Pure sarcasm, he said, "And what of it?"

"And I don't know what," Shawn said. "Not exactly. But we were warned about trying to figure out our location. And I can't help but notice you and Everett's daughter have been getting cozy, fast. So maybe Shelby Hyde just wanted a clear road, one less rival for your fickle affections."

"And what, she sent Ashley packing?" Chase shook his head. "First, it's not any of your fucking business, and second, that sounds crazy."

"Yeah? Well, where is Brick?"

Chase said disbelievingly, "Shelby said she suspected Ashley had this thing for Brick."

Shawn just shook his head. "I really do believe Shelby said that to you. I believe that because it's consistent with my theory that, for whatever reason, Shelby wanted you for herself.

But I don't buy the notion of Ashley running off with Brick. Jesus, she abhorred the son of a bitch. Surely you could see it, too."

Hadn't Chase said that very thing to Shelby? Still, he hated agreeing about anything with Shawn, presently.

Watching Chase, studying his face, Shawn said, "Knowing where we've been, thanks to Ashley, and having cleared off all that cyber spy stuff from my computer gives me certain advantages over our terrible hostess. That, and spending time with others than that conniving, slutty orphan in that crazy compound."

Chase said, "You trying to say something there, because I don't really sense a point."

"I'm getting to it. Had a few drinks with Brick while you were sparking the Hyde girl." Chase started to react to that, but Shawn pressed on. "Brick was all proud of this Mustang of his," he said. "Took me out to the garage to show it off to me. Stupid Ford looked like some teenager's wet dream—all wrong for a steroid jockey pushing AARP eligibility."

"Is this rant really headed somewhere?"

"Yeah, it is, pal," Shawn said. "I was surfing area news sites before we got hustled out. There was an accident up there by the Hyde place. A Ford Mustang went off the road and roared down the mountainside. The guy driving it was seriously injured. Report said a woman was taken to the hospital, too. She was transported a bit before the man. Some still-unidentified young woman. Cops were theorizing she was in that crashed Mustang, too."

Chase was belligerent. "So you're thinking Ashley did run off with that bastard?"

"I'm thinking she might have been in his car," Shawn said. "But I'm not saying she was there by choice. They took the woman off a chair-lift downtown. The ride's mountain terminus is close by the crash scene up this way."

"How badly was this woman hurt?"

Shawn had wondered how long it would take Chase to pose that question. "Reports were sketchy," Shawn said. "I just don't know." He'd toyed with trying to call the hospital, trying to get a phone connection with Ashley. Two things stopped him: he didn't trust the new disposable cell phones Shelby had provided them, for one thing. For another, Shawn also thought Shelby might be looking for Ashley now, and anything he might do to reveal her location or identity could give Shelby a critical leg-up.

Chase chewed his lip. "It may not even be them."

"It may not be. But it's a hell of a lot of coincidence if it isn't," Shawn said, raw-voiced.

"I'm going to confront Shelby about this," Chase said. "Put it to her cold and see what she says. It's not like it matters now about keeping her mountain retreat a secret, right?"

"I'm not sure confronting Shelby is the wisest way to go. Not for you and me, and particularly not for Ash."

"Well, it's my thought for the moment," Chase said, irked again to hear Shawn call her by a pet name. "I'll think more on it, since you say we have some time, probably, before we're sprung from this van, but it's the way I'm leaning. It's the way I'm leaning hard."

Several car lengths behind them, Shelby tore off her headphones and tipped her head back against the seat. She switched off the button on the receiver console that allowed her to eavesdrop on Shawn and Chase's conversation in the van ahead.

Goddamn them!

Well, at least she had some time to figure out parries to any of Chase's eventual questions about Ashley and the accident, or about Brick's whereabouts.

Shelby twisted in her seat. She expected some sting from the new tattoo above her backside, but it seemed to have finally subsided.

She, said, "Franklin, when we get to the airport, I've got a task for you. I'm going to call ahead and arrange a second flight. We're putting Shawn Dalton on a plane back home. I'm done with him now in terms of the contracts and all that stuff. All he is now is a drag and a danger. So you get Shawn in hand when we get to the airport. Don't hurt him, but get him on the other plane. I'm sending him back to New York City. Can you do that?"

Franklin nodded. "Natch."

Shelby wrinkled her nose. "Natch? What does that mean?"

"Short for 'naturally'. Means I get it."

"Then just say that next time. And keep both hands on the wheel."

"Just going to put him on a plane?"

"He's my attorney," Shelby said, "at least for now. So, yes, you're just going to put him on plane and send him packing."

46

For the moment, Ashley had some distance on the car she was certain was pursuing her.

It was hard to keep one another in line-of-sight in the dark and hairpin curves of the mountain road. If they reached a straight-away, Ashley thought she might be overtaken. Even if that didn't happen, once they reached the gridlock of downtown Gatlinburg's teeming main drag, it would be too easy for her pursuer to simply walk up to the side of her car, maybe smash a window, or just shoot her in the head and disappear into the bustling sidewalk crowds.

She was making a curving, dipping turn when she saw the private driveway curling back into the woods. The pavement was wet from the salting and shoveling so tire tracks abruptly veering from the main road wouldn't alert her followers.

Ashley turned off and palmed into the driveway some distance, switching off her lights and kept her foot off the brakes as she did that. Three seconds later, she saw the headlights of the other car sweep by the mouth of the driveway, showing no signs of braking.

She tapped her brakes and flipped back on her headlights. Grimacing at the discomfort it caused her surgery site, Ashley wrapped an arm around the seat and backed down the driveway and back onto the mountain road.

She shifted into drive and began to follow her follower.

Shelby chewed on a fingernail, nodding and gripping the cell phone to her ear. She cursed and folded closed her phone.

Franklin said, "What's happened?"

Shelby sneered at him. "You know your boy we left back at the house? He's an idiot, and too-slow-by-half."

Franklin split his attention between Shelby and the road. "Why do you say that? What's happened?"

"Ashley actually pulled up in the driveway about twenty minutes ago," Shelby said. "She evidently took down my address. Your boy Luke was slow responding, or he could have grabbed her on my driveway apron. He could have ended this, fast. Killed the stupid whore. Instead he tried to follow her. Dumb-ass lost her somewhere along the road down to tourist town."

"How the hell did he do that? It's a two-lane with no forks."

"Exactly," Shelby said. "He's an asshole. You tell me how he fouled it up. I'd really love to know." This look. "This goes badly, it's on you in the worst way."

The heater in her hotel was on the fritz and only seemed to run at high.

Ashley stripped down to her underwear and folded one leg under herself. It wasn't yet ten p.m. She opened up her laptop, booted it up, then looked up Selma's cell phone number. She sat the phone on the bed and punched in the numbers.

The über literary agent said, "Ashley? Honey? I was start-ing to get worried that I haven't heard from you or Chase in, like, *forever*. How are things going with the Hyde daughter? How are things simply going?"

The manic edge in her own voice made Ashley wince. But she couldn't help it. She blurted out, "It's a mess. I... I know this is going to sound absolutely insane, but it's all true, I swear to you, Selma."

47

Shawn slid out of the back of the van and stamped his feet in the snow, rubbing his arms. He said, "So where are you spiriting us off to now?"

Shelby's gaze drifted to Franklin, who shouldered up next to Shawn. She said, "Actually, I'm afraid this is where we part ways, Shawn. I thank you for putting up with all these crazy precautions regarding my privacy. Thank you for taking the time to come here and help me finalize contracts with Chase. But that's all done now. So Chase and I are going to go ahead and knuckle down to work on our book. I've got you confirmed on a private flight back to New York. Infinite booze and a four-star meal as you take the ride."

She leaned in then and hugged Shawn—no particular warmth or sincerity in that gesture, Chase thought—then she kissed the lawyer's cheek.

Shawn frowned, one hand still holding on to Shelby's arm. "What the hell is this? You're sending me packing? Really?"

"Like I said, your work's done. The legal work. Contracts are all signed." Shelby smiled and patted Shawn's cheek. "You really were very sweet to put up with all this. I'm very grateful for all you've done for my family and, particularly, for me. I'm sure we'll meet again."

Shawn said, "Chase hasn't interviewed me yet. Hasn't asked me about my memories of your father. About our conversations years ago. And those manuscripts—I need to look at them. My obligation to your father requires me to vet any—"

"There'll be plenty of time for that later," Shelby said. "When Chase gets back to New York City himself, I mean." A chilly peck on the cheek. "You have a safe flight now."

Shelby showed Shawn her back. She called out, not even turning to look back at him, "I'll call you in a couple of weeks…" To fire your ass, was implied.

Franklin took Shawn by the arm, urging him toward the terminal. "About twenty minutes before we're cleared for take-off, brother. Your luggage is being moved right now. Let's get you somewhere warm and set up for your next flight. But we need to hustle, 'cause I'm with them." He jacked a thumb back in the direction of Shelby and Chase.

Shawn half-turned; Chase was looking back, too. Shawn shot Chase a confused look. Chase simply shrugged and continued following Shelby toward a Jet Stream, a slightly smaller craft than the one that had carried Ashley, Shawn and Chase to Tennessee from New York City.

Chase said to her, "So where are we going now? Home to Kentucky?"

"No," Shelby said, "not there. That hasn't been home for a long, long time."

48

S elma said, "I can wire you some money to rush you back here. We need to get together, ASAP, Ashley. We really need to strategize and fast."

"To strategize about Chase, yes."

"Uh, sure. And also about what's happened to you." Selma, hesitated, then said, "And if something should happen to Chase, we need to think about all that, too…"

Ashley almost lashed out at that, not liking where she anticipated Selma was next headed. Selma already sounded prepared to write Chase off. Despite everything, Ashley wasn't yet prepared to leave Chase twisting. She said, "I'm not sure I shouldn't call the police."

Selma didn't miss a beat: "You shouldn't. And you were so wise not to after that terrible ordeal—you were so wise to call me first."

"You really think so? Because more and more, I think I should call the cops, Selma."

"Absolutely not," the Hyena said. "Think about it. We don't know who Chase really is, do we? Let's just say there's the possibility he is Everett Hyde." Ashley could tell from the tone of the Hyena's voice that Selma was clearly hoping that was so. Selma said, "If that's where we are now, well, think about the legal ramifications for Chase. Everett. *Whoever*… Shit, you know what I mean."

"No, I'm not sure I do," Ashley said.

Selma sighed. "Look, if he is Everett Hyde, then Chase defrauded his insurance company. Florida taxpayers' money and police resources were wasted investigating a death that never happened. I think Chase could be criminally charged over all that. Certainly sued. Hell, you can sue anyone for anything these days. Maybe even win."

"Hadn't thought of that," Ashley said. If by some outside chance Chase was Everett Hyde, all Selma said about the legal ramifications for his long-ago actions was too true.

Selma sighed. "How could you think about that, with all the crazy things happening to you? That's why I'm so impressed you've kept it together as well as you have. Why it was such a smart thing to call me first. So shrewd of you, dearie. The important thing right now is to get you safely back here to civilization. We need to get you back to me."

"I'm going to drive to New York," Ashley said. "With all this surveillance this Hyde woman has at her disposal, I'm not sure I could buy an airline ticket without her somehow finding out. So I'm going to drive home. I'm going to leave very early tomorrow morning. I want to try and see my doctor before we meet. Need to make sure I'm not risking infection or something worse." She paused, took a breath and rubbed her side. "And, God, could I use some pain pills about now…"

Selma said, "My own doctor is not particularly, well, let's call it, fusty. I'm pretty sure I can get you some Vikes. Some Percocet, too. Whatever you prefer. Something even to stave off infection. Where exactly are you, sweetie? I'll have prescriptions phoned in for you on the jif'."

"Huh-uh," Ashley said. "I don't want to be that specific. Like I said, there seems to be so much surveillance and electronic spying employed by Hyde's crazy orphan, I don't rule out the possibility even your phone's compromised. You should be very careful on your phones at home and at work, just in case."

"Can you actually tap a cell phone?"

"I really don't know, so I'm erring on the side of caution."

"I might know someone who does know things like that," Selma said. "I'm going to call him now. I may also bring him along to meet with you. To make sure I'm not followed getting there. You're right, Ashley, we have to be very careful going forward."

Ashley ran her fingers through her hair, getting it out of her face. She suddenly felt very tired. "If he could call the prescription in to the Pigeon Forge CVS, that'd be a godsend." Ashley had passed the pharmacy driving to her hotel. It was less than two blocks away.

"Is that a good idea telling me that? You said my phone might be tapped."

"I'll figure out a safe way to get the meds, don't worry. If I leave early tomorrow, I should be back in the city before nightfall. If the doctor doesn't take too long with me, I can probably meet you around eight tomorrow night. I'll get a message to your agency's office with a place we can meet."

"Great! But be careful, Ashley. I'll be worried sick about you until you're safe with me." It almost sounded true.

"You be careful, too," Ashley said.

She hung up the phone and fanned her face with her hand. The hotel room was stifling now. Ashley stripped naked, and, despite her exhaustion, Googled the county auditor's website. She keyed in the address for Shelby Hyde's mountaintop compound and punched in the command for a property and parcel ownership search.

Cute: the holder of the title on Shelby's land was some outfit dubbed "Dashiell Hunt, LTD"—a name lifted from the protagonist of Everett Hyde's first novel.

She checked her email to see if there was any response from Chase or from Shawn. Perhaps even from Shelby herself, though what she could possibly have to say Ashley couldn't imagine.

There was nothing but an accidentally ironic piece of spam for painkillers and an email from her mom. Ashley wrote a brief note back to her mother, promising she'd be home in a night or maybe two. She logged off and collapsed back onto the bed, sprawled naked atop the sheets, covered in a thin sheen of sweat.

Despite the nagging ache in her belly, Ashley was asleep in less than two minutes.

49

Their private jet coasted to a soft stop. Chase said, "So where are the funny black-out sunglasses? The blind-folds?"

Shelby reached across and took Chase's hand, smiled. "I wholeheartedly trust you now." Chase squeezed her hand back, then let go and unfastened his seatbelt. He shrugged on his winter coat. "No, you won't need that," Shelby said. The jet's door opened with a hiss of escaping, pressurized air; the door dropped down onto the tarmac in stairs position. A hot wind blew into the cabin.

Stooping for the low ceiling, Chase draped his winter coat over his arm and stepped down onto the pavement into the blast furnace wind. He held his left hand out to steady Shelby as she descended the stairs. Chase could see the silhouettes of palm trees in the distance. Their fronds brushed together in the lazy wind. He said, "If you tell me we're anywhere but in Florida, I'm going to question this trust of yours."

"We are in Florida, darling, yes." Shelby smiled and stroked his cheek with the back of her hand. "Western coast."

"So you have another compound here?"

"Sure. But compound is more than pushing it. That's a terrible term for a second home." She smiled. "It's just a small house. Cozy. Very, you know, intimate."

Chase nodded, then decided to fire his last bolt. "Listen, I've been meaning to ask. I heard word there was a car crash back in Tennessee. Some vintage Mustang like the one Brick was always bragging about. Seems there was a woman who maybe was in the car—"

"Huh-uh," Shelby said curtly. "Wasn't him. Not them." Shelby batted it away with a hand as if it was an irksome fly. "Whatever. It just wasn't them, I swear."

She smiled up at him, leaning in impulsively for a kiss. "Aren't I just going to eat you alive when we get home?"

50

She lay on her back, watching the orange glow around the curtains deepen as the sun rose. The pain at her surgical site had eased, but was still a worry.

Ashley struggled up onto her elbows and checked the alarm clock. It was five in the morning. She must have gotten cold at some point in the night despite the hyperactive heater, because the sheets and comforter now covered her to just under the chin.

Wincing at the discomfort it caused in her side, she pushed down the covers and reached to the nightstand. She scooped up the television remote and flipped on the local news, watching until she got a weather report. It seemed she could expect flurries all the way back east. Christ, it figured, didn't it? She couldn't catch a break.

Ashley kicked off the covers, stood and swayed a moment, feeling dizzy. There was a plastic liner in the ice bucket. Ashley thought she might pluck it out, press it over her bandages with her left hand and somehow keep them dry while she showered.

But she decided it wasn't worth heightening her risk of infection.

She printed out a message she'd send via the hotel fax machine to Selma's agency suggesting they meet at Havana Central, just off Times Square.

Then she dressed, tying her hair in a ponytail and hiding it under her souvenir Smoky Mountain ski cap. She slipped on a pair of sunglasses.

Ashley drove past the pharmacy and pulled into an adjacent parking lot. She sat parked there, idling, watching the pharmacy for a few minutes to see if she could spot any spies. There were no cars in the parking lot except for the ones out back, where the employees would be required to park.

She made sure her car doors were locked, then drove up to the 24-hour drive-thru window and picked up her prescription.

Ashley scooped her change from the bag and tossed it into the caddy between the seats. She split her attention between the road and the rearview mirror, looking for tails.

Hers was the only car on the road at this early hour.

Confident she wasn't being followed, Ashley steered into a Starbucks on the edge of town and ordered a large black coffee and a cinnamon scone.

Eating her scone, she checked her notes taken down longhand from Google maps. She washed the first pain pill down with coffee. She got back out on the road and dropped the hammer.

Many hours later, in Lexington, Kentucky, Ashley stopped for more gas and bought a fish sandwich and Diet Coke at a McDonald's. She ate her disappointing sandwich while grabbing glances at horse farms lining either side of the interstate.

It was dark for several hours before Ashley reached New York City. She didn't trust that her own place wasn't being watched; maybe her folks' place back home, too.

But Chase was presumably still with Shelby. *Bastard.*

Ashley decided to hazard it and settle into Chase's apartment, at least for the night. It didn't seem to Ashley the Hyde orphan would squander resources staking-out Chase's place when he was right there with her. Wherever there was. So long as she avoided using Chase's landline, Ashley figured she'd be okay.

More practically, she already had some stuff in Chase's apartment, including clothes and a toothbrush, shampoo and other things she might need soon.

And her cell phone was still there, too, gathering dust on Chase's writing desk.

She dropped off her rental car and took a cab into the city. On the way, she called her doctor. He assured Ashley the next morning would be plenty soon to check her surgical site and that she shouldn't worry about showering, though a bath was a different matter for the moment.

The taxi rolled up in front of Chase's apartment building.

Before she got out, Ashley took a long hard look around. She saw nothing or nobody suspicious. She paid her driver and then continued watching the street as he unloaded her bags from the trunk.

Safely inside Chase's place, Ashley cranked up the heat and turned on some lights. She began charging her cell phone. Then she stripped and took a long, hot restorative shower, washing away the scent of the hospital and medicine and old sweat. The piping hot water soothed the stiffness in her shoulders and back from the long drive and drew some of the dull ache from her bruises.

Ashley looked around the place, her chin trembling. The last time she'd been here Chase was still Chase, they each had their new book contracts, and Ashley was innocently imagining a life together as a writing couple in her dream city.

Now?

She turned on Chase's sound system and found a Lana Del Rey CD she'd given Chase for Christmas. It was still in its shrink-wrap. That told its own story, didn't it?

Rueful, she unwrapped the CD and cued up the singer-songwriter's "Ride."

She sat on the couch, head in hands and tried to steel herself for what was left of the night ahead.

51

Chase traced his fingers across the table top, leaving shiny twin trails. "Pretty dusty," he said, staring at his fingertips.

"Didn't exactly plan for us to be here tonight," Shelby said. "Didn't have time to call ahead for a cleaning crew to spruce it up. Still, it's not so bad, is it?" She sat down on a couch, looking around.

"Not at all," Chase said. "I didn't mean it as criticism. Honestly."

It was funny: Shelby's Florida retreat reminded Chase a bit of the hypothetical Florida hideaway Ashley had fantasized for herself a few days before, a rambling Spanish-style mélange of stucco and terracotta roof tiles, shaded by tall old palm trees and hidden at the back of an overgrown, twisting private drive, easily missed because of the tropical underbrush nearly obscuring the driveway apron.

The interior of Shelby's Florida hideaway looked like it was inspired by an old episode of *Miami Vice*: leaning hard on Art Deco and pastel color schemes.

"Either way, we'll go out to dinner tonight, somewhere along the beach," Shelby said. "While we're out, I'll have the place dusted and swept."

Chase nodded. "Sounds very nice, eating out, I mean. We going to dinner right now?"

This carnal smile. Shelby said, "Not *right* now." She held out a hand to him. He could hear the ocean behind the house.

Chase took her hand, thinking she wanted him to help her up. Instead, she pulled him down.

Chase was lapping gently; she was bare there, just like Ashley.

He sensed the tempo of her counterthrusts mounting.

Shelby's fingers tangled in his hair and her back arched. Her head thrashed side to side and her thighs trembled against his cheeks. Panting, she said, "Come up here, you." He did that. Smiling, all bedroom eyes, Shelby dragged a trembling hand across Chase's mouth.

Her hand drifted to the back of his neck and urged his mouth to hers. With her other hand, she guided him inside.

Chase felt the tip of her tongue pressing against his teeth and he obediently opened his mouth wider.

Moving with her, between kisses, he said, "Maybe this is a mistake."

Shelby, all breathy, her lips still brushing his said, "Really want to stop?" Her eyes searched his, urgently: "Really want to do that? *Really?*"

"No."

She screamed as they climaxed together.

The second time, he was on his knees, behind her, and slipped out. "Damn," he said, taking himself in his hand and trying to reposition himself. As he did that, Chase stared at the small of her back. There was a tattoo there, rather reminiscent of Ashley's. But Shelby's tattoo read "*Festina lente*."

He said, "What does it mean?" He was fumbling to get back inside her.

Distracted, frustrated because she was on the verge of another orgasm when he had slipped from her body, Shelby said, "What? What does what mean?"

"Your tattoo. What does it mean?"

"Make haste slowly."

"Huh?"

"Forget it." Shelby reached between her legs and helped to guide him again; she groaned as their bodies were once more joined.

Shelby again screamed when she came, came alone this time. Chase seemed to be having trouble climaxing again. Shelby figured maybe it was because of all the wine.

He slipped out again, and again fumbled to reposition himself, even as Shelby lay there, bathed in sweat and trembling from her orgasm, chin and cheek pressed to the carpet.

She said thickly, "No, that's not quite the right place." Guys always seemed to try for that, eventually. She remembered then what she could hear of Ashley and Chase together when she was spying on them. Shelby remembered Ashley balking when Chase attempted to take her the same way. *Well...*

This husky edge in Shelby's voice: "But, you *can* do that to me that way. I mean, if you want to."

Chase did, so he *did.* When he finally came, sprawling half across her, his cheek pressed between her shoulder blades and his pubic hair ticking her ass, he snarled. "You may be the death of me." As he said it, his lips brushed her slick back.

Shelby said, "I never imagined I could come that way. But I did. We're just too good together."

She twisted her head just enough that Chase, still laying half atop her backside, his elbow carrying his weight, could see the side of her face.

His eyes searched the single one of her hazel eyes that he could see.

This wicked smile on her face.

Shelby said, "Who's my daddy?"

52

Ashley asked to be seated in a segregated dining area with a drape that could be pulled shut for privacy.

She sweet-talked the host, a handsome enough, twenty-something Cuban dude, into closing that drape. As he did that, she took up a seat next to a framed print of Yousuf Karsh's famous portrait of Ernest Hemingway. Papa looked bulletproof in a massive, leather-fortified, cable-knit, turtle-neck sweater.

Ashley was staring up at the long-gone author when her waitress, a pretty Latina, asked if she'd like a drink while she awaited the rest of her party. Thinking of Papa, Ashley ordered a mojito. It came with a green swizzle stick shaped like a lissome Cuban looker with a high-riding breasts and unending legs. The plastic woman was wearing some form-fitting dress with a high hemline that appeared to be whipped by a tropical breeze.

The drink was delicious. Sipping, Ashley browsed the menu and settled on a Cuban sandwich with sweet potato fries.

"Ashley?"

She looked up from her menu.

The woman standing there between the parted curtains had long, manicured nails. Something about those nails made them the first thing you noticed. They looked like they could do real damage. The woman was somewhere between forty and forty-five, Ashley guessed. The woman was also Botoxed to the outer-edges of utter immobility.

Her hair was blue-black and looked lacquered enough to weather a tsunami. The woman's skin was olive and her eyes charcoal black. She was expensively tailored. There was no doubt in Ashley's mind the woman could be anyone other than the Hyena.

Selma Lindscott said, *"Oh... my... Gawd!* I *so* screwed up! Fuck me harder! I *so* should have gotten a photo of you before I started shopping our book, Ash. I'm going to kick Chase's ass—well, whoever he is—for not telling me what a hottie I have in you. Oh, my God, Ashley, even after all you've been through, don't you look good enough to lick top to bottom and eat alive? Oh, shit, I think I've cost us at least ten thousand dollars on your advance!"

Ashley stood up uncertainly, putting out a hand. "Selma?"

"Who else?"

The über agent ignored Ashley's offered hand and instead embraced her, briskly rubbing Ashley's back. Selma's perfume overwhelmed Ashley's senses. "You poor kid," Selma said. "How's the appendix?"

"Trashed. I mean, gone. Which is also to say, okay, so far." Ashley hesitated, lightly patting the Hyena's back, then said, "You're sure you weren't followed?"

"No danger of that," Selma said, somehow winking with that alabaster face of hers and pulling out a chair. She shrugged off her coat, folded it and draped it across the back of her chair. Selma sat down, crossed one olive leg over the other, and snatched up Ashley's menu. She turned straight to the beverage page.

Selma parted the curtains with one hand and called out, "A pitcher of Rose Sangria."

She closed the curtain and reached across the table and squeezed Ashley's hand. "Like I said, no danger of anyone following. Another of my clients, you can call him Ace because he likes that, and I mean, *a lot*—saw to all that. He's ex-CIA, ex-Special Forces. Ex-cop. He writes that series of men's adventure novels. You know the books I mean? *The Iron Seal* series?"

"Oh. Sure." Ashley had never heard of the books.

"Slam-dunk bestsellers, every one," Selma said. "Frankly, I have to get plastered to plow through one of those manuscripts of his. Mostly just to edit for grammar and spelling, which is appalling in his first drafts. So far as plot and so forth, I don't get it, not at all. But I poached him from a rival. I did that because he's a monster bestseller for the guys, and if it ain't broke, don't fix it, right?"

"Makes perfect sense." Ashley sipped her mojito. "So where is Ace?"

"Parking the car. He had some elaborate routines we went through to make sure we weren't tailed. He thinks we were followed from my place, but he swears we lost them. Still, he's parking about seven blocks from here and going through some multi-car, taxi dodge. He positively lives for this cloak-and-dagger stuff. Aren't we just lucky to death to have him?"

"Uh, sure. How'd you get here?"

"Ace dropped me off in the pass-through of the Crowne Plaza on Times Square. I ran into the lobby—not easy to do in these do-me shoes!—out the front door on the other side, and grabbed another cab we'd called ahead to reserve. No way anyone could follow us like that."

"Clever."

Selma held up a hand. "Down to cases. Do you think Chase is really Everett Hyde?"

"I have no idea." Ashley wiped some beads of condensation from her cocktail glass with her thumb's tip. "Chase swore it couldn't be so. He said the timetables don't work. Seems there was a time, when Chase fleetingly thought himself that he might be Everett Hyde. By the time I confronted him about that, he'd changed his mind. Chase was adamant it couldn't be that way."

"Well, he's not the most reliable source for anything, now, is he?"

Ashley almost snapped back at Selma for that, but got herself under control. "Pretty hard to argue with that," she said.

"So, your gut instinct is that he isn't Everett Hyde?"

Ashley sensed Selma would have arched her eyebrows for emphasis, if only she could move any part of her face.

Realizing she was in danger of staring, Ashley shifted her attention from her agent's rather unsettlingly still features to her own drink. "Honestly, I haven't decided," Ashley said, staring in her glass. "I think it's still a slight possibility."

"*Oh...*" There was definite excitement in Selma's voice; animation in that part of her, at least. The waitress brought Selma her pitcher of sangria. "You want?" Selma held the pitcher aloft with both hands.

Ashley smiled and shook her head. She said to the waitress, "*Uno mojito, por favor.*"

Selma said, "You speak *Cuban*! Isn't that just so darling?" She poured herself a glass from the pitcher. "When in Rome, I guess. Tell me about Shelby Hyde."

"Apart from the fact that she tried to have me shot, I know nothing more about her now than I did before we left," Ashley said. "I never met her. I was too sick, like someone was trying to bore into my belly with a baseball bat."

"Sounds like my over-endowed date last night," Selma said, then shifted gears when she saw Ashley was in no mood for humor, black or otherwise. Selma squeezed Ashley's hand again. "So you think they are still in Tennessee?"

"I think they bolted from that compound. Whether they're still in the state of Tennessee or not is another question. I'm betting they've moved on from there."

"We should wait to talk about that aspect of things until Ace arrives," Selma said. "Meantime, let's discuss some practical business strategy. Your novel is all but locked down now. Your editor told me she isn't going to be burying you in notes, just some minor line edits. Mechanical tweaks. Isn't that great? And it also means you've got a lot of time open well ahead of you. So for book two, or maybe even one, I'm thinking memoir."

Oh, no. Ashley said softly, "A memoir about what, exactly?"

"About all this, of course. All that's happened to you these past few days." Selma held up a hand as she saw Ashley was about to raise hers. "*No.* Don't dismiss this, honey," the Hyena said. "Look, this whole thing may be very costly. Extricating Chase from this vile woman's clutches, I mean. And we're on our own nickel, at the moment. So I say, let's get one of the major houses to help underwrite our rescue efforts. We'll work some expense codicils into the book contract, up front."

"I'll think about it," Ashley lied.

The curtain abruptly parted again.

Ashley flinched on first site of the imposing man standing there.

She was staring at Brick's lost twin. The man was probably older than Brick, but somehow he was even more formidable-looking to Ashley. The stranger was at least six-four, maybe six-five. His head was shaven, but he had a black moustache and goatee… And these unblinking brown eyes. He wore tight jeans and a leather jacket, cropped at the waist. His black T-shirt was stretched tight across his barrel chest. He said, "Howdy, ladies."

Selma said, "Ashley McKnight, meet Robert Sterling. Call him Ace."

"Call me Ace," the man repeated, sticking out a hairy hand you could hide a softball inside. The man's hand engulfed Ashley's.

The big man let go, grabbed a chair by its back and swung it around. He straddled the creaking chair and crossed his big arms across its back.

The waitress said, "Drink for you, sir?"

Ace eyed Ashley's mojito and then Selma's sangria. The Hyena circled protective arms around the pitcher. He frowned and said, "Double espresso for me, Senorita." The man's voice sounded like it was coming from the depths of some deep cave. He smiled at Ashley and Selma. "Guess it's caffeine from here to the end. Got to stay sharp, huh?"

"Very," the Hyena said. "Ash has been telling me horror stories about this woman and her army. This orphan, she's surrounded by mercenaries, I think. Ashley, and another man there, this attorney named Shawn who confided some things to Ashley, well, they both had the sense this guy Brick, at least, was a soldier of fortune. But not in your league, hombre." Selma smiled and squeezed the man's arm. "No match for you, I'm sure."

To Ashley, Selma said, "Ace writes the *Iron Seal* adventure series. Also a physical fitness book and companion DVD, and a guide on firearms for crime and mystery writers."

"That last is called *Don't Shoot Yourself in the Foot,*" Ace said. "You know—'cause of the way these pantywaist writers always screw up when it comes to writing guns? Friggin' dilettantes putting suppressors on revolvers and the like. Netted myself a Fairy Award nomination for that book."

"Barry Award," Selma corrected him.

"That, yeah." Ace drained his espresso at a pull, holding onto the waitress' arm with his other massive hand. Smacking his lips, he said, "How about you bring me two more just like that one, honey?"

The waitress nodded and slipped back through the curtains. Ace winked at Selma and Ashley. "Save the skirt a trip, you know?"

"That's so thoughtful," Ashley said.

"That's me out of the gates," Ace said. "I'm old school." He gave Ashley another long, hard look. "Toots, I'm thinking I want you to have my babies."

The Hyena pressed a manicured finger to her strangely still lips as Ashley began to balk.

Ace said, "Here's what I mean, Ash baby. I made some calls to that hospital you escaped from. Holy God, what you did to that mercenary asshole, Brick! Gave me real wood, just hearing it described. Here's the damage report: son of a bitch's eye is gone. He's got massive brain damage and has lost all motion on one hemisphere: a dead arm and leg on one side. He's Quitsville, for keeps. You flat *trashed* his ass."

Selma, mid-sip, nearly sprayed Sangria on her raw silk wrap. "Dear Lord, Ashley! You're like, *who*? Gina Carano? Some action babe. I'm *so* looking forward to your book about all this."

Ashley shot Selma a cross look. "I haven't agreed to—"

"How in God's name did you do all this to that asshole?" Selma refilled from her pitcher.

Ace said, "She hit him with a metal tray, it seems. As to the brain damage, clever minx here grabbed a hypodermic needle and shot the cocksucker up with a jugular full of air. Fucking inspired under the gun. Ash gave the son of a bitch a massive embolism."

Ashley winced. My God, she had all but killed the man. She felt sick inside.

The Hyena seemed impressed enough. "You're joking!"

Ace drained another espresso. "Fact is, the sorry son of a bitch is facing a future of adult diapers and drool cups. A real man facing that would eat his gun." He turned down his mouth. "But this cat is being moved to a nursing home, they say. Christ, how sorry an end is that?"

"Bet he'd shoot himself if he could use a gun anymore," Selma said. "Sounds like he can't." Selma reached across and stroked Ashley's cheek. "Aren't you the marvel?"

Ace nodded. "Well, like I said, doing all that damage to a man like that one—and I've researched him a bit by the way, and the fella was far from inept—well, that's why I want Ashley here to be the mother of my children. Brick's just so much head cheese, now." Ace smiled at Ashley. "He's just seriously, irreparably fucked."

Selma said, "Ashley, I see it like this. We'll have Chase's book, if it can still happen. We'll have your memoir. Then Ace will have his own account of his phase of the operation: logistics and all the macho stuff. You know, all the tough-guy stuff that makes the guys get wood reading Ace's novels. Between the three books, we'll have our own franchise, and if we get you all on the talk show circuit as a threesome, well, this will be major stuff like the book world hasn't seen in, oh, *forever*."

Ace grinned, raising his third double espresso. "A-fucking-men to that sweet vision!"

Ashley plucked the green swizzle stick from her drink, her fingers tracing its edge, trailing up the Cuban cutie's long legs, over the swell of her belly and defining her full, up-thrusting breasts. "This notion of me writing such a book—"

Selma shook her head firmly. "Ash, sweetie, we simply can't afford what Ace calls an *aggressive extrication* out of pocket. We need financial support for this, and I've already made some calls and know I can get it for your book, in particular. As a matter of fact, we're going to auction tomorrow afternoon."

The bald man winked again.

Ashley sighed. She took a deep drink of her mojito, realized she'd drained it. Ace leaned back through the curtain and called, "Two more espressos and another of these mint-leaf drinks my honey here is drinking."

Ashley dug her knuckles into her eyes and then drummed fingernails on the tabletop. She said to Selma, "So what's the plan, assuming I agree to this scheme of yours?"

Selma looked to Ace. He leaned in close, said to Ashley, "Any idea, any at all, about where Shelby might have taken this Chase cocksucker after you escaped?"

"No," Ashley said. "But I figured out where we were. It's a place allegedly owned under some DBA called 'Dashiell Hunt, LTD.' That's clearly a front—Dashiell Hunt was the narrator of Everett Hyde's first novel."

Ace slammed a fist down on the table, making their cocktail glasses jump. "Well, now, there you go! Fucking perfect! Start of business day tomorrow, we run a national title search on Dashiell Hunt, LTD. Then we'll have 'em! I'll bet real money on that."

Ace presumed to pick up Selma's glass then, it was half full and Ace drank all that was left. "I'm already fucking loving the way this is going," he said, smacking his lips. "Prospects for the fun ahead makes me harder than Chinese algebra."

53

The restaurant didn't look like much from the front. Once inside, or rather, once out back on the open-air patio, the view of ocean across the narrow beach was sublime. The full moon silvered the water and the lights from distant cruise ships were just visible here and there.

The food, too, was nothing particularly fancy, but wonderfully prepared. They were sharing a plate of fried plantains and some bits of batter-dipped alligator meat. They had a sweating pitcher of margaritas. Shelby wore another little black dress that showed a lot more skin than the first one he'd seen her in. The dangling hurricane lights swayed by the sultry breeze cast an eerie blue glow in her hair.

"I hurt, wonderfully and *everywhere*," Shelby said, smiling wickedly. "You're a marvel, such staying power."

"More like such drunkenness," he said. "I need to throttle back after tonight on the liquor. I mean, unless you want your father's biography to read like something composed by Charles Bukowski on an epic bender."

"No, we can't have that," Shelby said. "I want us to have a classic book, your very best." Her eyes drifted from Chase to the ocean. The sound of a boat horn found its way across all that water, back to where they were sitting. It was getting late, and there were only two or three other couples still eating. The bar on the other hand was still doing brisk business as sun-burned men and women looked for hook-ups before last call; nearly all of them appeared to be horny and sloshed tourists.

But hell, who was he to judge? Chase figured that, sans sunburns, he and Shelby probably looked about the same to the hired help—Shelby's bare shoulders and long, shapely legs looked winter-pale alongside those of the bronzed, dishy waitresses.

They both looked like out-of-towners. *Still.* Shelby was very attractive. There was a real resemblance to Ashley—no denying that.

But Shelby exuded sex with her wild eyes and a worldly air. And in bed? Well, she seemed game for anything. He could easily see himself losing a month to just loving this woman, raw and wrong.

Shelby freshened their drinks. He said, "Work is going to be harder if we continue along with this other."

She made him say it. "What other?"

"Us. As lovers."

"You regret us, already?" Shelby frowned, looked very sad.

"No, but... Well, I don't work like this. Or I never have."

Now she smiled and sat back in her chair. Shelby reached across the table with a long, bare arm and squeezed his hand, rubbing its back with her thumb. "What, you didn't bed Ambrose Bierce's great, great, great-niece? Didn't find some lost love child of Adam Garrett's to fuck breathless while penning your book on the missing poet? Couldn't find some lusty, long-lived sleeping bag partner of Everett Ruess' to bunk down with after a honest day's writing?"

Chase just shook his head.

"I'm sorry, Chase. I didn't mean to make light of it. I know you're a professional. This with us is new. Let's enjoy it to the max for a few days. Besides, you've got a lot of reading—all those manuscripts—to get through before you can really start the writing, right?"

He sipped his margarita with his free hand. "Yes, you're right."

"But no reading tonight."

He smiled. "No. Not tonight."

54

B efore she left Havana Central—left the Hyena there with a fresh pitcher of sangria and Ace with another double espresso—the mercenary turned author had scooted his chair around closer to Ashley's. Under the cover of the table, he had pressed something metal, cold and heavy, into Ashley's uncertain hands.

Startled, Ashley had looked under the table, her eyes widening. The gun was sleek and big and looked very deadly to her inexpert eye.

"Just keep your hands under the table," Ace had told her. "This switch right here? That's the safety. Flip it into this position, like this—" he guided her thumb, "—and you're ready to misbehave. We get some time in the days ahead, I'll get you to a range, show you properly how to use this baby."

Ashley said, "You're kidding, right? You want me to carry a gun?"

"That bitch tried to kill you," Selma said. "Didn't she do that? And you were lucky to get away from that monster Shelby sent after you in the hospital. Precautions are in order, Ashley."

"Ms. S is right," Ace said. "So, flick this switch, then you point it, like a finger, middle of the body of the man you want to put down. Just shoot for the biggest part of the son of a bitch. This is a real man-stopper. Two, three slugs to the torso, damned near anywhere, will drop anything short of a rhino. Baby makes little holes going in, but fucking big holes tearing through and out. Shoot 'em in your apartment, or indoors, wherever you're staying, and it'll likely be written off as an invasion situation. In that case, it'll ultimately be okay in terms of self-defense. It's called the Castle Doctrine or such like. If you have to do the bloody deed anywhere else, you call me first, if it's feasible. We'll square it somehow."

He passed Ashley a business card, one of those thick-stock cards embossed with a photo. This picture was of Ace, naked to the waist—all glistening muscle—and gripping two big automatics in either hand. The card also included Ace's email address and cell phone number—both easy to miss relative to the much larger, blood-red scream type trumpeting "The Iron Seal!"

Ashley slipped the card in her pocket. As she did that, Ace flipped the safety back on and said, "Put it in your coat pocket now, honey, before the waitress or some bleeding heart, pansy ass wanders in." Ashley did that, shooting Ace a look as his hand settled on her knee. His hand was trembling a bit, probably from all that caffeine. That, or advanced Parkinson's.

Ace had squeezed her thigh once with his big, warm hand, smiled, and then released her leg.

Ashley was walking fast, her head down and shoulders hunched, blinking back the cold drizzle. Her left fist was clinched and thrust deep in her coat pocket. She kept forgetting about the big gun crowding her right-hand coat pocket, repeatedly trying to fit her hand inside and then remembering again. Eventually, she slipped both hands into the pockets of her low-rise jeans, cursing their tightness—trendy, ass-showcasing pants just weren't made to accommodate hands in pockets.

Her cell phone rang. Ashley struggled to free her hand from her pants, frowning at the deep impression the edge of the pocket left in the back of her hand. She could actually see her pant's stitching in the imprint left in her flesh. She turned her hand over and checked the caller I.D. on her cell. "Caller unknown."

She tapped her screen to answer, said, "Hello?"

The connection was immediately broken on the other end.

55

He hung up the restaurant's pay phone as soon as he saw the shapely shadow on the floor.

Shelby arched an eyebrow. "Who are you calling?"

"My agent," Chase said. "But no answer. Probably at some literary gig." Chase racked the receiver and took her arm. "It's New York City, so there's always some literary event. For Selma, life is one unending launch party, I think."

"I settled the bill," Shelby said. "Ready to go home?"

Chase smiled and took Shelby's arm. "All ready."

"I'm pretty buzzed," Shelby said, locking her arm around his and leaning hard on him. "So you'd better drive." She passed him the keys to the rental car.

They left the air-conditioned restaurant and emerged into the sultry, now nearly empty parking lot. The waves crashed on the beach behind the restaurant. "We should eat here again tomorrow night," he said. "I really love this place." He opened her door, held her hand as she swung her long bare legs in, and then closed the door behind her.

He slid in behind the wheel, got her started, and then reached to turn the air conditioner on. Shelby pulled his hand away from the console. "Let's roll down the windows," she said. "I want to smell the ocean."

They did that, the wind knocking around their hair. "You're right," she said, pulling a lever to change the angle of her seat and then tipping her head back against the headrest.

"What am I right about?"

"About it being time to ease off the liquor. I'm a little drunk. Again. Just this side of unpleasantly drunk. Room-spinning drunk."

"We could stop for coffee."

"Starbucks hasn't found these parts yet," Shelby said. "I'll make some coffee back home. I'm a pretty good cook, too. Had to be, given the out-of-the-way places we lived."

"It must have been hard," he said.

Shelby cast him this sidelong glance. The wind whipped her hair in her face. She pushed it away with a clumsy hand. "What do you mean?"

"Growing up with all this, the precaution. All the solitude. The intense privacy. Must have been very tough, darling."

Shelby shrugged her bare shoulders. He suddenly wanted to massage them—to kiss her back between her shoulders blades, the back of her slender neck, covered with that soft down. Shelby called above the blast-furnace wind howling through the windows, "It's what I've always known."

"How'd your mother come to all of that? Was it her natural impulse, too, or was it at your father's insistence? Did it just, you know, become her way of life?"

Shelby twisted around in the seat, her back to the car door. As she drew her legs up under herself, he caught a glimpse under her short tight skirt—saw she wasn't wearing any underwear. "Are we on the record? Are you playing writer now?"

"It's just you and me," he said.

"Well, then... Like you said, it just kind of becomes your life. And being a Hyde, it's expected in some ways. Part of the appeal that keeps people buying and obsessing over Daddy's books—his strange life and the mystery of what became of him and why."

He said, "And your mother? She didn't fight it?"

"Mother bent to father's will," Shelby said. "Or I suppose it happened that way. I'm largely an enigma. No photos of me out there. No friends who could sell me out or sneak a shot with a camera phone or the like. Because I'm a cipher, I can venture out a little. Sneak out into the world under some assumed name. It's the great advantage of having never been photographed and of nobody knowing what Shelby Hyde looks like. For the most part, I get to have the life I want."

She smiled, her head on side. "Be honest? What were you expecting meeting me? Did I live up, or down, to your expectations?"

"You exceeded my expectations," he said, "by leagues."

Shelby smiled knowingly, stroking her wind blown hair back out of her face with slender fingers. "Because you expected a freak. Some pale, ascetic and bug-eyed hermit, yes?"

He smiled. "Maybe a little."

"Hardly surprising, or novel. Were you really calling your agent back there?"

"I really was."

"Turn left there. Two lights, then another left."

Even with the windows open and exceeding the speed limit, it was still hot in the car. He dragged his forearm across his forehead. His shirt stuck to his back.

"Slow down, darling, the driveway's just ahead."

He palmed the wheel. Foliage brushed both sides of the car as he pulled into the hidden driveway. He shifted into park and shut off the engine.

Shelby kicked off her shoes, left them there on the floor of the car. She slipped out the door, then pulled her dress over her head. She stumbled a little, and, now nude, threw her dress through the car window. Her nipples were already erect. The clouds across the moon cast deep shadows across her belly and thighs. "We'll go around back. The beach is pretty private. A swim will sober us up, but not get us *too* sober so we becoming boring." She smiled. "I like you reckless and uninhibited." The smile became wickeder in a way that made him hard: "I like you experimental."

He watched her long back as she tiptoed around the house. He kicked off his shoes, stripped off his shirt and shucked off his pants and underwear. He gathered them into a bundle and tossed them through the open driver's side window of the rental car.

He lost sight of her in the surf. Passing around to the back of the house, he saw a wire overhead, trailing from the house to an adjacent pole. It wasn't a thick wire like a power cable. There was another of those, much higher overhead. He was also passing by a satellite dish now. So the slender cable was likely a phone line; Shelby's place must have a landline.

She was standing in the surf now, beckoning him to her. Her pale body was glistening, her hair slicked back and the surf creaming around her thighs, lapping at her bare pubes.

He thought maybe he looked ridiculous, slogging through the sand with this bobbing hard-on, but then her hand was there, and he forgot about appearances.

56

Ashley had walked more than a mile and her hair was wet from the cold drizzle. It was only another seven blocks to Chase's apartment, and despite the fact the rain was picking up, she decided that soaked as she was, it was pointless to take a cab now.

The rain began falling faster, hard enough to sting her face. She ducked into a recessed doorway for shelter. From somewhere above, she heard "Adiemus" playing. The flute solo left Ashley feeling lonely and strangely empty.

She really was alone in the city, nothing like close friends at work. The girls at the office were frivolous and lacked focus in Ashley's eyes. The day job was a trudge for them, and their nights were a floating party from bar to bar, cadging drinks and hoping the next fleeting lay might be a keeper.

Chase was the only person Ashley had in the city. If he was lost to her, she was truly alone now. Maybe it was time to head home to her folks. Or perhaps somewhere else, some place where she could stretch a dollar and try to live as a fulltime fiction writer.

Now that she had her book contract, what her father had repeatedly said was at last true in a sense: she could write anywhere, she supposed. The challenge before her now was that of building a loyal readership, the struggle to remain published in a treacherous, too fickle and volatile marketplace and threatened industry.

God, but she was lonely tonight. All alone in the most bustling city on earth.

The rain slowed to a drizzle and she ducked her head and resumed her soggy walk to Chase's place.

On a whim, she called information, got the home number for Professor Adam Greenwood. It wasn't yet ten p.m., Eastern: she tapped in the number with her thumb.

The professor sounded alert enough, brushing it off when she apologized for the lateness of her call. It comforted her to hear his voice. Ashley remembered time spent in his cozy office, talking about writing over tea on drizzly gray afternoons, a little like tonight's soggy weather. Pleasant hours passed with this grandfatherly, wise old man.

Tonight he asked some fresh questions about Chase's Hyde project.

Ashley told him a little about the past few days, sans accounts of murder attempts and medical traumas. She paused and asked, "Have you ever heard of Bobby Bristow?"

"Why, yes." He seemed quite surprised to hear the name. "Relatively recently, I learned of this man. Why do you ask?"

Ashley decided to risk it. She told the professor what Shawn had told her about Everett Hyde's ill-fated "best buddy."

The professor took a deep breath, then let it out, slow and hard. The sound of his released breath against the receiver prompted Ashley to pull her own phone away from her ear—it sounded a little like thunder.

Adam Greenwood said, "I first heard of this Bobby Bristow from Carl Thompson, Everett's first would-be biographer."

"The one who was hanged," Ashley said.

"Well, found hanged, dear," her former professor quali-
fied. "Frankly, I thought Bobby was apocryphal. Carl disa-
greed, rather strongly. Something else I regret doubting him
about, now. Doubting poor, ill-fated Carl, I mean."

"What did Carl tell you about Bobby?"

"He didn't really tell me anything," the professor said.
"Carl's call was a bit like yours just now began. 'Have you
heard this name?' Like that. And I hadn't heard the name, not
ever. Fact is, you've just told me more about Bobby Bristow
than Carl ever did. Probably more than Carl himself knew. The
idea that there was someone along, riding shotgun with Everett Hyde on that last, crazed run down into the Keys? That's a
revelation. And it's hard for me to get my mind around it, at
odds as it is with decades of myth. God, how I would love to
spend an hour with this Shawn fellow."

"Not sure how forthcoming he'd be." Ashley didn't even
know where the Hyde family lawyer was now. She didn't know
how deeply allied with Shelby Shawn might still be.

Ashley talked a few more minutes with the professor, covering a couple more blocks in the process. "I may need to call
you again, Professor. Is that okay?"

"Absolutely. I look forward to it. And next time, call me
Adam. You're not my student anymore."

She smiled. "But you'll always be my favorite professor."

She heard the frosty smile she remembered in his voice.
"Kind of you to say."

Still smiling, Ashley slipped her phone into the interior
breast pocket of her coat. It really was good to hear her professor's voice, something familiar and comforting in that under
her present sorry circumstances. She pulled her coat's zipper
up higher, nearly to her throat. The rain was coming down
still harder, mixing with sleet. A stray snowflake twirled down

here and there. She frowned, after trying again to thrust her hands into the pocket of her Levi's.

She shoved her hands into her coat pockets, wrapping her right hand around the butt of the gun Ace had given her—the only way her hand fit in the pocket around the big, cold firearm.

And then Ashley was suddenly glad for the gun in her hand.

As she slid into the revolving door of Chase's building, a man slipped into the door with her, bumping her heels with his toes and wrapping a hand around her left arm.

In her panic at being accosted, and in this small space, Ashley thought she'd tear free when the door reached the opening into the lobby. She'd twirl around and kick the door back against her attacker, trapping him in there. Then, if need be, she'd empty the big automatic into the revolving door's compartment, just as Ace had instructed. She'd spend the whole clip until the man dropped.

A familiar voice said, "Thank God! Thank God you're safe, Ash."

Smiling uncertainly, Ashley said, "Shawn?"

57

They lay on the beach a long while, Chase flat on his back and Shelby on top, smiling cunningly and Kegeling what was left of his erection. For a time, the tide licked their feet and calves before retreating and then returning. Now the rising tide was forcing them to lift their heads to keep them above water.

"We should move," she said, reluctant sounding.

"That or drown."

She stood up, kneeling and resting her hands on her trembling knees. "God, I've seriously wrecked some muscles this time."

Chase stood up beside her, trying to ignore his cracking knees. He moved to wrap a hand around her waist, then feeling the sand there, he settled on trying to brush clean her back and bottom.

"That'll take forever," she said. "Follow me."

She had a shower spigot attached to a smallish back deck. She pulled on the chord and stepped under the water, squealing at its coldness. Her teeth were chattering when she finished.

"I'm going inside for a hot shower," she said. "You suffer this one, until I'm out. After, I'll make us a little something to eat. I'm hungry. Aren't you hungry again?"

"A little."

"Good answer."

He watched her until she disappeared around the corner, stopping just long enough to smile back over her shoulder. Chase stepped under the cold water, shivering and reminding himself to retrieve their clothes—at least his wallet and her purse—from the car before locking it up and heading inside.

The phone was ringing when Shelby opened the door. She checked to make sure Chase wasn't on her heels.

Shelby bit her lip, then picked it up. "Yes?"

"Calling for Ms. Shelby Hyde."

"Speaking." *Who the hell?*

"This is Detective Barry Peterson, out of Tennessee."

"Yes, detective?"

Her mind raced. Was it possible Brick had somehow said something to compromise her? Perhaps he had done that before Ashley rendered him a near-vegetable? If so, what could he have said? Shelby cursed herself for being dopy from booze and sex, maybe not fast enough on her feet to lie effectively.

Or worse, might Ashley have actually called in the cops on her? Would that silly bitch really risk putting Chase in jeopardy in that way?

The detective stumbled a bit, then said, "This is rather…" he sighed. "The autopsy results are back," he started again.

Now Shelby was truly thrown. "Autopsy results? Whose autopsy results?"

"The ones on your mother." The cop sounded confused. "You know—from the autopsy you requested through your counsel several weeks ago, via a Mr. Shawn Dalton? You personally assumed the cost of exhumation. Or, rather, Mr. Dalton handled that for you."

"I requested no autopsy for my mother." Shelby's heart was freshly racing. She was sweating profusely despite her recent cold shower and the chilly air conditioning. She watched the front door, prepared to hang up if Chase walked in. She said firmly, "I never requested an autopsy. I certainly never agreed to have mother exhumed."

"Well, Mr. Dalton has your power-of-attorney, and all the papers were certainly in order." A pause. "And either way, we have the results now, and, as we do, we have to pursue some things. This has become a criminal investigation."

"What things? How, criminal?" Shelby hated the way her heart was pounding. She could feel her pulse in her ears. She was struggling to modulate her voice, striving to convey something other than panic. "What in God's name is going on?"

Peters said, "Your mother was being treated for cancer, yes?"

"That's right."

"You were primary caregiver, were you not?"

Shelby bit her lip. Now she saw where this was heading. She scrambled for a lie. "Uh, not *really*. We have a lot of hired help. Mother's primary caregiver—I mean, in terms of administering medication and the like—was a man named Joseph Thorton Arick."

The detective asked her to spell that. There was the sound of some paper rustling. Shelby sensed the man had his hand over the mouthpiece of his phone, conversing with some cohort. He said, "Well, now, that's interesting because—"

"Mr. Arick was recently involved in a car crash," Shelby said. "He was also something of a, well, a security expert in charge of the family compound."

"Jack of all trades sort," the detective said. "Is that it? Medic and mercenary?" Detective Peterson sounded dangerously dubious. And that stress of his on "mercenary"—that couldn't be an accident, could it?

"That's about it," Shelby said. "Unfortunately for us both, his condition is quite grave. The possibility of any significant recovery almost hopeless. Or so I'm told." She heard the rental car's doors slam and knew she didn't have much time left before Chase straggled in.

"Mr. Arick was attacked in the hospital where he was recovering from his car wreck," Shelby said. "It's why I left Tennessee last night. I was frankly terrified. Afraid I might be in danger."

"Right. You haven't asked about the results of your mother's autopsy."

"Of course. I'm frankly rattled by this call. And by the attack on Mr. Arick. Rattled by the fact that our longtime family attorney seems to be running off like this, undirected. What did the autopsy reveal? It *was* cancer, wasn't it?"

"Oh yes, that's what killed your mother in the end." A dramatic pause for effect, something Shelby figured the stupid detective picked up from too many prime-time cop shows. "It's what the autopsy didn't turn up that has us quite interested. That's what might be criminal."

"And what was that?"

"Your mother was on a regimen of medications for her cancer while she was between sessions of chemotherapy and radiation. Well, she was prescribed these medicines, anyway. The prescriptions were all filled. But we found none of them in her system. She either wasn't administered her meds, or, she was given placebos. We really need to talk to you, Ms. Hyde. Over the phone just won't do. We need a face to face session with you, immediately."

"I plan to be back in Tennessee early next week. Can I call you to arrange a time?"

"We'd like to do it well before then. We—" She could hear the front porch slats squeak. The doorknob was turning.

Shelby said, "Well, then, it's agreed. I'll call you first thing Monday morning, then."

She hung up the phone as Chase wandered in naked and soaked to the bone. He said, "It's raining, now." He dropped this sodden bundle of clothes and personal items on the floor.

"I thought I heard thunder," Shelby said. She was very aware of Chase's focus on the phone.

"I've been doing the math," Shelby said, relieved to hear her voice was something close to normal, even nonchalant sounding. But she knew she needed to hurry: nothing saying the cop wouldn't go persistent on her—call her right back, over and over, if need be. "I think you should shower, a hot shower, and dress, darling," she said. "I'll get the food underway, then I'll clean up. Time I finish my showering, it should be time to eat."

"Okay. If you're sure."

"Move that sweet ass of yours," she said.

She smiled, watching him until he disappeared into the bathroom. When the door closed, she lifted the receiver on the phone; took it off the hook. She waited until she heard the shower turn on, then she rummaged in the kitchen and found a butcher knife. She wrapped the knife's wooden handle in a dishcloth for precaution. Then she padded outside, still naked and shivering.

Shelby moved a deck chair into position and slashed the phone cord at its terminus at the house, near the roofline.

She went back inside, put the now-dead phone back on its cradle and tossed the knife in the sink.

Shelby was in the shower now. Chase waited until he heard the spray and the sound of the shower door sliding closed—

the change in the sound of the water as it began to strike her bare body—then he scooped up the phone.

No dial tone.

Nothing.

He pushed the receiver button a few times, but still heard nothing.

He heard the shower turn off, heard the door opening again. Shelby had showered fast. He slipped the receiver back onto the rack.

Chase tiptoed back into the kitchen and began stirring the chowder from a can he'd promised to tend to while she bathed.

She walked out in a big bathrobe, briskly running a towel over her hair. "Going okay?"

"Going just great," he said, stirring the pot.

58

"**A**re you pointing a *gun* at me?"

Ashley glanced down and realized she looked like some sorry character out of a television show: the gun was levered up in her coat pocket, its muzzle outline unmistakable. The barrel was pointed somewhere in the vicinity of Shawn's crotch. She figured she looked like some stock character simultaneously trying to hide a gun and rob a bank.

She said, "Well, yes, I am, as a matter of fact."

Shawn nodded slowly. "Good. That's good. You should be on guard against that twisted little monster and her minions. I'm relieved you're taking precautions." He smiled, his hands out from his sides a bit. He was deliberately doing that, she realized, keeping them where she could see them. "I just thank God you're okay," he said. "I was worried as hell for you when you suddenly went missing. I didn't buy Shelby's explanation, not at all."

Shawn spread his arms for a hug.

Ashley thought, "it takes real guts to mock the void." She told herself she'd shoot Shawn dead if he tried anything. If he tried anything at all.

Ashley thought about it, then pulled her left hand from her pocket. She reached an arm over his right shoulder and patted Shawn on the back. He closed both arms around her, one hand resting familiarly on the swell of her hip. All the while, she kept her right hand in her pocket, twisting the gun up so it dug into Shawn's belly.

His brow furrowed, Shawn looked down at her, said, "That really is a gun, isn't it?" He tried for a joke. "Not just happy to see me?"

Ashley searched his eyes, so close in hue to her own she noticed. "Happy enough to see you, but, yes, it is a very big gun." She figured that admission bought her room for a lie. "And I know how to use it if you mean me harm."

He hugged her harder. "God, no, I'm just relieved you're okay."

"I'm glad you're safe, too."

"It's good you're seeing to your own safety with this thing." Shawn continued to hug her tightly to him, forcing the gun's muzzle deeper into his own gut by doing that. "I was fearing the worst for you when you and Brick went missing about the same time. I really figured you for a goner, Ashley. You had me terrified."

"Prove it."

His brow furrowed. "How, exactly?"

"Walk a few paces ahead of me," she said. "You're going to buy me a coffee, decaf because I need to sleep, Shawn. Try anything other than buying me that coffee, and I will shoot you."

This incredulous smile that swiftly turned into a frown. "You really mean that, don't you?"

"I've had a really bad forty-eight hours, Shawn. A true nightmare. So I really don't know what I wouldn't do at this point. Frankly, I feel about half-wrapped."

"You must also be freezing, soaked through like that."

She said, "By the time we get to the bar, given the way it's raining hammers out there, you're going to be every bit as wet as me, Shawn."

He smiled uncertainly. "Then maybe we could run there?"

It was an Irish bar, just around the corner. Somehow, Ashley and Chase had never made it inside the joint, despite its proximity to Chase's pad. The bar was tended by a thirty-something, honest-to-God Irishman. He said in a smooth and comforting Galway accent, "What'll it be, dear?"

"Decaf coffee," Ashley said.

"Irish it up?"

A smile. She said, "Sure, just a little. Could use the extra jolt."

Shawn slicked his wet hair back with his hand, hesitated, then said, "Red wine."

The bartender, tallish and Black Irish, said, "Merlot?" Some mocking there in his Celtic lilt.

"Cabernet."

"*Ah*, then." The bartender made this face at Shawn.

But Shawn let that go. He looked at Ashley's coat pocket. She still had the gun trained on his gut. He said, "Shelby sold Chase on the notion you got your nose out of joint over something about him, some 'secrets' Chase was allegedly keeping from you. And Shelby evidently led Chase to think you might have run off with Brick. That you had the hots for the ape."

She said, "*Yuck.* If either you or Chase actually believed that, then I've got some serious soul-searching ahead of me."

"My reaction was derision," Shawn said.

"And Chase?" Ashley rued the tone of urgency that crept into that question.

Shawn said, "He got there, but he's frankly a good bit slower on the draw. At the risk of angering you, my regard for the guy eroded pretty steadily once we reached Tennessee."

"I didn't ask." Ashley chewed her lip, then took another sip of her slightly spiked coffee. "Still, you're here, professing concern for me, tolerating a gun pointed at your crotch. And Chase?"

"Yeah. Go figure that." Shawn sipped his wine. "Well, I got booted off the tour bus. Shelby dismissed me. Then she took off with Chase. They bolted for parts unknown."

"Dismissed you how?"

"Shelby said all the legal work was done. Then she had one of her steroid stooges hustle me onto a plane back to here. It was all pretty rushed. I never saw it coming."

"And Chase?"

"Like I said, headed for parts unknown. Still with her, so far as I know." Shawn paused a long time. Ashley didn't try to fill the silence. After a while he said, "They're intimate now."

"I beg your pardon?"

"They're lovers already. That was obvious. Maybe, thinking you had left him, Shelby seemed a rebound bit of fun for Chase. She's certainly pretty enough. Even looks a bit like you, although you're far more attractive. But for her? Whatever they have now, it runs deeper from her direction. I think she had sights set on him from the start." Shawn sipped his wine. "Has Chase tried to contact you?"

Ashley shook her head, still trying to fathom Chase in bed with the Hyde orphan. God, everything was a mess. It seemed like everything was steadily being taken from her, one big piece at a time.

"Not as far as I know," she said. "I drove all the way from Tennessee today. I wasn't really reachable. I need to make it an early night. I have a doctor's appointment early tomorrow. Lost my appendix along the way. Need to make sure I'm not infected since I had to bolt the hospital back there in Tennessee."

She remembered then what he'd asked about attempts to contact her. She said, "Still need to check my email." Ashley covered her mouth as she yawned. "I really need to go soon, Shawn. I'm so tired I can hardly think."

"I can imagine."

"Exactly how'd you find me, Shawn?"

"I wish I could say it was something brilliant on my part. It wasn't. That said, I don't think you have to worry about Shelby or her minions replicating my tactics."

Ashley said, "And what exactly were those tactics?"

"There was a car accident up on that mountain. A car like the one Brick bragged to me about owning. Thanks to you tumbling to our location, I was sporadically checking Gatlinburg area news via the Web. I saw the report on the crash. And I saw the items about this amnesiac young woman police thought might also have been in that car wreck. I made some deductions, decided pretty firmly in my mind it was Brick's car that went off that mountain, and that you had been inside, maybe even caused the accident."

"Right on both counts, counselor." Ashley drank some more coffee, very aware of the way that Shawn was watching her, focused on her mouth, her lips. Well, she didn't have time to worry about him looking at her like that—no time to fret about some interest he might have in her. Maybe Shawn saw her as easy pickings after his revelation about Chase's moving on. Still, he'd correctly deduced her situation and been the first to find her. That counted for something, she guessed. It certainly impressed her on some level.

Ashley said, "Did you share your deductions with Chase?"

Shawn shook his head slowly. "I did. He was skeptical. I don't think he could emotionally let himself believe it even if he was inclined to follow my theories. Not after the way he was comporting himself. The way he just let you get away from him. But to be fair, I told him about ten minutes before I got the boot. It's possible Chase was still coming to terms with what I told him. Maybe he's come around since." Shawn didn't sound too convinced of that.

Ashley stared at her empty mug. The bartender was there again. He said, "Another, then?"

Tired as she was, Ashley said, "Sure." She took her right hand from her pocket finally. She flexed her hand. It was stiff from gripping the butt of the gun for so long.

"This mean you're not going to shoot me, Ashley?"

"Not before I finish my second coffee, anyway. We got a little sidetracked in our conversation, Shawn. You were going to tell me how you found me tonight."

"I was desperate to find you," he said. "Worried as hell. I needed to know you are okay. I figured you'd be cautious about Shelby and her yen for surveillance. Figured you'd avoid your own place. As you've done, obviously."

"Obviously."

"When we left New York a few days ago, we left from Chase's place, so I know where he lives. I knew you'd both left your cell phones in Chase's loft. Your mutual literary agent had given me your cell phone number, along with Chase's. I called your number a little bit ago. When you answered, I knew you'd risked entering Chase's place, apparently safely. Then I figured that it was a reasonably good place to hide. If

Chase is with Shelby, why should she spy on Chase's place, right?"

"Right. Smart. You could have said hello when you called a bit ago."

"Yeah, I should have. But I was afraid you might hang up on me. That I'd lose my only chance to talk. Given my business relationship with that woman, well, you'd be right to wonder about my allegiances. What the hell happened to you up there on that mountain, Ash?"

Ashley looked him in the eye, waiting to gauge reactions. "Your client tried to have me killed," she said. "Brick was taking me out to shoot me. He planned to put me down like some sick dog. He said he was going to dump my body off the road somewhere, then scatter my belongings in dumpsters around town." She paused, searching Shawn's face. "And you don't look at all surprised." Her hand drifted back toward the right pocket of her coat.

Shawn saw that, said, "No, it's not like that, Ash. Not at all. Fact is, I think Shelby has killed before, maybe several times. Now tell me everything that's happened to you, and in detail, please."

59

"Your phone doesn't work," he said.

They were standing at the sink, Shelby washing and Chase drying their dinner dishes. "I tried again to call my agent. Not even a dial tone."

"I noticed that after our swim. Bills are all paid, so I'm thinking lightning strike, maybe. Doesn't really matter. I mean, a lot of people have given up landlines, now."

Chase said, "On that note, maybe you could loan me your cell phone."

She smiled, "I'd be happy to oblige. But in the frenzy to leave Tennessee, I forgot my phone charger. I managed to make just one call before the battery died. At least I got that call in." She paused, said, "You do have a passport on you, don't you?"

"Your lawyer insisted upon it as we weren't sure where we were headed when we left New York. Not sure if we might not end up in Canada or Mexico."

"What a relief," she said. "It's great you have it." That was no lie.

"We're moving again. Is that where you're headed with that question?"

"Right. To Mexico. Land of Margaritas, spicy food, great beaches." She might have added, *and next-to-no danger of extradition.*

"We just got here," he said, stowing the last of the dishes.

"My boys got word that news crew has caught up to us, or nearly so."

"Where are your boys?" Chase realized he hadn't seen any of Shelby's stooges since the airport. "What's become of the praetorian guard?"

"Close by. Or they were," she lied. "They've taken the manuscripts and gone on ahead of us. Readying things there." Another lie. She'd shipped the manuscripts ahead, herself. She'd always envisioned going to her place in the Yucatan. Florida was simply a weigh station. "We'll leave early tomorrow. Crack of dawn, to coin a phrase."

"Shelby—"

"Don't worry, darling." She smiled and stroked his cheek with the back of her hand. He needed a shave. "The next place we go, nobody we have to worry about can follow." Shelby was thinking of Tennessee flatfoots bearing murder indictments as she said that last. And Shelby liked Mexico. Life in the Yucatan would stand her just fine.

He shook his head. "Shelby, I can't just keep—"

"Running?" This look in her eyes... her eyes that were so much like his own eyes, he realized for the first time. The similarity unsettled him.

She threw down her dishtowel and stepped into him, pressing her hands to his face and forcing him to look into those too-familiar hazel eyes of hers.

"I know, darling." She kissed him, hard and deep. Her tongue was in his mouth. His body was responding, pressing against her belly. Her hand drifted down there, rubbing him through his pants. "I know all about you, my love. Mother's researchers stumbled on it. About your memory, about your... accident. Mom was so thrown by what she found, I guess—by its implications—that she dropped it right there. That's why she never sent that email she had drafted, asking you to write the official biography. She became terrified at what the researchers were finding. When she died, and I ran across their reports, *I* was thrilled. And I had them dig deeper. I know everything."

"What?" He said between deep kisses, "What do you know about me?"

"About your accident in Florida, so many years ago."

Shelby was fumbling with his zipper, then his belt buckle. "I know about your memory—its loss, I mean. But now we can be together, like we were meant to be. Be safe together in Mexico. You can write again, and we'll be together and love one another." She kissed him again and he didn't fight it. She had his pants open and she was working at him with her still-damp hand.

Looking into his eyes, her lips still brushing his mouth, she said, "We can be family again."

60

Ashley frowned at the array of empty glasses and coffee mugs before them. She was starting to fear the check, starting to hope Shawn was treating.

And she was dreading the prospect of undergoing an early morning doctor's examination in the wake of what was shaping up to be a near sleepless night.

The bartender plunked down another coffee. Ashley smiled her thanks. After so many, what could one more hurt? And to that end, at least the nagging ache in her side was gone for the moment.

She had excused herself to the restroom a few minutes ago; Shawn had drifted to the jukebox. Now Lucinda Williams was huskily singing *Ventura*.

"That's a favorite song of mine," Ashley said.

"She's a recently discovered new favorite for me," Shawn said.

In fact, he had discovered Lucinda, and about half-a-dozen other new favorites, while poking around Ashley's computer in Tennessee, while browsing through her most played songs in her iTunes library.

"A lot of earthy yearning in her songs," Shawn said. "And God, that voice and what it can communicate. She's a true poet."

"Her father was a poet," she said. "Guess a way with words runs in the blood in that family."

Ashley warmed her hands over the coffee—she was all but done drinking and now wanted it mostly for its radiant heat. "You said Shelby might have murdered before."

Shawn sighed and leaned in, resting his elbows on the bar, staring at himself in the mirror behind the barkeep.

Ashley said, "Chase is still with that horrible woman. That woman who may be having my place watched, maybe thinking to finish what Brick started back there in the mountains."

Shawn put it out there, naked, this tone in his voice that reached her. "Despite it all, you really want that man back?"

"I don't even know that man," Ashley said. "Not really. The man I knew was a construct. A creation. So no, I don't want him back, not like that. But I feel an obligation or a responsibility to try and help him. I'm not yet sure why that is, either, but I do."

She paused, then said it. "Even if it turns out he is Everett Hyde."

Another Lucinda tune started up, *Those Three Days*. It was a song suited for late hours, confessed regrets and melancholy comradeship. "He and me are over, that's pretty certain," Ashley said. "But that woman? I have to take a shot at helping Chase if she's a danger to him."

"And you've got that crazy memoir about this mess that goes to auction soon," Shawn said dryly. "Can't put that in jeopardy, can we? Have to play out the hand to ensure the book deal."

"At best, that's a means-to-an-end," Ashley said, waving a dismissive hand. "If I even go ahead with it. I haven't signed anything. The notion gives me butterflies, frankly."

"What it is, is everything I feared for you," Shawn said. "I mean, sidetracking into nonfiction. Such a criminal waste of your talent. I was dearly hoping you'd lay off nonfiction."

"I appreciate the concern, Shawn, I truly do. But it's a one-shot."

"I surely hope so."

"It is. Now, you were going to tell me about Shelby Hyde and murder."

"Right." Shawn took a drink, a deep one. "I had Amanda Hyde's body exhumed recently," he said.

That prompted a near spit-take from Ashley. She put down her coffee mug and dabbed at her chin with a cocktail napkin. "You did what? And why? I can't believe that Shelby would—"

"Shelby didn't. And I was operating on a hunch. Shelby didn't know. The way the papers were drawn up all those years ago by Everett, I have the authority to act on hers or on Amanda's behalf in certain circumstances. I have very broad latitude in certain arcane areas. This was one of them. Shelby is clueless regarding what I was doing. Or she was. I got the call just a bit ago—Amanda Hyde's death is now being investigated as a homicide. I assume by now that the police, if they can reach Shelby, have told her about what's going on. They're probably demanding an interview with her. Be interesting to see if she hauls me in as her counsel. She really has no one else at the moment."

"Not bloody likely you'll get that call, given what you've done," she said. "Isn't that going to make Shelby furious? She'd have to see it as a profound betrayal."

"There have been intimations, indications, that she was edging up to trying to fire me," he said. "She wants her own infrastructure in place, her own people in place, top to bottom. Sycophants, I suspect. Not people who care about nurturing and maintaining Everett's literary legacy. That was one of Everett's directives to me, his strongest in fact. My first responsibility is to protect his literary legacy. Funny as it sounds, I'm still more Everett's employee than Shelby's. And I have serious reservations about publishing his posthumous writings. So I decided to go for the potential scorched-earth policy to best protect my primary client. Besides, if Shelby is the object of a criminal investigation, her ability to exercise certain business options is, at the very least, profoundly compromised. You know how it is—get yourself sued and try to take out a loan. Try to buy a house or even a used car? It's all but impossible."

"I guess it really is total war between you two," Ashley said. Then, "I thought the Hyde widow was killed by cancer."

"Oh, she was. But Amanda was also deprived the medication that for several months had kept her cancer in check. The theory would be that Shelby deprived her mother of her life-saving medications in recent months in order to clear the way to take over management of the Hyde literary estate. It wasn't lost on me that as soon as Amanda's health began its last, precipitous decline, the drive to put out all of this long-languishing material of Everett's—material that Amanda was obligated to destroy—quickened. The drive for an official biography kicked-in to overdrive then."

"It's incredible, the notion Shelby might have done that to her own mother," Ashley said. "What a messed-up family."

Shawn shook his head. "What family isn't?"

"Mine's pretty normal," Ashley said.

"Makes you rare and lucky," Shawn said. He nodded his assent for a refill of his wine glass.

"How was your family, Shawn?"

"Pretty messed-up, as a matter of fact. Broken-up too early, like so many are. More now than then, even. Folks always at one another's throats, kids watching it all unfold and blow to pieces. Infidelity. Christ. The happy American family is a lie, so far as I can see."

Lucinda was singing *Minneapolis*, another of Ashley's melancholy favorites. She smiled and propped her chin on her fist. "What, you played the whole album, Shawn?" She raised her eyebrows and nodded at the jukebox.

"Nearly. The ballads, anyway. So what is next, Ash? You get some clue and run off with this counter-mercenary? This Iron Seal? Hell, it seems a little like *Mad Magazine*, you know? *Spy vs. Spy*? You dash off with this crazy man to confront Shelby?"

Ashley smiled, looking in her drink and stirring it with her straw. "Kind of the plan, though I'm hoping for more competence on the part of the so-called Seal than *Mad Magazine*. More like James Bond. Bourne, at the very least." She smiled with tired eyes. "I mean, it's what's to be expected of that Ashley McKnight, angel of vengeance, right?"

Shawn laughed. "That's almost hysterically funny," he said. "Until you think about the fact that these men are textbook mercenaries. Sociopaths, at best."

"I know how serious it is, Shawn," Ashley said. "That fight in the elevator brought it all home for me. Believe that."

He looked at her, studying her, "I'm sure it did." He closed a hand over hers. She didn't move to pull her hand away. "You're a marvel, you know? Chase is such a fool to have let you slip through his fingers. If you were mine, you'd never have ended up in that car with Brick. If you were mine—"

Now she slid her hand out from under his. "Have to be up early," she said.

"So you said." He smiled and gestured for a check, briefly scoped it, then slapped down a credit card.

"I want to come along with you two, wherever this all takes you," he said. "Hell, you may need an attorney to help swab up the aftermath." Shawn smiled, said, "Particularly if you do go into full and fetching angel of vengeance mode."

Shawn scribbled on the bill with the pen the bartender handed him, then slipped his plastic in his pocket. He stood and extended a hand to Ashley. She took it, and he tugged her to her feet. She was unsteady, and he pressed a hand to the small of her back; she smiled uncertainly but let his hand stay there.

He said, "I'm wiped out, too. But I need to find a hotel for the night. My place is being watched by Shelby's stooges. Maybe watched on the off-chance you might make it back here and look me up. I got home, threw my luggage on the bed, then wandered down to Starbucks for a coffee. Coming back, I spotted these gorillas in the street."

Ashley thought about what Shawn said—if he should decide to risk getting back to his place at some point, then he could be followed back to her, later. Or he might be made to tell where she could be found.

Ashley said, "You can have the couch. But I'm locking the bedroom door, and I'm barricading it. I'm also sleeping with my gun under my pillow."

Shawn beamed. "That's my girl," he said. "And thank you, sincerely. You're one of the good ones."

He squeezed her hand again. "And I'll feel so much better having you in sight. I've really been sick with worry about you, Ash. What you've gone through? I swear I'm going to see my so-called client pays for this, one way or another. God, what a monster that young woman is."

61

More wine had been a mistake, but there you had it: Shelby uncorked it, and Chase drank it. Heedlessly and hungrily.

More shattered inhibitions ensued. More reckless, tawdry behavior. But this time it reached this whole new crazy level.

Emboldened perhaps by her earlier flirting around the edges of her belief about who Chase really was—stoked by that as much as by the potent and smoky Spanish wine she had unearthed, she had growled in his ear at certain moments during sex this time. Sometimes it sounded like she cooed "Everett," but more often, and fairly unmistakably, it sounded like "Daddy…"

But Chase went along with all that, just as he had gone along with the wine.

Content in his knowledge of who he was—at least that he certainly couldn't be Everett Hyde—he played her dirty, twisted, but—and no denying this—rather sexy decadent and forbidden game.

Certain that there was no foundation to her claims regarding his identity, he went along, even calling her "daughter" as she climaxed a last time. He'd said it at her desperate, intoxicating urging while in the throes of her last, mounting orgasm.

Hell, was it really so different from the crude urgings he had shared with Ashley and some others from time to time?

Coarse words whispered into ears to describe one another's most private parts and what they intended to do to those places?

Because he knew it was a game—a fantasy, albeit a dark one, even more than a tad twisted—it was okay, really. Just another sexy indulgence. A fantasy. Seemed just that to Chase, anyway. Or it did until the devastating pillow talk, after.

Chase had made the mistake of trying to gently pick it apart in the afterglow. "That was wild, dirty fun," he said, short of breath. "But you know I can't be your father."

That earned him a smirk, one he would never forget. This sultry and derisive smile under bedroom eyes, those eyes that were the unsettlingly near-echo of his. Shelby went and said it. "C'mon. Look at our hair. Our eyes. Even our smiles. Consider our drives. Get real. We *look* like family. We're blood, and this is what we've both long wanted, what both our lives and your art have long pointed to."

Queasy, Chase stayed at it, trying to push his points home. Soon, both of them were poised at the edge of dangerous exasperation. He played his ace then, the suicide note and its impossible chronology. The timing that precluded him having written the note.

He felt this triumphant smile spread across his face as he played his card, a smile he realized was angering Shelby.

Her irritation prodded her to parry back more viciously than she might otherwise have done. With a single blunt statement, Shelby knocked it all out from under Chase.

It came like a body blow. "Oh, the note," she said. "You'll remember, it was undated. Your argument stands on the date the suicide note was entered into police custody. The date the letter entered into the investigative stream. Fact is, mother had the note quite some time before it was made known to the police. I guess she was in some kind of denial. I suppose she hoped it was a cruel hoax of some kind. Whatever. Important thing for us is you could easily have written that note."

"But I didn't." His voice sounded shrill to his own ears, even verging on panic.

Her fingers traced his lower lip. "Now that you're back, now that we know who you are, we can see the best doctors. We can bring you back to the man—to the writer—you were. You can finish your great novel. Revise the others to perfection from the standpoint of your mature voice. You'll be the champ again."

Chase shivered, felt goose flesh everywhere. "I'm not Everett Hyde."

"A DNA test would settle it, fast. I'll submit to one, and eagerly, if that's what you need to convince you, to settle your mind on this. How about you? Take a test?"

He realized then that her hand was wrapped around his penis, stroking him. He was responding, despite it all.

"I'm not your father," he said, acid, now.

Her eyes blazed. "Well, until you decide to trust in chemistry, trust in this science: Everett Hyde left one hand-written note. A single handwriting sample. It was a very passionate unsigned letter to my mother. I bought an inscribed copy of your first Bierce biography. It was a long intimate inscription to the woman you were with when the book was published. Guess when you went separate ways, she decided to make some quick cash. Either way, the inscription was so long that the graphologists deemed it an excellent sample to compare against."

Chase's heart was pounding; his ears were burning with his mounting blood pressure.

"I consulted three handwriting analysts," she said. "Tops in the field. They all reached the same conclusion. It was a certain match. You wrote that letter, no question."

He tried to argue further, but eventually gave up in the face of her conviction.

What was it to him?

He knew the truth.

If Shelby wanted some tawdry incest fantasy, some sexy Elektra trip to spark her in bed, what did it really cost him? Hell, he'd already gone along once with it. And it wasn't a sin if he knew it wasn't wrong… right?

Shelby had slid down the bed then. She'd taken him into her mouth. It had gone on from there. With all the angst, all the alcohol, he didn't come again, despite the crazy gymnastics she put them through.

Despite her husky, wrong-headed cries and pleas. Despite that word growled over and over in his ear—*Daddy, oh, Daddy.*

His nightmares that followed were hellishly vivid, disjointed.

The people populating them lacked faces, as they often did.

But there were plenty of voices. Wild accusations… Gunshots.

He groaned at the remembered impact with the pavement, remembered landing on his bullet-riddled arm. The hard, bloody tumbling in the car's wake. Broken teeth.

A last scream, hollered from the open door of the car: "Fucking Judas! This isn't over!"

Another still-more disturbing scream, lusty and full-throated: "Oh, Daddy!"

Chase awoke in a sweat, his heart racing. He lay there trying to regulate his heart-rate, listening to Shelby's steady, even breaths. She was still out, hadn't been awakened by his thrashing. Ashley slept lightly—would have shaken him out of his nightmare before it drove him from sleep. Shelby slept right through it. But Shelby had to be exhausted from the sex, the liquor... the swimming. And, of course, from the running.

He could forgive her for sleeping through the end of the world in her present state.

He checked the clock radio: three a.m. The air conditioner was between cycles and he could hear the ocean, the crickets.

Something ran across the bedroom window above the bed, making scraping noises and casting an arresting shadow on the bedroom wall. He realized it was just a lizard.

His eyes fully adjusted to the dark, he carefully turned on his side and looked at Shelby naked atop the damp sheets.

He was infatuated with her, dangerously so. Their sex was raw and edgy and a big part of it, sure. Even this thing of her thinking he was her father—a *daft* notion—was potently erotic when he let himself play with it for carnal effect.

If he really believed what she thought to be true, it might be something else. Then he remembered the hard-on he'd been given by the incest passages in her father's books. Well... he knew it was just a dirty game. And this time with her, it was exciting on its own. A kind of lusty lark.

He had real money now, or he would soon, when the contracts were fully processed and the advance paid him. He'd have more money than he ever imagined amassing. Money like that could buy a man freedom. And options.

And Shelby was very much her own woman, despite the fact that she was approximately the same age as clingy, needed-mothering Ashley.

Shelby was archly independent, with her own money and these great houses here and there. He smiled, thought, *Welcome to your next new life.*

And conversation—writing talk—was different than with Ashley.

Shelby just appreciated the words and a story well-told in the way an intelligent reader should.

Ashley dwelt on process, subtext and angles of attack. She did that as if she and Chase were remotely the same kinds of writers. As if that engaged him. He'd told Ashley the truth: his interest in fiction extended only so far as it related to or informed his biographies of the various writers whose lives he'd chosen to chronicle.

He knew enough to recognize Ashley's writing was good enough to risk showing Selma. But he didn't really get it, in some ways. Or maybe he just wasn't the right gender to fully appreciate Ashley's first novel.

Chase wondered what had become of Ashley. He thought about what Shawn had claimed about the car accident back there in the mountains. He entertained trying to reach her by phone, just in case she'd not been in that car. In case she'd made her way back to the city. If he could get some time away from Shelby, maybe he'd try to make that call. Maybe tomorrow he'd do that, sure.

Shelby smiled in her sleep, making him smile. She whispered something that sounded like "Oh, Daddy."

God.

Still, he felt himself stirring. He smelled of her, baptized in her brine. Hard now, he slid down the bed, gripped her calves and pressed her legs back against her chest, opening her most private places to him. He remembered a phrase from one of her father's novels—a mention of a sex act reputed to seal a pact with the devil. Hyde called it "the unspeakable kiss."

He put his tongue there, began to probe. That awakened her.

62

This insistent, but gentle, rapping.

"Ashley? Please don't shoot me through the door. It's Shawn. It's six-thirty, and I wasn't sure when your doctor's appointment is."

"Thanks," she said hoarsely. Ashley checked the alarm clock. "You were right to wake me."

She slid naked from the bed, still exhausted. She tugged on Chase's too-big-for-her bathrobe. Remembering, she reached under the pillow, retrieved the gun and shoved it into the pocket of the robe.

Shawn was standing in the door when she opened it. He was dressed, clean-shaven. He looked pretty fresh for all his drinking and the very late night they'd shared.

"I opted for the first shower," he said. "Borrowed Chase's razor. Hope he doesn't mind. Actually, to hell with him if he does." Shawn's hands were behind his back. When he suddenly moved them to the front, Ashley almost reached for her gun.

But his hands were full. He handed her a cup. "Ran to Starbuck's. Coffee, black. There're a few assorted scones, too. If you're allowed to eat before the doctor."

His other hand was thrust out, palm up. Two white pills there. "Aspirin, for your side."

Ashley took the pills and the cup from his hands, muttered, "You're maybe my hero now." She realized she regretted not looking in a mirror before opening the door. She said, "I must look like twelve kinds of hell."

Shawn took several steps back to clear a path to the bathroom, his arms stretched in a pose suggesting crucifixion. He said, "All things considered, I think you look sublime."

She walked back into the waiting room, a hand pressed to her side. Shawn tossed aside the magazine he'd been trying to stoke some interest in; he stood up. "The verdict?"

He thrust his hands in his pockets, mindful Ashley's right hand was in her coat pocket again, her gun pocket as he'd come to think of it.

"All is well," she said. "Got a prescription for some new pain pills, though I'm loathe to use them. Kind of tired of feeling doped or drunk."

"But you are okay?"

"Fine. Just have to come back in a few days to have the incision site checked again. Thanks so much for coming along, Shawn."

He shrugged. "Until I know what kind of sustained surveillance I might be under, and to what end, I'm kind of at a loss for places to go. And I like watching you." Again, that could be taken a couple of ways.

"Yeah, well, anyway thanks." Ashley's brow furrowed. "I'm sure my friend Ace can think of something to help us out there. About your place, I mean."

He smiled crookedly. "Maybe so. But I loathe the prospect of a bloodbath in my building's lobby. With those types in the mix, I sense violent escalation could be a real risk. Hungry?"

"I could eat."

"Preference?"

"No," she said, then, "Yes. Still a little early, so we might need to kill some time first, but Italian."

"Know a place?"

"I do," she said. "We can walk to it."

"It's raining again." He nodded at the window behind the receptionist's desk. It was a lashing rain.

"It's real close by. And with the construction, we'll be under scaffolding all the way."

"Okay, then. Italian does sound good. Comfort food."

He realized she was still hanging slightly behind him. "Still got that gun?"

"Yeah."

"And still don't trust me?" They stepped in to the common corridor. He pressed for the elevator with a thumb.

"*Still* being careful. But maybe coming around."

A smile. "That's… encouraging."

They had come up in the elevator in a crowd. This time, the car was empty. Sensing she was troubled by that, Shawn held the door with an arm so she could slide inside. She went straight to the rear corner and put her back up against the place where the walls of the cage met. "You suddenly seem much more uneasy," he said.

"Think about what I said about the last time I was alone in an elevator with a man."

"Right," he said softly. Shawn put his hands in his pockets and stepped into the elevator, staying to the opposite side of the cage. "You'll have to get the button."

She nodded and reached across to the panel on her side and punched the button for the lobby with her left index finger.

He said, "God, what you went through, Ash. I hate Brick for that. Shelby, too."

Ashley nodded. "Should be hearing from Selma, or from Ace, and quite soon," she said. "I can have him work something out about your luggage. Have the stuff picked up from your place and delivered to Chase's place, if you don't mind bunking on the couch for a time. At least you'll have fresh clothes, your own toothbrush."

"The couch was comfortable enough. And long. So that'd be perfect." He smiled. "If you're sure. So far as Ace fetching my stuff for me, let me think some more about that." He kept his hands in his pockets and his back to the wall, giving her plenty of space. "How'd you sleep last night, Ash?"

"Funny dreams. Well, not funny so much as warped. But I slept pretty solidly." She shrugged. "Actually, that's not true either. After the compound, the quiet there, and after the hospital, even forty stories up, all I heard was sirens and car alarms. Horns all night long. I grew up in the country. Always takes me a while to adjust to the city when I've been away from it for a while."

"Me too. Probably be a day or two acclimating to the town's noise again. I was born in the boonies as well. Only child."

"Me too."

"Probably what makes us write," he said. "Well, you're the writer. But all that time alone, sort of fires the imagination, you know?"

Shawn stepped out first into the lobby, drawing a look from an elderly woman. He looked back over his shoulder at Ashley, then said to the old woman, "I'm her hostage." That drew him another cross look from the old lady.

Ashley said dryly, "That flavor of humor is a real risk in this city, even now."

"Suppose that's so. So I'm a fool. What's new?"

They'd nearly reached the front door when Shawn grabbed Ashley's arm and pivoted her around.

"What the hell, Shawn?"

"Franklin. One of Shelby's stooges. He's out there by the door."

That sent her reeling. "Did he see us?"

"I don't think so. Let's hope for a back door in this joint."

"How'd they find us?"

"They found you," Shawn said. Ashley shot him a look.

He said, "Shelby's researched Chase. Done deep background checks on you both. God only knows what she knows about you." Shawn suddenly held up a finger in this Aha! gesture. He said, "Is your doctor's information on your laptop?"

"They confirm appointments via email," Ashley said. It dawned her then. "At the compound, when they had my computer…"

"Right," Shawn said. "And then you escaped the hospital—"

"And they assumed I'd check in with my own doctor if I made it back to the city." She shook her head. "But to watch this place, my place, maybe your place? That's a lot of surveillance."

He said, "They wouldn't have to do that—watch this place, I mean. You said the doctor confirms your appointment times via email. We never changed your email passwords. Just didn't occur to me, at the time. So via Webmail—"

"They're still monitoring all my email," Ashley finished for him. "When we get back to the loft, I'm changing my passwords."

"Of course," he said. "But first we have to get out of here."

They reached another set of revolving doors on the opposite side of the building. Another muscle-bound man was standing guard there. His back, for the moment, was to the door.

"Got to be another one of them," Shawn said, steering Ashley back around.

"I think so, too," she said. She chewed her lip, thinking. "I could call Ace on my cell."

"He's not much use to us unless he lives upstairs here somewhere. Especially at this hour, it's the height of the commute. The Iron Seal would likely be a long time reaching us."

"Guess we're lucky they didn't catch us coming in," she said.

"Oh, I think that was calculation, too," Shawn said. "You missing a scheduled doctor's appointment would give the cops a timeline for an eventual investigation. You disappearing after your last known obligation, on the other hand?"

He looked around the lobby. His gaze settled on the men's room. He said, "We have to take a calculated risk, here, Ash. Well, this risk is really all on your end, sweetheart. It's you they're hunting. They let me walk away, more or less. I think I can get you out of here, but you have to trust me."

There was a sign in front of the women's restroom noting it was closed for cleaning. Shawn picked it up and moved it in front of the men's room.

He held out his hand. "Now, you have to trust me completely, Ash. You have to give me your gun."

63

Chase made a point of getting up early. He showered, brewed some coffee, then waited until Shelby was in the shower.

Fearing she might make it another quick washing up, he slid out the front door and jogged around to the side of the beach house. He intended to check the phone line's connection to her house, to see if some wire had perhaps been torn loose in the storm.

It was windy and the clouds were low and black. He could hear the surf crashing behind the house. Sounded like rougher seas.

Chase turned the corner and stutter-stepped.

The phone line dangled limply from the end of the utility pole, its end coiled in a lazy arc on the grass.

The end of the cable was cleanly severed. The exposed wires were still shiny—looked freshly cut.

Chase didn't recognize his own life as it stood now. He wasn't sure about himself anymore. Not that he believed he was Everett Hyde, or that he was sleeping with his own daughter. Not that at all. Nevertheless, Chase didn't fathom his own apparent low drives. And he didn't sense his newly found darkside really had a bottom. That frightened him more —this sense of having no boundaries. Chase suddenly scared himself.

This voice at his back, startling him. The voice said, "Yes, she's cut clean through. Really recently, too, right? No salt corrosion on those wires. Or did you notice that?"

Startled, Chase twisted around in his crouch.

A stranger held up a leatherette identification wallet in his left hand. It contained some kind of license from what Chase could see of it. The stranger said, "Name's Marcus Byron. You're Chase Alger, right?"

Rising slowly, Chase said, "You're police?"

"Private investigator," the man said. "Close enough."

"Not from where I stand," Chase said. "No badge, no authority…"

"I've already contacted the local police," Byron said. "It's protocol—they know where I am, and why I'm here. Frankly, they're very interested in all that. Oh, they'll leave me to do the heavy lifting, but when the time comes, we'll be hand in glove, no worries there." A pause then, "You didn't deny you're who I said you are, so I take it I'm right about that."

"Take it anyway you want." Chase wet his lips. He said, "What are you doing here?"

Byron's mouth turned down. "Going to talk more to you for starters, Chase."

"What are you really doing here? Also, since you're so very keen on rules and protocol, you must know you're trespassing." Chase checked the front door; he hoped Shelby was still lingering in her shower, wouldn't come stumbling out now.

"Far as I know, *you* have no rights here, either," Byron said. "I don't think you have the right to order me off the property or to grant me the right to stay standing right here." A smile, then, "If it makes you feel better, we can take a little stroll out behind the shrubs there and have this talk on the sidewalk—do it on public property, if it really matters to you."

"Suppose it doesn't matter in the end," Chase said. "Let's talk."

Byron said, "Right, let's go straight to it. I really appreciate that, you know. Need to get back to the clinic to see my boy. It's his birthday. He's been very sick."

Rory was seven today. Byron's ex-wife had agreed the three of them would share the day. The poor kid was finally coming back from the chemo, from all the radiation treatments. Rory's outlook was far from optimal, but the doctor's were letting in a little light lately, willing to make vague projections about long-term prospects. That was new, and it was good, and it annoyed Byron to have to be standing here, talking to some dishwater fugitive, regardless of the money it might make him. This gig chasing some forgotten writer's crazy daughter was a lucrative windfall—one badly needed with his boy's mounting hospital bills.

So Byron just wanted to verify this Shelby Hyde was here in this little beach place. He also needed to get some sense of this man Chase Alger's role in all the dark stuff back in Tennessee. When both of those goals were achieved, he had to update his client, this lawyer in New York, who would make the final decision about calling in the cops on the two. Meantime, Byron would be winging it back to his boy and to his estranged wife who was, lately, warmer to him.

"Short form, there are some very nasty concerns back in Tennessee regarding Miss Shelby Hyde, who, I presume, is inside there, whose place this is. Cops back there are looking for her, urgently. They want to talk with her, right now. My job is to help point them in the right direction. You two tore out of Tennessee the other night with no forwarding address—that never looks good, you know. Maybe it wasn't your intent, but you both ran like you're were in fear of making some Most Wanted list."

Chase shrugged. "What's any of that have to do with you? We're here for business reasons."

"Think again," Byron said. "I've been hired by an interested third-party to see if maybe you two weren't right here in this little hideaway. And here you are. You should probably know I was here last night, too. I even took pictures of you two out there in the surf. I emailed a few of the more discreet pictures to my client to prove I'd likely found you. Pictures were grainy, open to a little doubt, so that's why I'm here to see you in person."

"You took pictures of us last night?" Chase was seething. "Pictures of us like that?"

"Well, of you up and moving around, not so much of the *other*. Those pictures I did shoot were taken from public property, by the way—this field adjacent to the house here." Byron shrugged. "For all you or I know, my client's emailed those pictures to the cops up in Tennessee."

"Who is your client?"

"Afraid that's confidential."

"You're a real piece of work, pal." Chase began stalking slowly toward the man, though he wasn't too keen about it. Byron went six-two. Probably had fifty pounds on Chase.

With his left hand, Byron slipped off his sunglasses, folded one arm, then tucked the other down the collar of his T-shirt—like he was getting his shades out of the way in case it came to blows. Chase realized the man had his right arm behind his back—was it maybe gripping a gun, Chase wondered.

He stopped walking toward the private investigator.

Byron said, "Now, the lady is inside, right? Why don't we both go in and have a little chat and just wrap this up."

"She's not here," Chase said. "I'm alone."

"That's a lie," Byron said. "You were both here last night. You came in that car there. That car hasn't moved. Take a look at the rear passenger's side tire."

Reluctant to turn his back on the man, Chase stooped, squinted—saw an intact egg pressed up against the inner, backside of the tire. If the car had backed up an inch the egg would have been crushed.

"This is my living," Byron said. "I've lived this scene more times than I can count. I know it's all new to you, but to me it's just muscle memory to an inevitable end. Frankly, seeing she's here is a technicality at this point. I might as well just call my client and let him call the cops. Then I'll stand back and let the system work."

Chase looked at the front door again. Thank God it was still closed. He said, "This thing back in Tennessee she's supposedly tied to. What is it exactly?"

Byron said, "Cops dug up Shelby Hyde's mother," he said. "This time they autopsied the body. The first time they didn't do that because the woman was very sick, possibly terminal, so why bother, right? Then suspicions were raised. Questions asked. There was enough to justify exhumation."

Jesus, Chase thought, now what? He said, "What kind of questions? The woman died of cancer."

"That's right," Byron said. "Question is, why'd she die of cancer? More specifically, at whose hands? See, someone wasn't dosing Mrs. Hyde with the expensive drugs the insurance company was balking at having to pay for."

Chase frowned. "What the hell are you saying?"

"I'm saying someone deprived Amanda Hyde her cancer meds. That's same as murder, my friend. That's certainly how the police see it. Now, why don't you walk me inside so I can chat with the lady, bless her dark little heart? Near as I can tell, your hands are relatively clean in all of this, buddy. You're maybe not an accessory. Not quite yet, anyway. From your expression, I'm guessing most of this comes as news to you. But now you do know, and so now anything you do will be weighed in light of that knowing."

"And you're not a cop," Chase said. "You're on private property. I want you to go."

"What I am is a licensed investigator in good standing in the state of Florida. I'm okay with some key police here. I'm also a licensed bounty hunter. Really, Chase, please don't put me to the test. You will not like the result."

It happened so quickly, Chase wasn't certain what he was aware of first.

Was it the jerk of Byron's head, the detective's panicked awareness of someone moving behind Chase? Or was it the fact that Byron seemed to indeed be drawing a gun from behind his back?

Maybe it was the roar in his ear that left Chase's head ringing.

Or maybe the way this *little red divot* opened up in Byron's left temple, burping blood. It did that just a fraction of a second before some of the right side of Byron's face, including his right eye, disappeared in a pink spray.

As Byron's body was still falling, spilling brains and bone chips, Chase turned, raising a hand to his deafened ear.

Shelby stood there, naked, her towel fallen off and clumped there at her feet. She must have come out the back door.

The gun in her hand, some kind of big automatic, was still pointed at the fallen man, held at the ready like he might actually get up and need killing all over again.

Chase's knees quaked. He gasped to catch his breath. He looked again at Shelby. Her gun hand was rock steady.

64

Alone, fighting her fear, Ashley approached the revolving door. The door comprised her greatest moment of risk, Shawn had warned her, and she should try at all costs to avoid getting in the damned thing, whatever else happened. Before she reached the door, Franklin turned and glanced into the lobby.

Unable to check himself from his jolt of recognition, Franklin cupped hands to the front window and pressed his nose to the glass for a better look.

It didn't take any acting, after that. Ashley recoiled, pivoting and running toward the men's room, just as Shawn had instructed.

Franklin burst into the revolving door, knocking down an old woman exiting on the other side, sending her tumbling onto the sidewalk in the hard rain.

For some stage-setting—and to alert Shawn to her presence—Ashley picked up the aluminum trashcan by its chromed, flapping lid and shoved it up against the bathroom door, and then stepped back deeper into the men's room.

Franklin exploded through the door, sending the trashcan slamming back into the half-wall that blocked those in the lobby from seeing the urinals on the other side of the door.

Ashley backed toward one of the stalls, begging, "*Please…*"

After that, things didn't go quite to plan.

Franklin rushed Ashley, shoving her backward.

His berserker attack sent her sprawling into one of the toilet stall doors. The door swung open into the stall and Ashley fell through, nearly striking the back of her head on the toilet bowl. Franklin closed a hand over her mouth.

Franklin spoke into his other wrist, some kind of sleeve radio like the FBI agents in the movies were always barking orders into. Franklin said, "Luke? We're coming to the back door to you! Have Ralphie bring the car around, now! I may have to hit the bitch to control her. If I do, she's going to be groggy, maybe even out cold. If I have to carry her, we'll say she's diabetic and we're rushing her to the E.R. I'll be there in less than a minute."

Ashley figured that stuff about hitting her was a warning to her to comply and clam up.

As Franklin was speaking into his sleeve, Shawn lightly stepped down off the closed toilet lid he'd been perched atop. Under the raised partition, Shawn could see Ashley was still sprawled on the floor of the adjacent stall. Franklin's feet were pointed toward the toilet bowl. Shawn could see Franklin's hairy hands, struggling to gain purchase under Ashley's body.

Shawn waited until Franklin had Ashley about halfway off the floor—his hands full—then opened his own stall's door and crept out.

Ashley, who could see Shawn approaching behind, didn't react in a way that would tip Franklin. As Shawn raised the butt of the gun behind Franklin's ahead, Ashley rolled clear.

The smack of gun's butt against the back of the mercenary's head made a crunching noise that sounded deadly to Ashley.

Franklin fell face first into the stall. His mouth struck the toilet seat. Something that might have been a tooth skittered across the tile, shooting under the raised partition and into an adjacent toilet stall.

Ashley got her tangled hair out of her face with one hand, clutching her side with the other. She hoped she hadn't torn any stitches. "Did you kill him?"

"How the hell should I know?" Shawn pocketed the gun and gripped the back of Ashley's neck. "First time I've ever done that, you know."

"He's still breathing."

Shawn said, "That's good, I guess." He stroked her cheek. "Lets get out of here, now, Ash. This bastard has got friends out there, remember."

"Where do we go?"

"Out the front door. Then we shake a leg." Shawn reached into his pocket and took out the gun. "Here, your security blanket. Check the door into the lobby and make sure those other two gorillas aren't out there, watching. I'll take care of him."

Ashley shoved her gun in her coat pocket and peeked through the door into the lobby: there was no sign of Franklin's sidekick.

She looked back; Shawn was backing out of the stall, closing the door behind himself.

Shaking his hands, he said, "Can't leave the guy just laying on the floor out here. I propped him up on a seat."

Shawn took Ashley's arm and they fast-walked across the lobby and out the front door onto the street. It was still raining hard. The old woman was stretched out on the sidewalk. Some people were gathered around her, speaking urgently into cell phones. A young woman was kneeling down beside the elderly woman, holding her hand.

Watching and feeling quite guilty, Ashley said, "Where should we go?"

He shook his head. "Away from here, and fast. Why not your Italian restaurant?"

"I'm not sure I'm hungry after all this. If anything, I feel a little sick to my stomach. But sitting down would be good."

They stayed under the dripping scaffolds, trotting the short distance to Ashley's Italian restaurant. There were sirens closing-in now, maybe from the ambulance called for the old woman they'd seen sprawled on the sidewalk on their way out.

On the street, beyond the scaffolding, rain bounced knee-high off the pavement.

65

Chase was standing there, looking at the dead man, and all he could think was, *Jesus Christ Jesus Christ Oh, Jesus Christ...*

It was like it ran on some hellish loop in his head.

He turned and looked again at Shelby standing there naked, gun in hand.

She terrified him; he wondered if she might shoot him next.

Shelby smiled uncertainly. Her smile chilled him. She said, "Darling, don't look at me like that. I heard what he was saying, the lies he was telling that the stupid police clearly believe. I had to do it, had to, for us. He would have blocked our driveway, may have already disabled the car—we should check that right now."

She put down her gun and picked up her towel, moving toward him.

"We have another chance now," she said. She stood on tiptoe and kissed him. "Mexico—we'll be safe there. Untouchable."

Everything, everything was gone because of it—he knew it. His dream book contract, his imagined *nouveau riche* life. Everything he'd known this past quarter century was blown to hell and gone now, just as surely as if she'd put the gun to his head and pulled the trigger.

66

Shawn was putting away his phone as he returned to the table.

The waiter was just clearing their dishes. Shawn thought Ashley looked fairly wrung out: two glasses of wine and releasing tension seemed a too potent combination after all that the morning had brought them.

She pointed at the phone in his hand and said, "Is everything okay?"

This expression she couldn't read, a kind of distraction she hadn't seen before. "Too soon to tell," Shawn said. "Awaiting more information."

Ashley nodded, slowly. "Any indication Shelby or her minions have been trying to get in touch? You know, maybe to fire you for exhuming her mother's body?"

Shawn crossed one leg over the other. "No. I don't expect Ms. Hyde can find the time to do that just now. As her counsel-of-record—I mean on all the property paperwork, the insurance, the rights contracts and so forth, on nearly everything—I am the one the police tend to call when they can't reach her. This thing with Amanda's death is heating up. I think they might actually indict Shelby."

"For murder?"

"So it seems. Families. I'm telling you, they're trouble." He said softly, "Families, they'll destroy you. Some blood is poison."

"A murderess," Ashley said, hardly hearing him. She massaged her temples with her fingertips. She shivered. "Then you think Chase is in even more danger there with her?"

Shawn thought about it, then waded in. "I think Chase is far from in danger, Ash. I think Shelby believes she's found her father."

She shivered and wrapped her arms around herself. "Really?"

"I really do."

"If they are intimate, and if Shelby truly thinks he is Everett Hyde then, *my God*. I mean, that's so far beyond sick."

Shawn nodded. "Pretty damned twisted for certain."

Ashley gestured absently at the menus stacked on the table next to their bottle of wine. "You may want to go ahead and order some dessert. I did that for myself already. Thought I'd found more of my appetite. Although now I don't feel so hungry."

"Maybe. Though I think I've had my fill, too." He flipped open the dessert menu, and resting his hands on its open pages, scanned his options.

He was surprised when she closed her hand over his, her thumb rubbing the matted hair on the back of his hand. "Thanks for all that back there," she said. "If you hadn't been with me, to protect me, I'm sure they would have me again now. I was going to walk right through that front door. I never saw Franklin until you pointed him out."

Shawn smiled, looking at their hands. "Forget it. Anyway, you might simply have outrun him. Those fools have made themselves insanely bulky—with your legs and athleticism, you'd lose them across any distance."

She said, "Run? Not with my side like it is. More wine?"

"No," he said. "I think we're both wined out, don't you?"

"After this, I thought we'd go back to the loft," she said. "It's a rainy day. It's a good day to loaf inside. Just hang out, I guess, while we wait to hear from Selma and Ace."

Shawn smiled and moved his hand from under hers.

Ashley started to frown, then smiled as he spread his fingers wide.

She slipped her fingers between his and squeezed, smiling at their tangled hands.

"That sounds a wonderful plan," he said. "Yeah, Ash. Let's do just that."

67

He was holding her in his arms, still trying to find his breath. His heart was still pounding. He kept thinking of the mess behind him—the bloody heap that had been a man, talking reasonably to him just moments before, calmly laying out what a monster this woman in his arms was.

Shelby said, "Probably nobody even heard the shot. Only place close by is the empty guest house, and with the wind and the waves? If nobody was driving by just now, we're probably just fine." *Just fine?*

She said, "You have to protect us now, darling. We have to think what to do."

It began to rain—a fine drizzle that would soon pick up tempo.

Shaking his head, Chase let go of her. He took a breath and forced himself to look at the result of her shot.

Flies were already at the bloody wound. He wanted to be sick. He said, "Why? He was just a private eye, had no real authority to stop us."

"A private eye and a bounty hunter," Shelby said. "Haven't you ever watched that idiot blond bounty hunter on TV? He wouldn't hesitate to detain a couple of normal people like us."

Normal people? Chase just shook his head. "He wasn't like the idiot on TV. He was trying to be reasonable." Chase wanted to push her for confirmation of Byron's claims regarding her mother's death. But Chase was still fearful of her, and she was still between him and the gun.

"If I only had a boat," Shelby said. "You could take us out there, and we could get rid of this thing that way." She gestured at Byron's body.

"I don't know how to drive a boat," he said thickly. Chase looked at his hands.

Shelby, standing close against him, trying to embrace him again, said, "Nonsense. When you ran down to the Keys with Bobby and took that boat—"

"I'm not the man you think I am…" He shook his head. Last thing he wanted now was a reopening of that crazy argument. "I don't know how to drive a boat," he said again, softly this time, sounding defeated.

She was right enough about the other thing, though. They needed to get moving, to get over some border they couldn't be dragged back across. If this shooting was ever tied to him, he was as doomed as Shelby.

Shelby said, "Well, we can't bury him here, even if I had a shovel. This ground, this close to the water, it's impossible to dig a useful grave." She was shivering now; a cold rain was beginning to fall. "That plane is still waiting to take us to Mexico. If we hurry, we can still make it."

He just stood there, dumbly blinking back the rain, looking at the body.

After a while he said, "That gun you used to kill him— that was *your* gun? Registered to you?"

"No, it was something Brick arranged for me," Shelby said. "He claimed the gun was clean. Let's go inside. I need to get dressed and get everything packed."

"You do that," Chase said. "Leave me the towel—I need to wrap it around his... head." He'd swallowed hard and said the last word though it didn't seem accurate enough to describe what was left. He had this idea about getting the man's keys, then pulling Byron's car into the driveway and hiding the body in the trunk. He could drive the car to... to where? In this heat, it was going to start to smell very soon, and there was so much development around the general area...

It was like Shelby read his mind. She said, "Every minute we stand here trying to think what do with that thing is another minute we don't have. Just pull it inside and throw dirt over the... you know." She didn't wait for an answer, just dashed inside, naked on tiptoe in the rain.

Alone there in the driving rain, soaked to bone, he surveyed the scene. They were fugitives now. Really runners.

Once they got to Mexico—if they even *made* it there—that was where they would stay, perhaps forever.

He figured he'd die down there, maybe after even growing old first. To the locals, he'd be some mysterious and probably wanted gringo with blood on his hands. Close enough.

Chase tried to get the towel around Byron's ruined face—as much to cover his one accusing eye as to contain the mess, then grabbed the man's ankles and dragged him inside.

He said aloud and rather bitterly to himself, "Welcome to your next new life."

68

Before they left the Italian restaurant, Shawn's cell phone rang. He excused himself again to take the call. He came back, looking a bit agitated. Ashley said, "Something wrong?"

"Just some headache with a client. Nothing I don't know how to fix. Already took steps to that end." He smiled, though not too convincingly. "Forget about it. We have some loafing to do, remember?"

They took a cab back to Chase's loft. After they got there, Shawn briefly ran to the corner store for some things—toothpaste, a toothbrush and a fresh razor.

Ashley took advantage of the time alone to change the sheets on the bed. Not that she thought they were necessarily headed there, but a part of her—a lonely, hurting part of her—didn't know if she'd put up much resistance if Shawn pressed for it. She was attracted to him. She liked his smile and voice. And when they talked about writing? That was bliss.

Shawn dropped his purchases on the sink, then they passed an hour listening to music—Tom Waits' *Rain Dogs*. They sat by the windows, looking down on the rainy city, lost in deep talk.

More of that talk centered on her than on Shawn, Ashley came to realize, but she went with it. They talked a good deal about Ashley's literary influences. They switched from Tom Waits' music to Lana Del Rey.

Shawn had pressed her again about the memoir, tried to talk her out of it.

"I just don't know," Ashley said. "Maybe I won't do it. Probably I won't. It is against all my instincts. And it's all been so crazy. Not sure anyone would even believe it."

Shawn's fingers combed through her hair. "Like the man said, life is what happens to a writer between drafts."

Ashley smiled, turning her head into his hand and kissing his palm. "I'm appropriating that one immediately."

"It's always been a favorite," Shawn said. "That one, and another, by Nin: 'We write to taste life twice, in the moment, and in retrospection.'"

"We've got to get you published, Shawn."

His expression gave her pause. She hadn't meant to sound superior; hadn't meant to lord her book deal over him, not at all.

Then she realized he maybe didn't take it that way. He smiled and said, "I write now simply because I love to write, Ash. It'd be great to have the stuff on shelves, but really, I'm writing for the sake of writing, in the end. I don't know that I really crave an audience or—" He hesitated a long time, then stroked her hair behind her ear. "Well, what you think matters to me because I respect your writing, Ash. I truly do."

Ashley smiled again and looked down at the city, at the people down there bustling and scurrying in the cold rain. "I'm told I'm going to get a light edit whatever that means. Not sure how I feel about that."

"Trust in your novel," Shaw said, stroking her hair. "I've read it and I'm here to tell you it's superb. You've written an amazing debut. It doesn't need work at all, really."

"Feels like there just could be more, maybe," she said. "Not sure what, but if I had more time…"

"You can run yourself crazy thinking like that, sweetheart. I'll burden you with one more quote. Wilde, this time. Oscar said no book is ever finished, only abandoned."

Ashley rested her head on her hand. "Now that depresses me."

"It shouldn't. It's the writing life, that's all. We're privileged—or at least you are—to be a part of it."

"How on earth did you end up a lawyer, Shawn? The way you talk about writing, with reverence and passion, I don't see how you ended up being some legal eagle."

"We all have day-jobs, Ash. At some point, anyway. How'd Eliot soldier on in that goddamn bank? William Carlos Williams was a doctor."

"I wish we had access to your computer," Ashley said.

He smiled uncertainly. "Why?"

"So I could read something of yours, Shawn. It's only fair. You've read my stories. You've read my novel."

Lana now in the background, *Video Games.*

He chewed his lip. "Okay, I'm going to risk it for you. I need to use your computer though, you know, to access my stuff."

"My computer's all yours." She smiled. "I mean, you already know all my passwords, all my access codes, right?"

Shawn's story was about a working man and woman who meet inadvertently in a hotel lounge. To their mutual surprise, the strangers drift into a night of passion. It was a marvelous character study, Ashley thought.

Much of the characterization advanced through sly, knowing, pitch-perfect dialogue and spare but evocative description.

"It's wonderful," she said. "Surely this is published somewhere."

He shrugged but looked very pleased by her reaction. "You know the short story market," he said. "There isn't one anymore. And, as you said of your own writing, there's maybe too much story in my stories. Probably far too much for the lit mags as they stand now. Things happen in my stories, too, just like you said of your own work. Guess you could call me another throwback."

Ashley impulsively leaned forward and kissed Shawn. Her hand cupped the back of his neck, the tip of her tongue parted his teeth.

Soon enough, he had her shirt and bra off and he was also naked to the waist. He was crouched over her on the couch, tonguing her nipples to aching stiffness when Ashley's cell phone rang. She checked its glowing screen.

It was Selma. Ashley said, breathy, "I have to take it."

"Sure, do it," Shawn said, his voice hoarse with passion.

Selma said, "Have you heard from Ace this morning?"

Ashley squirmed a bit as Shawn stayed at her right breast, suckling gently. She bit her lip and tangled her fingers in his hair, giving a not-too-convincing shove to push him away. A shove he ignored. "Uh, no," Ashley managed. "I haven't."

Shawn was unsnapping her jeans as he kissed her offered throat. Selma said, "Ashley, are you ill again?"

"No. Well, I just came from the doctor. My doctor. He gave me some pills."

"Groggy then?"

Ashley raised her hips so he could pull down her jeans. "That's it." Shawn pulled them down over her feet and tossed them aside. He kissed his way down her flat belly, careful to avoid her right side. He tongued her through her panties. "I'll let you know if I hear anything," Ashley managed.

"Good, rest up," the Hyena said. "I'll call Ace myself. I'll do it right now."

Squirming, losing herself to it, Ashley hung up her phone. She managed to turn off the ringer and pitched her phone onto the side table behind her head.

Shawn had her panties down around her ankles. He was kissing her there, and she realized there was some friction. At first she thought it might be his face, his beard to be exact, but he had shaved just a few hours ago. She realized then it was her own body—her pubic hair was growing back. She said, "Sorry, I haven't been able to get back to—"

"Don't," he said thickly, not stopping what he was doing. "Grow it back. I prefer women to—" The rest was lost as he thrust his tongue more deeply into her, setting her legs to trembling.

She was still under him, her legs wrapped around his hips. Shawn's breath was coming hard against her throat; his face was buried in her damp hair. The rain lashed the windows and glassware and bric-a-brac vibrated with the thunder. Ashley thought she could actually feel the subtle sway of the building in the high winds.

It was a fact: Shawn was a better, more attentive and passionate lover than Chase.

Maybe it was just because it was the first time, and he was determined to please her, but Ashley sensed it would always be so with Shawn. He lingered long in her after, held her close to him afterward.

She was content to spend the day on the sweat-streaked, distressed leather couch that was sticky in spots now.

At least the couch would be easy to wash clean; sheets Ashley might have felt driven by guilt to burn.

Here she was, having abandoned sex with another man in Chase's own place, a place she had more or less come to think of as her own the past few hours.

Shawn finally rolled onto the floor and rose on unsteady legs. "Afraid I really have to check my messages," he said.

"Me too."

Shawn scooped up his new cell. Naked, he walked into the bathroom, tapping his phone's screen. Ashley watched him go, then picked up her blouse and spread it under herself since she was sitting up. She picked up her phone and checked its screen. One new call: Ace. She tapped to return his call.

"Christ, you had me worried," Ace said. "Then Selma got hold of me and told me you're on some pharmaceutical holiday. You lucid now, baby?"

"Sure." For some reason, Ashley was uncomfortable talking to the big man while she was naked. She grabbed a pillow and held it over her breasts. "What's happening?"

"We're booked on a flight tonight if you're up to it. Florida. Seems Ms. Hyde has a little place down there: a little beach house owned by a certain Dashiell Hunt, LTD. I've got some friends in intelligence. Had me a report of Ms. Hyde having booked her own flight south yesterday."

That set Ashley's heart beating. "You're sure?"

"No doubts, baby."

"Look, something darker is going on with that woman," Ashley said. "Something we didn't know before. I'm not sure we can just charge down there and confront her like we thought." Ashley told Ace about the exhumation of Amanda Hyde's body and the possible murder charges coming from Tennessee against Shelby Hyde.

Ace listened, then said, "All the more reason for us to do it now. If the media gets hold of her being arrested on matricide and so on, we're both going to be racing a bunch of goddamned straight-to-paperback True Crime writers to try and get our books to market first. That won't do. We'll be royally fucked."

"I'm frankly more concerned about us getting Chase out of—"

"A better reason to do it the way we discussed, then," Ace said, cutting her off. "Look-it, if your ex is hobnobbing with this woman, and if she's even half the killer those hick cops think she is, lover boy's going to end up dead or an accessory, mark my words. Now, I'm going down there to the fucking Sunshine State, and I leave in five hours. I'm taking a couple of tough boys with me, so we'll be safe enough, if that's your fear."

Ashley sighed. "No, it's not. I'm coming with you. I have some things to catch you up on, too."

"Give it to me now, short form, baby."

Ashley did that, a quick account of her brush with Franklin and about Shawn coming to her rescue. She mentioned then that Shawn might be coming along with her.

Ace said tightly, "I don't like him tagging along, not a damn bit." He sighed. "But if you vouch for this lawyer, I guess I'll go along 'cause you sound adamant."

"I am."

He cursed, then gave her directions so she could find him at the airport.

Ashley hung up. She cocked her head; the shower was running. Smiling, she tossed aside the pillow, scooped up her now stained blouse and wadded it under the sofa to deal with later. She tiptoed into the bathroom, tried the knob and found it unlocked. Ashley could just make out his dim form through the steam and the pebbled glass of the shower door. She slid the door back and he smiled, making room. Shawn said, "Look, I hate this so much, but I'm going to have to be going soon. I'll probably be gone just a couple of days."

Ashley frowned, her palms pressed to his pecs. "Where are you going?"

"Business trip I can't avoid. I'll catch a cab to my place. Just pick up my bags already there and hop the plane. If I'm followed, fine. Let them chase me around the Windy City. Be fewer of them for you to deal with, at least."

He smiled sadly and cupped her chin in his hand. "God, how I hate this. Especially after these past couple of hours. They've been heaven. I hope me going away for a day or two doesn't bring you to your senses about what we've started here."

"Have we started something?" She said, "And if we have, is it something you want to continue?"

A long kiss. "Oh, yes."

She smiled. "Good. The timing is terrible though. Ace called. He's tracked down a piece of property owned by Shelby Hyde in Florida. It's—"

Shawn rapped the shower wall tiles with his knuckles. "I could have given you that Florida address if I knew you wanted it, honey. I keep underestimating you," Shawn said, shaking his head. "You are so slick."

Ashley said, "Ace used what I found in Tennessee, this shell or front called Dashiell Hunt, LTD, to find the Florida property."

"If I only knew you were looking for it…"

"It's where we're headed, tonight." Ashley hesitated. She said softly, "Any other property I should know about? In case this one is a bust?"

Shawn licked his upper lip and shook his head. "If there is, speaking as her legal counsel, I don't know about it, either."

He leaned in and kissed Ashley then, slow and hard. He pulled away; she was reluctant to stop. He said, "Make that trip if you feel you must, honey. But let that Ace go through the door first, and make sure you have your gun with you. Or better, wait for me to get there, won't you? Give me twenty-four hours and I'll be able to join you. We'll all go in together that way. Promise me?"

"I can't promise that," Ashley said. "You act like I can actually control Ace. But that's clearly not in the cards. And he's afraid events might overtake us. I'm not sure he's not right."

"Try to do it for me?" Another hard, hungry kiss.

"I'll try," she said. It sounded to her ears like the empty promise it was.

"After we get out of here and dry off, I'll give you my cell phone number," he said. "You can call me there with the information about where I can find you."

Ashley pressed her palm to his heart. "How soon do you have to leave?"

Shawn kissed her again. "Well… not this very second of course."

69

Chase had deluded himself that increasing relief might come at intervals along the path of their white-knuckle dash down to southern Mexico.

He thought some stress would lift once they had cleared check-in. Maybe more would dissipate when they boarded the private jet, and still more when they were at last airborne.

Most profound of all, he anticipated, would be the relief that would come when the pilot announced, as Shelby had instructed him to do, that they had crossed into the safety of Mexican airspace.

That announcement had finally come. Shelby squealed and mixed them drinks. She handed Chase a margarita on the rocks.

He sipped. It was a heavy pour on the tequila, almost too bitter to enjoy. He guessed then Shelby was aiming to keep him drunkenly numb to memories of their bloody morning. He put the drink aside.

Shelby, for her part, seemed strangely unperturbed.

He said abruptly, "What the hell is to become of us? I really wonder."

"We'll let things cool down," she said with a half-smile. "A month, two months. Maybe a year, if that's what it takes. We'll pass the time, getting tans, making love and eating good food and swimming to stay fit against all the drinks we'll be enjoying. And we'll work on getting you back your memory. We'll take stock. We'll bide our time until it's safe to announce you're back."

He decided to let that insistent implication that he was Everett Hyde pass again. At least for now. Instead he said, "Exactly how much of what that private detective was saying to me did you hear?"

"I didn't kill Mother," Shelby said. Her hazel eyes stared into his, unblinking. "That must have been Arick," she said. "He was a problem, though it took me time to see that. He was trying to take over, exert more influence as he wheedled his way into the family business. He was the one who found and directed mother's personal nurse. I was a fool to trust that bastard, and my misplaced trust cost Mother, dearly. I was just a fool. Just as I was an idiot to trust Shawn Dalton. He doesn't know his place, either."

"But you did kill Byron," Chase said gently.

"I did. But it was, well, it wasn't an accident, but it was a kind of... reflex. Something that just happened because I saw no other way. He would have detained us, waited for the police. Where would I have been then, my love?"

Shelby shrugged her shoulders. "I'd be lost, of course. After just finding one another, we'd be pulled apart again." She thought about harder, watching his face all the while. She said, "The more I think about it, really look back on it with a cold eye, the more I see it was self-defense. He saw my gun, though it wasn't pointed at him when I was coming up behind you. Out of reflex maybe, he reached for his own gun. So I shot first. Instinct. I was protecting us. Please stop worrying, darling. Nothing can touch us now."

This far-away look passed over her. "We have nothing to worry about but our dreams tonight. You know—dreams or nightmares—about what happened to us this morning. About what *we* had to do." She put her glass down alongside his. Shelby said, "We'll have to help one another through those nightmares, won't we?"

She began fumbling with his belt. He said, "What are you doing?"

"Cockpit door is locked. Crew has orders not to barge in. We won't be disturbed." She pulled his jeans and underwear down around his ankles. She raised her dress—no panties—and straddled him. He cursed himself for his ready erection.

Her tongue was between his lips. "Just this now," she said. "Just this." She thrust more frenziedly against him. "Just this, father."

EVERETT

"Identity is the theft of self."
— Estee Martin

70

They'd almost missed the place, swathed as its driveway was with under- and overgrowth; a riot of long untended shrubs and trees.

Ashley and Ace sat sweating across the street in dark rental sedan, the engine off and the windows rolled down. Ace had decreed dark clothes be worn in case they ended up going in at night, so Ashley wore black jeans and trainers and a long-sleeved black T-shirt. She'd brought along a black baseball cap, but it was too hot to wear that in the car. Tired of lifting her heavy hair off the back of her neck, she finally knotted it off in a ponytail; pushed up her sleeves and raised her shirt and tied it off below the edge of her rib cage, revealing her bandaged belly. She fanned herself with a copy of the folded up local paper.

Two of Ace's "friends"—one a Florida native who'd provided ordinance—were creeping around somewhere inside Shelby's jungle of a front yard.

Through the open car windows, Ashley could hear the slap and draw of the distant tide. Some big bird, maybe an old heron, flapped its heavy wings, gaining just enough altitude to avoid smacking the hood of their car.

Walkie-talkie crackle startled Ashley, then a voice: "Skipper, we've got meat."

Ashley arched her eyebrows. "Meat? What does that mean?"

"A body," Ace said. Ashley swallowed hard. Ace said into his walkie-talkie, "Elaborate."

More crackles, then: "Male. Took a cap in the face. At least twelve hours dead. Shot him outside and dragged him in, from the looks."

"Any signs of any other bodies?"

"No, just this one. Phone line's been cut, too."

"I'm on my way in," Ace said. "Goes without saying, don't touch anything."

"We're not calling this in, Skipper?"

"Let me look first, but chances are not." Ace said to Ashley, "You better wait. This guy was shot to death. It's going to be bloody. And he's been there a while. Bugs and birds may have been at him. And in this heat, he's already much the worse for wear."

Ashley nodded, uncertain. She got out her phone. "I said we're not calling the police," Ace said. "Or I don't think we are."

"I was calling Shawn, checking in," she said. "Telling him what we found."

"I'm not sure that's a good idea, either," Ace said. "I forgot to mention. After you told me about this attack at your doctor's office, I fished around. Seems a man was found dead in the ground-floor men's room. It was Shelby's man, Franklin."

Ashley said, "He was definitely breathing after Shawn slugged him."

"Either way, no cops until I say. So no lawyers either, right?"

Ashley put away her phone and tipped her head back against the seat. "I'll wait here," she said. "Just wait. No calls."

Ace softly patted her check with a big, hard hand. "Atta girl."

Shelby's Yucatan beach house too vividly evoked her Florida hide-away: substitute sand for grass and swap out adobe for stucco and you were almost there.

Shelby had a thumb hooked in the back pocket of his jeans. "What do you think?"

Chase managed a smile he surely didn't feel. "It's great."

It *had* to be. It was maybe where he'd be spending the rest of his haunted life, however long that was to be. He said, "But what if someone follows? What if they find us like they found us in Florida?"

Shelby kissed him. "Nobody can follow us here," she said. "Nobody else knows this place even exists. Not even mother knew. This was a private gift, left me in trust. It became mine when I turned eighteen. It was a last gift from fath—" Shelby stumbled, smiled, and kissed him again. "From *you*. It's your secret writing retreat. Where you wrote much of your second and third novels, according to the sealed note you arranged to have turned over to me when I came of age. Given to me by a lawyer other than Shawn Dalton, thank God. Some one-shot special estate attorney." She leaned into him. "You're such a strategist."

She hugged him close and wrapped her arms around Chase's waist, her cheek pressed to his bicep. "Only two people on earth know that this place even exists: Everett Hyde, and his loving daughter. So we're really safe now."

Shelby kissed him again, passionately, and smiled. "So, if only you and me know about this place, you see now how secure we are, don't you? She beamed up at him. "Nothing can touch us now."

71

The smell of the ocean was strong through the open car windows. Ace called over the wind shear, "I suppose we could have headed back tonight, but I'm frankly wrung-out after this ragged-ass day. We'll crash at the hotel. Head back north in the morning."

They'd driven off from the bloody scene without calling into report the dead body in Shelby's little beach house. Their silence was another tactic on Ace's part to buy them time until they could figure out a way to get some lead on Shelby and Chase's whereabouts—a frankly mercenary bid to preserve their exclusive material for their respective books. It was wrong of course—downright criminal—but Ashley went along.

She pressed Ace for a description of what he'd found, but Ace demurred, just mumbled, "Brains and bugs and a lot of blood, baby. Leave it at that, sugar."

"But who was he?"

He shot her a look then, said, "What, you think I poked around the body looking for identification?"

Ashley held her ground. "Honestly? Yeah, I do."

A terrible smile. "Well… you'd be right. He is a private investigator. Or he was. Guy named Marcus Byron. It looks like it went as my guy says. Some kind of confrontation outside. Dude got himself capped in the head and his body dragged in. Some dirt and torn up grass thrown over the bloody trail. Strictly amateur hour. Whoever did the hauling threw up next to the body. That's DNA, potentially. If it belongs to Mr. Alger... Well, you know. More nails in the coffin."

They checked into a hotel, not far from the airport. Ace said, "Boys and me are going to get a couple of drinks. You joining us? Your rounds are on us, hon'."

Ashley smiled knowingly. "I'll bet. Sounds good, though. But I'll catch up with you in a while. I need to stop by my room first, check my email."

Ace said, "When you get tired of doing that, you come to the bar. Me and the boys will show you a good time."

"Sure," she said.

Her room was the usual anonymous hotel suite. This one had a writing desk, at least. She was feeling dehydrated and decided to treat herself to an overpriced soft drink from the hallway vending machine—something caffeinated to fire her brain while she plowed through her email. As a kind of afterthought, she remembered her loaner gun. She took it from its hiding place in her luggage under her underwear and stuck it in her pocket, hiding its grip under her untucked T-Shirt.

Swinging her plastic Coke bottle by its neck, she walked down the long common corridor, back to her room. She slid the key card into the lock, waited for the red light to turn green, then began to open the door.

There was a sharp punch to her right kidney that nearly caused Ashley to pass out. A hand closed over her mouth. She tried to bite the hand, but it closed tighter, cutting off oxygen. She was manhandled into her room and slung across the bed. She landed sideways across her luggage. Her attacker snarled, "Scream and it'll go a lot worse for you."

72

He followed them to the cantina, idling in the dirt lot with his headlights off while they parked their car.

Shelby was driving. She slid out from behind the wheel and clutched at the car door to keep from falling. It was no revelation to their watcher she was drunk: her weaving during the fifteen miles between the beach house and the cantina had convinced the man tailing them someone very intoxicated was at the wheel.

Now she slammed the driver's side door—too hard—giggling and leaning against the car to stay upright on her stiletto heels.

Chase shambled out of his side of the car and closed his door—not quite so hard as Shelby had—and walked carefully around the back of the car.

In the parking lot light he suddenly looked older than his years. Chase wrapped an arm around Shelby's slender waist. Chase seemed dangerously sober... and wary.

Their watcher couldn't decide whether it was an affectionate or a pragmatic gesture on Chase's part grabbing her like that. Without his support, Shelby likely would have ended up on her world-class ass or on her face in the dust.

As the couple made their way into the cantina, their shadow turned on his car's headlights, palmed the wheel and headed back to the beach house at speed.

He dropped off some of his supplies, then parked his rental car in front of the neighbor's house—if you could truly regard a structure so far away as neighboring. He jogged back to Shelby's beach house. He broke out a bedroom window with his elbow, knocking out stubborn glass shards with knuckles, and undid the latch. The man slipped in through the window and began turning on light switches with elbows while pulling on latex gloves.

There were several sealed cardboard boxes in the living room. He pulled out a utility knife and began slitting packing tape and tearing back box flaps. He found manuscripts. Lots of them. He read a few things here and there. Christ, wasn't it every bit as bad as he remembered?

One manuscript, however, that unfinished work—now, some of that was bloody marvelous. It was intended to be his masterpiece. It was so much better than he remembered.

But he couldn't bring it to a finish all those years ago. Now, with much more time under his belt—maybe his unconscious working at vexing plot problems during all those intervening years—well, hot *damn* if he didn't know how to drive that one home.

A rueful smile: in some, he guessed, the dream dies hard.

He picked up that particular manuscript box and opened the front door and carried it to the edge of the yard. He stashed the box in a tangle of trees by the end of the drive-way—something he'd retrieve later.

He wandered back inside, sweating now, and rummaged around some more. He found a couple of guns. He emptied their clips and put the bullets in his pocket. He shoved the empty clips back into the guns and returned them to their hiding places.

For another thirty or so minutes, he continued to search the house. Then he went back outside and fetched the first of four five-gallon plastic gasoline containers. He emptied them throughout the house, the stench so strong it set his eyes to watering.

He shut off every light but the one in the bathroom, the only windowless room in the house. He closed the bathroom door, leaving only a crack open to better hear outside.

He pulled out a paperback copy of *Rain Dogs*, the last of the three novels he had published under *that* name—a dog-eared copy he had snagged from one of the bookshelves in the bedroom. The spine of the book was broken. Given Shelby's sexual proclivities, he suspected that was a result of myriad one-handed reads.

Alas... what a piece of work that sorry, twisted child had turned out to be. He wondered if it was all inside her from the jump, or if his books had done it to her. The latter prospect chilled him.

Sighing at the bloody mystery that was Shelby, he sat on the edge of the bathtub and started to read.

Car doors outside; slamming closed hard—too hard—from drunken shoves.

He turned off the bathroom light and tossed the paperback onto the top of the toilet's water tank.

He crept into the living room, sat on the couch and pulled out the automatic. He screwed in the suppressor.

Giggling, Shelby swung open the door and held it for Chase. They had some plastic bags in their hands. Must have stopped for provisions.

Shelby flipped the light switch with her elbow, her arms weighted with bags. She wrinkled her nose and said, "That smell!"

She saw him, saw the gun, and dropped the bags.

He leveled the gun at her belly.

This gasp. Shelby said, "Shawn?"

73

Ashley was in agony from the punch. She couldn't find the wind to muster a scream, but she managed to roll off the bed before he hurled himself across her.

Her attacker landed belly first on the bed where she had been. His arm tipped her open suitcase backward off the foot of the bed, spilling its contents. His gun flew from his hand.

Ashley skidded backward against the wall, her belly burning from where her gun's butt had dug into her surgical site. She was racked by bouts of nausea. She forced herself to her unsteady feet.

He was spread-eagle, belly-down on the bed, his head hanging off the side of the mattress and hands frantically groping for his lost gun. He grasped Ashley's ankle. He twisted her leg and Ashley fell, her head slamming into the lid of her suitcase. Something hard was digging into her left breast.

Still unarmed, the man scrambled off the bed, moving to pin Ashley to the floor with his body.

Ashley forced her hand between them, wrapping her hand around the butt of her gun. She strained to twist its muzzle into his belly. Snarling, he wrapped both hands around Ashley's throat.

"Fucking bitch," he said. He slammed her head against the floor. Ashley saw splashes of color. She was gagging, unable to breathe.

She pulled the trigger of the gun, frantically, over and over.

The gun's recoil, reflected back by his bulk, actually amplified by it, nearly broke her wrist. But the point-blank hits to his stomach suppressed the sound of the shots.

His hands fell from her throat.

Ashley felt something warm against her belly and crotch, felt it through the cotton of her T-shirt and her jeans.

Her attacker groaned, tried to raise himself on his fists, knuckles digging into the carpet. Ashley kicked frantically at the floor as his weight lifted, skidding backward from under him.

Raising a hand, grasping again at her ankle, he reached a last time, then coughed blood into her suitcase and collapsed across it.

Ashley's cell phone was on the floor next to her hairbrush. Rubbing her throat with one hand, Ashley pushed buttons with the other.

Ace answered immediately. Ashley dimly heard laughter, some woman's voice… music. It took Ace a few seconds to grasp it. He repeated, "A man just attacked you in your room?"

"I shot him, over and over." Ashley's voice was raw and cracking. She almost sounded androgynous to her own ears. She feared her windpipe might be damaged. And she was shaking now, began sobbing as she stared at the dead man on her floor.

Now *Ace's* voice was different. He said urgently, "Bucky and me, we're running to your room, Luv."

"I think I'm going to black out," she mumbled.

"Don't you do that, darling! Get to the door and open it for me! Do it! We're almost there, sweetie, do you hear me? Do you understand me?"

Ashley staggered to the door. She pulled down on the door handle and swung the door open wide. The doorknob slammed into the rubber stopper on the wall and rebounded. Ashley shoved an arm into the crack to keep the door from locking again.

Her cell phone tumbled from her numb hand. She fell to her knees. She was seeing spots. With a shaking right hand, she grabbed the plastic "Do Not Disturb" sign and tugged it from the knob. She wedged it in the door between the hasp and its catch.

Then she blacked out.

74

"Shelby... Chase," Shawn said. "Please, close the door and lock it behind you. Then you both take six steps inside and get down on your knees."

Shelby snorted. She said, "Are you fucking kidding?"

"Down on your knees, Shelby." Shawn pointed at the floor with the end of his gun. "Do it, both of you. I have no intention of underestimating either of you when it comes to potential for mayhem. After all, one of you is now a killer in the eyes of the Tennessee law. One of you soon will be the same sorry thing in Florida."

Shawn nodded at Shelby and said, "Don't think about engaging in brinksmanship with me, Shelby. You have no grasp of my boundaries. Truth be told, I don't think I do anymore, either."

Seething, Shelby closed the door and twisted the deadbolt. She knelt down.

"You, too," Shawn said to Chase. "On your knees, buddy. Might want to take up prayer while you're down there." He shrugged. "You never know, right? There *might* be something on the other side."

Chase looked from Shelby to Shawn and back again. "Are you insane?"

Shawn took aim and fired a shot about an inch from Chase's right foot. He said, "On your knees, Bobby! Get down there, Judas."

Shelby looked at Shawn, incredulous. "What the hell are you talking about? He's not Bobby Bristow! He's Everett Hyde!"

Shaking, falling to his knees and raising his hands as he settled onto the carpet, Chase said, "Just who the hell is Bobby Bristow?"

"You are," Shawn said.

"He's Everett Hyde," Shelby said, nodding at Chase.

Shawn shook his head. "You poor twisted sick child," he said to Shelby. "He's not Everett Hyde."

Shelby wasn't backing down: "He is—mother thought so. I know he is. All the evidence—"

"Is wrong," Shawn said, cutting her off. "He's Bobby Bristow, the bane of my tortured existence. The monster who brought us all to this bloody crossroads."

She said, "How can you say that? He—"

Shawn pointed a thumb at his own chest. "I know, because I'm Everett Hyde."

75

Ashley had the vague sense of being lifted, carried. Voices…

One of Ace's guys said, "We caught a break, Skipper. Blood's pretty much all on her or in her luggage. Though everything of hers still in the suitcase is a wreck. All of her pants and shirts. Slack and blouses. Whatever the hell the skirts call 'em. All she's got to wear out of here is some under-things."

Ace: "Good. Good about the suitcase catching all that cocksucker's blood, I mean. That is a hell of a lucky break. Get her clothes sizes from the tags. There was a discount store we passed on the drive in. Pick her up some stuff, Buck. The rest goes into that luggage along with some big stones. Toss it off a bridge. Get her a new suitcase, too. Once I get her in the tub, I'll give you my plastic to pay for it all."

"And the meat, Skipper?"

"Out the sliding glass door there," Ace said. "We'll wait until we've got a clear shot at hustling him out the back door and down the beach. Take his wallet, rings. His wristwatch, if he has one. Then we'll toss him in the tide to cover for the lost blood. Let some crabs get at him and hope the cops take it for a mugging gone bad."

Then Ashley felt her pants being peeled down; she heard water running. Ace said, "Here, take these clothes, too. They're soaked through with the son of a bitch's blood."

Ashley was naked and she could feel warm water. She felt rough hands briskly rubbing at her. She could smell perfumed soap, the cheap acrid stuff hotels always seemed to spring for.

Ace said, "Christ almighty, what a fucking mess. Still Ashley, taking down a gorilla like that? You *have* to have my children. Holy Christ, even our daughters would be like fucking Amazons."

76

Shelby pointed at Chase. "*He's* Everett Hyde. Now put away that gun before I decide to do more than fire your ass, Shawn."

Chase looked at Shelby with stricken eyes. He said thickly, "You swore Shawn never knew about this place. Think about it, Shelby. You said only you and your father knew about this place. And here he is." Chase jerked his head in Shawn's direction.

"Listen to him, Shelby." He looked around the room and smiled. "My old writing get-away. Hasn't changed much at all, really."

Shelby was still fighting it. "Everything, everything mother's people found that so scared her, everything the investigators found for me in the past few weeks, it all points to Chase being my father. Everything. All of it."

"Can't argue with that on the surface," Shawn said with a sad smile. He shrugged. "But it also points to Chase being Bobby. Sick and evil as you are, I actually feel sorry for you, Shelby, learning it like this."

Chase said, "Who the hell is this Bobby?"

"Bobby Bristow," Everett said. "My best friend. *Heh.*" His eyes went far away, and he said, "You were always there for me, Bobby. Always with me. From the time we were kids to that last run down to the Keys. We were always together. Inseparable. Mostly from your direction. Good Christ, what you cost me, times over."

Shawn smiled again. The expression unnerved Shelby and Chase. Shawn said, "Tonight, Bobby, we settle it all. Tonight you finally pay the piper. You and this pretty little mess you've been coupling with these past few days. And cheer up, you two, if you try something crazy, a bullet from me must surely be better than a life rotting in prison."

He pointed his gun at Shelby. "Tennessee cops have got you on matricide, thanks to me. You'll not be going back to Tennessee... no longer meddling with my legacy."

His gun wavered between Shelby and Chase. "The Florida cops have got one or both of you on murdering Byron. That poor man was working for me. I was hoping to catch up with you two in Florida. My investigator was to detain you. When another under my hire confirmed Byron was killed, I figured you two would run here. You had to get out of the States, to escape extradition. So it had to be Mexico. But it ends tonight. The only thing that would make it better for me is you remembering, Bobby, remembering all the ways in which you've poisoned my life over the years. All the things that drove us to this moment."

Shelby was looking sick, the truth of who Shawn was finally settling in.

Shawn settled back into the sofa, crossing one leg over the other. He said, "Hands in your pockets, Bobby. Make fists. Then you can rest your hams on your heels. Get as comfortable as you can in that posture. I'm going to do what I do best, now. I'm going to tell you a little story. See if I can't jog that fritzy memory of yours, Bobby, old pal."

77

"The hollow we lived in was pretty remote, and pretty poor," Shawn said. "Sun only reached there about seven hours a day. That remote. Not many kids, so when our folks learned about one another, about you and me and the fact we were about the same age, Bobby, well, they pushed us at one another. I was already a kind of loner, living in my head. Very bookish, much to my old man's consternation. You were a different breed of kid from me, Bobby. Kind of a punk, really. But you had a brain, and you were a reader, too. Had your own way with a phrase, after a fashion.

"But you were the tough one, the daredevil. You were the one who pushed me to the boundaries. Got me in all kinds of trouble. At first, it was the usual kid stuff—shooting out windows with B-B guns and shoplifting candy and the like. Looking back, I guess you were a thrill-junkie, Bobby. But it ran deeper even than that. As we moved into our teens, I resisted more often. You seemed to compensate by doing darker things, all on your own. Oh, I stood by as witness now and again, but more observer than participant.

"Everyone said we could be brothers, Bobby. Even now, we look enough alike, I think, that many would confuse us for blood. We grew tall, early—grew 'like weeds,' as Old Man

Sloane, who took us along fishing with him back in the day, used to say.

"You'd always preferred my family to your own, Bobby. Particularly my mother. I just didn't know how deep your interest in Mom ran." Everett arched his eyebrows. "Any of this bringing anything back for you, Bobby?"

Chase just stared at Shawn. He looked from the gun to Shawn's eyes and shook his head. "I don't remember any of this."

"Really?" Shawn said, disappointed. "Well... we push on. You were so fond of my family, Bobby, that you at last broke me down and dragged me into one of your evil nefarious schemes. But this one was the most evil of all. This one revealed you for the sociopath—the homicidal psychopath—you are at base. You threatened me, browbeat me into silence about your brake job on your parents' car—the one that sent them off that bend on that mountain road to their deaths. The so-called tragic accident that bought you a ticket into my house. The one that officially made you a member of my family, the very family you then set about systematically destroying.

"Things were strained between my mother and father about then. Economy was bad, and despite everything he was doing to try and keep us all fed and under a roof, Mom picked at Dad something fierce. She went at his manhood. He was working three jobs, putting years on himself and his face and so tired all the time he could hardly think straight, and it was never enough for that woman. He took a job as a long-hauler finally. The money was good, but it kept him away too long, a week at a time, or more. You and me were both about fifteen then. I took on one of Dad's old jobs to help out. You couldn't seem to be bothered to do the same. You didn't lift a finger to help pay your own way, let alone help the family. In time, I came to figure out why that was. I'd leave school and go to the docks to hump boxes, sweating to death in those sweltering truck bays. All the while, you were back home, sleeping with my mother. You were tall enough, good-looking enough, I guess, she could get around the fact she was having sex with a child. Creepier, she was bedding a boy who looked so much like her own son." Shawn shook his head. "So sick…"

He frowned and switched his gun to his other hand. "To be honest now, I didn't tumble to it at the time—the fact you were screwing my mother. That came much later, Bobby. You told me so yourself, years later, when you were scared and angry and trying to twist the knife. But I believed you when you said it. It made a lot of other things click for me. You told me all this when I was driving you down to the Keys with me that last time. You thought we were going down there for some fishing and carousing. You were looking forward to sleeping your way around the Keys with a procession of tanned beach bunnies. You've always been led around by your cock. You may not remember who you are, but you're really still the same person. The same poisons and dark drives are still inside you, even now. To coin a phrase, that's your permanent fatal error, Bobby."

Shelby said, "This can't be true. He may not be Everett Hyde, but he *can't* be Bobby Bristow. I have a letter—an unsigned, undated, but hand-written love letter to my mother written by my father. I had the writing compared to samples of Chase's handwriting. The match is exact."

"Oh, the love letter. Yeah, I remember it well." Shawn took a deep breath, let it out slowly. This darkness settled in his eyes. "I still remember when I found that note," he said. "I guess I should have burned the cursed thing on the spot. In a sense, I guess it brought us all here tonight. As much as any-thing else did, anyway." He smiled at Shelby then. His smile was a pained one and it made her flinch.

"I'm sure that handwriting matched his just as perfectly as you say, darling," Shawn said. "It would *have* to. Because Bobby here wrote that letter to Amanda. To your mother. First he slept with my mother, then he began sleeping with my wife. Some fine friend, aren't you, Bobby boy?" Shawn's gaze shifted then from Shelby to the man on his knees at her side.

"You were sleeping with Amanda for about six months before I found out," Shawn said. When I did find out, I thought about killing you on the spot. But I just couldn't see costing myself any more because of you. Seems I'm just not a killer like you, Bobby. Not like you and surely not a mur-derer like you either, Shelby. You'd already tainted so much of my life, taken so much from me. Wrecked it all. So I took a breath, and I thought about it. *Plotted* my way to a new plan. I was struggling with the fourth novel. Couldn't finish it and had all those other go-nowhere manuscripts in these boxes sitting here. Stuff I knew would harm my literary reputation. So I came upon this new scheme. My three published novels were starting to make me real money, to accumulate signifi-cant foreign translation interest and film options. That last money was good and easy, and I knew my stuff was adapta-tion-proof. Once the suckers in Hollywood knuckled down to trying to adapt my books, they all ran into the roadblock of all the internal monologues that drive my novels. So I took that money and ran, content no film would ever see the light of day."

Shawn paused, remembering those dark, endless, tension-filled hours sitting in his writing room, struggling with his fourth novel, striving for a kind of literary perfection that might stand down the critics who, he sensed, were waiting to pounce after lauding his first three novels. That was the critics' way, after all—elevate you, then tear you down.

They were laying in wait, he knew it.

They would savage his fourth novel even if it achieved brilliance. They'd knock him down, let him flounder for another couple of books, then call some other, later and possibly even lesser novel a "return to form," or a "comeback."

He'd seen it before. He was a student of the craft and the Canon. He knew the literary life and the game in all its sour iterations. After all, they'd done it to a legion of others. It was just his turn in the barrel.

If he was going to die, there was no better time like those months after the universal praise reaped by his third novel. He had a window, an opportunity, to go out young and to leave a beautiful corpse, so to speak: his three perfect novels.

"For years, I'd already been functioning as my own agent," he said. "I had an agent, but he was a construct. Just some business cards and a letterhead. A voice on a phone. I was that man. So after learning about you and Amanda, I decided I'd make myself a posthumous writer—goose the value of my work in that way. Escalate my already snowballing reputation and literary standing. I'd kill myself. Then, I'd administer my literary estate in the guise of my own attorney. And so was born Shawn Dalton. I put all the parts in place. Set it up so when I died Amanda would find the papers that would direct her to Shawn Dalton, a lawyer granted extraordinary powers of attorney. I was prepared to be a good guy about it, and I was—saw to it that Amanda and Shelby were well provided for. I siphoned off enough rights money here and there to keep myself in a decent state while I tried my hand at writing under different names. Writing different novels that didn't bear the impossible weight of Everett Hyde's previous three works. I've got two alternate and very lucrative writing identities now.

"But I'm going off on a tangent," Shawn said. "I put all the machinery in place for my post-Everett Hyde existence, then I planned our little ill-fated fishing run down to the Keys, Bobby."

Shelby said, "This is all insane. I can't believe this."

"Don't look so sad, darling," Shawn said. "Look at it this way. You desperately wanted to sleep with your own daddy. Well, you've done that. Anyway, the final straw—the one that pushed me to action—was Amanda's confession she was pregnant. We'd been distant for some time. I didn't quite know why. Didn't know it was because she was in love with Bobby. Well, I did the carnal math and I knew I wasn't the father of Amanda's baby. The devil was in the details, the numbers didn't lie. For a time there, I wanted to murder Bobby and Amanda. But I still had some affection for her."

Shawn pointed his gun at Shelby. "And you, kid, you were an innocent player in all this. As much a victim as me. Or you were back then, anyway. You were no monster like you are now. So I determined to push ahead with my plan. I convinced Amanda I was making that run down to the Keys with Bobby to try and patch things up, to strike some kind of, well, rapprochement, one that wouldn't lead to desolation among the three of us.

"Amanda was so desperate at that point, so frantic for some way out of her sorry position, she embraced the lie. Bobby fell for it too."

Shawn paused, studying Shelby. She was looking hard at the man on the floor next to her. Her bottom lip and chin were trembling. "That's right, Shelby dear. That's your father, right there. Bobby Bristow, Judas and ne'er-do-well journalist-turned-biographer. He's really your blood, Shelby. So you got your darkest dream in the end, honey. You bedded Daddy. Only Daddy isn't the writer you thought he was. Some sorry break, huh, kiddo?"

Shelby and Chase both looked quite ill, now.

Shawn frowned, looking harder at Chase. Something was changed in Chase's expression. Chase said, "You got me in that car, and you shot me!"

Shawn nodded, his face dark. "It is coming back, isn't, old friend? I thought that would make this perfect. But it doesn't."

He shook his head. "I keep veering. Sorry. Yes, Bobby. Things went crosswise, early. We were in Miami, screaming at each other as we were driving through South Beach. You tumbled to my intentions. So I shot you, twice, right there in traffic. It was hasty, bloody—shots fired in white-hot anger, not even aimed. We were going about forty or so when you rolled out the door and onto the pavement. I thought that fall alone would kill you. It *had* to, because we were in traffic and the strip was narrow—I couldn't just u-turn to chase after you to finish the job, even if I had the stomach to do that. I couldn't abandon my car to do that on foot, either... couldn't leave it there for the police to trace to me.

"So I ran. I went down to the Keys and executed my plan. Faked my death. Bided my time and waited to hear that you bled out or died from head injuries jumping out of that car. I tried to trace you, but without success. In time, as Shawn, speaking through a handkerchief and biting on a quarter to change my voice, I phoned Amanda. Poor grieving mess—I wondered at the time if the tears were for me or for you, Bobby. Either way, she bought my ruse, all the way up. She believed I was Shawn Dalton. In time, Amanda and I took advantage of a partial torso that washed up to fabricate that story about Everett and his honeymoon tattoo. A lie agreed to and a convenient body to free up my estate.

"For years, it all rolled along nicely." Shawn gestured at the boxes sitting on the floor. "I thought Amanda had executed my order to destroy all that drivel. If I'd known she wouldn't do that, I'd have done it myself before I left. God knows, I might have saved some of my soul if I'd done that. Maybe spared some other lives.

"Years passed. My literary reputation grew. Amanda got sick and Shelby got greedy. Our girl here started getting crazy notions. Biographers were starting to coming knocking, trying to latch on to my fame like remoras. Shelby wanted to publish my scraps, all the stuff I'd held back and thought Amanda had set fire to. At the same time, Shelby rightly feared the right persistent biographer might harm the legend that had grown up around me. Any light shed on my shadowy past was a threat to the empire, so she began hiring out killings—a would be biographer here, a screenwriter there." He shook his head. "I suspected what she was up to, but to my shame I didn't raise a hand. Hell, I didn't want any biographies out there, either, for pretty much the same reasons."

Chase looked at Shelby and said, "How many people—"

"He's lying," Shelby hissed.

"Here's the crazy part," Shawn said. "Here's the stuff you can't make up. In her hospital room, bored one day, Amanda picked up a biography from a lending library cart. It was one of your books, Bobby. One of your biographies. Amanda recognized you instantly from the dust jacket photo. She wanted to connect with you a last time, to talk, so she contacted her trusted solicitor to reach out to you, under the pretext of commissioning a Hyde biography that you would write."

Shelby was watching him closely now, trying to put it together. Shawn helped her do that: "When your mother succumbed—died because of you, let's not loose sight of that—you found just enough of her notes and diaries and paperwork to set your own mind spinning. You thought Amanda had found Daddy, so you appropriated your mother's Hyde biography gambit. By kismet, fate—you indeed found Daddy here. Once you two were put on a collision course, I knew I had to take a more active role in protecting my own legacy.

"Put yourself in my place," Shawn said. "You've written some books, Bobby. I assume you did so with a sense of pride and dedication, if you're at all capable of real emotion. I poured my blood and soul into my writing. I was the guy in the chair all those hours and days, alone and pounding out words in the dark of morning while the rest of the house was asleep. I was the guy working in my office, crafting these novels while the rest of the world watched TV and sports and frittered their squandered lives away. My art. My effort. My novels and legacy. But Amanda, then Kathleen, and then these biographers, and lastly you, Shelby—you all contrived to take what was mine and warp it. Tried to publish my sorry leavings your mother was duty-bound to burn. You were going to do all that for mere goddamn money."

78

Ashley was still mostly numb, sitting in the car clutching an aluminum coffee travel mug that Ace had filled with rum and Diet Coke.

Her whole body ached. She felt like one giant bruise. Her voice was coming back, but her throat bore bruise marks shaped like fingertips.

Gretchen Peters was singing *Germantown* on the radio.

"Finally getting cool in here," Ace said. He flicked switches on the driver's side console, raising the windows. He twisted up the air conditioner a couple of notches. "Sorry you'll be flying coach, but we all agree it's best to get you out of here, and I mean now, Hon'. Sooner the better, right? Clearly, Shelby is still gunning for you. If you look at it from that freak's perspective, she has to take you out to have any prospect of a future. That is, if she dodges homicide charges coming out of Tennessee. If she avoids fallout from that dead guy on her front lawn here."

Ace slipped an envelope from atop the dash and passed it to Ashley. He flipped on the dome light. "Through channels, I managed to get this. You said you never saw Shelby Hyde in the flesh. Figured you might be curious. This is her passport photo."

Ashley slid the photo from its container. She was startled by Shelby's resemblance to herself.

He glanced at the photo. "She looks like you—beautiful, I mean. Like they say, no judging books by their covers. Not that book anyway." He nodded at Shelby's photo.

Ashley said, "How the hell did that man at the hotel find me?"

He ran a hand over his sweating scalp. "I suppose Shelby must have posted someone to watch the house after she fled the joint. That bastard you put down drew that duty, I suspect. He must have followed us from her beach house back to the hotel. I blame myself for not paying enough attention."

"Makes sense," she said. "What happened to him? I mean to his—"

"Dumped in the ocean behind a hotel a couple of doors down," Ace said.

Ashley shivered, chilled by the notion some poor person, maybe a couple out for a romantic stroll on the beach, or some elderly beachcomber—maybe even some child scrounging around for shells—might find the man's corpse.

"Hey, kiddo," Ace said, "sorry for that bath and all, but you were pretty out of it and covered in all that—"

"Say no more. It's okay, really. I'm so grateful for all you've done." She looked down at her replacement clothes. She shook her head at her hip-hugging, low-rise jeans that she barely managed to get snapped, at her cropped T-shirt that said "Porn Star In Training" across the swell of her breasts. "Who bought these again?"

"Bucky—the one with the teeth," Ace said. "Wal-Mart cowed him, on account of that big packed parking lot. So he hit some other joint. I know that shirt is a bit much. Hot as it is, I could give you mine to wear instead. Doubt any airport hump will give me grief for going bare-chested."

Ace's T-shirt was soaked through at the armpits. He smelled pretty ripe after all the mayhem. After all the lugging around of corpses and giving baths to naked crime victims. "No, I'll cope," she said. "Thanks, though." She sipped her half-ass Rum and Coke. "This hits the spot, thanks for thinking of it."

"You're in shock, honey, whether you know it or not. What you did is going to slam home hard for you, eventually. Maybe real soon. It'll drag at you even though it was self-defense and fully justified. Even if that cocksucker deserved much worse. You're going to suffer guilt for what you did, even though you shouldn't. But you will. It's only human. Best thing, I find, is to drink hard. You should look up an old boyfriend, maybe, or find a new one." Ashley thought she heard a hopeful note in that last. He said, "Burn it out in bed and with booze for a week or so. Then soldier on. That's my earned advice to you."

She thought about that. She said, "You've killed many men?"

"A few," he said. "Some even deserved it."

He said it with such nonchalance, Ashley decided he wasn't showboating or playing the hard-ass "Iron Seal." She said, "You really think this woman will stay after me?"

"She has to," he said. "You're too big a threat, even an undying menace to her. She has to take you out. Now, when you get back there to the city, you need watching after. My crew is spread thin, but so is Shelby's now, I'm banking. So Selma will meet you at the airport. Place she lives is like a stockade in most ways, so you stay inside there with her until I call. Hopefully, I'll phone soon and with an all-clear."

Ashley said, "You have some idea where Shelby might be now?"

"I hope to." He smiled and reached over and squeezed her knee. "All thanks to you, by the way."

Ashley sipped more of her drink. It wasn't really taking her anywhere in terms of a buzz yet, but it did soothe her throat. She said, "How so?"

"You took out that hump, this Luke Assman, and what kind of a dumbass name is *that*?" Ace pronounced it Ass-Man. He said, "Bucky swears to me it's pronounced Oz-Mon. But it looks like Ass-Man to me. Anyway, you doing him got us his wallet, his key card to his room. We tossed his bedroom and got some more things. We got his phone and snagged a shit-load of phone numbers and emails from that. Solid clues that we can work. We'll find the bitch."

"And then?"

His gaze roamed from the road to Ashley and back again. "Really going to make me say it?"

"I guess so, because I have trouble believing it."

"She's tried to kill you, more than once."

"You could call in the law on her."

"Yeah, if I was a goddamn fool. Look, if Shelby has any sense at all, and I give her credit for that, she's out of the country now. Probably Mexico. That puts her beyond the reach of the humps in the Tennessee and Florida police departments. And we still have that other high damned hurdle—losing containment of *our* story. We have books to protect. So you lay low. Let the Seal do his work, Sweetie."

"His work?"

"Don't make me say it," he said again.

He didn't have to. It was clear enough what he intended.

Ashley sat in silence, trying to think of some way, any way at all, to protect Chase and coming up blank. Chase had lied to her in the very worst way. He wasn't the man he pretended to be. But then he said he didn't know who he was, either. A part of Ashley still believed him, regardless of what Shelby thought, or had maybe made Chase believe.

And that dead private investigator?

Chase couldn't do that, he would never do that. Shawn said Shelby was culpable in her mother's murder; she'd ordered Ashley killed.

But Chase? He might still stand apart from all that.

Ashley tipped her head back against the seat, trying to think of some argument she could make to Ace to spare Chase but again coming up short. She kept turning it over in her mind, thinking, *I'll think of something. I've got to think of something.*

79

Shelby said, "What do you want, *really*? Money? The manuscripts back? What?"

"Money I've got, Shelby," Shawn said. "Really, all the money I need. And the manuscripts? I want what I always wanted. I want this sorry stuff destroyed, just like your mother was obligated to do. So I'm seeing to that tonight, as I should have done myself years ago—just more to feel guilty for, more that brought us all to this sorry place."

"That's crazy," Shelby said. "You can't burn it! It's plenty good, and your readers have a right to—"

"They have a right to what I allow them," Shawn said sharply. "It's my writing. My literary reputation you're mucking around with, girl. You're not an artist, not a creator. You don't get it at all. I didn't write these novels for the money. Hell, I was flabbergasted to receive the money I did for that first book. All I ever wanted to do was write, on my own terms, and you know what? I did that. My books went from my desk to my readers, same as unmediated. I was never really edited. I printed the books I wanted to put out under my byline. What you're trying to do is immoral. It is the worst form of treachery, of disrespect."

Shawn shook his head and sighed at the man on his knees by her side. "If you were really a writer, Bobby, you'd understand what I mean. But those biographies you crank out, each one is just another hired-gun job to you, I'd wager. Words on a page, money for words. Is that how it goes for you, Bobby? Because that's not how it is for me. I sense for you there's no striving for the perfect passage, no reaching for what Fitzgerald called the golden moment. I don't write for the cash, and it should be clear by now I was never in it for the celebrity. Being a writer is a sacred calling. Your kind sullies it."

Chase said, "What then? If not the money and notoriety, why do you do it?"

"I thought I made it more than clear by now—it's all about the craft," Shawn said. "Everything for the story and the characters. But they aren't mere characters to me. They're real people. That's what I'm protecting here tonight, protecting it all again, as I've had to in the past, God forgive me. I'm protecting the sanctity of my novels. I'm preserving a legacy and a legend—three perfect novels. My life's central purpose. The one thing I leave behind when I finally really go."

"The other books in these boxes are good," Shelby insisted. "Better than your peers' books."

"My peers? That's truly damning with faint praise. And those other works of mine may or may not be good," Shawn said, "but what they are not is transcendent. Those three published novels under my name are as near to perfection as any novelist dares hope to come."

He waved an arm at the gasoline soaked boxes. "This all burns."

Chase just looked at him, shaking his head, unable to find the words.

Shelby said, "And you're going to do what, kill us and leave us to burn with your writing? Please, you can't possibly—"

"Oh, I'm sorely tempted to do that very thing to you both." Shawn shook his head sadly. "Bobby here deserves to die, he's earned murdering a thousand times over. And you, Shelby? You're a stone killer. I can see I haven't reached you with any of this tonight. Not a flicker of remorse or guilt. You're evil, Shelby. Truly evil."

Shelby's chin trembled. "And faking your own death, making everyone who loves you believe you're dead, that isn't wrong? That isn't evil?"

"A necessary evil," he said. "Anyway, I'm not going to kill you, not either of you. Hell, I'm letting you leave together. You'll be wanting to do that fast, because when this place goes up, there's going to be fire trucks and police here in droves. You two are going to get back into that car you drove up here in, and you're going to leave together. Hell, you more than deserve one another. I don't envy you the nights or days ahead. Don't envy you the paranoia of the one knowing too well what the other is."

Shelby said, "But I can't just disappear, I've got your estate to manage. Our shared futures depend on—"

"Nonsense," Shawn said. "Your future is behind you now. I'll see to things as my attorney, just as I've always done. You're going to be a fugitive soon, darling. If some cop back in Tennessee decides to contact some TV reporter to help in their manhunt, you're going to find your own kind of fame, honey. You'll soon have your own biographers, I figure. And Chase, here? Irony of ironies, I guess he just becomes another of those guys he loves to write about—another missing man of letters."

Still on his knees, hands in his pockets, Chase snarled at Shawn, "All this to protect, what, a literary reputation? Jesus, was is that in the end?"

"Everything," Shawn said. "Hell, ask this little witch at your side. It's probably the one thing she and I see eye-to-eye on."

"It's crazy," Chase said.

"You only think that because you're not a writer in the pure and fullest sense," Shawn said. "That young woman you discarded to chase this homicidal one at your side? Ashley's the real thing, Bobby. A pure writer, like me, in my innocent prime. And if she's under my tutelage? Then the sky's the limit for Ashley McKnight. I pity you maybe not being around to savor the works to come from her hands. But then, Bobby, I doubt you'd ever really grasp it at the deep and meaningful levels. Ashley's an old soul, Bob. She's a real artist. And no killer, no nonfiction hack or mercenary angler. You're a sell-out, Bobby. Ashley? She's going to be a master. She's my redemption."

Chase said, "Are you saying Ashley's with you now?" His lip curled. "You and her are together?"

"What do you care, Bobby?" He nodded at Shelby. "You tossed her aside for this one. You traded up. Or you thought you did, didn't you?" Shawn frowned. "Already feeling the old buyer's remorse, Bobby? Don't worry, this one's likely a short-lived mistake. I don't see you having legs as a couple."

"Unbelievable," Bobby said. "You kill me, take my girlfriend and—"

"I told, you I'm not going to kill you," Everett said. "Not going to kill either of you. Hell, there's hardly any point in doing it now. You've already killed yourselves in the truest sense."

He pointed at the box. "I've already taken your guns and stripped them of ammo. You're going to leave your phones, your computers, your passports—all of it—right here, to burn. Your future—shared or apart—so long as you both last, is here in Mexico, now. I'm burning everything else of yours along with my own unworthy words. You take the money you're carrying, that car out there, and you leave with your many sins and each other, God help you both."

Shelby balked. Shawn fired another shot into the floor between them.

He watched them quickly drop their passports, driver's licenses and credit cards into the gas-soaked boxes containing his holographs. He kept a gun pointed at their backs as they walked slowly to their car parked outside, moving like crash survivors.

When their get-away car's dust trail at last disappeared in the twilight, he went back in, sighed and struck a match.

Shawn threw his latex gloves into the closer of the two burning boxes.

He trotted down the driveway, already sweating in the humid night air. He stopped just long enough to retrieve the box with his single worthy, unfinished manuscript.

He knew he could complete that work now; Everett Hyde's literary legacy would soon enough stand at *four* transcendent novels.

But that was all. No other posthuma.

No biographies or Hollywood bio-pics.

He'd see to that, just as he always had, through litigation where Shelby had opted for murder. He'd bury them in paper.

It was his right as creator.

He loaded the box in the trunk of his car and drove in the direction opposite the one taken by Shelby and Chase.

Shawn heard sirens in the distance; smiled at this big orange and red glow in his rearview mirror.

80

Selma spread her arms wide, hugging Ashley so tightly to her that it hurt. The Hyena said, "You poor kid! But God, can you imagine how what's happened to you this time will play in our book? I'm definitely thinking Jennifer Lawrence has to play you." She thought about it some more, then said, "Or maybe Lauren Cohan."

The über agent frowned then, her hands resting on Ashley's shoulders. She pushed Ashley back to arms' length.

The Hyena gave Ashley this hard, head-to-toe look, then back up again. "Ash, honey, don't you dare take this personally, but when we get to the promotional point, publicity, interviews and so forth, I'm putting you in the hands of another of my authors. Shelly Caprice, do you know of her?"

Bone-tired, Ashley said, "I'm sorry to say I don't. I—"

"You *don't* know her? I guess I can *see* that. Well, Shelly is *huge* in her circles. Her newest is called, *You're F-ing Wearing That?*"

81

Ashley…
She was some kind of young woman. She'd reached him, down deep, as no other ever had. They had spent the morning in bed, making one another crazy, making love in Chase's old place. Ashley, apparently mourning Chase's loss less than he would have expected, had exploited that confusion and more or less taken control of the place, assuming the rent payments.

Ashley had quickly made the loft hers—redecorating with advance money, tossing much of Chase's stuff and moving in her own. Filling it with family pictures. That was an alien concept to him, but they were her pictures, her family. He found it charming. And that surprised and delighted him.

Today was Ashley's very private housewarming party. One they meant to spend mostly in bed.

She'd chosen Lana's *Ride* as background music for their reunion sex. Ashley had just climaxed again—on top during their lovemaking because of the sensitivity of her lower back from the last of her laser tattoo-removal procedures—when he began his gentle counter-offensive again.

He prodded Ashley about the need to focus on her own fiction. He argued she should just drop the whole prospect of a Hyde memoir.

She pole-armed him. "Stop there, because I've already decided against it on my own," she said. "It's just not me. I'd be doing it for money, not love. I'm a fiction writer. That's what I am."

He kissed her so hard and for so long they were both left breathless. When she could manage it, she said, "Now it's just a matter of working up the courage to tell Selma. The Hyena is going to want to have my head for backing out on that deal."

He smiled and kissed her again, tenderly this time. "At least you know a great lawyer if it comes to that."

That was when Ashley let some more drop about Ace and his own Hyde project. About another of Selma Lindscott's clients, a psychiatrist, who was writing some kind of case-study book on Hyde and Chase. This Selma Lindscott was turning him into a cottage industry, goddamn her. He'd have to bury her in litigation, too, he supposed.

But all things in their time. For the moment, he just wanted to savor this time with Ashley, his fiction writer-lover. If she'd been the woman when he was in his youth, when he was writing those three books? God, what a different road it might have been. It hurt to think he might have had that life.

But then Ashley dealt him a body blow.

She leaked to him stuff not yet made public.

Stuff Ace had gotten access to through unspeakable back channels and murky old military connections who had gone over to law enforcement or transitioned into FBI work.

Now that Chase had gone missing—had become something of a tabloid mystery himself—some of Shelby's hired-gun experts were starting to try and shop their own stories, to solicit payment for prime-time TV interviews.

One of them was the graphologist who claimed to have matched a love letter in Everett Hyde's hand to the handwriting in a dedication of a book—a personal note written by one Chase Alger.

Ashley was by his side, stroking her fingers through his chest hair as she explained this all to him. His fingernails raked softly through the soft, short hair returning between Ashley's legs.

Seemed that the Hyena also had this graphologist in her sights for some book, too.

Then it hit home with full fury. Oh God, this could be a whole *different* kind of disaster.

Ashley confirmed it: "The Hyena—Selma—sent me some PDFs of covers for reissues of Chase's old books that the publisher is wanting to rush back to press. The reprints will read 'Everett Hyde, Writing as Chase Alger.'"

He saw spots then, felt like he might actually blackout or at least have some kind of gasping panic attack. This was so much worse than books about him. This was an expansion of his literary legacy he never dreamed might occur. This was a waking nightmare.

She frowned and said, "Are you okay, Shawn?"

"Yeah… I, well, this is awkward." He managed a smile. "You better stop right there, darling," he said. "We may end up some kind of enemies through the courts. Not you and me per se, but your agent and I. Chase's publishers."

Ashley's frown deepened. "What do you mean?"

"I'm left to coordinate and handle—to protect—Everett's literary legacy… all of his works. If Chase has been determined to be Everett Hyde, via handwriting samples, or whatever, well, Chase's works belong to the Hyde estate. They therefore belong to me, or so I would argue. I'm probably going to have to file an injunction, pronto, to stop publication. Get Chase's publishers to lay off. Tie them up until we can work out all these rights issues. Let his books go out of print, if I have to."

And that was probably going to mean finding himself some real and costly, top-shelf entertainment or copyright attorney now.

Ashley nodded slowly. "I should have kept my mouth shut, I guess."

"I'd have found out anyway," he said. "I'll keep you protected, don't worry."

It was all spinning out of control. It was too big to get his arms around, just yet. Maybe through the courts he could neutralize some of the threat. But he couldn't do much to stop this shrink's book. He couldn't do much to stop the Iron Seal.

If the courtroom failed him, there was one other unthinkable possibility—to return to the world as Everett Hyde.

But what would that do to this life he was starting with Ashley?

One crisis at a time, he told himself.

"I'm thinking about a vacation," he said. "Some island somewhere. Couple of weeks of sun, surf and hedonism. Private beaches. Maybe Jamaica. Would you come along?"

Ashley smiled uncertainly. "You're sure about that, Shawn? I mean, if you're going into battle, your time is going to be spoken for."

"I have partners. Hell, in this day and age, we do more electronically than face-to-face in courtrooms, anyway. And this may take years to sort out through the courts."

Ashley smiled. She kissed him passionately. "Sounds wonderful," she said.

She frowned, then Ashley said, "I'm going to want to consult with Ace, though. See if there is some way to get a gun down there for me. It's sick and wrong, but it's kind of truly become my security blanket. I still can't quite believe it's all over, the threat to me, I mean. You never know, you know? Especially if we head south, to Mexico..."

Everett Hyde kissed Ashley again, tongues tangling.

He said, "Nothing wrong with some precautions, Ash. Like you said, darling, you never know. You never know what might happen next."

He thought, *But not to you, Ashley.*

She would always be safe, he swore to himself, because he loved and respected her, writer-to-writer.

EPILOGUE

Ace Sterling sat at his desk, combing through his morning's emails.

One particular item with a subject line that caught his eye. The subject line read:

EVERETT HYDE PROPOSITION

Ace guzzled some coffee, then clicked to read the pithy message.

> *RS:*
>> *I've read with interest, and growing ire, the reports of your Everett Hyde project.*
>> *One chance: Drop it or face the consequences.*

Annoyed, Ace typed back, one finger at a time:

> *Bring it on!*

He hit send, then turned his attention to other correspondence.

A few seconds later, his computer chirred, "You have mail!"

Ace scrolled to the top.

There was a new message there, a delivery failure notification marked "Permanent Fatal Error."

ABOUT THE AUTHOR

Hadley Colt is the pseudonym for an internationally acclaimed author. Hadley Colt's previous novels were published in several languages to excellent reviews and high praise from fellow writers who've declared the author's work, *"subtle, moving and tragic"*, *"non conformist"*, *"bold and extravagant"*, *"reviving"*, *"an explosive mix of humor and action"*, and who has been described as *"an erudite with formidable imagination"* and a *"master of suspense"*.

To learn more about Hadley Colt, visit *http://hadleydcolt. blogspot.com/* and *www.betimesbooks.com*
Follow Hadley Colt on Twitter: *https://twitter.com/HadleyColt*